PRAISE FOR A

"There are still books being written that you cannot put dow... . *Beach Lawyer* . . . is just that kind of read."

—*American Bar Association Journal*

"A page-turner."

—*Bloomberg Law*

"A fast-moving, interesting, exciting ride . . . This book is hard to put down."

—*Portland Book Review*

"*Beach Lawyer* is a multilayered tale of backstabbing, greed, and manipulation that continually surprises readers with where Duff's mind takes them."

—*Chattanooga Times Free Press*

"A roller-coaster ride with twists and turns and unexpected happenings . . . great read."

—*Fresh Fiction*

"Great legal suspense."

—*Great Thoughts*

"So tense . . . I found myself holding my breath . . . A great summer read!"

—Nancie Claire, *Speaking of Mysteries*

THE
BOARDWALK
OPTION

OTHER TITLES BY AVERY DUFF

Beach Lawyer

The Boardwalk Trust

THE
BOARDWALK
OPTION

AVERY DUFF

THOMAS & MERCER

Text copyright © 2019 by C. Avery Duff Living Trust
All rights reserved.

Published by Thomas & Mercer, Seattle

www.apub.com

Amazon, the Amazon logo, and Thomas & Mercer are trademarks of Amazon.com, Inc., or its affiliates.

ISBN-13: 9781503904828
ISBN-10: 1503904822

Cover design by Kirk DouPonce, DogEared Design

Printed in the United States of America

This book is dedicated to my friend Thorpe McKenzie.
Sui generis.

PROLOGUE

Boneyard . . . Boneyard . . . Boneyard . . .

A rock-strewn surfing spot where Sunset Boulevard ended at Pacific Coast Highway. That end-of-the-road surf spot's name kept rolling around inside Robert's head as he fought the churning wall of seawater that had clutched him seconds earlier and now flung him toward the steep face of the shale cliff.

Desperate, he grabbed a breath of air and shielded his head from the impact bound to come—and there it was. For a moment in the churning liquid mass—one second? three?—he blacked out. When he opened his eyes, he found himself in a foot of seawater, dazed in the darkness. Still alive. His arms felt like someone had beaten them with a baseball bat; the cliff had shredded the right side of his body raw.

All around him lay algae-slicked rocks and canted foundations of houses that had fallen from the cliff top decades ago.

Standing, he could just make out the empty mouth of a ravine, fifty yards down the rocky beach. He could still picture it as it had been mere minutes earlier, but this time a man walked out of its graffiti-marred mouth onto the stony beach. A familiar weapon dangled from his right hand.

Now, seaward, just visible, here came the next set of waves, their tips feathering white on eight-foot faces, rolling toward him.

Avery Duff

His eyes flashed to the ravine. To the armed man. Then to the serious incoming surf and the cliffs behind him. Next time, he might not be so fortunate.

Locals called this place Sunken City, and as he started to make his move, he wondered if this was the place where he would die.

CHAPTER 1

Two Weeks Earlier

"Not too many people know about the Constitution."

Those words had just been uttered by Robert Worth's prospective client, "Three Belts" Childress, a man who always wore exactly three belts, none of them inside his belt loops.

"The US or the California Constitution?" Robert asked.

"Say what?"

Maybe it was just another crazed day on the Venice Beach Boardwalk. After all, the Santa Ana winds had been blowing hot off the desert and through the passes all day. A crazy-making wind, Los Angelinos liked to believe. This same offshore surge and rising heat had turned Catalina Island a sick-canary yellow and had driven termite swarms from the boardwalk's concrete cracks for a one-and-only shot at mating.

An hour ago, Robert had set up his office—a lightweight, faux-bamboo conference table and canvas beach chairs—on the ocean side of the boardwalk. The Mini Cooper–size slot was where he'd practiced since leaving his legit Santa Monica law firm a couple of years ago.

Beside him, his live-in girlfriend, Gia Marquez, studied a LexisNexis printout of a legal case for her summer clerkship. Kicked back in her chair, she dozed in and out beneath her long-brim VB Surf Shop hat.

He might've dozed, too, but for Three Belts taking up his offer to the public: a free quarter-hour consultation.

Robert took another stab at it. "The US Constitution or the California Constitution?"

Three Belts appeared poleaxed by the question but kept his seat and forged ahead.

"So anyways, my car's booted for excess parking tickets, and being how I'm a sovereign citizen, I'm not paying, and you need to have my back in court, bro."

Sovereigns. Each claimed to be his own ruler, not the government. Sometimes based on the *Magna Carta*, other times on sunspots or irrelevant language from the US Constitution. The upshot was always the same for rules they didn't like: *You're not the boss of me.*

Robert nudged Gia. "My colleague, Ms. Marquez, handles the firm's sovereign cases, and she's never lost one." True as far as it went.

Gia stirred, slid down her knockoff, two-for-$7 Ray-Bans, and sized up Three Belts.

"Stand up, turn around," she said.

Three Belts complied. Apparently, the command of a beautiful woman outweighed that of LA parking enforcement.

"I don't like his case," she said.

"Why not?"

"I don't need a reason for doing or not doing anything. Am I right, Three Belts?"

Logic wasn't Three Belts' strong suit. Robert wrapped it up.

"Mr. Childress, go to court. Good chance the officer won't show, and your case'll be dismissed. If he shows, pay the tickets, or tell the judge why you shouldn't. But do not mention this sovereign business to the judge, no matter what."

Three Belts left, certain to ignore the advice. Gia slipped over into Robert's lap, melting into him.

"Masterful," she said, stroking his palm with her index finger.

"Baby, this is inappropriate. We're in the workplace."

"I hung up your closed-for-the-day sign."

No such sign existed, but why argue? Her sun-warmed body exuded coconut oil and vanilla, and her fingernails snaked into his hair.

"Not tired out, are you?" she asked.

"C'mon, who you talking to?"

"Not even after last night?"

About last night—*drained* was a better description than *tired out*. He and Gia were trying to get pregnant. Maybe *trying* wasn't the right word. *Striving* was more like it. Striving to have a child together, and they'd been striving like demons for the last month.

Before he could answer, familiar voices reached them across the wide deep-sand beach behind him.

Retired LAPD cop Erik Jacobson trudged toward them, lugging a boy under each arm: the twins, after their three-hour swim. Erik Junior and Hans, half-Thai, half-Swede dervishes, blonded-out by the salt and sun. "The lads, ages six and six," Erik liked saying.

His wife, Priya, strolled beside him—floating, it always looked like—with their towels and boogie boards. By the time the clan reached the boardwalk, Erik's 260-pound body was drenched in sweat as he let the squirming boys slide off his ever-pale body onto the ground.

"What was Three Belts up to?" he asked.

Robert said, "Can't say, dude. Attorney-client privilege."

Gia added, "Sorry, *Oso*, attorney-lover privilege." *Oso*. Short for *Oso Polar*. *Polar Bear* being Erik's Latino nickname.

"Who is Three Belts?" Erik Junior asked.

"A man who wears three belts," Erik explained.

"Why, Daddy? Are his pants too big?" That from Hans.

"Every day he wears three belts?" Priya this time. Eccentric Americans still puzzled her.

Erik said, "Yes, Priya, he wears three belts every day."

"But why? We want to know why," Robert and Gia took turns asking, piling on.

Erik sighed. "Lesson number one in the parenting biz. Once you're out of the lads' spin cycle, you get out clean and count your blessings."

Priya waved to someone up the boardwalk. All of them saw who it was—Raymundo Reyes. A man with only a casual acquaintance with life on the straight and narrow. For that reason, among others, a constant pain in Erik's ex-cop ass. Wearing a black leather jacket, a lime-green tank top, and black skinny jeans with zippers down the pant legs—*zippers to nowhere*, Erik called them—he held a soft leather briefcase with no handle under his arm.

Erik's sons made a beeline for Reyes, who exchanged high fives with the boys. To them, Reyes was a movie star who'd given them a *Street Cred 6* poster for their bedroom. The star of that movie had been a Latino actor, *El Sueño Azul*, the Blue Dream. But Reyes' tiny image did appear in one corner of the poster as Thug #7. No doubt at all in Robert's mind—that poster irritated Erik every time he looked at it.

Yet something in Erik's expression, watching his sons with Reyes, went beyond irritation.

Reyes approached them and gave Gia a hug.

"How's it going, Reyes?" she said.

"Keeping it, Gigi." Short for *keeping it real*, Robert guessed, with *Gigi* being long for *Gia*. "She still with you, Roberto?"

"I know, it's a miracle."

"Mystery to me how you two layabouts rate such fine women."

Reyes wasn't bold enough to hug Priya; instead, they high-fived. Once, with Robert, Reyes had referred to Priya as *The Asian Sensation*, given her striking looks. Robert had told him, "Never call her that if Erik's around."

"By *around*, you mean . . . ?"

"I mean, Erik's still alive."

On the boardwalk now, Reyes asked, "Still working on that tan, *E-Rik?*"

"What you know about working, Ray-Ray?"

"What you call bein' at the film market, Great White?"

"You say *film* or *flimflam*?"

These two could go at it all day. Both of them street-smart men who came at problems from different angles. Erik found the bottom line quick; Reyes tended to take you all the way up to Alaska and back again.

Robert had met Erik five years ago before Erik had retired from the LAPD, when he'd still worked out of the Venice substation. Smart and loyal with an arid wit, a first-round draft pick among men you'd want beside you in the trenches. Gia and Priya had become friends, too.

"Not that she's innocent," Gia once told him. "I mean, she worked reception in that Bangkok hotel where Erik met her, but she always tries to see the best in people."

And Reyes? In spite of his tenuous grasp on the up-and-up, Robert and Gia liked what they actually knew about him, but both preferred leaving his street activity to their imaginations.

Gia took Priya and the boys over to their Ozone apartment for a beach-sand hose-off. That left Erik and Reyes to have at each other.

Erik said, "Nice briefcase, Ray-Ray. Most guys just carry their PB&J in a Ziploc."

"No handle, making it a portfolio case, not a briefcase."

"My bad. Perfect size for toting around your mug shots."

"Mean headshots?"

"No. I said mug shots, and that's exactly what I meant."

It was getting hotter than Robert liked. Even though he knew Erik would never swing on a man eighty pounds lighter, Reyes wasn't one to back down, either.

Robert stepped in and asked Reyes, "Saw your text. What was it you needed to talk about?"

"Business, *Roberto*, and it ain't none of it yours, E-Rik."

CHAPTER 2

Once they were alone, Robert took a seat across from Reyes.

"What's up?" Robert asked.

"Let me do it up legit, *Roberto*, sign all your digital papers."

Same as he did with all prospects, Robert took a photo of Reyes' driver's license, and Reyes DocuSigned Robert's release form.

"Legit as it's ever gonna get. Let's hear it."

Reyes placed his portfolio on the table and unzipped it with a flourish. The insides were neat. No PB&J, but a stylish pen set and two manila folders.

Excuses he could give Reyes jockeyed for mental position: *I don't do criminal defense work; I don't know anything about traffic court;* and his old standby: *Sorry, I never once tried a case.*

But here came Reyes' curveball: "You probably don't know it, for the last little bit, I been involved in a movie. My own script, my own project."

"Congratulations, I had no idea."

He could've added, *I don't know jack about entertainment law* to his litany of excuses, but that wasn't entirely true. A lot of movie deals involved basic contract law, although laced with complex union requirements for writers, actors, and directors, and with other terms outside his comfort zone.

Plus, what he couldn't say to Reyes: these low-budget indie film projects never went anywhere for one simple reason—they were terrible.

"What's up with your project?"

"Couple things. First off, I got somebody interested in it. More than a little interested, but there's a few hitches I need help on."

"Hitches are my business. *More than a little interested* means . . . ?"

"This here. T-Mack Films, straight outta Dublin, Ireland. Met 'em over at AFM." The American Film Market. "That's all the skinny I have on 'em and copies of me and T-Mack's back-and-forth."

He handed Robert the larger manila folder. Inside, a clipped-together sheaf of T-Mack's promotional materials and Reyes' emails with the company. The CEO's name was T. O. Macintyre. *T-Mack, got it.*

"Did you two come to an understanding about your project, or what?"

"Pretty much. Far enough to where we were discussing budgets and actors. Then something came up on my end, and things got off track."

Okay, here we go.

"Thing is, I got this letter from the guys optioned my project."

"So, your project was under option, but you were out in the market with it?"

"Project wasn't under option anymore, but I *was* out in the market with it."

"What happened?"

"Dude, we gonna run over my free quarter hour. What's your rate?" Robert stared at him until Reyes said, "Friends and family, I hear you. So first off, that option happened. I signed with some hotshots over on Abbot Kinney."

"Let's see your paperwork."

From the second folder, Reyes handed him a contract: *Option Agreement.* The parties were Raymundo Reyes and 333 Film Ventures,

LLC, with offices on Abbot Kinney Boulevard in Venice. Hip central, a mile away from where they sat.

Robert skimmed the option. Its first paragraph showed 333 Film Ventures optioning from Raymundo Reyes "a project currently titled: WALK STREET HITS." Flipping to the signature page, he saw that each party had signed.

Robert hadn't heard of 333 Film Ventures, but there were hundreds of small movie companies around town. Most came and went after burning through other people's money without getting a project completed, much less sold in the marketplace.

He looked up. "And your problem is?"

"Not too sure about that. See, the option, it's over and done, and T-Mack's interested in it."

"Interested in *it*? What's *it*?"

"What I already shot. *It*."

"And you're saying the option you signed had expired . . . was *over with* . . . and now T-Mack's interested?"

"Interested up to a point, yeah."

"Great, way to go."

Reyes didn't elaborate, unusual for him. In fact, he looked nervous.

"How'd things get off track?" Robert asked.

"See, this movie thing, it's important to me. I know you're book smart and smart-smart, too, and I don't want you thinking I'm some dumbass, ran off and messed up, doin' things on his own."

"The book-smart thing's overrated. From what I hear about the movie business, you've got just the right kind of smarts to succeed."

Reyes nodded. "This buzzkill right here's why I texted. Why me and T-Mack got off track."

He slid a piece of paper across the desk. A snail-mail letter from 333 Film Ventures.

As you know, the Option Agreement ("Option") between the Company and you has expired by its own terms on the expiration date set forth in the Option. Anything in said Agreement to the contrary notwithstanding, by this letter, the Company expressly reserves all rights it has, may have had, or will have in the future with regard to the optioned material or any expression thereof, including, without limitation, the characters, plot, and any alterations, or additions thereto in every medium, whether such medium is now in existence, or is developed hereafter.

Best of luck,

Trevor Reid III

That letter told Robert that Reyes' option must have deviated from the norm. Every option that Robert had ever drafted, if it expired without being exercised, left both parties to go on their merry, or not-so-merry, ways. But always free and clear of each other.

"Trevor Reid. So is Three Thirty-Three Film Ventures connected to the Three Thirty-Three Hedge Fund?" A fund he'd seen mentioned in the financial press.

"Brother-sister outfits, yeah."

"Your project was optioned by a company owned by Trevor Reid's hedge fund? The fund with offices in Beverly Hills?"

Reyes nodded. "Beverly Hills, what I hear."

"It's amazing you pulled that off."

In a town full of people writing and running around with new scripts—fifty thousand scripts a year, or so he'd read—only a handful made it as far as Reyes.

"And I think you were smart to show the letter to T-Mack. Lots of people needing a deal would've held it back. In fact, in the independent-movie business, *most people* would've held it back and worried later about the fallout."

"Well, see, that bullshit reservation letter's not from Three Belts Childress, a'ight. It's from Three Thirty-Three up in the Beverly Hills. Say I went ahead and signed with T-Mack, held back that letter, and down the line, we started shootin' something. Everybody's high on life, but here come Three Thirty-Three sayin', 'Hold up, bitch. Y'all must not a' seen my letter to Mr. Reyes about my client's rights.' Then T-Mack, he'd be sayin', 'Shuck that FUBU beret, Raymundo, and get your ass over here!' At that point, picture's done. Word gets out about me, I'm done, too."

A sophisticated analysis, street or otherwise. Robert agreed with every word.

"Why didn't you show me the option before you signed?"

"My thinkin' was, I let you look at it, you'd tell me what all's wrong with it. And if you talked to Three Thirty-Three, maybe y'all get sideways, and they get pissed off, me being a nobody bringing a lawyer to the table."

"Let's call you *an unknown*, all right?"

"Unknown superstar, I hear you. But most likely, you'd tell me not to sign, and I'd know you were right, and where would that leave me?"

Robert nodded. "At some point, you gotta step up and take your shot."

Much more than a kernel of truth lay in Reyes' words. Deals between unequals could be lost simply because the weaker party had the audacity to hire his own lawyer.

"Fact is, *mi abogado*, I read it over lotsa times before signin'. Didn't look sketchy to me."

"Okay, then, tell me how you saw the option working."

Not an idle question. Reyes had an unusual, intelligent take on just about everything.

Reyes said, "I mean, they pay me my option money up front, right? And if they want to, they can pay me more in a year—a lot more—or buy me all the way out anytime they want, for *a lot, lot, lot* more, and own the whole thing."

So far, sounded like a typical option.

"What else did you agree to in the option?"

"Well, I gave Three Thirty-Three what they like callin' *a warranty*, pretty much like you'd get buyin' a new car. I'm sayin' I own the script, just me, thought it up myself, and didn't rip the ideas off from nobody else."

"What happens if you're not telling the truth about that warranty stuff?"

"That case, I hafta pony up what Three Thirty-Three already paid me, plus pony up for any trouble they got into for believing me in the first place. They had a long contract word for it. Can't recall it just now, us sitting here."

Indemnification. Reyes had gotten the hang of its meaning better than some lawyers he knew.

"What'd the option say about their lawyers getting involved?"

"Push comes to shove, and they sic their *abogado* on me? I gotta pay *their* man for coming after what I owe. What's that cost, a thousand an hour?"

"Close enough."

"But if I'd raised hell about those warranties, what's Three Thirty-Three gonna tell me?" Reyes laid on his best Richard Pryor white-man voice: "You are aware, are you not, Mr. Reyes, if you are not lying to us about your warranties, you have nothing at all to worry about?"

In his street voice: "Same time, I'm thinking, 'I'm lying to y'all? I'll just go home, pull my big screen off the wall, bring it to your office. That way, you already picked me clean.'"

By this point, they were both grinning about the big screen. Reyes gave book-smart guys too much credit; he'd just ripped through one month of first-year law school contracts class.

13

The fact remained, the letter from 333 Film Ventures where the company claimed to *reserve all rights* in the optioned material after the option expired seemed unfair. Overreaching, at minimum. Still, Robert knew that he was bound to find incredibly punitive language in Reyes' option allowing postoption rights. Language that Reyes had either missed or misunderstood.

"Telling you where you stand, Reyes, that's really all I can do."

"Hear you, *Roberto. Gracias.*"

He could tell that something else was bugging Reyes. "What else?"

"Got a little situation with Roland Jakes, young cat over on Abbott Kinney, runs Three Thirty-Three Film for the big boys."

Big boys meant the 333 Hedge Fund. Reyes slid a piece of paper across the desk. A copy of an email from RJ, who had this salvo for Reyes:

> Hey, Ray Man,
>
> Just a heads-up—I filed our material with the Writers Guild. On the cover page, I reflected my participation in *Walk Street Hits* like so: By Raymundo Reyes and Roland Jakes. With all the time I put in, wordsmithing and honing the material, I know you'd agree that sharing authorship was the only fair thing to do. Real sorry this didn't work out. Maybe we'll pick it up again down the line. Peace out, bro. RJ.

Even Robert knew the importance of writing credits in the movie business. Credits told the world who was due the laurels—or the blame—for a screenplay. A sole writing credit—Reyes only—was considered best of breed.

"What'd RJ contribute?"

"Hmm, lemme think. Oh yeah—not a damn thing."

"Nothing at all?"

"I mean, look, I spent time over at his office working out the second and third act of the screenplay, and we'd go up on his tricked-out roof to hang, and he'd talk about how he *pictured* the story—and he can only *picture* it one way. Lucky for me, what he pictured was things he'd seen in cool movies and wanted to copy, so he'd come off cool, too."

"Like . . . ?"

"Like Uma's wig and Glocks."

Uma's wig?

Reyes said, "Had to have a guy pulling out his Glock, holding it sideways. RJ, he'd tell me, 'Outta nowhere, out came the Glock.' You and me both know it's coming outta *somewhere*, but okay, I played along. 'Love it, RJ, keep those sweet words flowing.' Everybody knows, on a low-budget gig, the gun's gonna be what the prop house has on hand, or whatever weapon I got lyin' around the house." Before Robert could comment on Reyes' *weapon* crack: "Hey, nothin's lyin' around my house, a'ight?"

"I want no part of that kind of bullshit. *Claro?*"

"That ain't me, *Roberto*. You know that, don't you?"

"I believe you, Reyes, until I don't. You said, *Uma's wig. Uma* being *Uma Thurman?*"

"Ain't but one *Uma*, and RJ pictures my movie *chica* wearin' a blonde wig with bangs. Same blonde wig Uma wore in *Pulp Fiction*."

"Blonde? I'm picturing Uma in a black wig."

"You, me, the rest of the world, but RJ's picturing blonde, so that's that. Oh, and every time we'd meet, he'd tell me he's gonna send me story notes, account of he couldn't turn off his creative juices."

"Uh-oh."

"Don't sweat it. No notes, not once. We'd always meet early afternoon, and by two, two-thirty, RJ's headed out drinking with an older guy, drove a drop-top Delta 88."

"Is this what they call development hell?"

"More like development flu. You treat it right, supposed to go away in a few days."

RJ's writing-credit issue would go onto the far back burner for now. The way they left it, Robert would take a serious look at the option and find out how 333 Film could possibly justify reserving any rights after its option had expired.

Walking home afterward, he recalled a game he'd made up with Gia after they'd gone to a screening of a particularly cringeworthy indie film.

Their game: Let's tell the director the truth about what he just put us through!

Their favorite entries had been: *At least your next movie can't be worse. What was the biggest lesson you learned from all your mistakes? Between the script, the acting, and the direction, which was worst? And please take your time.*

He'd help his friend out of a jam if he could, but to Robert's way of thinking, it wasn't the worst thing in the world if Reyes' indie movie never saw the light of day.

CHAPTER 3

Robert rounded the corner of the alley onto Ozone, where he and Gia lived. Ahead of him, the Jacobsons poured from his gate into the street.

Erik clapped and shouted, "All right, boys, load up in the Beast!"

Parked beside Robert's vintage Bronco, the Beast—the family name for Erik's Yukon—looked like the Bronco's roided-out sibling. As Robert approached them, Erik held back from his family as they piled into the Beast, something on his mind as he laid a hand on Robert's shoulder.

"What's up?" Robert asked.

"Listen, man, I know you and Reyes—Gia and Reyes, too—you have a relationship, and that's cool by me. But my situation's different. I don't want my kids around him down at the beach—on the board-walk, especially. Hey, it's us adults, okay, I can deal, talk a little smack, nobody gets hurt. But my boys? That's not happenin' anymore, and Reyes asks me why, I'm not gonna be over-easy telling him. I can't have my boys thinking he's their uncle Ray and wind up around him that day somebody sprays bullets at Reyes over some gang beef or whatever turf war's on the menu."

That explained the earlier concerned look on Erik's face.

"Hundred percent your call, I get it, but Reyes isn't gang affiliated."

"Not in it, but I gotta believe he plays in that sandbox from time to time. And about the boys? You don't really get it yet. Not quite yet, from what Priya tells me."

"Gia told her we were trying?"

"Priya can't keep a secret. But look, when you do *get it*, you'll get it as big as I do, maybe bigger."

He had no grounds to argue with Erik on either count. Gangs had sprayed bullets down here before. As to what kind of father he might become? Time would tell.

After the Jacobsons pulled away, he removed Gia's handwritten sign from the Bronco's windshield: *I'm Old! Please Drive Me Away!* For reality-based reasons, she believed that the Bronco wasn't as reliable as it had been in its last-century heyday.

As he headed up the stairs to their apartment, he looked over at the two-story clapboard house on the same 35-by-120-foot lot but in front of theirs. If he and Gia wanted to buy it, they had first dibs.

Two months ago, he'd been picking up his mail from the walk-street mailbox when he'd spotted his landlord, James McCabe, lying on the floor inside. He'd called 911 and ridden with him to the hospital. In his late sixties, James had lapsed into an insulin coma tied to metastasizing cancer. Robert had visited him in the hospital and brought him his mail; James had never made it home.

A month later, James' lawyer contacted Robert. James had put Robert in his will a year before his final curtain.

"For six years, you always paid your rent on time, and James wanted to offer you the lot and two structures at a bargain price."

"There's family back east," Robert had said.

"He couldn't stand 'em, but they'll get the proceeds of the sale. Big decision, I know, but James noticed a woman started living back here with you, thought you two might be serious."

James had that right.

Fortunately, money wouldn't be a problem. Robert had banked $1.4 million from a settlement with his former law firm, plus another $750,000 from his share of a personal settlement from one of the firm's senior partners, Jack Pierce, who currently lay comatose in a Santa Cruz hospital.

Gia's financial situation was similar after selling her family's Brentwood home. Originally her parents' residence before she'd been orphaned at sixteen, her home had become a teardown sandwiched between upscale six-thousand-foot homes. One neighbor wanted her lot for a tennis court; the other craved a swimming pool. The swimming pool had won out, and Gia had recently pocketed more than $1 million.

He'd never questioned the turn of events that had brought them together. Years ago, they'd met when she'd been his firm's office manager, and he'd been working soul-crushing hours as a senior associate. Even though they'd flirted, he'd kept his distance because they worked together; she'd kept hers, too—along with her own secret life. But as a result of a soul-searing experience, they'd bonded, and he'd left behind the formal practice of law to set up shop on the boardwalk, taking on only clients who interested him.

Now, as he opened the door to their apartment—Gia had named it the Love Shack—he had a game plan for tonight: work through Reyes' situation and avoid physical contact with Gia until his work was done.

CHAPTER 4

A large living space with mullioned windows and open rafters. Their walls glowed orange and pink as the dimming sun slow-danced with the horizon. Robert had commandeered the dining room table-slash-desk to study Reyes' situation.

Nearby, Gia had stretched out on the couch behind her own work.

"Got time for a question?" she asked.

She'd already tried luring him to the couch with bogus questions.

"I'm not biting, okay? I'm working, same as you."

"This case is about offer and acceptance. Look at what I'm offering."

Confident she'd just exposed her breasts, he said, "I'm not looking over there."

"At what?"

"At your breasts."

"How'll you know unless you look?"

"Seriously, lotsa women have gotten pregnant from one—just one—look from me."

That got a laugh. An aptly named throw pillow whizzed over his head.

He'd just reread Reyes' option agreement with two goals in mind: deciding whether he could help Reyes and, if not, whether Reyes had a case good enough to attract a decent trial lawyer.

Reyes had been correct about how the option worked: 333 Film had optioned his project for $10,000 for one year—meaning that as the project took shape, they had the exclusive right during that period to decide if they wanted to buy it. At the end of the first year, they could renew the option for another year for $25,000. Robert didn't know if the payments were high or low, but $10,000 up front was decent money for a guy with no track record. Decent, too, was the $500,000 that 333 Film would pay to buy Reyes' project outright if they decided to produce it.

His next task: locating a clause in the contract allowing 333 Film to reserve all rights even after the option expired. *Reserve all rights* was incredibly broad language, and its vagueness could mean whatever 333 Film decided it meant, including, he guessed, the absurd position of still having an option on Reyes' project.

From Reyes' emails, Robert saw that 333 Film had dropped the option at the end of the first year—that had been months ago. No language in the contract granted 333 Film any rights to Reyes' project after the option expired.

Score one for Reyes.

Next order of business: Was T-Mack one of countless indie-world bullshitters or the real deal?

Leafing through T-Mack's promotional materials, Robert saw that its five movies had made it to the Edinburgh International Film Festival, the Venice Film Festival, and the Toronto International Film Festival, among others. Nothing about Cannes or Sundance, and Robert had never heard of any of the movies. But each festival, Google told him, was legit.

He studied one of Reyes' email threads with T-Mack:

T-Mack: Everything I've seen so far makes us very excited about what you've done. I think it would be great if we put our heads together, tried to iron out the details.

Reyes: Think it's great. Let's nail it down. Quicker the better. Tomorrow too soon?

T-Mack: Loews lobby, 9:00 a.m.? We'll go from there.

Other emails discussed budget—anywhere from $1 million to $2 million, depending on cast; when Reyes would complete the last two acts of the screenplay; payment for Reyes' writing services; writing credits; when and if Reyes might direct the movie.

Then came the bad news from T-Mack:

Raymundo,

Sorry to read that letter from 333 Film reserving rights postoption, and no, there's no need for me to read over your option agreement. No matter what it says, or whether 333 Film's claim is valid or not, they are backed by very deep pockets and made their position clear. Movies are hard to make and making good movies, even harder. What I've learned—start each project with every reason to succeed, not with ownership problems hanging over your head. Appreciated your honesty showing it to me, and if you can persuade them to release that claim, we can try to pick up where we left off.

Robert called Reyes, who must've been holding a finger on his "Answer" button.

"What'd you think?"

"Gia's here. Mind if she can hear us?"

"A Gigi legal twofer? Hell no."

"Even if you didn't sign it, did you and T-Mack ever put together a deal memo nailing everything down?"

"What you see in the emails, that's it."

"Did anybody at Three Thirty-Three Film know what you were up to with T-Mack?"

"Not that I know of. I's glad to be shed of RJ, and I never laid eyeball one on T. Reid Three."

Gazing out the window, Robert reached the same conclusion as Reyes: by sending that letter, 333 Film had wrongfully put a cloud over Reyes' project. They had gone out of their way to screw him and had acted in bad faith. From his five years of drafting contracts at his old firm, Robert knew that in every California contract, both parties were obligated to act in good faith, even if the contract made no mention of it.

Acting in bad faith would put 333 Film in breach of the option contract. What then could Reyes—either through Robert or with a trial lawyer—do about it?

Under the California Business and Professions Code, Robert believed 333 Film had committed an unlawful business practice. Sending that letter had been what the code called *unscrupulous and oppressive*.

The code provided for injunctive relief. As Reyes might describe that kind of relief: "Hey, man, reserving rights was oppressive and unscrupulous, so y'all better cut that shit out!"

Helpful to Reyes? Maybe, maybe not.

Now he looked into whether 333 Film had committed a *business tort*. *Torts* were civil wrongs that entitled Reyes to sue for monetary damages. Two business torts might apply, but after two more hours of legal research, he believed that California law wouldn't let Reyes through either door. Either because an actual contract between Reyes and T-Mack must be in place—it wasn't—or because 333 Film had to actually know about Reyes' dealings with T-Mack—and according to Reyes, it didn't.

With little to no prospect of collecting monetary damages, Robert concluded, Reyes would be hard pressed to find a decent trial lawyer to take his case.

Gia said, "*Hola, chico,* you need to come over here."

He didn't look up. "Can't. Working."

"Something I need to tell you."

From the corner of his eye, he saw that she was fully clothed, breasts sheathed.

"Please?"

He took an easy chair across from the couch, the coffee table between them. She got right down to it.

"*Walk Street Hits.* I was in it."

"*It?*"

"Whatever *it* is, I had a couple scenes in *it,* and I feel kinda bad about not telling you."

"Hey, you helped him out, I get it," he said.

"He asked me not to tell you. Said you'd tell him not to make it, and that you'd be right, but he was doing it anyway, even though he respected you."

"Oh," he said, flattered and trying to hide it.

No way could he be pissed off about Reyes' choosing Gia. On several of their nights on the town, legitimate directors had asked Gia to read for a part. Sure, it was always part come-on, but movie people seemed to discern a hard-to-pinpoint *something* about her.

"What was it like?" he asked.

"Couple of scenes was all I did. First one, I was *the chick* sitting at a table alone, looking around, not saying anything, lighting a cigarette. Oh, and I signaled the bartender to bring me the check. Nobody was really over at the bar, so I pretended—sorry, I mean *I acted.* I leave some money on the table and walk out. And there was a scene where I was driving a car, alone, and I parked on a dead-end street. He told me to look to my right, so I did."

"What was there?"

"Nothing. I mean, later there will be something there, but not yet. Reyes said he'd use a stand-in for me for the rest of the scene, so I took off for class."

"What'd he tell you about being *the chick*?"

"Let's see. At first, he said"—imitating Reyes now—"'Just be y'self, Gigi. Cool as cool can be, a'ight?' But that didn't work."

He knew why. No matter how she came across to the world, Gia didn't think of herself as cool. She was a little shy and held back because of it, which, in fact, actually made her cooler.

"So he came up with something that worked," she said, heading for the kitchen. "Want anything?"

"No, I'm good. What'd he tell you that worked?" he called out.

She came back in and sat at his feet with leftover taco salad from Mercedes Bar and Grille.

"In the bar scene, Reyes said, 'Try this, Gigi. You sittin' here, thinkin' about *Roberto*. He's late, and you not sure where he's at. Maybe y'all had a fight, nothing atomic, just a day-to-day, pick up y'socks, toilet-seat-up kinda beef.'"

He smiled. "What about your driving scenes?"

"He told me to look worried, not frantic, so I pretended to be driving the Bronco, knowing it could break down any minute."

She loved throwing shade at the Bronco; he loved catching it even more. Looking back on it, he must've glanced away. One of her hands snaked up his shorts. The other slipped under his waistband from above. A pincer movement, ripped from the pages of Sun Tzu's *The Art of War*.

No escape; his surrender was complete, and she took no prisoners.

❧

By the time Robert woke up an hour later in the chair, Gia had gone to the gym and texted him a variety of "I love you" emojis.

A shower, the rest of her taco salad, a quart of Gatorade later, and he was back at work. Asking himself: What were the chances a decent trial lawyer could overcome all the obstacles Robert had already uncovered and win *damages* for Reyes?

Winning money. Item Number One for any trial lawyer. No doubt, Trevor Reid's two companies had *damaged* Reyes as laypeople viewed that word, but legal damages differed.

Sargon Enterprises v. University of Southern California was the guiding California Supreme Court case. *Sargon* made it clear that California courts awarded money damages only if the damages were not too speculative. By speculative, the court meant damages not certain to ever occur—like Reyes' project, with no contract and miniscule chances of getting made. Or damages that were too uncertain in amount—again, like Reyes' project with an unknown director and unknowable final box office numbers.

Sargon said Reyes' prospects were not good. Not. Good. At. All.

That night, over a late dinner, he asked Gia, "How many friends of friends' indie screenings have we gone to?"

"Indie movies? Ten, maybe? Fifteen?"

"What'd they all have in common?"

"Low budgets, bad lighting . . ."

"You're overthinking it—every one of 'em sucked. And the person who made it, when the lights came on, remember that look they all had?"

"Yeah, beaming, so proud of what they'd done."

"Proud of what they'd inflicted on us, and smart people, too. It's right in front of them, and it sucks. How's that possible?"

"Making your own movie," Gia said. "I guess it makes people crazy."

CHAPTER 5

The next morning, Reyes wanted to meet Robert at the Wee Chippy, a fish-and-chips joint just off the boardwalk on Westminster Avenue. Robert was early and found out that Wee Chippy's window didn't slide open till noon.

He spotted Reyes walking up Speedway and forced himself to stay on an even keel. Sure, he was pissed off about what Trevor Reid had pulled. Whether Reyes' project was the next *Godfather* or the next *Plan 9 from Outer Space*, sending that reservation-of-rights letter was unfair and wrong.

They grabbed cold-press coffees from Groundwork in the Morrison Apartments, where Jim Morrison of the Doors fame had lived back in the sixties.

As the men headed north up the boardwalk, the Santa Monica Mountains found their way through the morning fog, and Robert explained the law to Reyes, whose first reaction came as no surprise: "After all the work I did on my project, I'm DOA in court?"

"I'm just telling you what the law says. At this point, you don't have a contract with T-Mack. You two didn't get far enough for a court to figure out if you'd ever be damaged, and if so, how much damage would've been done."

"My project's in the hit-man genre, not some art-house flick. Even got a star who's in it."

"What star?"

"You already tellin' me nothing matters, nothin' I can do. I get myself right up to the door, bangin' on it, they jam me up, and you sayin' *nothing doing*?"

"Not what I'm saying at all. What Three Thirty-Three Film did was an unfair business practice. I think you could prove to a court that Three Thirty-Three's screwing up your prospects going forward."

"Cuz Three Thirty-Three's letter's an *oppressive and onerous* business practice."

Guess Reyes had been listening earlier; bad news took time to filter through anger.

Robert said, "Yeah, and you'd ask for an injunction against them telling them to quit making their bogus claims. I'm guessing it'd cost you less than ten grand."

"What about how they damaged me?"

Damage again. Robert tried to be patient.

"Think about it, Reyes. You're a first-time director in negotiations with a buyer, and you haven't nailed down most of the deal points. You have no track record making movies, good or bad, so I don't think a court lets you get your case to a jury. I could be wrong, but that's what I think. The movie business is risky as hell, and nobody knows what audiences are going to like next week, much less next year."

"How about *Blair Witch*? *Clerks*? *Napoleon Dynamite*? *El Mariachi*? *Paranormal Activity*? *Saw*? All of 'em low budget. All of 'em killed. All of 'em by first-time directors."

"Even *I* know about those movies, Reyes. Want to know why? Because they broke out. Movies like that almost *never* break out. That's why I know about 'em—because when it happens, *it's news*."

"But they do, right? Break out."

"Course they do, but you didn't get far enough along with T-Mack. Look at it this way. If Warner Brothers called today and offered you ten million for all your rights? Think T-Mack could tell them to get lost because T-Mack had you under contract?"

The answer was so clear, Reyes didn't bother to answer.

Robert said, "I'd be pissed off, too, and I am, but that's not the same as having a good case and finding a decent lawyer to try it. So, look, we'll send Three Thirty-Three a cease-and-desist letter, let 'em know the impact their letter already had. We'll put 'em on notice, so next time—"

"Won't be a next time. Got a bunch of business cards from around town, but they all fly-by-nights."

"What about Paul Dickerson? Can he help you out?"

Reyes shook his head. "Not for something like this."

Peter Paul Dickerson was an LA investor-billionaire who had bought and sold the entire seven-film *Street Cred* franchise. Reyes claimed to know Paul quite well—always skimping on their friendship's details—so Robert didn't know if he'd been bullshitting about it or not. With Reyes, it was always hard to tell.

Robert said, "I'll work out a letter for you, get my old firm to send it out on their letterhead."

"I hear you, thanks. But Three Thirty-Three? They're big dogs, *Roberto*. They don't get off the dime just because they start getting letters."

Reyes' conclusion was far more right than wrong. Robert hated seeing the crushing impact his legal news delivery was having, but he'd already spent seven or eight hours on Reyes' problem. A bill for $4,000 or more would've been in order at his old firm.

Even so, seeing Reyes' beat-down expression, he found himself offering, "So, look. Why don't I meet with this RJ character, see if I can get him to drop his claim to a writing credit?"

Reyes brightened. "You'd do that?"

"I'll give it a shot. Anything you can tell me that might help me deal with RJ?"

"Show up right at two p.m. He's always blazing up a bone right about then."

CHAPTER 6

The next morning, once Gia bounced off to work, Robert dragged out his computer.

Articles in the trade magazines *Variety* and the *Hollywood Reporter* confirmed 333 Film as a three-year-old start-up funded by the 333 Hedge Fund. Turned out, Roland Jakes was related to Trevor Reid by marriage. PR puff pieces quoted RJ talking about his lifelong love of film, with Trevor putting in his two cents about moviemaking being essential to the fabric of Los Angeles.

With RJ in mind, Robert drafted a short release for him to sign, giving up his bogus writing credit. At 1:45 p.m., he paid his tab at the Rose café and headed the four long blocks over to RJ's office on Abbot Kinney Boulevard, a walk that confirmed how much Venice had changed. Gunfire had been replaced by espresso-machine steam as twenty-year liquor-store leases expired and trend-blazers moved in.

Once Robert arrived, he hit the intercom, gave his name, and was buzzed inside the three-story building. Sandblasted cinder-block walls supported a freestanding metal staircase. A blond maple desk rested on blue-tinted concrete floors, and the receptionist—blonde, too—sat behind it.

About forty, dressed for success, she gave him a big smile and said, "I know you. I saw your picture online. You saved that little girl. The Beach Lawyer, right?"

The little girl, Delfina Famosa, had been his last client. After Robert had pulled her from the clutches of a psychopath, the story had made news in a big way.

"Sometimes. Other times, I'm Robert Worth."

"I'm Lane Lang all the time."

"Like Superman's evil girlfriend?"

"That's my evil sister, *Lana* Lang. What a bitch." Somehow, her seen-it-all vibe didn't come across as jaded.

"Roland Jakes, is he in?"

"As in as he ever is. And this is regarding?"

"Raymundo Reyes."

"*Walk Street Hits*, sure. RJ's on the roof deck. Go on up. He doesn't get too many celebrities like you these days."

He crossed the polished concrete to the stairway and climbed to the third floor, which gave onto a forty-by-thirty-foot deck. At its far end, a flat-top canvas tent sheltered two couches and a Plexiglas coffee table.

Halfway down the deck, RJ leaned against the railing, midtoke, and so far, Reyes was batting a thousand about RJ's habits. Spotting Robert, he exhaled an epic blast of cannabis smoke and stubbed out his j.

As Robert approached, nothing about RJ told him he minded a stranger finding him getting baked at work. Taller and heavier than Robert, RJ looked like an ex-jock, midthirties. A wannabe hipster going to seed.

Robert said, "Robert Worth. You're RJ, right?"

"Got that right. What's cooking, my man?"

They shook hands. RJ's palm sweated onto Robert's; he wished they'd fist-pounded instead.

"Glad I caught you. I dropped by for a client I just picked up. You know him. Name's Raymundo Reyes."

"Ray Gun Reyes, ma' man. *Walk Street Hits*, ma' bitch. Shit, you win some, right?"

"Not sure what you mean by that."

"Project's done, over, fried. Ray Man'll never get anywhere without us."

If Reyes' project ever got anywhere—as remote as that possibility was—credits would be arbitrated by the Writers Guild of America West, and RJ would lose. But his friend needed a win right now, and given how busy RJ had been screwing Reyes, Robert decided to get busy, too.

"If Ray Man's project's not going anywhere, you mind letting go of your writing credit?"

"Why would I do that? What do I get?"

"Look, RJ, I hardly know Ray Man, but I gotta take something back to him, anything. You feel me?"

"Just remind him how the two of us gutted it out, blood, sweat, and tears. It's not his; it's ours."

Looked like RJ believed his own rap—another deluded prick in a business full of them.

Robert shrugged and said, "That might fly. Your herb any good?"

RJ cupped it in both hands like a prizewinning squash. "Best in the biz, cuz. C'mon, let's chill."

Over in the tent shade, they took opposing couches. RJ fired up the joint, took a hit, and handed it to Robert.

Robert said, "Man, I should be working . . ."

"Hey, when in Venice, right?"

His play on *when in Rome* was actually clever; Robert wondered where RJ had stolen the line as he fake-hit that j and made a big production of coughing it out.

"Good shit," he said, wiping his dry eyes.

"I pick up the *chicas* from over at Viceroy, tell 'em I got this office down here on AK, right?"

AK? Abbot Kinney? Was that a thing?

"Get 'em up here on deck central, they lose their shit, and that ain't all."

"Bet they do."

That's when Robert realized—a whiff of inhaled smoke had tilted him off-center. For some reason, he recalled Reyes' bad joke about having weapons around his house in East LA.

"How well you know Reyes?"

"We're tight as any two bros can be."

"So, you've been to his place over in East LA?"

"Not, you know, recently."

Meaning *not ever*—passing through East LA en route to Palm Springs didn't count.

"Scary place, scary people, man. I didn't know what I'd gotten into going over there," Robert said.

"Ray Man's keeping it real, right?"

Was there a cliché RJ wouldn't use?

"Too real for me. It was rough."

"The criminal element? Any Glocks come out?"

Robert pressed his palms into his eyes to keep from laughing.

"There was something in the air—not dope. I mean, a hardcore vibe. One of his guys was getting ready to go up for murder one, home for one last visit."

"No way, cool."

A cool murder one wasn't doing the trick, so he upped the ante.

"Another dude over there? He and another guy just got out of the joint on mayhem charges."

"*Mayhem's* a good title for a flick. Hold on."

RJ Googled *mayhem* on his iPhone.

"Somebody already used it, but I's right."

He reached over for a fist bump; Robert bumped him back and said, "That's a movie. This was real, trust me. You have any idea what mayhem is?"

"Some bad shit, right?"

He knew the answer but Googled the California statute on his iPhone anyway.

"Here you go, *mayhem*." Then Robert read: "Every person who unlawfully and maliciously deprives a human being of a member of his body, or disables, disfigures, or renders it useless, or cuts or disables the tongue . . ."

He looked over at RJ. "*Cuts the tongue.* Can you imagine how bad that would hurt?"

RJ stuck out his tongue and squeezed it. "A ton, I bet."

Robert started reading again: "Or puts out an eye . . ." He looked up. "*Puts out an eye?* Really? How? An ice pick or what?"

"Who's down with doing shit like that?"

"Guys over at Reyes', is what I'm telling you. Listen to this. '*Or anyone who slits the nose, ear, or lip.*'"

"Slits the lip?"

"What it says. That's who's guilty of mayhem, and that's who I was trying to eat tamales with."

"What kind of sick-ass friends does Reyes have?"

"Not friends, bro. *Family*, and that East LA family water runs deep. Hey, you want to stay on Reyes' bad side, that's your business." Standing, Robert said, "The good news for you is . . ."

He didn't finish on purpose.

Standing too, buzzed and alarmed, RJ asked, "What's my good news?"

"Your weed's primo. Besides, I don't want to rep Reyes, so I'll tell him straight up: 'RJ said he worked his ass off, wants his writing credit, and if you don't like it, Reyes, go fuck yourself.' How's that, m'brother?"

"I didn't say *go fuck yourself.* Did I?"

"Didn't you?"

As RJ's worry inventory grew, a car horn blared below. RJ and Robert looked over the railing at a metallic-blue Delta 88 Oldsmobile convertible. Top dropped, a silver-haired man mashed the horn.

RJ called down, "Yo, Dav, cool it for five. I'm taking a meeting!"

Dav shouted up, "No way, man, time to boogie!"

RJ turned to Robert. "That there's my boy, Dav Concha. Forget my writing credit, man. Life's too short. Got that release?"

Robert pulled up the one-page release on his laptop, showed it to RJ.

"Any tricky shit in here?" RJ asked, skimming the document.

Nope. The tricky shit had just happened.

"Not in the document. It deals only with *Walk Street Hits* and releases any creative credit you might've had."

Once RJ DocuSigned the release, he gave Robert a business card and hurried for the stairwell. Robert took his time leaving. On his way down, he checked out a series of photographs staggered at eye level.

Near the top, Trevor's wedding photograph: Two couples, captioned *Trevor and Marguerite Reid, Jerry Baugh and Kay Miller. Malibu, California, 2003.*

Robert's first look at Trevor Reid. Short, his curly black hair framing a scowl that might require surgical removal; the other man, Jerry, was Trevor's external opposite: tall and powerful with a winning smile.

On the next level down, several more shots. A barren landscape with a rapids-filled river in the background. Two men held a fifty-pound salmon; a huge feathered fly hung from its mouth. The caption: *Trevor and Jerry, 2005, Ponoi River, Russia.*

Their expressions matched the other shot—a scowl versus a smile.

Next, at the same barren locale, Trevor and Jerry posed with a gray-haired Russian man between them. This caption ID'd him as General Sergei Popov. Saluting, surely drunk, he neither scowled nor smiled—he leered.

On the second floor, he saw RJ's nameplate on a door at the end of the hall. Three other office doors lined the hall, one of them ajar. He could see that the office was empty. He walked over to a second door, this one closed, and knocked softly. No answer, so he opened the door and found this office empty as well.

Down in the lobby, he grabbed a cup of espresso with Lane and shot the breeze. Turned out, she'd moved to the beach from Echo Park, near downtown, signed a long-term lease, and just learned from RJ that she'd be out of a job next month.

That explained the empty offices. Three Thirty-Three Film was on the verge of closing shop, prompting Lane finally to say, "Trevor Reid is rich, and he's a jerk. Guess it beats being a poor jerk, but that's about all I can say good about him. Got a job opening at your firm?"

"Sorry, Lane, I'm not really set up for a receptionist."

"Oh, did I say, *job opening*? I meant, *let's get together for a drink.*"

Not jaded, just having fun. Flattered, he begged off. Left the office and made it around the corner to Electric Avenue, where Reyes waited for him.

"How'd it go?"

"RJ's writing credit is history."

"Bravo! Either ya' brains or ya' signature gonna be on the Beach Lawyer's dotted line."

Reyes' version of the famous *Godfather* quote.

"Only way I roll," Robert said as Reyes DocuSigned the release.

Robert forwarded it to the email address on RJ's card and was about to wish Reyes luck when Reyes said, "Thing is, I still want you to see what I shot."

"Give me a copy. Gia and I will try to watch it tonight."

"Naw, naw. See, I shot it on sixteen millimeter. Want you to come over to my crib and watch with a crowd."

With people? An hour's drive from here, sometimes two with traffic, for an indie film? How much abuse did Reyes want to put him through? Was he being punished for lying to RJ?

"And bring Ms. Gigi Marquez. No doubt she'll want to see herself."

"I'm sure she would, but look—"

"Everybody—and I mean *everybody*—loves it. So'll you, guaranteed."

At this point, Robert hit his limit. For anyone besides Reyes, he'd have never looked at an indie-movie problem, option related or otherwise. He wanted to get out of helping anymore without rubbing too much more salt in the guy's wounds.

"Everybody? Guaranteed?" Robert asked.

"Like I just said."

"Think that Erik would go for it?"

Reyes didn't miss a beat. "You get him over there, and hell, yeah, he'll be my biggest fan."

"Tell you what. If Erik likes it, I'll try to fix things with Trevor Reid—the whole thing, all in. But if he doesn't, never mention your project to me again. How's that work for you?"

Cornered or confident? Hard to tell with Reyes.

"Like I said, *jefe*, everybody likes it. You get E-Rik over to East LA, he will, too."

⁂

Back at Ozone that night, Gia asked, "Let me make sure I heard right. If *Erik* watches what Reyes shot, and *Erik* doesn't like it—you're off the hook repping the movie?"

"That's the deal. A thumbs-down from Erik, and I'm off the case."

"Is there another Erik I don't know?"

"Nope."

"Erik rolling to East LA to watch Reyes' whatever? I can't see it."

"That's what Reyes was counting on when he didn't back down, but I was thinking, what if *Priya* wanted to see *you* in a movie? She has no idea how much these indie projects suck, so she'd want to go. Then Erik has to tag along. Once he goes thumbs-downs, I'm a free man."

Gia started getting into the spirit. "What if Priya thought I was *starring* in the movie?"

"Hey, for all we know, you *are* the star."

She was already calling Priya. "Erik's opinion is the last word? Reyes is that confident?"

"Nope, that deluded. I can see it now. His movie's over, lights come on, and everybody's cockroaching for the exits. And there stands Raymundo Reyes, *beaming.*"

She spoke into her phone. "*Sawatdii, ka,* Priya. How're you? So, listen, did I ever tell you I was in a movie? No, I'm not a movie star, but guess what? Reyes made a movie I was in, and you, me, Robert, *and Erik* get to watch it."

"What's she saying?" he asked.

"Something about Reyes winning an Oscar, and now she's screaming and telling the boys."

All right!

CHAPTER 7

Two days later, Erik didn't look at all chipper as Robert drove the I-10 through early-evening traffic downtown, headed for Reyes' screening. Priya and Gia rode in the Bronco's back seat; Priya was still stoked about viewing Reyes' masterwork.

Erik's final objection to the movie-viewing trip had been security, but once he'd learned Reyes' *mamacita* would be the guest of honor, he'd folded.

Robert told Erik, "You know what a showman Reyes is. It'll be cool."

"Showman? That's what you call him now?"

"Just tell him what you think, no need to spare his feelings."

"No worries there, my friend." Erik actually smiled.

In the back seat, Gia pointed outside and told Priya, "That's the LA River."

Its meager flow trickled along a hundred-foot-wide concrete culvert.

"That's no Chao Phraya," Erik said to Priya. The major river flowing through Bangkok.

Priya said, "Chao Phraya is called *mother water*. LA River looks like a sad child."

A few minutes after getting on the Pomona Freeway, they passed Boyle Heights and exited onto South Lorena Avenue. When Robert parked near Reyes' place on Second Street, Priya leaned up from the back seat and whispered to him.

"Gia will have a baby soon."

"How do you know?"

"I see it happen in my dreams," she said, and opened her door.

❧

By the time Robert and the others walked into the red-carpeted side-yard driveway at Reyes' address, they were running late. Ahead and to their right sat Reyes' mother's two-story house. On her front porch sat a lit-up glass cactus with a Santa hat, and beside it, a three-foot-tall papier-mâché Frosty the Snowman. Christmas year-round at the Reyes' family abode.

Garlic-and-onion-suffused food-truck smoke hung in the air, drawing them toward the rear of the lot. A mariachi band on break wore black suits embroidered with silver buckles; wood tables offered *raspodos*, *tacoloquitos*, and *calaveras*—sugar skulls.

A handful of guests milled around; another twenty or so sat on folding chairs inside Reyes' crib, a converted three-car garage on his mother's lot.

Here came Reyes up the driveway, his iPhone camera raised. Beside him, his mother, about sixty, walked with the help of a red-and-green hand-carved cane. Her braided hair had streaked natural gray.

"Just like the Oscars," Priya said, in her black-and-white cocktail dress and matching heels.

"Almost exactly," Erik said.

Reyes started his patter, his iPhone still rolling. For the first time ever, Robert hoped that Reyes would start throwing shade at Erik.

"*Mami,* these are the people I invited from Venice and Mar Vista. Erik Jacobson and his wife, Priya, from Thailand. Erik is a retired LAPD officer. This is my momma, Gabriela Reyes."

"All the way from Thailand, really?" Gabriela said. "And LAPD? So very nice to meet you, Erik."

Reyes said, "And right there's Robert Worth and his sweetheart, Gia Marquez."

No *Yake* for Jacobson? No *Gigi* for *Gia? Asian Sensation* would've been too much to hope for.

Gabriela said, "Gia? Raymundo told me you were in his movie."

"Hope I did okay."

"I haven't seen it yet, but he said you stole the show. *Roberto*, you're the one my son calls Beach Lawyer?"

"Among many other things, Gabriela. Sorry we're late, had a few lookie-loos on the 405."

"All that matters to me is that you came."

A gracious, well-spoken woman. He couldn't help watching Reyes, proud as could be of her. A twinge of guilt pinged him about what was getting ready to happen.

Reyes gave a hand signal, and a mariachi trumpeter blasted out horse racing's "Call to Post."

"Time to head inside," Reyes said. Then: "Really appreciate you coming, Erik. I have special seats for you and Priya up front. Hope you both like the show."

"Hope springs eternal," Erik said.

Reyes handed both Robert and Erik a thin folder.

"Copy of the screenplay, for you two only. You'll see why."

Gabriela asked Priya, "Mind if I take your husband's other arm?"

Priya said, "No problem, plenty to go around."

Reyes said, "*Mami*, you're in back with me. Your footstool's already set up."

"Raymundo, I plan to sit up front with Mr. Jacobson and his wife." Then to Erik: "How many years were you with the LAPD?"

"Twenty and out," Erik said as they disappeared inside.

Watching them go, Gia said, "Can you believe it?"

"So far, none of it," Robert said.

A simple *Walk Street Hits* poster hung on the door. A red-and-white map of Venice Beach, a bull's-eye centered on Windward Circle. The credits showed that Reyes had written, edited, and directed it—whatever *it* was.

"*Walk Street Hits!*" Reyes shouted. "Let's do it!"

Robert grabbed a cold Victoria from the tub, took a gulp, and headed inside behind Gia. They sat in the third row. Erik, Priya, and Gabriela took their reserved seats in front.

Gia whispered, "Look, Erik has an entourage."

"No laughing unless it's a comedy."

The crowd was buzzing as Reyes took the podium—an overturned crate. Robert couldn't help grinning at the movie posters behind him: *Clerks, El Mariachi, Paranormal Activity,* and *Scarface.* Reyes thanked all the guests who'd worked on his project and mentioned that the two male leads couldn't make it—they'd found paying work.

Reyes waved to a good-looking guy just walking in the back door, a daypack slung over one shoulder. The guy waved back.

Gia asked, "That's Paul Dickerson, isn't it?"

The billionaire Reyes claimed to know well.

"Think so."

Reyes shouted, "Looks like everyone's here, so let's have us some fun!"

CHAPTER 8

In the dim light, Robert read paragraph one of Reyes' screenplay:

EXTERIOR. VENICE BEACH—MORNING.

Every beach has guys who hang around and don't do shit. Here's two of 'em, thirty and up, walking along the bike path. Since they got nothing better to do, these two argue a lot and bet each other with money they don't have. Neither of 'em's all that smart, especially the big blond guy. Let's call 'em Dude 1 and Dude 2, the blond guy holding down the #2 slot.

Robert had read screenplays before. *Heat, The Godfather, Deadpool,* several others. This was much more conversational, like Reyes talking to the reader. Good or bad? He had no idea.

Gia read it, too, and whispered: "You and Erik? Not all that smart and don't do shit? Love it already."

On the screen:

The movie's credit sequence: A single Venice Beach postcard. On the flip side, a felt-tip handwritten list of the actors' names, including Gigi Marquez.

Bottom of the postcard: *WALK STREET HITS. Every bit of it by Raymundo Reyes.*

Reyes' Two Dudes walk along the deserted bike path.

> Dude 1: *I wouldn't say the waitress was smokin' hot.*
> *She was more what I call pretty.*

> Dude 2: *Wrong, I'd say she was smokin' hot 'cause*
> *that's what she was.*

> Dude 1: *That girl works over at the Cuban place?*
> *Now that one, she's smokin' hot.*

> Dude 2: *A smokin' hot waitress at the Cuban joint—*
> *which one you mean?*

> Dude 1: *The smokin' hot one, like I just said.*

A bike rider speeds by and shouts, "Bike path, douchebags!"
The Two Dudes are oblivious.

> Dude 2: *There's three smokin' hot ones at the Cuban*
> *place.*

> Dude 1: *No, they's only the one. The one I'm talking*
> *about.*

> Dude 2: *At the Cuban place? They's three.*

> Dude 1: *Wait up—which Cuban place?*

> Dude 2: *Ain't but one Cuban place.*

> Dude 1: *No, they's two Cuban places.*

Dude 2: Wanna bet?

Robert found the Dudes engaging. Gia was smiling, too. As the Dudes kept walking, they made a $100 bet about the number of Cuban restaurants in Venice.

Around the room, the crowd looked like they were into it. Robert scanned his script:

INTERIOR BEACH BAR—MORNING.

There's a bartender behind the long wood bar. He'll look exactly like me, if I can't find a good-enough actor to play him.

Back on-screen:

The Two Dudes sit down at the bar with takeout coffee cups from another joint. Reyes stands behind the bar.

Bartender: Told you two about bringing coffee in from outside.

The Two Dudes ignore him.

Dude 1: Want to hit the surf later?

Dude 2: Surf's no good today.

Dude 1: Said on the surf cam it's supposed to be good.

Dude 2: Gonna get blown out early, be terrible.

Bartender: Ocean's a hundred yards away. Get up off your asses, go look.

Robert liked Reyes' acting, not overdoing it just because it was his movie. And directing? Most of the attention was on the Two Dudes, talking about whether there was a red tide, whether it was unhealthy to swim in it. The Bartender told them it was deadly, then offered to pay them to go for a long swim.

That's when Gia's character—Chica in the script—walked in the bar. Took a table by the window wearing a red cocktail dress with matching heels and an Uma-style, *Pulp Fiction* wig—blonde, not black. Reyes must've conceded to RJ's only script note of value.

"God," Gia whispered to him, hiding her eyes.

"Doin' great, baby."

Back on-screen:

Chica signals for the Bartender. He walks offscreen, leaving the Two Dudes.

Dude 2: Think she's a pro or not?

Dude 1: Stops by here for a cup of coffee first thing in the morning, looking like that? Gotta be a pro.

Dude 2: A pro looks like that has a limo already picking her up. Nah, she's right off a heavy civilian date. Guy fell in love with her—look, she's checking her phone. He's ringing her up to see if she made it home all right.

Dude 1: Does it burden you always being wrong? She's checking her phone for her next customer—cuz she's a full-time professional sex person.

Chica leaves. After some back-and-forth, the Bartender lets the Dudes use his car to follow her and find out who she was. One word of caution: the front passenger door might stick a little.

Inside the Bartender's car. A pistol-shaped air freshener dangles from the rearview mirror. Dude 1 drives up Venice Boulevard. Chica's white sedan is ahead.

Inside Chica's car. Chica looks worried, not overdoing it.

Dude 2: Man, if she'd let me, I'd brush her hair for two hours.

Dude 1: Feet are the key. Women insecure about their feet. Why they spend so much money buyin' shoes.

Dude 2: She ain't lettin' you nowhere near her feet, dude.

Dude 1: Why? Cuz she's lettin' you give her hair a thousand strokes?

Chica turns onto an industrial-looking street, stops where it dead-ends. A car is already parked across from hers. She cuts the engine.

The Two Dudes stop fifty yards back from the parked cars. A concrete wall looms beside the driver's-side door. A red-haired woman exits the other parked car, strolls toward Chica's car, gets in. From here, it looks like the two women are talking.

In the script, the second woman was called Red.
"What's going on?" he whispered to Gia.
"Told you, I never saw what happened. Shhh."
Back on-screen:

Inside the Bartender's car. The Two Dudes watch Chica and Red through their windshield.

Dude 1: They gonna get it on. A Tinder hookup. Lovers! What'd I tell you!

Dude 2: Hell no! That's what I told you! You owe me a hundred bucks!

BAM—muzzle flash from inside Chica's car. Blood splatters her front windshield. The Two Dudes jump back.

Beside Robert, Gia's nails dug into his arm; the whole room jumped.
Gia whispered, "Me or her?"
Gia's character fell over.
"You didn't make the cut."
Back on-screen:

Chica's passenger-side door swings open. Red gets out. Stops and looks right at the Two Dudes. As Red slowly approaches their car, Dude 1 cranks the car over and over. It catches, then dies. Then again.

Red reaches for a pistol.

The way Reyes directed this part, Robert felt trapped inside the car with the Dudes. They screamed at each other. Dude 2 tried to bang open his door. Like the Bartender said—the door sticks a little. Dude 1 hit the wiper switch by accident—his wiper blades bumped across the dry windshield. Loud like the car's cranking engine.

Dude 2 tried kicking out his window; his soft flip-flops didn't do the trick.

Gia squeezed his hand. Up front, Priya hid her eyes; so did Mamacita. Erik leaned forward, intense, as Dude 1 tried to open the driver's-side door. That concrete wall blocked his way out. Dude 1 started honking the horn. More noise and tension as Red eased between that wall and the car. Stopped at the driver's window and shattered it with her pistol.

Back on-screen:

> *Both Dudes cower. Red's face comes into frame in heavy makeup, eyeliner. Next comes the gun. Red pulls off her red wig. Gives her head a shake—she's a man.*

Robert can see that it's *El Sueño Azul,* the Blue Dream, star of the *Street Cred* series. The Latinos went nuts. So did Gia, who jolted him with elbow shots.

Back on-screen:

> *Red peers in the window at the Two Dudes.*

> *Red: Need new wiper blades, Danica.*

> *Dude 1: I know, but it's not my—*

> *Red reaches inside and shuts them off.*

> *Red: Who sent you?*

> *Dude 1: Sent us? Nobody.*

Dude 2: Swear to God, we were just following the blonde chick.

Dude 1: Shut up!

Red: Following her, but nobody sent you? Why didn't you say so?

Red stands. His face leaves the side window. Red is going to split! The Dudes sag in relief. Then Red leans down again. Dude 1 and Dude 2 jam themselves against the passenger door, eyes fixed on Red's pistol.

Red: Who? In God's name? Sent you?

Red's pistol muzzle almost fills the screen. Feels like the audience is going inside the barrel as the screen fades to black.

Robert turned to Gia, sagging. A cliff-hanger. Before either of them had spoken:

BAM! A single gunshot blasted from the movie speakers.

Everyone in the room jumped. As the lights came up, Robert and Gia stood along with the rest, clapping and whooping it up. All of them turned toward Reyes in back, where Paul Dickerson, facing Reyes, too, clapped like crazy.

Up front, Erik raised his two big thumbs high overhead so that Reyes couldn't miss them. Robert's eye caught the thumbs-up, too.

Amid the applause and cheers, Robert gave his next client a nod: up-and-coming screenwriter and director Raymundo Reyes.

And his face was *beaming* because his movie was good.

Walking up Second Avenue, away from the two-story house, Chet Archer heard the roar from the unit at the back of the property. He stopped and looked, wondering what was going on. A white Taurus sedan pulled up while he was still looking that way.

Chet knelt and ran his hand over the vinyl decal on the passenger door—two interlocking circles with firefighter icons inside each one. There were matching Los Angeles County Fire Department insignias on the driver's door.

Chet got inside and rolled down Second with Sonny Mars. Both of them in their early forties and dressed in rayon-polyester-blend suits and clip-on ties from Al Weiss Men's Clothing downtown.

Sometimes Chet called himself half-Asian, sometimes half-Latino, depending on the situation. Truth was, he didn't know or care about his father. But Sonny, the one driving, didn't have any racial leeway. He looked like what he was, a white boy through and through.

Chet took off his clip-on. "Just heard a bunch of people yelling, back of the house."

"Cockfight, Amway meeting, or what?"

"Not sure what."

Sonny asked, "Think we should stick around? Wait for him to come out?"

"Cockfight could last all night. No telling how long he'll be in there."

Chet noticed a vintage Bronco parked on the street.

"Don't see many of those anymore, do you?"

"Wouldn't take that car if you gave it to me."

Bottom of the hill, they took a right, headed for the Pomona Freeway.

"Still want to see the Museum of Ice Cream?" Chet asked.

"Not today, I don't feel so hot."

Chet couldn't remember a day when *not feeling so hot* wasn't true about Sonny.

Didn't matter, not yet. They had a few days still before anybody died.

CHAPTER 9

The crowd around him had thinned out, and Reyes made introductions. "Robert Worth, Gia Marquez, this is Paul Dickerson." They shook hands all around.

Peter Paul Dickerson, sometimes called PPD in the news. Charismatic in chinos and shades, that leather daypack slung over his shoulder. Robert read somewhere that Paul was around fifty, but seeing him, he'd have guessed early forties.

"Wasn't his movie great?" Paul asked them.

"Loved it," Robert said. "Smart, funny, I was sweating it at the end."

"A little bit sexy, too," Paul said, smiling at Robert but talking about Gia.

Gia nodded her thanks. He liked how Paul handled Gia's on-screen sex appeal: without a come-on.

"Her first time acting," Robert said. Then to Gia: "You killed it."

Reyes added, "Blonde Uma killed it dead."

Robert knew how much Gia disliked being the center of attention. True to form, she thanked them and said, "Beer run, anybody?" No takers as she headed out the door.

Paul pulled a cream-colored envelope from his backpack and handed it to Robert.

"Reyes wanted you to have this, and I hope you and Gia can make it. Beach casual, should be lots of fun." He held up a second envelope.

"My wife wanted to make sure I gave this to Priya Jacobson, so excuse me, guys."

They watched him walk down front where Erik, Priya, and Gabriela still sat.

Reyes said, "Take a look inside, Roberto."

He opened the envelope: an invite to Paul's home, a charity fundraiser for something called Capri Foundation. Before he could quiz Reyes about it, Reyes said, "That's for Paul's spankin'-new foundation. That right there used to be my ten-grand backyard ticket."

"*Your* ten-grand ticket? You should use it. C'mon, I just met the guy."

"Don't sweat it, that ticket's comped. I'll be in the front yard with the small fry, but you'll be in back with all the *machers*." The Yiddish word for *big shots*. "And one of 'em's gonna be Trevor Reid. Paul's gonna make sure you two hook up for a chat."

"Wait—Reid and Paul are friends?"

"The two of 'em went to college together, run into each other around town time to time. Friends? I couldn't say."

"Does Paul know what's up between you and Reid?"

Reyes shook his head. "I won't bring no sad story to Paul. That's the last thing he'll be hearing from me."

Looked like Reyes had banked on Erik liking his movie, planned this in advance. A party meeting would work better than what Robert had planned: camping out in Trevor's office till Trevor agreed to meet him.

"Remember Lane Lang?" he asked.

"Double El, sure, a bright spot in that shit show."

"She's no fan of Trevor Reid or RJ, might be an asset down the road, and she's gonna be out of a job. Any way you can find her a front-yard ticket?"

"Just found it—I'll bring her along with me."

In front, he noticed Priya bowing to Paul, hands clasped. A *wei*, the Thai gesture of respect. Beside them, Erik was in deep conversation with Gabriela.

"Paul and Priya? What's that about?" he asked Reyes.

"Paul's wife, Lawan, she and Priya go to the same temple. Both of 'em from the same province, too, back in the old country. Why's your plus-size pal spending all this time with my *mamacita*?"

"I'm sure your name hasn't come up. So, tell me, what's Paul like?"

Reyes turned to him. "Paul's not *like* nothin'. He different, easy. Not a pushover, I seen him be hard. You know how he came over to East LA today? A limo? Some top-secret Uber class we never heard of? Hell no. Took Metro Rail, got off at Indiana, walked over here like Joe Lunch Box."

Metro Rail with a downtown transfer? A rare choice for a Westsider.

Reyes said, "And he's not just riding Metro. He's seeing things other people don't see, like what kinda concrete they usin' at the Metro station. And a year down the road, maybe it dawns on him, 'Hey, they not making enough a' that concrete,' and he buys a plant somewhere. Thing is, all this shit's going on and more, and Paul's still easy."

Easy. A good word for Paul. Down front in an East LA garage, talking to three strangers. Now, Paul, Priya, and Gabriela all turned to Reyes. The women blew Reyes kisses.

Erik put his arm around Gabriela's shoulder and busted a smile, special delivery to Reyes.

Reyes said, "Son of a bitch. The hell's *Oso Polar* doin' with *Mami*?"

Taking up rent-free space in Reyes' mind. Robert joined Gia outside so Reyes didn't see him laughing.

❧

After dropping off Erik and Priya, Robert and Gia decided on a late dinner at Osteria Venice West, just off the boardwalk. At a sidewalk table, they skipped the wine and ordered branzino and tagliatelle with wild mushrooms and norcia black truffles.

While they waited, he asked, "On the way home, what were you and Priya laughing about in the back seat?"

"Before or after you borrowed jumper cables?"

On the street in front of Gabriela's house. And, yes, a small crowd had gathered.

"After."

"You mean after everybody started chanting, 'Go, O.J., Go'?"

He took her hand. "That was just you, baby. Everybody else was feelin' the Bronc power. What was going on with you and Priya in the back seat?"

"She shared some of her Thai wisdom. If I like sour food, I might be pregnant. Having an ugly baby keeps bad spirits away. If I dream about a snake, I'll meet my soul mate. Then I told her I didn't need to *dream* about a snake."

"How much do I owe you for that?" he asked. "When we were leaving Reyes', I heard Gabriela mention some kind of promise Erik made to her."

"Priya showed Gabriela pictures of the boys, and she wanted to meet them, so Erik promised he'd bring them by her house."

"Score one for the lads. Erik says Gabriela asked him to have a talk with her son about his . . . let's call it his *lifestyle*."

"Oh, God. Erik declined, right?"

"Count on it."

He understood why Erik might be drawn to Gabriela. He'd lost his mother when he was three. Never really knew her, he'd told Robert, and he'd been raised by a father who had never remarried.

"Your parents would be real proud of you," Robert told Gia. "In law school, clerking, and in a movie."

"Especially Mom."

Gia's mother had been an avid moviegoer and had chosen *Temple* as her daughter's middle name. After Shirley Temple, whom Gia's mother had adored.

He recounted to Gia what Reyes had said about Paul being *easy*.

"Easy, sure, confident, laid-back. Wearing off-the-rack brand names, nothing showy except the Tom Ford shades. Those were water buffalo horn and gold, twenty-eight hundred and up."

"So, look, about Mr. Laid-Back Billionaire? When I'm out of town, he's not allowed anywhere near Ozone. Or the beach. Or the Westside."

"He lives on the Westside."

"Then he needs to buy a house out in the desert for when I'm out of town."

Their food came. The smell of garlic and herbs swirled in the air, and the waiter left.

Gia said, "Paul does have *that thing*."

"What *thing*?"

She fork-fed him a truffle. "That thing you have tons more of than he does, McLovin'."

CHAPTER 10

Chet looked out the second-story window of Hobart's Vinyl Wraps at downtown LA's Fashion District. Everywhere he looked, developers had grabbed up crap warehouses and turned them into what they liked calling *artist lofts*.

Like thousands of LA hipsters woke up one day and decided, "I want an artist's loft where it's hotter'n a two-dollar pistol three hundred days a year, people pissing the sidewalks in front of the free toilets."

Behind him, Hobie Hobart, the shop's owner, had just used the words *recipe for disaster*.

"I hear you, Hobie," Chet said, with no idea why Hobie had used the phrase. "That's a definite recipe for disaster."

A few minutes ago, Hobie had started his lecture series about two-millimeter vinyl being the best thickness to use when custom-wrapping a vehicle.

"Like I told you back when I did that Brinks van wrap, Chet, you start out with cheap vinyl, and you're asking for trouble."

Chet said, "We don't want trouble. Do we, Sonny?"

Sonny leaned against the wall, always okay with Chet taking the lead. "Last thing we want's trouble."

Hobie looked at him and his half brother like most people did. Here Chet was—ethnic mutt at 185, shaved head, and a hard look he'd cultivated in the joint. But white-boy Sonny was the one you'd better look out for. Long arms, a lanky frame, hair combed over like a civil-service desk jockey, but what went on inside Sonny's head made him a world-class dude to avoid.

Their dealings with Hobie had started a few years back. Sonny and him had slipped up and paid Hobie full retail on that Brinks wrap. So getting paid was what Hobie'd come to expect. Since then, they'd found out Dewey, Hobie's brother, was doing time outside Delano. That changed things, so before this job—for two wraps this go-round—they'd had a word with Hobie.

Chet had told him, "You know that better'n I do, your brother pulled a mandatory-five stretch for convenience-store armed robbery. Dewey ever mention he's in the same block as Quince Vale?"

"Once, maybe."

Dewey would know damn well who Vale was; every inmate feared him.

"See, Vale's already doing life without parole, so he's inclined to take any piecework he can find. That's P-I-E-C-E to provide for his loved ones on the outside."

Chet went on to explain how Vail maiming Dewey was a $1,000 job; taking Dewey's life would set Chet back another $3,000.

"Better for everybody, Hobie, if Vale stayed out of it."

Seemed to Chet that Hobie got the point: Do these two wraps free—one van plus the sedan he'd already fixed up with the fire depart-ment decals—and do your brother a favor at the same time. But today, just a week after their most recent chat, Hobie was lecturing them about using cheap vinyl years ago.

Chet said, "See, Hobie, you're the one picked out the cheap vinyl, not us. So you're flat-out wrong about that."

Hobie raked his hands through that charcoal-gray brush cut. Looked like reality about Chet and Sonny was dawning on him again.

Hobie said, "No, no, like we agreed. This time's all on the house."

"Online, they rate Dewey's jail only two stars off thirty-five reviews," Chet said. "One of 'em said the place was filled with psychotics prone to random, violent outbursts." He looked at Sonny for the punch line. "Right, Son?"

Sonny said, "Yeah. And that's the guards it was talkin' about."

Hobie didn't bother smiling at their guard joke. "Let's go downstairs. I'll show you how your van wrap came out."

Downstairs, he walked Chet and Sonny around their van.

Chet asked, "Any problems we should know about?"

"A few small air bubbles under the vinyl, is all."

Hobie. A solid professional with a Better Business Bureau plaque in his office.

Hobie said, "If the vehicle's not properly prepped coming in, the problem doesn't lie with the installer."

Chet waited for Hobie to figure out his own mistake. Across the room, Sonny turned on a flared-nozzle heat gun Hobie used to apply vinyl.

Chet shook his head; Sonny turned off the heat gun.

Using Sonny now would be a waste. Soon enough, Chet would start reminding Sonny of slights made. Planting thoughts, or taking Sonny back to prison in his mind, priming Sonny's pump in case Sonny's simmer needed to boil right quick.

Chet couldn't resist verbalizing the heat-gun threat. "You said it scorched vinyl between two hundred seventy-five and three hundred degrees, so you set it at two fifty. You point it wrong, bet it'd burn your face off."

Hobie finally paid full attention about those air bubbles.

"Bubbles are my bad, Chet, but no shit, something you need to know on this van." Hobie walked him around to its back doors. "I have no idea how to make every single thing back here look exactly like your pictures. A real artist, a painter, could finish these two back windows up right, but I lack the wherewithal."

That's the spirit, Hobie. Chet could see what Hobie was worried about and didn't care.

"It's not like we'll be sneaking inside the CIA or the Vatican. Leave it as is, we're cool." Then Chet said, "Landlord gonna price you out of this spot or what?"

Hobie said, "Got less than a year left. After that I'll probably move to—"

Hobie stopped. Chet would bet anything Hobie regretted bragging about his Mexican beach house a while back. Things didn't come to Chet all at once like they did with some people, but something was taking shape, back of his mind. After finishing this new job they'd been hired to do, maybe he'd swing back by Hobie's and ask nice for the key.

"After that, you'd think about moving down to Ensenada, right?" Chet asked.

CHAPTER 11

"That's what you call beach casual?" Gia asked Robert in their bedroom.

"My version," he said, in a blue blazer, T-shirt, jeans, and Reefs.

She pulled on purple hip-huggers, tucked in a faded Gap black pocket tee, and slipped into purple Nike trainers.

"If there's a potato race, I'll dominate," she explained.

An hour later, holding hands on Capri Drive, they meandered its uphill grade north of Sunset Boulevard toward Paul's estate. One of those perfect LA nights where the wind played tag with the palms, eucalyptus, and acacia. Red roses mingled with orange-and-purple birds-of-paradise, both flowering beneath blazing yellow trumpet trees and magenta bougainvillea.

Ahead of them, Erik and Priya strolled arm in arm. Erik in board shorts, Priya wrapped in a sarong, both invited because of Priya's Wat Thai connection with Paul's wife, Lawan.

On Amalfi Drive now, party traffic built as they drew closer—UberX's, Mercedes, Teslas, and Beemers.

Across Rustic Canyon lay Will Rogers State Park's oasis of horses, stables, and hiking trails. Rogers' heirs had owned a lesser-known property across Sunset. In the sixties, Beach Boy Dennis Wilson had rented it, and his frequent guest had been aspiring musician-songwriter-lunatic Charles Manson. Only a few months passed before the Manson Family moved out and went on to commit the brutally infamous Tate-LaBianca murders over in Benedict Canyon and Los Feliz, putting a dagger in the West Coast's peace-and-love era.

As they neared the top of the hill, security checked invitations against their list, and guests poured though the estate's wide-open, wrought-iron front gates. That's where Erik and Priya headed.

Robert and Gia stopped at the VIP side gate in the estate's ten-foot wall.

Gia squeezed his arm and whispered, "We're VIPs. Finally."

Inside the wall, they strolled along a trellised wooden pergola. Robert caught glimpses of the $1,000-a-couple party in the tented front yard. A massive open bar serviced by ten bartenders, Buddhist monks in saffron robes—and wasn't that RJ with the Delta 88 driver, crowding the bar?

At the end of the pergola, Paul's backyard opened up on fifty or sixty fellow VIPs mingling on a one-acre rectangle of unmanicured grass and trees, an infinity pool, and a pool house by the canyon. A fresh-dug barbecue pit smoked off to their right, where staff loaded slabs of ribs onto platters.

A jazz trio eased through standards on a small stage, and the air smelled sweeter than Robert could ever remember.

"From the orchids," Gia said, pointing.

Orchids clung to tree limbs and trunks and decorated ten or twelve tables randomly spaced around the yard. Even the Thai spirit house had orchid offerings. According to Priya, these miniature temples housed evil spirits, and leaving offerings—like orchids and shot glasses of Fanta strawberry soda—kept evil spirits out of the main house.

Paul waved them over to a circle of five people, where they shook hands with the group.

With the last guest, Paul said, "And this is my wife, Lawan."

Lawan said, "Reyes told us how much he values knowing each of you."

Gia said, "Never a dull moment."

Lawan. Soulful to Priya's joyous, and unlike Priya's, her English was quite good. Five seven, an orchid in her long black hair, arched eyebrows framing her dark-brown eyes. Easy to see why Mr. Easy had been smitten.

Like Erik once joked with him: "I have no recollection of meeting Priya, but we have two kids, so it must've happened."

A half hour later, Paul led Robert and Gia over to a barbecue bar. Each of them took on a plate of hot ribs and ate with their fingers. Robert never quite saw how Paul pulled it off, but he found Gia and himself standing alongside a short man with black curly hair and a familiar scowl.

Paul said, "Robert Worth, Gia Marquez, I'd like you to meet Trevor Reid."

They shook hands all around. Trevor wore a dark chalk-stripe suit, a tailored cream-colored shirt with cuff links, an open collar. Wall Street casual.

Paul said, "Trevor and I go back quite a ways."

Trevor nodded. "We met in college. Paul was our token hippie down at San Diego State."

"I showed up from Colorado in a VW van, hair down to my ass. Even then, I was a cliché."

"He came to California for the weather, stayed for the money. Who knew that all hippies ever wanted was a potload of dough?"

Paul took the ribbing in stride.

"Nothing wrong with money, Trevor. Depends on what you do with it, and what it does with you."

Paul slipped away on party business. Trevor turned to Robert and Gia.

"Money didn't change me at all. I was always a dickhead."

"Amen to that."

That comment from a massive man in a sauce-stained jumpsuit. He'd just stepped behind the barbecue bar. Robert had noticed him ferrying slabs of meat into the house for guests out front. Jerry Baugh, the best man in Trevor's wedding photo, who'd also held that monster salmon with Trevor in Russia.

Trevor leered at Gia and asked, "What's so special about this guy, rates a girl like you?"

Ignoring him, Gia licked Jerry's sauce off her fingers. "This sauce is so damn good."

Jerry said, "It's the ginger, lemongrass, a few Thai peppers. Gave it a little bit of Thai flavor for Lawan."

Robert picked up a bottle of barbecue sauce from the bar. Its label: *Cannonball BBQ Sauce.* "This yours?"

"Not what you're eating now, but close. More a prototype than a product."

Trevor said, "Earth to Gia?"

She gave in to his question. "If I had to pick one special thing about Robert, I'd say it's that he doesn't know when to quit."

"Whoa! That could mean lots of things."

"It does," she said.

Lawan appeared at Gia's side. "Have you seen the canyon view from the pool?"

"Not yet. Mind showing me?"

That left Robert alone with Trevor and Jerry. Robert didn't want to dive in to Reyes' problem; he dug deep for small talk with a guy he already disliked.

"Three Thirty-Three, that's an interesting name. Does it have any significance?"

"Not to me, so much. Marguerite, my deceased wife, came up with it."

Jerry asked, "Didn't she say it was a lucky number?"

"While she was alive, I have to admit, Marguerite *was* damn lucky, so I didn't buck her about picking those numbers."

Robert asked, "You're superstitious?"

"Every serious investor is superstitious."

"Athletes, too," Jerry added.

Robert hadn't done a deep dive on the 333 Hedge Fund, Trevor Reid, or Jerry Baugh. From what little he'd read, the pair had started a hedge fund together in 2006 but closed it down after taking some big hits. Trevor had resurrected himself with the 333 Hedge Fund, with Jerry serving as its chief operating officer.

Trevor said, "Half of investing is confidence. Confidence in your thesis, in your analysis, in yourself. Confidence leads to conviction, and conviction sets me apart from the bovines."

Despite Trevor's abrasive everything, Robert was impressed.

Trevor watched Jerry plating a stack of ribs and said, "Jerry once had confidence, didn't you, Jerry? Then you got burned." To Robert: "Not him, really. *My fund.* Tell him about Prison Max, Jer."

"Ancient history. No need to travel down that road again."

"No, no, I love revisiting mistakes. Prison Max—that was Jerry's greatest hit for this fund—cost me a boatload of money. They say invest in what you know, but what do you invest in when you know absolutely nothing?"

Robert wondered when Jerry was going to crush Trevor's windpipe with one of those big paws. If he did, Robert would've held Jerry's coat.

But Jerry just said, "Hey, Robert, don't assume it's the booze talking. Alcohol actually mellows him out."

Trevor kept peppering Jerry with insults.

"Fixing lawn mowers in your garage, that's what you're best at. Nail up a sign on a tree: *Will Sharpen Blades.*"

"Trevor's right, in his own charming way. I should've run a machine shop—if he only knew the tales my garage could tell."

Robert was ready to start talking sports, anything but this, when Jerry emerged from behind the bar.

He shook Robert's hand. "Trevor says money can't buy friendship, but it can lease loyalty. And my lease, Robert? It's up next week. Hallelujah!"

Trevor said, "Can't come too soon for me. Glad you're leaving the fund, you cheap bastard." Then to Robert: "Best way to make money in any market—find out what Jerry likes, and go the other way."

Jerry looked to the sky. "Give me strength, Lord. Excuse me, gentlemen. Time for my state-mandated piss break."

Witnessing Trevor's vitriol up close had actually helped Robert. He wanted to avoid this kind of bad juju when he brought up Reyes' problem.

Jerry headed toward the pool house; Trevor wasn't done.

"I'm too damn loyal to friends and family."

An odd statement from an odd man. Hard to imagine any truth to it.

"Know why I kept Jerry around all these years?"

"Not exactly sure."

"Cheapest man on the planet. Goes over expense reports like a chimp looking for lice. Keeps those other pricks working for me honest."

Trevor grabbed a bottle of barbecue sauce.

"Cannonball. That's a good name. Came from Jerry 'The Cannon' Baugh."

"Cannon Baugh, got it." And he liked it.

"Played quarterback in high school. He'd have been All City if we hadn't had such a shit team."

"High school friends, I had no idea."

"College, too. Jerry picked up a scholarship to San Diego State."

"Division One, damn."

"They recruited him as a QB, but he didn't cut it and crapped out junior year with an injured ACL."

"Tough break. Looks like he's still in great shape."

Trevor wasn't much of a listener; he picked up wherever he wanted.

"Know how hard it is to break a new barbecue sauce?"

"Difficult, I imagine."

"Impossible. What Jerry's gonna do? Stand in a grocery aisle and hand out free samples on a toothpick? 'Have you tried my sauce? Goes great with everything.' Except making money."

One minute, Trevor insulted Jerry to his face. The next minute, behind Jerry's back, he showed almost-human emotions about the guy. With normal people, the sequence was just the opposite, but so far, he'd witnessed nothing normal about Trevor Reid.

Trevor asked, "What do you prefer investing in?"

Robert saw a chance to sit at Trevor's feet, the only location that might help out Reyes.

"I'm not much of an investor. Any advice on the stock market?"

"Stocks? You're what, early thirties?"

"Good guess."

"Guys like me—and guys who pick stocks—we've got another decade or so before artificial intelligence obsoletes us. Finally, the retail suckers'll believe AI performance numbers and stop paying brokers for useless advice. I'll be obsolete, too, but I'll have cashed out by then. Now, a guy your age?"

Wasn't that his original question?

"Put your stock money into an index fund, average in over time, don't ever watch the financial channels, and don't brag to your friends what a hotshot investor you are, because you're not. Over the long haul, you'll beat damn near everybody in the world—except me. Know why?"

"Patience?" A guess.

"Patience is a given. You'll win because you made one bet. A long-term bet on the US stock market—and you did that, and only that, *with conviction*."

Hard as it was taking advice from a jackass, Trevor made sense—park your money in a passive vehicle with low fees, add to it occasionally, and forget about it.

"Thanks, Trevor, I really appreciate it."

"Paul told me you might have a piece of business with me?"

Good. He'd waited long enough, and Trevor brought up Reyes' situation on his own.

"Actually, yes. I'm an attorney. A client of mine, a friend of Paul's, actually, dealt with your film company down in Venice."

"RJ's small-ball thing at the beach. What of it?"

"My client's project's called *Walk Street Hits*, and somehow, after Three Thirty-Three Film's option expired, he received a letter from the company reserving all rights to his project."

He didn't mention that Trevor had signed the letter. Good chance Trevor had forgotten about it; no reason to bait this particular bull.

Trevor said, "Follow you so far."

"The option expired by its own terms with no mention of the company having any postoption rights, so I'm pretty sure the letter was some kind of oversight."

He'd almost said *some kind of mistake*, then autocorrected, given Trevor's deformed persona.

Trevor said, "Not sure I follow you. Got an example on this postoption rights thing?"

"Sure. Instead of a script, let's say Three Thirty-Three optioned a warehouse and—"

Trevor put his hand on Robert's shoulder and smiled. A genuine smile, the first one all night.

"You know, Paul and I go way back, so I shouldn't dick around with you. I know everything there is to know about options. I traded them. I wrote them, and I turned down a seat on the Chicago Board Options Exchange. That letter you're worried about? It was prepared in my office, at my direction, and *I* signed as CEO of Three Thirty-Three Film."

Deliberately obnoxious and insulting. Not what Robert thought he might hear: *I never discuss business in a social setting*, or *Let me look into it, get back to you*. Anger quickened his pulse.

"Take a deep breath, lawyer man. It's your client's problem, not yours."

"Mind telling me why you sent the letter?" Robert asked.

"Because I paid up for a nonentity like your nobody client. I gave him a shot, and if he ever—*ever*—gets any action on it, he'll need to go through me."

"What if my client agreed, if he ever sold the property, you'd get all your option money back before he took a dime?"

"We could do that, but where's my upside?"

"Did you ever read the option? If you did, you'd know that what you're saying is wrong."

"Know what? Maybe I am wrong. Maybe your client gave us those rights in another document. Or maybe he had a conversation with RJ— or was it with me? A conversation giving me those rights out of sheer gratitude. But in order to prove that conversation never happened, your client would find himself in, I'm afraid, protracted litigation."

"That never happened, and we both know you're acting in bad faith."

"Harsh words. Isn't that why we have litigation?"

"Pointless litigation, sure."

"Pointless and protracted, even better. I have my lawyers and your client has you, so let's all go be big boys and do what big boys do."

"You'll be hearing from us," Robert said, already wanting to take back his weak cliché.

"Look forward to it. And free-spirit billionaire Paul Dickerson? Don't get taken in—he's a just a money-grubber like the rest of us."

Don't leave anybody out. What about that asshole Gandhi?

Trevor walked away. Robert snagged a champagne from a passing tray, pissed off.

He looked around the yard. Party staff carried in covered, galvanized tubs, setting them down here and there. As he walked toward the pool, he crossed paths with Jerry and raised his flute.

"Best of luck on your barbecue sauce."

Jerry glanced over at Trevor. "You know, I once knew another Trevor Reid, a gracious gentleman."

"I don't follow you."

"Trevor's father, a terrific guy."

"What the hell happened to his son?"

Jerry laughed. "Nobody knows. Not even his father. He's actually a loyal person, but his loyalty comes at a very high price."

His eyes looked bloodshot. Could've been from smoking barbecue for the last day or two. If Robert had to make a bet, he'd say that Jerry had been crying. Just raked over the coals in public, humiliated by a lifetime friend. Made sense.

Jerry took a deep breath and looked around. "This scent, these Royal Thai orchids, they're so beautiful." With that, Jerry walked away.

Robert joined Gia by the infinity pool, its far edge merging with Rustic Canyon. Party staff came around with clear plastic boxes, asking for cell phones and keys. Other puzzled guests forked over their gear, too.

"What's going on?" Robert asked Gia.

"Beats me."

Strolling back to the bar for more champagne, they drew even with the bandstand. As he slipped his arm around her waist, he noticed Trevor and Paul in the shadows across the yard.

Both men vibed angry; each gestured aggressively. He made out raised voices. Saw Trevor push Paul in the chest.

Paul raised his hands, palms up—*it's over*—and turned his back on Trevor.

Trevor must've lost his mind. He shoved Paul in the back, still yelling.

Without looking, Paul ripped a hard side kick that caught Trevor in the solar plexus; Trevor folded, went to his knees. Paul grabbed him by the jacket, pulled him to his feet, and dragged him over to a security post. Trevor disappeared into the pergola with security.

Gia had seen it, too. "What the hell?"

"Only so much of Trevor that anyone could take."

Paul walked toward the bandstand. Passing by, he asked Robert, "Any luck with Trevor?"

"Not really. Hope I didn't cause you any trouble."

"Wasn't you. Trevor's a prick, always will be." Paul grinned. "Hey, let's have some fun!"

He jumped onstage and grabbed the mike. As he spoke, guests pulled in to listen.

"Ladies and gentlemen, well, friends, really, if I may have a small part of your attention, I want to thank each one of you for your donation to the foundation. Your generosity, well, you already know how generous you are, and that's why you were invited. Our foundation is just getting off the ground, but our goals will be, I promise, pure, and Lawan and I will keep you abreast of developments. Speaking of my wife, I want to thank Lawan for leaving her lovely Isan province to join me here in this dreary part of the world."

Nearby, Lawan smiled in embarrassed appreciation.

"Recall, if you will, that beach casual was the order of the night. With that in mind, just in case Lawan was homesick, I offer my own version of the Thai water festival, Songkran! Check out those tubs around the yard. Look inside."

Guests meandered over to the tubs. Inside the nearest one, Robert found an assortment of filled squirt guns. He grabbed a green pistol, tossed Gia a blue one.

Paul said, "Come on now, we gotta move!"

A squishing noise came from underfoot as sprinkler heads popped into place and began spraying water over everyone.

"Our first order of business—take out that drone!"

Paul pointed at the sky. A drone hovered overhead, floating up and down. Part of the party? No way to tell as Paul jumped off the bandstand.

It was on! Guests fired at the drone; the drone ascended fast, taking off for parts unknown.

A cheer went up; guests began running around the yard. Robert and Gia joined in, too, squirting each other, firing at strangers, slipping and sliding on the wet grass. The whole backyard, a soggy mess, everyone screaming.

Gia tackled him by the pool, clinging to him as they plunged underwater and stayed there. Random lights sliced the surface, making magic, shimmering images. For a moment, peace claimed his heart, being paired with this woman who took no shit and always backed him up.

As they surfaced, other bodies piled into the water beside them; more and more bodies filled the space and sent a wave of water off the pool's canyon end.

They ducked under again. Reaching inside Gia's jeans, he cupped her buttocks and pulled her close. She wrapped her arms around his neck and screamed voice-bubbles into his ear.

"I love you!" her popping bubbles told him.

His bubbles let her know: "I love you, too!"

✥

"Rich people gone wild," Sonny said to Chet from their hidden spot in the canyon trees.

That's how Chet saw it, too. Yard sprinklers turned on, middle of a party, all of 'em running around with squirt guns and cutting loose.

Chet said, "Let's beat it."

After two hours of watching, they moved out of their hide. Neighboring lots had terraced cliffs cut into the canyon's steep grade.

Some had built railroad-tie retaining walls; others had gone upscale with cypress and exotic hardwoods. Point being, Chet knew, to out-spend your neighbors.

This lot differed. Behind the rear fence lay a tangle of English ivy, ice plant, and a mess of vines. The foliage made for slow going but would leave their presence harder to detect.

A calm night so far—until that first wave of water rolled down from the pool and soaked them. Screams filtered down from the party even louder than before.

A second wave splashed down and drenched them to the bone.

Ten minutes later, they made it to the main trail. Chet had shucked his wet shirt, zipped it inside his daypack. Sonny kept complaining about his condition.

"Freezing my ass off now."

"Take off your shirt. It's fifty-five, no wind, you'll heat up in no time."

"Point is, I'm wet, and I've had a fever."

Sonny's health made up only half the reason for his grousing. The other sour half, Chet believed, was generated by the people who'd just soaked them. Chet had planned to wait longer before planting the anger seed inside Sonny, but now looked like the time was right to start.

"You can't blame 'em, Son. You had a pool and all that money, what'd you do with it?"

"Squirt guns?"

"Had 'em when I's a kid, same as you."

"When you's a kid, yeah. Got one now?"

"Looked silly, didn't they?"

"Yeah, they looked foolish."

Farther up the trail, Sonny finally took off his wet shirt and tied it around his waist. Shivering, he ran his hands up and down his wiry limbs, all of them thinner than you'd ever think, considering most of what he ate had been fried first.

Sonny said, "Immature rich people, trying to feel young again."

"*Rich People Gone Wild,* that'd be a good cable show."

"Already seen it, but they call it something else. *Housewives* of this and that."

"Way of the world, guess it ain't gonna change. Same way up in the joint, ones with all the juice gettin' treated special. Same as what we see on the greed show." He meant *American Greed.*

Sonny said, "All those crooked white-collar turds on that show? Tell *white collar* to the ones had their savings cleaned out."

"I hear you." Chet eased his rich-people needle into Sonny again. "What's it like, you think, having so much scratch you can give it away?"

Sonny shrugged. "Them having so much, it makes me angry sometimes, Chet."

"Way of the world, like I said. Nothing we can do about it."

Sonny said, "Not yet."

Once the party cruised to an end, Robert and Gia, both buzzed, wandered their way down Capri toward Sunset.

Erik had texted: Left early. Duck problem. Then a duck emoji.

"Duck problem?" he asked Gia.

"Ducky Joe, the family duckling. Hans named him."

Was that the best pet name ever? He'd named his first dog Tommy. Inadequate at best. The brilliance of Ducky Joe's name grabbed him and wouldn't let go. Or maybe he was drunk.

They walked past two men standing at the curb: Delta 88 throwing up, and RJ texting somebody.

From behind them came RJ's voice: "Hey, Worth! What's with you and that dick, Raymundo? He said you're still his lawyer!"

Robert kept walking with three quick thoughts: *Don't ruin this, RJ.* Then: *Don't let him ruin it, Robert.* And then: *Dammit, Reyes!*

Footsteps closed behind him, and Robert put himself between RJ and Gia.

"See you in a minute," he told her, and she kept walking.

"Thought you were dropping Reyes as a client?" RJ said. "Where's that bogus release I signed, you lying cocksucker?"

Robert knew that RJ was soft, but he was a big boy, and Robert didn't like standing below him on the grade. He circled uphill until he was even with him.

"You have my card, call me tomorrow."

"Stick your card up your ass!"

RJ squared off, feinted a couple of jabs. Robert didn't bite, so RJ started to swing—a looping right hand.

"And fuck that bitch you're—"

With never made it out of his mouth. Robert ducked the round-house and bulled his shoulder into RJ's gut. RJ's heels hit the curb, and he toppled back into a bank of ice plant. Robert body slammed him.

"Cool it, RJ! Cool down!"

RJ bucked. Robert pinned down his neck with a forearm and kept up the pressure.

"I mean it, dude! Cool it!"

A knee to RJ's nuts was next, but RJ stopped thrashing. Robert stood up and left him in the succulents' bed. He caught up with Gia, grabbing a few deep breaths, and headed downhill with her.

"You okay?" she asked.

"Yep."

He didn't care about RJ's problem with Reyes' release. RJ had the signed document, and if he wanted to attack it, the burden of proving Robert's mayhem tall tale would be on RJ, not Reyes.

Good luck with that.

Until now, Paul's party had been an unexpected treat. Watching Paul handle himself, a learning experience. *Easy*, like Reyes had said. More than that, he'd handled ten things at once—throwing a party, setting Robert up to meet Trevor, kicking Trevor's ass, making an off-the-cuff speech, and raising $500,000 or more for his foundation, all without breaking a sweat.

An authentic person. Not *a phony* like that cruel little man, Trevor, had said of him.

He decided Reyes had it wrong, too. Paul Dickerson wasn't easy; he made his life *look* easy. So why couldn't Paul help make Reyes' life a little easier, too?

CHAPTER 12

The next morning, Robert kept his ten o'clock conference call with Philip Fanelli, who'd been his mentor at his former firm. Philip brought him up to speed on winding up a lawsuit Fanelli's firm was handling for Robert, Gia, and the Boardwalk Trust.

Last year, his client, Delfina's father, Teo, had been murdered by a full-time psychopath. That left nine-year-old homeless Delfina as the only beneficiary of a family trust; Robert had been chosen by the court as sole trustee. He'd hired Philip's litigators to sue the killer's estate on behalf of all three of them. Both Robert and Gia had suffered real emotional distress during Delfina's kidnapping and rescue and would wind up being compensated, too.

Once their business was done, Robert caught up with the latest from Philip. Philip and his fiancée, Dorothy, planned to marry in one month. Still madly in love, no doubt about it, but Philip had let *his beloved* wrangle him into salsa lessons so that they could perform a solo salsa number at their reception.

"In front of everyone, Robert. And it's not dancing, it's torture."

"What's the problem, Philip? Just loosen those hips, tap into your Latin roots, let it go."

Fanelli was half-French, half-Italian.

"One day, you, too, will marry the woman of your dreams. I can only hope the salsa is front and center at your reception so you can look back at your lack of empathy with deep regret."

An hour later, Robert met Reyes at his office on the boardwalk.

Robert told him about his unsuccessful meeting with Trevor at the party, and how Trevor had outlined a scenario: Reyes verbally giving postoption rights to Trevor's company out of gratitude.

"Reid's sayin' *I told him* he could have the rights?"

"What he said, yeah."

"Never said nothing like that to him or RJ, either one."

"I believe you, Reyes, but now we know Reid is willing to lie about what happened."

"Said in your text you had some ideas. I'm eager as can be to hear 'em."

"Then check this out. After talking to Trevor, I started thinking: Why not mention to Paul about helping out with Trevor?"

"He already tried to help out."

"Look, he's invested in movies before. Paid a bundle for the *Street Cred* franchise, didn't he?"

"Yes and no. See, a *chica multimillionara* in the Philippines had already agreed to buy it from him for ten million more than he paid, so he never really owned it. And besides, Paul told me once, he liked helping people who didn't need help. People who showed him they'd get where they were going without him."

"That was before he saw what you'd shot. And he liked your movie, right?"

Reyes nodded. "Went on and on about it."

"What if I told you Paul and Trevor don't get along—*at all.*"

78

"Knew they wasn't all that tight, but when I heard Trevor's coming to the gig, paying the ten stacks, I thought they's good with each other."

"Paul can't stand him, said he'd always been a dick. Oh yeah, Paul dropped Trevor with an MMA kick to his gut."

"Whoa, and me and Lane Lang hangin' in the front yard with RJ, missin' out?"

Given Robert's tussle with RJ, he thought about schooling Reyes on keeping quiet about his legal business. This wasn't the right time.

"Look, Reyes, Paul already knows without your ever asking that you'd love him to be involved with your project. No way does he think you've been sitting around, waiting on him to help you out."

Reyes began to brighten. "If Paul wanted in, say, as an investor, he could help pull Reid from out my ass. And maybe juking Reid puts a little cherry on top for Paul."

"A big, fat cherry."

"Gonna see Paul coming up." Grinning, he said, "Think I'm gonna step up and get some help."

They pounded fists.

"I'm headed to the desert with Gia for the weekend. Let me know how it goes."

Their first night in Joshua Tree, Robert and Gia stayed in a silver Airstream camper, cooking chicken wings and grilling vegetables outdoors on a grated firepit. Without ambient light, the sky lit up in the desert, bright and calm, and gazing into it from a lawn chair, he recalled their last trip to the desert.

That time, they'd brought Delfina, in part to share with her some hidden family history. Their visit had included a stay at the 29 Palms Inn, a desert oasis where her father had once stayed as a child with his own family and met a former park ranger turned soul singer, Jesus Stone.

For Delfina's sake, Robert had reserved the Forget Me Not cabin at the inn. Beside the cabin's hearth, he'd explained to her that this very cabin had provided a single-night's respite from her father's childhood, otherwise ravaged by drug-and-alcohol-addicted parents.

The next day, he'd introduced Delfina and Gia to Jesus Stone. Meeting Jesus was a memory that had stayed with her father until the day he'd died.

"Wow," Delfina said, and hugged Jesus for a long time.

Jesus had performed at a bar gig that night, singing Temptations hits with his Motown-style group, the Disciples. From the bandstand, he'd announced, "Tonight, I have a special guest from Los Angeles. I knew her daddy, Teo, way back when. He passed away recently, so this next song, I'm dedicating to Delfina Famosa and her daddy, Teo."

Jesus put his heart and soul into "My Girl." Halfway through Jesus' number, tears began streaming down Robert's face. Something about the pain and redemption of the Famosa family churned his own emotions to the surface.

Robert's extended family still lived on their farm up in Gilroy, self-proclaimed Garlic Capital of the World. A simmering Shakespearean stew. His schizophrenic father lived above the garage beside the family farmhouse, where Robert's mother had decided: *Hey, why don't I shack up with my husband's brother?*

Last year he'd reconciled with his first cousin Rosalind, his closest childhood friend, but it remained to be seen whether there would be more family fence-mending in his future.

This weekend the trip with Gia was peaceful, not emotional, romantic more than sexual, and by the time Sunday night rolled around, they'd each felt touched by what Jesus called *the desert vibration.*

On their way home, as they passed Gramma's Country Kitchen in Banning, he asked Gia, "Did you see any jackalopes this time?"

Made-up desert creatures, jackrabbits with antelope antlers.

"Not this time." Gia smiled and took his hand.

Their last trip, Delfina had been doing homework in the back seat when Robert asked, "Are you going to report to the class about desert jackalopes?"

Delfina had said, "No, Robert, jackalopes aren't real animals."

"That can't be right," Gia had said. "I saw a big herd of 'em last night."

"Jackalopes are just for fun." Delfina leaned up and kissed his cheek, then Gia's. "Jackalope kisses," she said.

A sweet moment. A few months earlier, they'd almost made up their minds to try for custody of Delfina when her mother had reentered the picture. Not fighting her had been the right thing to do, but even so, that jackalope moment had led to long discussions that put them on the road to becoming parents.

That night, as Robert gassed up near the beach, he sneaked a look at his texts for the first time all weekend.

Reyes had reached out to him with a series of messages, starting midday: Give me a call. Call me. Let's talk. Hear about Paul?

He texted: My office, 10:00 a.m.? and got back a thumbs-up emoji.

CHAPTER 13

A coffee break sounded good to Robert after an encounter with his tenth prospect of the morning: a millennial in a texting frenzy wearing an *It Doesn't Matter* tank top.

"Yo, Kafka, anybody home?" he asked.

Nada came in reply, so he set a *Back Soon Maybe* placard on his conference table and headed down the boardwalk to Groundwork for a slab of caffeine.

Strolling back to his office with an iced cold brew, he spotted Reyes three long blocks up the way. Right away, Reyes looked different to him. His usual swagger gone, his shoulders slumped.

He guessed that Reyes' pitch to Paul about his project hadn't gone as planned. He was about to wave when Reyes stopped, looked landward. Raised his hands and went to his knees.

Robert's instant reaction—*this was the gangbanger scenario Erik had warned him about.*

Instead, cops swarmed onto the boardwalk. Guns drawn, they shouted orders at Reyes, who got spread-eagled on the asphalt in a hurry.

Robert ditched his coffee and jogged toward the pileup. Must have been six cops shouting, "Don't you move! Hands behind your back now! Cuff him!"

Once they'd secured the cuffs, he was close enough to hear Reyes ask, "What the hell's going on?"

"Are you Raymundo Reyes?" one asked.

"Why you askin'?"

"You're under arrest for the murder of Peter Paul Dickerson. You have the right to remain silent. You have the right . . ."

What? Paul was dead? Reyes killed him? That was insane. Reyes' eyes met Robert's: *What the fuck?*

The cops pulled Reyes to his feet, led him away, and Robert followed them.

The closest one grazed his pistol. "Sir! Move away! Don't make me ask again!"

His hands went up; he stopped. "I'm his attorney."

The cop checked out his board shorts, Reefs, T-shirt, and shades. "Me, too."

"I'm Robert Worth, Mr. Reyes' attorney, and I want to know where you're taking him."

"If you're really a lawyer, you already know the answer."

They put Reyes inside their squad car. On its trunk, in massive gold letters: *SHERIFF*. A kid with a jungle camo forehead tattoo shot a grinning selfie with the squad car before it took off. Oblivious tourists ate their churros and fried Oreos, already back to boardwalk business as usual.

Paul Dickerson, killed? *Don't go there yet,* Robert told himself as he headed toward the Bronco. First, find out where the LA County Sheriff's Department had taken Reyes.

Like every other corporate attorney in town, he knew next to nothing about Los Angeles criminal jurisdiction, city or county. LA County covered an enormous area. Almost a hundred actual cities containing at least a quarter of California's population.

Where the hell to start?

He texted Erik to call him ASAP and drove to the closest station he could think of: Culver City Police Department. Out in the parking lot, he saw no sign of Reyes, that swarm of deputies, or any squad cars.

Parked on Culver Boulevard, he recalled a multistory criminal court building by LAX. Did the county book prisoners there? This time of day, the drive could take an hour, so he pulled out his laptop instead and Googled the killing.

A headline appeared on his screen: "Peter Paul Dickerson Slain in Palisades Riviera Home."

The initial articles revealed that Lawan had found Paul's body Sunday morning when she'd returned from an overnight visit with Thai friends in Chino Hills. She'd let herself into the house with the maid, who had just arrived, and they had discovered Paul's body in the foyer, where he'd been brutally beaten to death. So brutally, in fact, that investigators speculated the attack might have been personal.

"You kidding me?" Robert said out loud, still reading.

The maid had called 911 while Lawan stayed in the foyer with Paul's body until the police arrived. The estimated time of death: between 2:00 and 3:00 a.m. on Sunday.

Yesterday morning, while he and Gia had slept soundly up in the desert.

He found it impossible to accept: that someone—*Reyes?*—had entered the Dickerson residence around 2:00 a.m. on Sunday and had beaten Paul to death. Burglary had been the apparent reason for the killer's or killers' presence. The LAPD had questioned both the maid and Lawan, who, the article said, was *distraught*.

Freaking out, no doubt.

No news story mentioned Reyes, other than a generic *Police are currently pursuing several leads*.

Not anymore. One of several leads was now in custody for murder.

Erik called him back. "You hear about Paul Dickerson?"

"Just now. I can't believe it. Has Priya talked to Lawan yet?"

"She drove out to their temple to pray. Not sure if Lawan was there or what. Damn, hard to believe all this."

"Awful, I know."

Given Erik and Reyes' history, he decided to hold back telling Erik about the arrest.

"So listen, I have a client who was picked up on the boardwalk, and I don't know where the cops'll take him."

"Where on the boardwalk?"

"At Park Avenue."

"Not Santa Monica, then. That's Venice. County sheriff?"

"Yeah."

"Felony or misdemeanor?"

"I'm gonna say felony."

"Crime committed in the City of Los Angeles?"

Palisades Riviera? He wasn't 100 percent sure.

"Gonna say yes."

"More likely than not, your guy'd be transported downtown for booking. Other than having you as a lawyer, was he a mental case or not?"

"Not."

"Then after booking, he'll wind up at the Twin Towers. In Tower One, down on Bauchet."

Once the call ended, Robert sat in his car and recalled the essence of Erik's earlier warnings: Reyes was trouble waiting to happen. At this point, Robert was nowhere near ready to agree.

His first instinct about Reyes: 100 percent innocent. Then again, last time he'd seen Reyes, he'd planned to meet with Paul about his project.

If Reyes had followed through, he might've had—at least—the opportunity to commit murder. But at 2:00 a.m.? And why? He decided to stop speculating. If he was right about Reyes' innocence, motive and opportunity were nonstarters because Reyes would have an airtight alibi.

Rather than heading downtown to chase Reyes though the system, he drove home to nail down what Reyes could be facing.

In his living room, Robert researched the California Penal Code. Granted, he knew even less about criminal law than he did about trusts and estates, but he remembered enough from law school to evaluate the basics. Or knew enough, some might say, to be dangerous.

Two hours later, he looked up from his research when Gia walked in the door and asked, "Do you know about Reyes?"

"I do."

"It's on the radio. I can't believe it."

"I can't either," he said, with slightly less conviction than he'd have liked.

He told her about Reyes' boardwalk takedown.

"You were there?"

"Right on top of it."

Last year in law school, she'd studied California murder statutes and confirmed what he'd just relearned about the punishments involved. California's criminal statutes provided enhanced punishment for so-called special-circumstances felony murders. Murders committed during the commission of certain named felonies, such as burglary of a residence. By statute, these murders became death-penalty eligible.

With investigators already speculating that a burglary had been in the offing when Paul was murdered, Reyes had as much legal trouble as the State of California had to offer.

"God, he must be freaking out. Is there any chance he's, you know . . . ?"

"Innocent or guilty?"

"Guilty?"

It pained him to say, "Always a chance."

Gia brought him up to speed on what Reyes could expect next. In three days, Reyes would make his first court appearance—his arraignment. The court would read the charges against him, Reyes would no doubt plead innocent, and bail would be set or denied.

"What about bail before the arraignment?"

"The court has a prearraignment bail schedule. For charges like this, there's no bail at all allowed before arraignment."

He wanted to visit Reyes, so he registered online at the Twin Towers website. So far, inmate *Raymundo Reyes* didn't appear in the system.

She asked, "Think they questioned him?"

"Think he'd let them?"

They'd watched enough *Dateline*, *The First 48*, and *20/20* to know that suspects, both innocent and guilty, opened up to detectives in the box—even after their rights had been read to them—and thought they could keep themselves out of jail with an alibi, by offering up another suspect, or by crying. Hopefully, Reyes' street smarts extended to avoiding that trap.

That night, Reyes' inmate number showed up online; Robert made an appointment for the next morning.

He and Gia followed the case online and on the local news until a report came in, finally revealing that Reyes' arrest had come from an anonymous tip called into the LAPD's Crime Stoppers hotline.

The Crime Stoppers tip: a car with plates matching Reyes' had been spotted in the neighborhood, speeding, around the time of the slaying.

After hearing that news, Robert and Gia turned off all media and walked out to the shoreline, where moonlight silvered the Pacific's wind-chopped surface.

"Remember those texts Reyes sent you yesterday?"

He nodded; he'd been thinking about them, too.

They went over them: the first one, yesterday afternoon at 3:14: Give me a call. The next at 4:48: Call me. At 5:30: Let's talk.

Then last night at 7:32: Hear about Paul?

Gia asked, "What do you make of them?"

"You first."

"Well, the first text was about six hours after Lawan found Paul's body. Over the next couple of hours, Reyes texted you two more times. Was that unusual?"

"Not when he had something on his mind."

He had assumed that all of Reyes' texts had been about his meeting with Paul, but it wasn't until the last text that Reyes had mentioned Paul by name.

"If his first text was about Paul's death, he learned about it pretty fast," she said.

"Too fast?"

"Pretty fast," was all she said.

"What'd you think about that Crime Stoppers tip?" The tip putting Reyes' speeding car in Paul's neighborhood in the early-morning hours.

"Same thing as you—*what the hell, Reyes?*"

"Reyes being in the neighborhood could be explained away. I mean, he and Paul were tight, Lawan's not home, boys' night out?"

"Sure," she said, but he could tell her heart wasn't all the way behind it.

Before they went to bed, he checked the internet one last time. New developments appeared online, none of them good for Reyes. He went back to the bedroom.

"LAPD says they found the murder weapon at Reyes' address."

She covered her face with a pillow and yelled, "Damn!"

In bed that night, he heard waves slamming the granite rocks of Venice Jetty, and Reyes stayed on his mind. Without really knowing it, Robert had been rooting for Reyes ever since they'd struck up a boardwalk friendship several years ago. He pictured Reyes' slumped posture on the boardwalk just before his arrest. His body language could've been caused by sadness about Paul's death. Or it could've been caused by something else.

Something like remorse.

CHAPTER 14

"So," Robert said in a Tower One prisoner meeting room, "Gia says hi."

Behind a thick plate-glass barrier, Reyes said, "Tell Gigi the same, and thanks for coming, *Roberto*. Know what's been on my mind, besides what you lookin' at?"

"Beats me."

"Last cup of Groundwork I saw you drinking. How was it?"

"What I drank was good. What I dropped on the boardwalk, dunno."

"Cold press?"

"*Sí, con hielo.*" Iced coffee. "How's your mom?"

"A'ight, hangin' in. Talked to her yesterday on my one outgoing call. She wanted to put up her assets to pay for bail, for a top-shelf crime lawyer. That's not happening, is all I know."

"Mind walking me through your thinking on that?"

"First off, you here as *mi abogado* or *mi amigo*?"

"I am your lawyer, so everything's confidential unless you waive it, or you tell me you're about to kill someone. Here as a friend, too, so I guess I'm here in a dual capacity."

Reyes grinned. "*Dual capacity.* Gonna write that one down."

"Just so we're clear, I'm not repping you on this case."

"Hell no, *chico*, I want to get outta here."

The joke was all too true; Robert smiled along with Reyes.

"Tell me about making bail, getting a good criminal lawyer, and your mom helping you out."

"Enough I'm living in her backyard, but she put in the sweat for what she has, took the risk, and I'm not taking none of it away."

Reyes filled him on how Gabriela had worked a behind-the-counter sales job for forty years, bought two rental properties, and did the maintenance herself—sometimes with Reyes' help if she could corral him.

"All in, she's worth what?" Robert asked.

"Gonna say seven hundred grand, seven fifty. Last five years, she been doublin' down on tellin' me to get my shit squared away, and look where I landed. Like I said, this's my mess, not hers."

He remembered that Gabriela had asked Erik to *have a talk* with Reyes; Erik had declined.

"Bet that's not how your mom looks at it."

"I's a kid, she used to walk me over to the Mariachi Plaza in Boyle Heights. Up high on a hill, downtown right in your face. She'd show me Macy's where she worked and show me this building right here, 'cept the twins was under construction back then. She'd tell me, 'When they finish buildin' the jail, all your bad-boy *cholo* friends gonna go live inside there. You don't shape up, they buildin' a special room just for you.' I's a wiseass even back then, asked her, 'How you know it's for me?' And she said, 'Got your name over the door, you little shit!'"

"She's your mother, wants to help you."

"No way she worked, saved, all those years to say, 'Now I can bail out my son, pay for his lawyer.' What she worked for's *her stuff*—not *her stuff unless I get in a jam.*"

Sitting in his cell for a while, Reyes might waver on his position.

Robert asked, "Public defender, right?"

"Yeah, going with a PD's how I see it."

"Met 'im yet?"

"In a couple days, at my arraignment. Paul bein' high-profile, I'm bettin' I draw a decent PD, won't sleep through motions call. I want a lawyer who acts like you but knows the judge's secret handshake. What's the news sayin'?"

"A hotline tip put your car in Paul's neighborhood around the time of his death."

"Finally got me some street cred."

Robert asked, "How'd you find out about it?"

His real question: *How'd you find out about it at 3:14 p.m. the day Paul was killed?*

"Maid called me, let me know about it."

At least that much made sense.

Robert asked if he minded talking about the aftermath of his arrest on the boardwalk.

"Not at all. Before they'd even booked me, they wanted a peek inside my cell phone. Told 'em, 'Hell no.' And after booking, they wanted me in their box for a little tête-à-tête."

"You said no, right?"

"No, I said let's go."

Oh, Jesus, no.

"Figured I knew my rights, don't gotta answer nothin', so wasn't much gonna be coming their way. They's the ones did all the talking."

"They talked to you about their case?"

"Not exactly. More like how they went about asking their questions."

"Sure you didn't tell 'em more than you thought?"

"*Positivo.* I'd say to 'em, 'Not quite sure what you mean by that.' So they'd ask it another way."

"Like how?"

"Like asking me, 'Maybe you can tell us why you were in Mr. Dickerson's neighborhood at two a.m.?' I'd give 'em a look like I's about half-smart, so they'd ask, 'Are you saying you don't recall speeding through the intersection of Sunset and Capri?'"

Sunset and Capri, a half mile below Paul's estate. So far, Reyes wasn't denying that he was there; Robert kept waiting to hear Reyes' alibi.

Reyes said, "I bet Capri and Sunset's something their hotline tipster told 'em."

"Think so, yeah."

"The detectives asked if I'd be surprised to hear someone said I almost ran over 'em, bottom of Capri. Now, Roberto, can you see a Latino from East LA hauling ass around that hood any time, much less two, three a.m.?"

"I hear you."

Reyes had overlooked the obvious—if detectives believed Reyes was speeding away from a crime scene, his Latino-in-Brentwood argument cut *against* his innocence.

"Did you tell the detectives your Latino-speeding theory?"

"Told 'em *nada*. Look, *Roberto*, if you in the box guilty, you freakin' out hearing them askin' this and that. You innocent? That's a different story. You listenin' hard to what's going on, not shittin' yourself. Not yet, anyway."

That had been the first time Reyes had mentioned his innocence, even indirectly.

"Detectives ask about anything else?"

"Wondered if I owned one'a them batons."

"The telescoping ones?"

Reyes nodded. "Looks small until you sling it at the ground, then it's badass. Musta been what they used to kill Paul."

They. A second vague assertion of innocence; Robert relaxed a bit.

"They?" he asked.

"He, she, them, *they*. Detectives asked me about where I bought *my baton*, where I kept *my baton*, was I missing *my baton*, who all I told *my baton* went missing."

"And you said . . . ?"

"Wanted to ask 'em, 'Is *baton* a French word?' But I just sat there, looking dumb as I could."

"The news said the weapon was found at Gabriela's house. That it had Paul's blood on it."

"If that's what they say."

Nonresponsive. Dreading the answers, Robert asked more direct questions.

"Know why the cops were at your house in the first place?"

"Gotta believe they's looking for me."

Evasive again. His bad feeling began to metastasize.

Your alibi, Reyes, let me hear it.

"Look here, *Roberto*, I know one thing's eatin' at you, so let me get to it. Paul dyin', I shed my tears about that already, and I'll shed more when I get outta here. But not right here and not now."

Not an alibi, but better than what he'd been hearing.

Reyes said, "You a good man coming down here. I know you got questions about me, and what did I do, but coming down here anyway. One day wouldn't surprise me at all you turnin' into a great man. But you see Paul, he was already a great man, more than I'd ever dream about bein' in my own life."

Straight from the heart. Robert knew that he wasn't entitled to hear anything more. So he'd wish Reyes luck, deposit the maximum in his prison account, and hit the road.

Before Robert could get the words out, Reyes said: "Y'see, *Roberto*, I was at Paul's when he was killed. And the cops knew it."

"How'd they know?"

"Might as well've told 'em myself."

Robert slumped back into the cold metal prison chair.

"You still here?" Reyes asked.

He couldn't find an answer. If Reyes had killed Paul, he was done with Reyes forever, no matter what Reyes might say.

"Give me sixty seconds," Reyes said. "You want to split after that, I get it."

"Sure."

That was all he had left to offer.

"What you never knew, Paul and me, we both insomniacs. Way we got to be so close, we used to drive around all hours of the night.

Sometimes we'd take my ride, usually his Aston Martin, or his Rolls Phantom, and hit the road. One time we drove north, far as Santa Barbara. East to Palm Springs another time.

"Lotsa times, we'd wind up at a family bakery on First Street. Pasteleria Luceros. Paul loved hittin' there around four a.m. because I know one of the bakers, and if I tipped him we coming? He'd make us the first batch of churros, hot from the oven, right out the back door. We'd down six apiece, couldn't stop, 'specially if I'd burned one on the drive over. If we stuck around the bakery a little longer, we had first crack at the day's *tres leches.*"

Three-milks cake was soaked in evaporated, whole, and condensed milk; only God and the baker knew how much sugar was added.

"You two insomniacs drive around LA some nights, eating churros and *tres leches?*"

"Felix and Oscar, I know, but that's how we rolled sometimes."

"Lawan was okay with that?"

"Sure, because it makes . . . it made Paul happy, and that's how she wanted him to be. Happy, same as her. And when she's gone somewhere, like she'd done that night, our drive was on, a hundred percent."

"So you were up at Paul's?"

Reyes nodded. "At his place, inside the gate. Drove around the side of the house and parked same as always. Lights were on inside—not all, some—no cars in the driveway, but I was gonna drive that night, so that didn't set me off. So I go to the kitchen door in back and knock. Not hard, light, you know, let him know I'm here, case he walking around bare ass inside."

"Okay and then . . . ?"

"And then nothing. Didn't hear him or see him, and that never happened before. I cracked open the door, called out, 'Hey, cover your ass up, let's get going.' Not my exact words but like that, and still nada. Now I'm thinking maybe he's taking a shower, still upstairs, so I walk around, front of the house, look up at the master bathroom. Lights off up there, whole second floor was dark, so, shit, I'm gettin' concerned, not *worried*, concerned, but I don't want be a pain in his ass if he's changed his mind."

"What about the front door?"

Reyes nodded. "What I'm talkin' about. Thought about ringing the bell, but ya' know, that never was our drill, so forget it. Went back to the car, phone's in the charger. Got in, thought about calling him. Thought about honking, said, 'Forget it' again, and drove off. About the time I hit Sunset, I rang him up, hands free."

Hands free? Wouldn't want a moving violation.

Reyes said, "Left him a message, something like, 'Hey, what's up, man? Where you at?' Maybe he'll hear his phone and say, 'Oh, shit, that must be Reyes.' When he didn't hit me back, a few minutes later, I hit him up again. One'a those, 'Not like you not bein' at home, gimme a shout when you get this.'"

"Oh, boy, *the call*."

"I know. The I'm-so-worried-about-you call. The one a husband makes after killing his wife."

"So, the LAPD can get your calls *off Paul's phone*."

Reyes nodded. "He had my cell number, my address, too. Never heard back from Paul, so now—inside here now—I'm thinking, by the time I knocked on the door, Paul's already dead."

Reyes sank into himself. His shirt pitted out, eyes watering.

"Peter Paul, damn, I miss him."

Robert had too many questions to sort through. The guard was knocking. Time was up.

Reyes said, "One thing you could do for me. Only person I trust to do this."

"Let's hear it."

"Lawan. Talk to her. Bring her to my arraignment."

"What?"

After a quick exchange with Reyes, Robert began to see what he was driving at.

CHAPTER 15

Lying on Erik's backyard lawn, Robert drank in the cerulean blue sky. Its depth filled him with . . . he wasn't sure with *what*. Gratitude for his life? Regret about Reyes' situation? Both at once?

Priya was inside looking for her phone and Lawan's contact information. Next to him, Erik Junior and Hans giggled, taking turns letting Ducky Joe peck cornmeal from their belly buttons.

Kid freedom, the best kind. The kind he'd had growing up in Gilroy. Not the same as the lads—there'd always been farm chores—but he'd had tons of kid freedom and a farm to be free in.

His mind wandered to his grateful drive away from Tower One. The distant, snowcapped San Gabriel Mountains he'd seen must remind inmates of simple pleasures left behind. Trains rolling in and out of nearby Union Station surely haunted them, same as Johnny Cash's prisoner had been tormented in Cash's classic song "Folsom Prison Blues."

Once he'd reached Erik's house, he'd used a garden hose to wash prison patina from his face, hands, and arms. That clinging chemical smell infused with nicotine and body odor from his brief brush with incarceration.

Priya called out from the upstairs deck.

"Erik! Hans! Where is Mommy's phone?"

"I don't know, Mommy," they said. They shook their heads, too, for emphasis.

"You *suah, suah?*" she asked, throwing in a little Thai-sty sass.

They said, "*Suah*, Mommy. *Suah, suah.*"

Soon as she went back inside, Robert spotted her phone in Hans' elastic waistband.

"You boys should help Mommy find the phone," he said.

"It's a game," Hans said.

"Mommy likes it," Erik Junior added.

So serious, he almost believed them. The sliding driveway gate started to open; Erik parked the Yukon outside his garage.

"Daddy!" both boys screamed.

Erik Junior set Ducky Joe on the grass, and both sons ran over to their father. Erik held two white sacks—looked like he'd brought takeout lunch for the family. Robert approached him, cradling Ducky Joe.

"What's up?" Erik asked.

"Needed a phone number from Priya."

Erik's broad face held none of its usual welcome. "Reyes was the client you asked me about?"

Robert nodded. Erik knelt down and fished Priya's phone from Hans' waistband.

"Please go inside and give Mommy her phone." When they started up with him, Erik gathered them. "Let's all be good boys and help out Mommy. You two get going, and we'll have tamales for lunch."

Something about Erik's tone . . . his boys caught it and took off inside. Robert put the duck back in his pen, then followed Erik into the kitchen, which opened onto a large living area with exposed ceiling beams—a full-on "We have two boys" disaster zone.

Careful about his sons overhearing him, Erik asked, "Dude, what the you-know-what? And don't give me any attorney-client you-know-what."

"Didn't want to tell you until I knew more."

"You didn't *want* me to be right about him, and I was. What a total," he whispered, "*asshole* that guy is."

Erik emptied two bags of Mexican food. Its sharp aroma reminded Robert that he hadn't eaten since his scone at downtown Urth Caffé, five hours ago.

"Smells good," he said.

"It'll taste good, too."

No lunch invite. Robert caught the name on the bag: Liliana's Tamales. Not far from the East LA bakery where Reyes and Paul used to grab predawn churros and *tres leches* cake.

"What takes you over to East LA?"

"Heard Liliana's had the best *mole poblano* in LA."

An answer, not the truth. He heard Priya and the boys heading down the stairs.

"Gonna stick with your story?"

"All day long."

"You visited Reyes' mom—Priya already spilled the beans."

The rest of Erik's family poured around the kitchen counter.

Erik asked Priya, "You told this guy where I was?"

"Robert ask me, I tell him. No *kwaam lap* from your friend."

"*Kwaam lap*. What's that word mean, boys?"

"It means *secret*, Daddy."

No secrets from your friend.

"That's exactly right," Erik said, clueless about the Thai word's meaning. He popped the lid off a red-sauce container. "*Phet maak maak.*"

Even Robert knew that meant *very, very hot* and that Thais could roll with the hottest *chiles* Mexico had to offer.

After Priya texted him Lawan's telephone number, Robert stepped outside with Erik, each with a plate of *chile rojo con puerco* tamales.

"How's Gabriela holding up?" Robert asked.

"About what you'd expect. Sure you want to go there?"

"Why not?"

"Know what your pal Reyes has his mom doing?"

"Yeah. Coming to visit him in prison."

"That, and running around town looking for a criminal lawyer. Getting her house appraised so she can put up bail for her dickhead son. Hardworking Latinos dropping by her house with tens and twenties to help her out. And if Reyes ever gets out on bail? He'll run, no doubt in my mind, and leave his mom holding the bag."

"Not gonna happen that way. First thing out of Reyes' mouth—Gabriela's assets are hers, not his."

"I believe he said it, but I don't believe it."

"Not asking you to. Reyes told me he'd take his chances with a public defender and won't let Gabriela put up her assets for bail or a lawyer. And I believe him."

"Believing him, *that's* your problem. Why do you need Lawan's number?"

"Something I said I'd do for Reyes."

"Do for him? With what they got on him?"

Robert shrugged. "You never know."

"Sure you do. When the weapon's found at his address, that's a good indication of guilt."

"Where'd you hear about the baton?"

"Gabriela. Cops were at her door, getting ready to question her on her son's whereabouts. One of 'em saw a baton sticking out from under Frosty the Snowman. Blood on it's gonna match Paul's, if it hasn't already."

"Prints?"

"Depends on how careful Reyes was wiping down the weapon."

This was the first time he'd heard about the weapon's exact location when found. It made sense to him that Reyes hadn't known either—he would've told Gabriela not to discuss any specifics of his case on their call.

Erik said, "I'm having seconds, maybe thirds, but you're cut off for having poor judgment in clients."

Priya joined them. "Lawan texted me, Erik. Tonight, you and I will go to Wat Thai. There will be a ceremony for Lawan's husband."

Erik winked at Robert and stood up.

"I was thinking, tonight me and the boys would barbecue some ribs, kick back, drink a few beers."

She hugged his waist, as far as her arms allowed.

"No, we must go. She is my friend. We went to their home as guests and must be respectful."

He grinned at Robert. This was the Jacobsons' usual routine.

"Come on, baby, your man's gotta stay at home, be a man."

"My man needs to pray tonight at Wat Thai."

Looked to Robert like she'd just hugged Erik even harder.

Erik said, "You and Gia want to come with us? We'll take the Beast."

CHAPTER 16

Four chanting, shaven-head Buddhist monks sat on a platform in lotus position. Purple-and-white orchids from Paul's party surrounded them. Seated on the purple-carpeted floor with Lawan, Gia, Priya, and Erik, Robert faced the saffron-robed monks and an easel holding a large photograph of Paul and Lawan.

The pair stood in an Isan Province rice field so vibrant with green shoots that the image appeared to vibrate.

"The field where Paul and Lawan first met in Udon," Priya had explained.

This forty-yard-long rectangular worship room soared three stories. The far end of the room held a fifteen-foot-tall golden Buddha. Nine umbrellas hovered over the Buddha's head, each one smaller than the one below, until the smallest created a pointed top; red-and-gold tables rested in front of Buddha; two golden, antlered deer poised watchful on either side.

Without knowing what the symbols meant, Robert thought the totality of the temple said *welcome*, same as the sea of smiling Thai faces seated around him.

Robert closed his eyes, and as the chanting monks continued, a humming grew in his head until it drowned out his other thoughts. Might've been one minute later or ten when water sprinkled his face. He opened his eyes and looked up.

A monk flung holy water at those seated before him. He smiled at Robert. Robert smiled back—he couldn't help it—and the monk's smile grew broader. He still didn't know what was going on but felt thankful to witness this transfer of Paul's spirit into the next world.

After an hour, the ceremony ended. Robert and Gia made their way to a counter by the front door and bought four plastic boxes filled with toothpaste, toilet paper, socks, and towels for the monks, who had taken poverty vows and depended on donations to survive.

Lawan joined them, made *wei*, and thanked them both for coming. Deep sadness had descended into her soulful eyes. An emotion not relieved by drugs but by something within.

Lawan said to Robert, "Priya said that you wanted to speak to me."

"It's very important, a legal matter, or I would never trouble you now."

"It is no trouble at all."

They stepped outside the temple, where two armor-clad terra-cotta warriors with fangs and swords guarded the front door.

"To scare away all evil spirits," Priya had told him as they'd first walked inside.

"When was the last time you spoke to the police?" he asked Lawan.

"Sunday, around noon. Again that night. Not since then."

"Do you mind telling me what they wanted to know?"

"Not at all. Where I had been the night before, what I saw when I came home, if anyone working at our home had argued with Paul. I think I answered all their questions."

"Surely the police called you back?"

She nodded. "I have not called them back. They made an arrest, a Latino, I understand from my Thai friends, but I've been in mourning, speaking to Forever Hollywood, and here at the temple."

"Forever Hollywood is . . . ?"

Somehow smiling, she said, "They provide cremation for Wat Thai. I think Paul would find their name quite funny."

He could see that she'd been living a parallel life, more Thai than American, since Paul's death.

"Paul wasn't exactly a Hollywood fame-seeker, was he?"

"The opposite. A special soul, I think, but I will always be biased about him."

"I missed out, not knowing him better."

Her eyes closed. A sound came from deep inside—sounded to him like *mmmph*. Her eyes opened. "This legal matter you mentioned?"

If possible, he wanted to hear her unvarnished version of Reyes' story.

"Raymundo Reyes. How well do you know him?"

"Quite well, but he was more Paul's friend than mine."

"Would you be surprised to hear that he's the Latino in jail for Paul's murder?"

He watched that information start to sink in, then led her through part of what the LAPD believed. That Reyes had been inside her home early Sunday morning and had killed Paul.

On her own, Lawan said, "They sometimes took long drives at night—very, very late—after traffic calmed down, and they would meet at our house."

"The night Paul was killed? Had they planned anything?"

She thought about his question. "They could've, easily. I was out in Chino Hills with friends, and it makes sense they would go that night. I wondered why Reyes hadn't come to the temple—he and Paul were close. He must be so afraid."

Her words came from her generous heart.

"Reyes cared very much about Paul, admired him, and I don't believe Reyes would've ever hurt him," Robert said.

"Of course not. How can I help?"

He told her about Reyes' arraignment, and she agreed to join him there. He made *wei*, best he could. She returned the gesture, smiling at his clumsy effort.

On their way home, Erik fielded a call and took it through his earphones. When they reached the Jacobsons' home, he took Robert aside on the back patio.

"That was Gabriela calling. She was crying because your pal wouldn't let her pay for a hotshot criminal lawyer."

Reyes, true to his word.

"And bail?"

"Won't let her pay."

"And?"

"Does Reyes have an alibi worth mentioning?"

Robert picked up on his change of heart. "Enough of one. Lawan just backed up that Reyes and Paul were often together, early-morning hours."

"If you need a top-tier, unlicensed investigator, maybe you could sign me up."

"I'll tell you up front—there are major problems with Reyes' situation."

"You mean *his case*?"

"It's not my case. I'm just helping out. Sure you want to come on board?"

"How else's he gonna finish his movie? I need to see how the damn thing ends. Do you think the bartender might've been involved?"

CHAPTER 17

Robert and Lawan spoke very little on their drive downtown to Reyes' arraignment. As they pulled onto the 405, he fielded a text from Gia: Trevor Reid on CNBC re: Paul. Will save.

He returned a thumbs-up emoji as traffic rolled to a standstill near Crenshaw Boulevard.

He said, "Trevor Reid is on the money channel talking about Paul."

"Not a complicated man. Simply a difficult one."

"Paul and Trevor don't seem like they'd be . . . friends."

"Knowing Trevor for many years did not turn him into Paul's friend."

By the time they made it to Clara Shortbridge Foltz Criminal Justice Center, they were still on time. After looking for a parking place and waiting in a jammed-up security line at the front door, they wound up being a half hour late to Room 30, felony arraignment court.

Lawan said, "Today, Los Angeles is running on Thai time."

Late, she meant.

"My fault," he said, and pushed through the courtroom doors.

Up front, a judge sat on a dais between the American and California flags. A low wooden railing and swinging doors separated the visitors' gallery from the district attorneys and public defenders.

As they took seats on a graffiti-gouged wooden pew, a full-bodied Latina sheriff's deputy in a crisp beige uniform paced the gallery. A Smith & Wesson M&P bounced on her right hip.

"Each of you will take off your hats, remove any headphones, and shut off your cell phones. Fail to do so, and deputies *will* remove you from this courtroom."

To his right, beyond the railing, stood a glass-and-wood prisoner holding area about forty feet by ten feet. Chain-link fencing had been bolted on top; a narrow opening in the glass sides allowed attorneys to confer with defendants.

A public defender, a woman in a blazer and slacks and black loafers with gold buckles, had been conferring with the only visible prisoner in the holding area: inmate Raymundo Reyes.

Now, she turned to the judge.

"Your Honor, my client, Mr. Reyes, waives a formal reading of the indictment and pleads not guilty to all of the charges against him. He does not waive his right to a timely preliminary hearing."

Boilerplate language, Robert was pretty sure.

The judge set the hearing ten days from today—the statutory time frame—subject to a defense motion to extend the date.

The judge raised the issue of bail, and for the next five minutes, the attorneys argued about whether Reyes posed a flight risk, the seriousness of his offense, his criminal record, ties to the community, and the danger Reyes might pose to witnesses or the victim's family if released on bail.

Robert already knew that, unless the judge set bail at a ridiculously low number, Reyes couldn't make bail on his own.

"You okay?" he asked Lawan.

"Amazing to watch," she said, as American justice unfolded.

The judge set bail at $1 million. To Robert's surprise, the judge said, "And I wish you good luck, Mr. Reyes."

From the holding area, Reyes didn't crack wise. "Thank you, Your Honor."

As Reyes turned to leave, Robert caught his eye. He raised his manacled hands and managed a nod to Lawan. A deputy then led him to a prisoner holding room behind the courtroom.

Reyes' public defender walked over to a district attorney; they began to talk shop.

Robert asked, "Will you be okay here for a few minutes?"

"Sure."

He walked over to the deputy's desk.

"Deputy, excuse me, my name is Robert Worth. I'd like to see prisoner Raymundo Reyes, if that's okay."

"Are you his lawyer in a matter before the court?"

"No, I'm his lawyer in another matter."

"Are we playing a game today where you might or might not be his lawyer?"

"I am a lawyer. I'm also Mr. Reyes' friend, and he asked that I—"

She raised her hand; it stopped him cold.

"Unless you represent him in this arraignment court this very morning, you are a civilian."

"Could I talk to his public defender? Don't know her name, but she's talking to—"

He realized that Reyes' public defender was gone. He turned, saw her heading out the back door.

"Anita Yates," the deputy said.

"Pardon me?"

"That's her name."

He signaled Lawan to keep her seat and caught up with Anita in the hallway. All around the hall, criminal lawyers conferred with clients; friends and families huddled in various states of fear and resignation.

"Ms. Yates, could I have a word with you?"

She stopped, faced him. "About?"

"Robert Worth, a friend of Raymundo Reyes. I also happen to be an attorney, not a criminal attorney, but I represented him on another matter."

"And?"

"I have information that will be useful to his defense."

"Why don't I give you a card and . . . ?"

"That's not going to work. I brought the wife of the deceased to court. She has information that could—"

She pointed to the ladies' restroom sign. He caught the hint of a southern accent when she said, "If you're still here when I get back, we can have a quick chat."

He decided against bringing out Lawan for the discussion. No point in confusing her with American legalese. Confused himself, he Googled *criminal preliminary hearings* in California; he'd just scanned the basics when Anita reappeared.

"You were saying that Mr. Dickerson's wife is with you? On behalf of the defendant?"

"In the courtroom, yes, on behalf of Mr. Reyes. And I think what she has to say will make the burglary element of the special-circumstances charge iffy at best. At the, you know, the preliminary hearing."

"Want to explain to me how you're going to make the burglary element disappear?"

"I don't want to tell you how to do your—"

"No, please, explain it to me. I'm all you-know-what."

Ears? Her tone fell somewhere between sarcastic and even more so.

"First, let's assume that Mr. Reyes was inside the Dickerson residence. He wasn't, but let's go with what the DA's saying, and assume that he was."

"Okay, let's."

"In order to prove burglary, the district attorney . . ."

"Call him a DA, it'll speed this up."

"For the DA to prove there was a residential burglary at the preliminary hearing—"

"That's Burglary One, okay? And down here, we call the hearing *a prelim.*"

He hated to admit it—he was starting to like her, breaking balls with her soft accent.

"Here we go," he said. "For the DA to prove Burglary One at the prelim, he'd have to show it was more likely than not that Mr. Reyes entered the Dickerson residence with the intent to commit a burglary."

"Stealing things usually tops on the list. That plus a murder gives you special circumstances."

"But if Mr. Reyes did not enter the house to steal anything, or to do anything else illegal, then there was no burglary. And the fact is, Mr. Reyes often came to the Dickerson residence at that time of night."

"At two a.m.? Were he and Mr. Dickerson romantically involved?"

"Not that I'm aware of. I mean, hell no."

He explained in detail the pair's unlikely late-night cruises and suggested that Anita's office might verify prior drives by interviewing the baking crew at Pasteleria Luceros.

Hearing this scenario, she fought a smile, caution bred no doubt by many trials and even more setbacks.

Anita asked, "If Burglary One gets tossed out, what would that mean for Mr. Reyes?"

A pop quiz?

"It would mean that Paul's murder didn't happen during a residential burglary. That would eliminate the special circumstance and the prospect of Reyes facing the death penalty or life in prison without possibility of parole."

As they headed back to the courtroom, Anita said, "If this story holds up, he'd still be looking at life *with* possible parole, but I agree with you, Mr. Worth. And that's pretty decent criminal work for a civilian."

※

A half hour later, Anita finished up her one-on-one interview with Lawan; they joined Robert in the gallery of the courtroom.

"Everything all right?" he asked Lawan.

Lawan looked at Anita. "I think so."

Anita said, "More than all right. Excellent news, same as advertised, Mr. Worth."

"Wonder if there's any way I can get on a list to see Mr. Reyes as a lawyer?" he asked.

More liberal visiting hours, longer visits.

"I'll put together an order today for the judge's signature. Show the order to the admitting guard at Tower One, and they will honor it. Want to watch me ruin the DA's day?"

Anita approached the DA inside the bullpen. As they spoke, he crossed his arms and nodded. Robert saw no change in his expression when she spoke to him. Just the same stone face.

When she turned away, Anita winked at him. Robert caught the DA closing his eyes, his body sagging just enough to notice.

CHAPTER 18

On the way back to Lawan's home, Robert answered her questions about what she'd just witnessed in court. Mostly, though, she was quiet. She dozed off, curled up in her seat the way that only women can manage. He couldn't imagine what she'd been through the last few days. A fairly new country, husband slain, cremation arrangements, LAPD grilling her.

On top of it all, she'd found time to help Reyes.

As he drove uphill on Capri, he said, "Lawan, almost here."

She stirred in her seat, looked around. A flicker of sadness before she sat upright.

Ahead of them, the estate's gate was open; she leaned forward.

"I wasn't expecting anyone."

About to turn in the driveway, he slowed. Three sharp knocks hit Lawan's window. She jumped.

Outside the car, a sweat-drenched woman wore visually unwelcome spandex, head to toe. Lawan lowered her window.

The woman was already talking: ". . . for your loss. I know you must wonder where we've been. Frederick and I only just now returned from Palm Springs."

Her sweat dripped inside the car onto Lawan's door panel.

"I want to bring by Bryan by to apologize for flying his drone over your yard. Lately, he thinks he's Vin Diesel or something."

"We didn't mind at all, Gretchen, it was good fun. And tell Bryan that he can still use the pool if there's an adult with him."

"Not until he apologizes. When's convenient for you?"

Already checking her calendar, the woman seemed to have no idea how pushy and thoughtless she came across.

When she was done, Robert continued into the driveway. A Flower's Flowers van had parked in front of the house. Lawan's maid waited in the doorway as two deliverymen lugged an enormous arrangement up the front steps.

He pulled up behind the van. Lawan watched the arrangement disappear inside, making no move to get out of the car.

She said, "Paul told me that Gretchen was a great teacher."

"I, uh, really?"

"He said it was helpful to talk to someone so transparent. She's going broke, and her husband cheats on her, but Gretchen still believes that *things* will make up for all of it. Paul said that she taught him patience and gratitude."

Her eyes brimmed. Robert was about to take a stab at changing the subject, but he was too late. Her hands came to her face, and she began to cry. Nothing he could say would ease her pain, so he didn't try.

In front of him, the van's driver shut the rear doors. The Flower's Flowers logo—a woven basket filled with a colorful arrangement—was split by the doors. Once they closed, the basket's design came together in the middle, with hand-painted vines creeping up the small rear windows.

"Those big flowers just now," Lawan said, wiping her eyes. "Bet anything they came from his lawyers."

"Nice."

"Not really." She turned to him. "Would you mind coming inside for few minutes?"

Robert and Lawan entered the foyer. The living room opened to his right—comfortable couches, lived-in, same as the backyard. A dining room to his left gave into a hallway leading back to the kitchen.

That new flower arrangement dominated a side table in the foyer. As Lawan checked the card, he avoided looking at the marble floor where Paul had died.

She replaced the card, then looked around the foyer, up at the ceiling. She seemed relieved.

"Paul's *phii thai hong* was still here last night."

"His . . . ?"

"His ghost. Paul died suddenly, violently. His spirit was confused about what happened. The monks, their chanting, he's free now."

"Good."

Priya believed in ghosts, too. Who was he to argue? He believed that Mike Tyson could mount a comeback anytime he wanted.

She handed him the card. "From Paul's lawyer, Hampton Bergen."

The firm of Belkin and Daniels. A Century City firm with a reputation for top-tier legal work and top-tier bills.

"I don't know Mr. Bergen."

"I do, but barely. He's called me several times already."

"I'm sure he has—"

"He didn't attend our party—made a small donation instead. Didn't come to Wat Thai to honor Paul—sent these flowers instead."

Before he could comment, she moved on.

"One answer I gave to the police wasn't entirely accurate. I told them Paul didn't have any misunderstandings with anyone. That day, my mind was focused on his death, his spiritual life, and I forgot to mention—"

"'Trevor Reid, I met him."

"Yes. *Him.* I still don't understand why he was there."

"I do know this. If Trevor came to the party to patch up something with Paul, he failed miserably. I saw Paul and Trevor arguing, fighting."

"Paul told me about it later. He was still angry."

"I don't blame him."

"Not at Trevor, angry at himself. He studied Muay Thai near Chiang Mai, and when Trevor struck him, Paul reacted on instinct."

"I'm surprised Paul didn't get a round of applause. Any idea why they argued?"

"No. I suggested Paul reach out to him. He said Trevor would take an apology as a sign of weakness, so Paul decided to examine his own actions and deal with that. Whether he ever had the chance, I don't know."

"A sign of weakness? Had they been in a deal together, some kind of negotiation?"

"Maybe both. Again, I don't know."

She explained that Paul had pushed her to get more involved in his business affairs. So far, she had resisted doing so.

She said, "In time, that would have happened. But it was important to me that Paul not be seen as marrying a younger Asian woman who was suddenly interested in his business affairs."

His money.

"Makes a lot of sense." And it did.

"I'd like for you to do something for me. It's about our charitable foundation. To hire you . . . I don't know exactly what to call it."

"I don't do foundation work. It's very specialized, Lawan, and the Belkin firm is tops in that area."

She nodded. "I want you to read Paul's business files. You will learn about things that I need to know, and I have a feeling you will learn things that might help our friend Reyes."

"Things about your husband and Trevor Reid?"

"Perhaps."

"Do you think Reid might be involved in . . . ?"

"As a Buddhist, Robert, we are taught to avoid hating others. Christians also strive for the same goal. As far as Mr. Reid is concerned . . . perhaps I am failing to practice my religion's teachings."

With Trevor now on the menu, a fire seemed to rekindle in her eyes; a fire lit up inside him, too.

"I'd love to help out, Lawan, any way I can."

CHAPTER 19

At the outset of Robert's next visit with Reyes, he was certain of one thing: he didn't like being inside Tower One any better the second time.

"What the hell happened to your face?" Robert asked.

"Altercation," Reyes said, touching his bruised eye socket.

"Thought you had a solo cell?"

"Man's gotta eat. He cracked me from behind in the dinner lineup."

"Did you tell Anita that it—?"

"I know the guy. Said his cousin didn't cop an invite to my screening and felt like I disrespected his cousin. Most days, his cuz like to lay up on the couch all day. Other days, he'd bag up some off-the-rack McCormick's, sell it like it's weed or Spice or Atom-Bomb potpourri. And he thinks I disrespected his cousin?"

He needed to vent; Robert got it.

"Did you meet with Anita Yates after your arraignment?"

"She dropped by for a visit, yeah. Told me about you being on the lawyer list and asked did I trust you talking about my case."

"Don't blame her. If I start shooting my mouth off, I could mess you up."

"Trust you a hundred, *Roberto*. Told her you could look at the case file anytime you want. Now that my Burglary One beef oughta go away at my prelim, that right there's *gigantesco*."

"Lawan backed you up. You nailed that one, Reyes."

"Anita was askin' me about Lawan, too—wantin' to know what the DA was gonna find out, he start lookin' into *us*."

Anita had asked him about any Reyes-Lawan angle, too.

"Look, the DA's gonna see Lawan's a beautiful woman, and I imagine she'll come into quite a bit of money, so Anita damn well better ask you about *us*."

Reyes nodded. "Know the problem Paul always had with Lawan?"

"Not sure I want to hear about that."

"Couldn't buy her any big-ticket bling. She wanted a Lexus sedan, not a Mercedes AMG 65, because it was dependable, lotsa room in back. Wanted him to help her family back in Thailand—same as he'd wanted—but he couldn't buy her nothin' flashy. She's not geared like that."

He nodded. "Help Anita every way you can, all right? I think you drew a good PD."

"Will do. For a second, let's talk in my dual capacity as a prisoner and a moviemaker."

Hearing *dual capacity*, Robert smiled. He bet Reyes had spent real time to work the phrase into this conversation.

"I never talked to you about your fee, so I'm giving you ten percent of *Walk Street Hits*. You got that coming, no matter what."

"Right now—even knowing one day it'll be the flagship of your billion-dollar empire—I consider it totally worthless. And so do you, because you're indigent."

"Got Trevor Reid to thank for that, but yeah, I won't wear my FUBU beret talkin' to Anita."

Without any prompting, Reyes jumped into discussing his case.

"Way I see the big picture, the DA'll still try to max out my sentence on simple murder. No way he wants to be looked at as soft on my ass in a high-profile case."

He couldn't argue with Reyes' sound conclusion.

"Now, *mi abogada*, she got other cases, needs to reshuffle her deck, so she'll be putting off my case. Besides, if she gonna make my Burglary One go away, she's already a hero. Hey, I'm not throwin' shade—but B-One getting tossed? The firm of Worth and Reyes left that under the Christmas tree for Anita Yates to open."

Their fictional law firm brought an involuntary smile to Robert's face.

Robert said, "Look, your PD's just getting started, and her investigator will find things neither of us ever would."

"But her investigator just got assigned from the pool, and I'm guessin' he's been working the Valley or Watts or East LA, and just moved over the hill to work EZ Street."

"Easy . . . ?"

"The Westside. Meaning he's still punchin' his Waze to see if Barrington runs into Sunset. Whereas, you?"

"Whereas me what?"

"You know me, believe me, and you my homie, and I didn't do none of what they sayin'. We both know who did."

"I don't know anything."

"Okay, let's be circumspect, a'ight. Let's not say Trevor Reid's name out loud."

Lawan had already mentioned Trevor, and up he jumped again. Robert believed Reyes and Lawan both had it right in suspecting him.

Robert asked, "What's your take on Paul's relationship with Reid?"

"You heard what happened at the party?"

"No, I saw it. Did Paul tell you about it?"

Reyes shook his head. "No, the maid. All the people who worked for Paul knew about it. If he'd just kicked Trevor's ass over that cliff . . ."

Reyes stopped, shook his head.

"You ever see anything else violent between Paul and Trevor?"

"Nothin' like that, no. But Reid's was the only call Paul ever took where . . . Usually, a call'd come in on Paul's car phone, and he'd say,

'I'm with my friend Reyes, so watch what you say.' Givin' the caller a heads-up, and they'd have their chat. Reid called him twice I know of. Once in the car, and Paul said, 'We need to talk later' and hung up. The other time, he called up at Paul's house, and Paul took it outside to talk. After he got back, he was—not angry, what's that word starts with a *g*?"

"Agitated?" Not a *g*, but that was exactly how Trevor had made Robert feel.

"Yeah, agitated, and you'd never see easy Paul agitated. How do you think Anita's investigator's gonna get in and around Trevor Reid?"

"Lots of ways to do that, Reyes."

"He'd be calling Reid for a sit-down, and Reid's putting him off a month, then another month till it's *Mr. Reid sincerely wanted to help out*, but Reid's lawyered up. Even questioning good guy Jerry Baugh—you think Reid would ever sit still for that?" Reyes leaned closer to Robert. "Way I see it, you already runnin' ahead of the pack, *Roberto*. What's the point you not catchin' that fox?"

"If I do stay with it, I'll need help."

"Talk to *Mamacita*. She can set you straight about—"

"I mean Erik."

"*Oso Polar* help? Shit, *Oso* ain't gonna go bird-doggin' clues for me. He's ex-LAPD, and LAPD put me in here. End of discussion."

"You done?"

Reyes looked down. "On him, yeah."

"I'm not. Why'd you let Erik have final say-so about your project?"

"I didn't. I never thought he'd roll over to East LA on my account."

Robert didn't let go. "But you risked it. Risked depending on a guy you're always sideways with."

Reyes just ran out of runway for the truth. "Fine. I knew the clip was good, and I knew he'd, y'know, put our beef to one side and shoot me straight."

"No matter what, right?"

"Somethin' like that."

"Something *exactly* like that. Want Erik to help out or what?"

Grudgingly: "Couldn't hurt."

Robert waited.

"Yeah, it'd be super-duper if *Señor Oso Polar* could find time in his busy day to help me out. Tell him I said so, would you?"

"Super-duper? If I run into Erik, I might mention it."

They talked a while longer. Jerry Baugh came up again—he might be willing to shed some light on Trevor. A downtown private club came up, too: Sprocket, where Paul and Trevor had each been members.

Robert had seen their ads: *Sprocket. Making LA Move.*

Reyes said, "Shit name, worse slogan, but Paul took me there couple times, and their Cobb salad's off the chain."

As they kept talking, nothing they touched on deviated from the faint, curved line from Paul's death to Trevor Reid. Robert had no problem admitting to himself that he looked forward to straightening out that line and drawing it in bold.

CHAPTER 20

The checkout line ran eight-deep at the 7-Eleven on East Olympic downtown. Most people were buying Lotto tickets and Big Gulps, but Sonny needed pork rinds and Shasta Tiki Punch for their weekly rooms over on West Sixth Street. Smart & Final was only three blocks away, but Sonny had insisted on coming here while Hobie removed the wrap from the sedan.

"S and F won't have an assortment at checkout. More like one brand boxed up that'll last a year or two. Same way they do with Slim Jims, and who wants to lug that bulk all around town?"

"Can't argue with you there," Chet said.

What good did arguing with Sonny ever do?

Sonny said, "Know that guy on TV sometimes, supposed to be so money smart? One they call the Wichita Wizard?"

"Wears those corduroy jackets, puffs that empty pipe?"

"Him, yeah. The one said his plumber paid more taxes than he did."

"Who cares what his plumber pays in taxes?"

"Not me. Sounds like his plumber's overchargin' him. So, anyway, speakin' of jerky, I was thinking . . ."

C'mon, Sonny, not jerky again.

"The Wiz throws a party every year. Why don't we go there?"

"To Wichita?"

"Yeah, and ask him what he thinks of the jerky biz. Profit margins, turkey versus beef, and like that."

Chet looked at Sonny in line. He was kidding around. Smiling Sonny was a rare sight, so Chet enjoyed it while he could.

Sonny said, "We'd need a business plan to show him, wouldn't we?"

"Hell no. We'd just say, 'Hey, dumbass, we had a business plan, we wouldn't be talking to you!'"

Sonny liked that one. "What if after puttin' it to him real nice, he still can't see reason?"

"Seein' reason, Son, that's what torture's for."

Sonny nodded, hearing that, then stepped up to the clerk and asked, "Tell me something. On a given day, ballpark number, about how much jerky do you sell?"

Chet couldn't listen to the jerky clerk-quiz again, so he went outside and chilled in their van. No pressure on them anyway. They'd laid the hammer down hard on that Latino; they had time to spare, mapping out their next moves among the rich and famous.

CHAPTER 21

At home that night, Gia fast-forwarded through a CNBC show and stopped when Trevor's face appeared on a split screen. She hit "Play" as Robert joined her on the couch.

> Interviewer: *"You and Paul Dickerson went back quite a ways, didn't you?"*

> Trevor: *"All the way back to college, Joe. We certainly weren't best friends, but I kept track of Paul over the years, even more so once we both settled in LA. I always respected him as an investor."*

"San Diego State," Robert told Gia.

> Trevor: *"A sweet guy, different, had his own way of going about things."*

> Interviewer: *"Have an example you could share?"*

> Trevor: *"Sure. When Paul worked in Japan after grad school, he noticed more and more young men staying at*

home, isolating themselves, lacking any desire to engage in one-on-one social activity. Hikikomori, the trend was called. Quite a bit later, he thought he saw a similar behavior trend back in the States. Dominoes way back when, then Facebook, Netflix, Amazon—he linked each one to a milder form of hikikomori, and because of that was an early investor in each. Or maybe he just got lucky."

Interviewer: "As Paul would've been first to tell you, I'm sure."

Trevor: "If you say so."

"What a prick," she said.
"And he's on good behavior."

Interviewer: "You've made quite a comeback since your first fund closed down. According to my underpaid research staff, that fund, called Marguerite, was named after your wife."

Trevor: "Marguerite, yes. I always thought she was lucky because, after all, she married me."

Gia said, "He's giving douchebags a bad name."
"I can't stand the guy. Don't make me laugh."

Interviewer: "I know many managers are quite superstitious. Rain Dunes—I recall that as the rather odd name for your beach house in Malibu Colony."

Trevor: "Named it as a nod to uranium, my biggest conviction buy at the time."

Interviewer: "U-rain-ium, got it. Wasn't there once a racehorse . . ."

Trevor: "I was once knee-deep in silver and named my filly Hey Gee."

Interviewer: "Ah, Ag. The elemental symbol for silver. Do the numbers Three Thirty-Three have any significance?"

Trevor: "Actually, that sequence was suggested to me by Marguerite before she passed away. Its impact? Well, the proof is in my fund's pudding, and that pudding is doing quite well."

Interviewer: "Okay, then, tell me, Trevor, what's looking good to you at the Three Thirty-Three Fund these days?"

Trevor: "Here's an idea, why not invest in my fund and find out?"

Interviewer: "A little rich for me. If I were an investor, could I find out what you're up to?"

Trevor: "You want to know what my fund's investing in? Now you're talking crazy."

Both men shared a TV laugh as the show went to commercial. Robert turned it off.

Gia said, "That fight at the party. Think Trevor had something to do with killing Paul?"

"Reyes thinks so. Lawan, too, but she's not quite as firm about it as Reyes."

"What kind of work does Lawan want you to do?"

"Something to do with her foundation or Trevor, or both. I'll know more after I dig into it."

Gia leaned back against the couch arm and slipped her bare feet under his nearest leg.

"She's beautiful, smart, alone. If she comes on to you now, it's not really about you. You know that, right?"

"Hadn't thought about it," he said, starting to get up. "Not gonna happen."

"Want to reboot that answer?"

He caught a rare edge in her voice. Sitting back down, he thought about how he'd brushed off her concern about Lawan. *Whoops.*

"I hadn't really thought about Lawan that way. Now that you mention it, if she did make a pass at me—because she was lonely, not because of me—I would never be tempted."

"Why not?"

"Because I'm smart."

For being with her. She knew that's what he meant. One of Gia's rare serious moments about *them*. In fairness, his only carnal lapse today had been remembering the deputy from arraignment court.

"Never gonna happen, baby, for every good reason in the world."

But for the first time in weeks, she went to bed without propositioning him.

It was still early. He decided to wait for an inspired approach to Gia in the bedroom. In the meantime, he educated himself online about hedge funds in general, Trevor Reid's in particular.

Hedge funds, he read, got their start in Manhattan—where else?—and differed dramatically from other investment vehicles (mutual funds, ETFs, index funds) because they had no self-imposed limits on investment style. Fund managers could invest in whatever they wanted. Everything from herds of live cows to diamonds to boxcars of corn. And they could also place bets *against* the prices of each one.

At the fringes of the hedge fund world lurked eccentrics and malcontents who generated plenty of bad press. The son who murdered his hedgie father for cutting his allowance; funds that stole elections in foreign countries; and Bernie Madoff, who sold pieces of a hedge fund that never existed.

Unlike other investment vehicles, hedge funds with fewer than five hundred investors didn't have to make their investments public. How much insight a fund allowed investors also varied from fund to fund.

He recalled Trevor's hammering the CNBC interviewer who wondered about the 333 Hedge Fund's current investments: Trevor saying, *You want to know what my fund's investing in? Now you're talking crazy.*

Another feature of hedge funds: if an investor wanted out of a fund, the fund had specified dates—*gates*, they were called—when an investor could withdraw a portion or all of his money. Whether fund values went up or down between those gates, investors had to wait.

All hedge fund managers like Trevor—whether swinging for the fences or grinding out single-digit returns—had two things in common: making money for investors and making themselves rich. They earned a 2 percent fee based on how much an investor had put in, plus a percentage of the fund's profits. That meant if a hedge fund had a kick-ass year, the manager's percentage of profits would kick ass, too.

Trevor had appeared on the investment world's radar since the Marguerite Fund started up. The best article was an early *Barron's* interview from 2007. A joint interview of Trevor and Jerry Baugh:

Trevor: When I came down in the nineties, Jerry was the only person I knew at San Diego State, and I wound up on his couch for quite a while.

Jerry: For only four short years, as I recall.

Trevor: Mooching is an art form. Between long-distance running, which I still do, and marathon sleeping,

127

which I now don't, I got interested in stocks. Started reading Value Line and hanging out in stockbrokers' offices. Back then, they still used Quotrons, but you could hang out and ask questions.

Jerry: Trevor was all about stocks, all the time. I was more interested in who was doing what around San Diego.

Trevor: Jerry and I teamed well. In the nineties, sleepy San Diego was a hotbed of tech investing, given the strong government presence there. The US Navy in particular. A ton of tech was going on, not the least of which was Qualcomm. Jerry arranged for me to meet a few of the principals early on—how'd you meet them, Jerry?

Jerry: Big fans of the football team. Because I'd played, they invited me up to their box to hang out after I was injured.

Trevor: Keep in mind that back then, meeting people was a lot more casual than it is today. And these were the people figuring out how cell phones were going to work, not using a sock puppet to sell puppy chow.

Jerry: Just to be clear, we have nothing against dogs.

Trevor: Unless the dog happens to be a stock! Don't let Jerry downplay his value added. He introduced me to great investors and to minds that were cross-pollinating with the university crowd back then.

Given that Trevor came across like a normal person in this article, Robert had no doubt this so-called interview had been written by a third party, then edited in advance.

Both Trevor and Jerry had each married not long after college, and each had stood as best man in the other's wedding. After college, Jerry pursued other interests while Trevor parlayed his tech research into several early-stage tech investments for a small base of clients out of LA.

Those early contacts became Trevor's investor nucleus for the Marguerite Fund.

During the mid-2000s, Trevor had become a staple on CNBC. Robert understood why: his confrontational style made good TV. *Maury* and *Springer* without the paternity tests and fistfights.

In one interview, Trevor and another pundit went head-to-head on Cameco, a uranium mining company.

According to Trevor, the stock was poised for a gigantic breakout based on spectacular uranium deposits in its near future. The other guy used past earnings numbers, projected them forward, and decided the stock was already trading too high.

Trevor lit into him.

"Two secret words, let's see if you've heard of them. *Cigar* is the first one. Want a hint about the second?"

The guy drew a blank. The anchors tried to laugh it off, but Trevor jumped all over the guy.

"*Lake* is the word, and Cameco's *Cigar Lake* deposits will become the richest uranium deposit in the history of mankind. No wonder your brokerage is considered second-rate—forgive me, second-rate at best."

Trevor had been right. The stock took off on the Cigar Lake news. Several years later, the underground lake had flooded; repairs would take years to complete and burn a ton of cash.

Trevor had been invited back on the show. If the producers had expected him to eat crow, they'd been keenly disappointed.

"My job as an investor is to know more than the other guy about every situation I invest in," Trevor said. "I knew there could be an engineering problem, and, if realized, the stock would get annihilated. That's why hedge funds are great—I can change my mind on a dime, and bet today against stocks I loved yesterday."

One thing was clear—Trevor Reid *always had to be right*. It must've devastated him when the Marguerite Fund shut down in 2010, almost two years after the big recession.

TV anchors had a ball reminding viewers how Trevor's hedge fund had cratered. Typical jibes: *Let's try to get our good friend Trevor Reid back on the air to talk about what happened to his highly touted fund. Highly touted by him. He's into long-distance running, isn't he? Looks like he's running from us! No callback from Trevor? Imagine that!*

Until his interview after Paul's death, Trevor had ghosted television. Even after he'd started up the 333 Hedge Fund—on his own, with Jerry as an employee only—in 2010.

Had Trevor learned a lesson about shooting his mouth off, antagonizing people? Based on Robert's dealings with him, the answer remained an unqualified *no*. The only lesson Trevor Reid had learned: *Stop being Trevor Reid on television.*

Only two more entries caught his eye: "Trevor Reid Sells Malibu Colony Home for Above Asking Price." The article sourced Golden Fritts, Broker to the Stars. That's how Golden billed himself—so did twenty other brokers.

Robert would've rewritten the headline: "Trevor Reid—Right Again!"

The final headline of interest: "Trevor Reid Throws Sprocket Retirement Dinner for Jerry Baugh."

Jerry had mentioned the dinner at Paul's party. Robert noticed its date: the same night Paul Dickerson had been killed.

And there it was. *Trevor's alibi.*

An hour later, he joined Gia, nudged her awake, and sat beside her in bed. She wore her *Bacon Is Always in Good Taste* T-shirt.

"Something I need to tell you," he said.

"Okay."

"At the courthouse, a female deputy walked around with a pistol on her hip, bossing everybody around, and it made me feel strange."

Already pulling him into bed, she said, "Strange how?"

"Aroused strange."

She straddled him, slipped off his boxers. "Don't say a word."

He closed his eyes so they wouldn't start laughing.

"How about if I make a noise?"

"That's okay unless the noise is a word. Now zip it, mister, and do what I say."

So, he did, and when he moaned later, she gave him a pass. By the next morning, he'd been granted a full pardon.

CHAPTER 22

Midmorning, Robert waited for Erik at the shoreline across from Ozone Court. Several hundred yards to his north, a circle of surfers had gathered in the ocean, holding hands. Called a paddle-out, the ceremony honored the death-by-drowning of local surfers, the death of a big-time surfer, or occasionally, a local nonsurfing tragedy.

Erik appeared by Robert's side—funny how quiet a man his size could be—and they took off north at a jog, headed for the Santa Monica Pier a mile and a half away.

Robert said, "I told Reyes you might come on board, help out."

"And he said?"

"He was plenty stoked about it."

Erik cut him a look. "Reyes? Plenty stoked about me?"

"Can you deal with *almost stoked*?"

"I can try." Erik pointed at the paddle-out. "Did I ever tell you about the Boneyard surfer?"

"Which Boneyard?" There were many Boneyards up and down the West Coast.

"North of the point break at Sunset Beach. Before you moved here. Get this: A guy's been in a serious relationship and gave up surfing for years. Then he gets depressed, and his shrink suggests he take up surfing again. So the guy finds his old board, waxes it up, and beats feet to Boneyard."

"Okay, got it."

"First time the guy paddles out—first wave—he gets caught inside. His leash gets hung up on a rock or something, and the poor guy drowns while his girlfriend's watching."

He looked over at Erik, waiting for a punch line. Erik kept his eye on the surfer circle, rising and falling in glowing gold water.

"No kidding?"

"None at all," Erik said. "Tell me what's what with Reyes' alibi."

He relayed Reyes' overall situation: his late-night drives with Paul, Lawan backing up the drives with his public defender, the Crime Stoppers tip, and Reyes' two calls to Paul's cell phone on the night of the slaying.

Erik chewed on that a moment. "A little more."

"At between two and three a.m., Reyes showed up at Paul's house. Paul was expecting him. Reyes opened the kitchen door in back and called out for Paul. When no one answered, he went around front, looked for upstairs lights, saw none, and gave up. Driving home, he called Paul twice, leaving messages asking if Paul was okay and saying that he was just there."

"Cops have both messages, right?"

"They must. Time-coded calls off Paul's phone."

"Ouch. 'Just calling to say that I'm the perp.'"

"This time, the messages meant what they said—*I was just at your house because we were supposed to hang out; where are you?* But they put Reyes there at or around the time Paul was killed."

"Damn. So even Reyes' alibi puts him at Paul's at zero hour. What'd Reyes' phone locator show?"

"He didn't give up the code. Left his phone in his car charger when he went to the kitchen door. I'm not sure if that hurts or helps him."

"They'll get a warrant, get his location from the phone company. In Palisades Riviera? I have no idea how accurate the result would be anyway."

"Good enough to put him in Paul's neighborhood, I'd bet. With Reyes' calls to Paul's phone, I'm not sure the DA needs to look inside Reyes' phone anyway."

Robert picked up their pace; Erik grumbled an admission that his Grand Slam Denny's breakfast might've been a mistake.

Robert said, "The Crime Stoppers tip ID'd Reyes' car at the bottom of Capri near Sunset, speeding away."

"Using just those two items, the DA can put Reyes *at the scene of the crime*, then *fleeing the crime scene*. Both damn near beyond a reasonable doubt."

"If I'm on that jury, I think you're right—at first. But now, the DA's gonna lose that Burglary One charge. That means the DA's got to assume that Reyes was invited inside the house, and after that, he and Paul started arguing about . . . about . . . ?"

"About *something*."

"And Reyes got so angry about *something*, he beat his friend to death in the foyer with a telescoping baton. Then Reyes sped down Capri for Sunset, headed home, and called twice to cover his ass."

Erik nodded, thinking it over.

"About Reyes' two phone calls," Robert said. "Lawan will testify that Paul and Reyes often drove around together, late nights, early mornings. So Reyes could've easily been at the house—but not inside. And he could've left the house without seeing Paul—who was already dead—and then called to ask if Paul was okay."

"So Reyes' two phone calls can be neutralized. I like it. A lot."

They high-fived on the run, then moved on to the Crime Stoppers tip.

Robert said, "You be the DA, and I'll be Anita, the public defender."

"Crime Stoppers tip, take one." Erik cleared his DA throat. "I have no doubt that Mr. Reyes was speeding away from the crime scene, a crime he'd just committed, when he was spotted near Sunset Boulevard.

Fortunately, an alert citizen called our hotline and gave the operator his tag number, leading to Mr. Reyes' arrest the next day. Have at it, Anita—by the way, love your outfit."

"Totally inappropriate, Mr. Jacobson. Now, if I may. The Crime Stoppers tip was meaningless in and of itself. Mr. Reyes could have been speeding, or could've been obeying the speed limit. Was the tipster an expert in calculating vehicle speed in the dark? We'll never know because the tip was anonymous, so the fact that Mr. Reyes was seen by a citizen, alert or otherwise, is irrelevant. He had been invited to the Dickerson home. When Mr. Dickerson didn't open the door, he left. If someone saw Mr. Reyes leaving the neighborhood in the early morning hours—*so effin' what?*"

"Gotta say, I like our guy's chances a lot better than before."

At the Santa Monica Pier's cool underbelly, Robert and Erik took a breather as bikes rolled past on the bike path. They took off the way they'd come, to the Venice Pier this time, three miles away.

Robert said, "Let's get into the killer's point of view from inside the house."

Erik asked, "You think he was still there when Reyes showed up?"

"Hang on and you'll see. On the ground floor, Paul's house has floor-to-ceiling windows. The killer could've heard Reyes driving in. *Definitely* would've seen his headlights and could've watched him park his car. Once Reyes knocked and opened the door, he'd have heard him calling out for Paul. 'Hey, Paul, it's Reyes, you here?'"

Erik nodded. "Killer's thinking, 'A guy shows up here at two a.m. calling out for Paul, so the guy at the door was expected to be here.'"

"*Expected.* Hell yeah, and at that moment—that's when Reyes turned into a good candidate to frame for murder."

"Think the killer called Reyes' tags into Crime Stoppers?"

"Why not? Maybe he'd scout up a pay phone, speak with a thick accent, and refuse to give his name, but that's the gist of it."

"Makes perfect sense that the killer was still in the house," Erik said. "Ready to talk about that baton at Gabriela's?"

"Only three possibilities with the baton," Robert said. "First, we both reject Reyes hiding it under our boy Frosty because he's innocent."

"Check."

"It's a baton, and cops carry them sometimes. What about LAPD putting it there to frame Reyes?"

"Rejected with cause."

"How so?"

"First off, batons are street-ready weapons, too. Plus, I know both the cops who found it, and they're Eagle Scouts, all right? They never had access to Paul's blood from the crime scene, didn't know the murder weapon was a baton, and on and on and on."

"I'd been thinking about that angle, too. If Reyes had a solid alibi—at that point in the investigation, they'd have no idea yea or nay—they'd be screwed for planting evidence."

"That, plus they didn't plant evidence."

Once a cop . . . "You already talked to the two cops, didn't you?"

"Of course."

That left them with one conclusion: the killer planted the murder weapon on Gabriela's front porch.

Robert said, "Maybe they followed him home. Maybe they got Reyes' contact information off Paul's phone after it rang, but somehow they had Reyes' tags and figured out where he lived. The killing occurred between two and three a.m. What time did LAPD set up shop to surveil Reyes' place?"

Erik said, "By ten thirty that night. That would give the killer from about three a.m. until ten thirty p.m. to plant the baton."

"Hours and hours. Oh—and let's not miss the obvious. Unlike LAPD, the killer already knew, *firsthand*, that Reyes had no alibi. Why? Because they, and only they, saw Reyes at Paul's."

"Beautiful, baby!" Erik shouted.

"Reyes left his crib around nine the next morning, showed up at the beach for our meeting. He was arrested on the boardwalk a little after ten a.m."

"Gabriela says it was around nine a.m. when LAPD showed up at her door to question her about Reyes."

"So LAPD watched him leave, *and then* went onto the premises?"

"Nothing wrong with that—nobody has a right to be arrested. The good guys had every right to build their case first."

Gia showed up and joined them for the Venice Pier leg of their run. They explained their thinking to her on the way down and back. Robert was relieved that she agreed with them.

That night, Robert and Gia ate take-home salmon sushi from Kifune.

Gia said, "I have one problem with what you and Erik came up with."

"A small problem, I hope. Want that last piece of sushi?"

"Go ahead, you'll need the energy later. So if the killer . . . or killers . . . were going to get away with it, why bother to frame Reyes at all?"

That morning, Robert and Erik had thrashed around in the tall grass of theory and timeline. They'd overlooked her simple question.

His first reaction: "The killer . . . or killers *wound up* getting away with murder, sure. But standing in Paul's foyer with his dead body, the killer didn't know yet that he'd pulled it off."

"Pretty good. That's all you got?"

"I don't know exactly why the killer framed Reyes, baby, but that's what happened."

"And Trevor Reid is behind it all?"

"Who better than him?"

"Not that I believe in clichés, but you know what they always say?"

"You'll tell me, right?"

"Better not. If I said, 'The surviving spouse is usually guilty,' I'd sound like a bitch."

CHAPTER 23

The next day around 11:00 a.m., Robert eased back from Paul Dickerson's desk and computer screen. Crossing to this second-story home-office window, he could look over the backyard, across Rustic Canyon to Will Rogers Park. Below him an unlikely scene unfolded.

Near the spirit house, Lawan sat with several other Thai women, prepping vegetables for lunch.

Erik liked to joke about Priya: "Thai people eat constantly. How can anyone eat that much?"

Closer to the pool, Erik had retrieved some of Jerry Baugh's smoked barbecue from the freezer, grabbed two bottles of Jerry's Cannonball BBQ Sauce, and was firing up the backyard Weber. EJ and Hans each wore plastic mullet wigs that Priya had bought them on the boardwalk, and played in the infinity pool; Priya lifeguarded in her homemade *Baywatch*-red one-piece. An unabashed fan of the show, she'd stenciled *Baywatch* across the chest.

Three hours earlier, Lawan had led Robert upstairs to Paul's office. On the desk, he'd seen framed photographs of Lawan and Paul: at the Great Wall of China, at a floating canal market in Thailand, and holding hands on the steep tram to Victoria Peak in Hong Kong.

She'd told him, "You'll be looking at his will and the papers for our foundation. There's more, too, I'm sure. Maybe some of it will help Reyes."

"Which papers are you comfortable that I see?"

"I'll leave that up to you," she'd said, sitting down at Paul's desktop computer. "First, though, this is my file."

She'd pointed to a folder on the desk. "I hired my own lawyer to work out my situation with Paul before we married."

"I don't think I need to look at your file."

"Robert, I was Paul's wife, he was quite wealthy, and we married recently. In Thailand, and all over the world, wives and husbands murder each other for money."

"Fair enough, Lawan, I appreciate it. If I find anything that helps Reyes anywhere, I'll disclose it to his lawyer no matter what."

"*Khawjai*, I understand. You are not my lawyer; you are doing Paul and me a favor."

He'd noticed the computer's password: *Lawan_samuur*.

"Lawan summer?"

"No, it's Thai." A deep breath. "It means *Lawan forever*."

"Sure it's not too soon for this?"

"No, but there will never be a good time."

Once inside Paul's documents, she'd pulled up a folder called *Capri Foundation*.

"If you have questions, text me *na*."

"Okay, *na*," he said. Okay, okay.

She'd left and he'd taken a seat at Paul's desk.

So far, so good—Paul Dickerson had given Lawan his password. Looks like he'd trusted her with everything on this computer.

Robert had started out with the foundation folder. Right away he'd seen why Lawan had been intimidated: long letters from the IRS cited tax laws and regulations; letters from Hampton Bergen's firm discussed the IRS letter in great billable detail; a one-hundred-page legal document set up the foundation, including broad language about its social, educational, religious, and charitable purposes.

After reading one—just one—of the regulations, he'd been tempted to text Lawan: Let's leave this crap for the lawyers.

He'd skipped the tax-law legalese, looking for a human angle, and came across letters between Paul and Hampton. More conversational, they began to explain why Hampton had shown such poor taste—if there was such a thing in LA—by calling Lawan repeatedly so soon after Paul's death.

Hampton was concerned that the foundation's five-person board of trustees hadn't yet been appointed beyond himself, Paul, and Lawan. The foundation needed a majority of three trustees to take action on anything. Now Paul was dead, and no third trustee had been selected.

Robert felt sure that Hampton wanted to assist Lawan in making their third-trustee pick. He could hear him saying, "How about using my law partner? He's knowledgeable about foundations, and he's right down the hall from me."

Moving on, several of Hampton's earlier letters had urged Paul to sign a proposed prenuptial agreement with Lawan. Paul had resisted; Hampton had persisted.

Later, with the prenup signed, Hampton had written Paul: *That decision will be best for everyone concerned.*

Lawan's personal file told a different story. She'd hired her own lawyer, who made it clear to Paul that she would not marry him without a prenup.

Even so, little doubt remained about Hampton's overall opinion of Lawan:

It was such a pleasure meeting your wife, Paul. I can only imagine how alien all of this arcane tax law must seem to her, not to mention American culture in general. (California in particular!) But I'm sure, that with our tutelage and patience, she will get the hang of it. It will take time, but we have plenty of that, don't we?

We? Our tutelage? Lawyer jokes would never go out of style.

Another one of Hampton's letters summarized Paul's estate plan. After paying Lawan under the prenup and paying off any other obligations, everything else in Paul's estate poured over into the foundation. Even though Lawan had been named Paul's sole executor, she had little to no discretion over what happened to Paul's money. Once he died, most decisions would be made by the foundation.

What Robert read confirmed that Lawan had relatively little to gain by Paul's death. She'd receive $1 million under the prenup—compared to an enormous settlement if Paul had died without a prenup. It meshed with what Reyes had told him: Lawan had turned down a Mercedes AMG 65, whatever that was, for a Lexus SUV.

Saint Lawan, he could hear Gia saying.

He was weighing which information to read next when a 333 Hedge Fund subfolder caught his eye. From there, it didn't take long for him to get to the heart of the beef between Paul and Trevor.

Paul had been trying to withdraw all the money he'd invested in the 333 Hedge Fund, funds Paul would've targeted for the foundation. But the hedge fund—i.e., Trevor—had been putting him off.

On his first attempt to withdraw funds, Paul had emailed the 333 Hedge Fund:

Trevor, I need to pull out at the next gate. We can discuss this anytime. Please advise.

Under the governing agreements, Paul's request didn't appear problematic. On gate dates—quarterly here—the agreements allowed investors to withdraw if the investor jumped through all the hoops.

Five days after Paul's notice to withdraw, Trevor had addressed Paul's request with a copy to Jerry Baugh: Paul, let me get this over to Jerry.

That was all Trevor had to say. So far. Now it was Jerry's turn.

Jerry: Your notice, once the fund received it, actually missed the gate date. Wait till next quarter. In the meantime, Trevor tells me there's a lot to like about the fund's performance.

Paul: I still have no idea how we're invested. Over the years, that has troubled me more and more.

Jerry: Have you looked at the financials with your year-end statement? The fund is audited every year.

Paul: No help at all. The financials were "prepared in accordance with generally accepted financial principles"? Nothing concrete there in terms of what the fund is doing. Thanks for trying, Jerry. Love your BBQ sauce!

Jerry and Paul went back and forth a few times, their tone always cordial; nothing came of it.

Next quarter, Paul learned that Jerry planned to retire; the problem landed on Trevor's desk again.

Trevor had found a new reason—a new excuse?—for denying his request. This go-round, Paul had mailed a certified letter to the address in his original contract, but several years back, the fund had notified him of a change of address and had used that minor defect in Paul's letter to deny his request.

The fund had been right under California law, which was brutally strict in rejecting notices that didn't go to an agreed-upon address—even if the notice, like Paul's, had been received and understood.

But for Trevor to play hypertechnical hardball with a friend?

No surprise, the emails between Trevor and Paul took a nasty turn.

Trevor: After all this time investing for you, this is the thanks I get?

Paul: My thanks was the fees I paid you to invest my money. This isn't about performance, Trevor. I've decided to use my money differently. Please deal with it.

Trevor: Again, this is the thanks I get?

Paul: I thanked you by entrusting you with $50 M. As it became $80 M, I talked you up every chance I had. Now, I want my money back. So simple, even you can grasp it.

Trevor: I have all of my own money in the fund. Our interests are 100 percent aligned.

Paul: One hundred percent aligned in what? What's your largest position? Still metals, like it was starting out? Something you have a track record doing? Or is it corn or pork bellies, or have you shorted both? Do I still have commodities exposure that diversifies my risk? I simply do not know.

Trevor: Ask Buddha, you money-grubber!

Money-grubber—the same insult from Paul's party.

More emails followed as these two went at it:

Paul: Nothing in eastern religion or philosophy dictates that I roll over for a gonif like you.

Trevor: Ommmm, Paul. Cool down, baby!

A few days later, the two men started up again.

Paul: Whatever happened to your original pitch? 'Don't worry about what the contract says, Paul, we're friends. I don't want to keep you in 333 if you don't want to be there, Paul. All that gates lingo is for new money, not people like you, Paul.' Was that hyperbole or was it lying?

Trevor: Before you get too self-righteous, check Section 62.5 (i) of your signed limited partnership agreement. Then take a magic carpet ride down to 71 (d) to see where you stand.

The first section Trevor cited, very common, stated that the written document was *the entire agreement.* Nothing mattered outside the four walls of the document: pitches, negotiations, conversations like *Don't worry about getting your money out, Paul, we're pals.*

Even though Robert knew of ways around this section, that path was a molasses-covered road with potholes. A lawsuit.

The second section read as follows: *Managing Partner reserves the unqualified right to deny any withdrawals whatsoever, for any reason, in Managing Partner's sole and absolute discretion, as long as Managing Partner has determined that to do so is in the best interests of the fund.*

Trevor's last email: By the way, Paul. The Managing Partner? That's me!

Trevor Reid, a confirmed jackass capable of generating ill will at will.

Then this incoming email just three days before the party:

Trevor: I want to buy a 10K ticket to your backyard, and two more tix for the front yard. If you will have me?

Paul: Beach informal dress code; Jerry smoking ribs in backyard!

Of course, Trevor had worn a suit. But there it was: Trevor's unlikely path to Paul's backyard. Robert had believed that Trevor showing up had been part of Paul's plan to put Robert with Trevor. Not so. Trevor had reached out for an invite.

But the pair's mutual animus explained what Reyes had witnessed between them firsthand: Paul's agitation whenever Trevor had phoned him.

From outside the house, the faint cry of screaming lads drew him again to the window. In the backyard, Erik fired a hose stream at a drone hovering over the pool.

Looked like all the fun was in the backyard, so he headed downstairs.

In the foyer, he stopped where Lawan had sat quietly with her mate until the LAPD had arrived. Where Lawan had seen Paul's ghost hanging out. Where Paul had been beaten to death so violently that the LAPD believed the attack seemed *personal.*

He understood even more fully Gia's concerns about Lawan. Her beauty was undeniable, and her mind was sharp, like her sense of humor. But Robert didn't have feelings for Lawan. He had a feeling *about* Lawan: admiration.

He passed through the living room, the same route Paul's killer would've used to track Reyes as he'd pulled into the driveway and parked.

Easy to see, easy to follow, easy to frame for murder.

What he'd seen upstairs explained the bad blood between Trevor and Paul, and would go a long way toward explaining Trevor's beatdown in Paul's backyard. Was it enough to give Trevor a motive to murder Paul? Or, given Trevor's apparent alibi, to have Paul killed? Was what he'd just learned enough to create reasonable doubt for Reyes' case?

He didn't know yet; time would tell.

Outside the house, mullet-wigged Erik Junior and Hans ran toward the kitchen door, each grabbing one of Robert's hands, leading him to the pool. On the way, they had a few things to share with Uncle Robert:

Did you see the drone? Did you see Dad shoot at it? It flew away, and Dad chased it next door. Did you see us swimming from inside? What were you doing in there? Do you like this pool better than the ocean? Do you like barbecue? I wish Ducky Joe could swim in Lawan's pool, don't you?

"Yes," Robert finally answered.

He'd covered everything but the pool-versus-ocean debate; they didn't seem to notice.

Priya and Lawan were waiting by the pool. Seeing how Priya's wet one-piece clung to her body, he guessed at the motive behind Erik's drone assault. Mostly, Robert knew, Erik was just putting on a show for the lads.

Erik barreled back through an ivy-covered side gate to the house of Gretchen, the spandex-clad neighbor.

"Pervy kid, flying that thing over here just now, buzzing Priya and Lawan, buzzing my kids."

"Did Bryan ever apologize?" Robert asked Lawan.

"Yes, Gretchen brought him by. Then they used the pool. Then they left."

Erik winked at Robert and went into full-on B-movie mode: "Drone Boy next door? I get him under the hot lights downtown, he'll fold like hot laundry."

Robert took Lawan aside and explained Paul's repeated attempts to pull money out of the 333 Hedge Fund, as well as Trevor's over-the-top insults to Paul. "Paul insisted on knowing what Trevor had invested in. Trevor refused to tell him."

"And we still don't know?" she asked.

"Not yet. I plan to find out."

"That's why they fought?"

"If you can call it a fight. I think Trevor came up here to make nice with Paul, but things went sour once they started to talk about it."

"Do you believe Trevor was involved in Paul's death?"

"Driving up here today, I did. And I still do, even more so. Mind if I quiz you about the foundation?"

"Not at all."

"How many trustees are needed for the foundation to make a decision?"

"Let's see, uh, three."

"And how would you pick that third trustee?"

"Honestly, I hadn't thought about it."

"Would you want Hampton to help you decide?"

"Maybe, but I don't believe he likes me very much."

Hampton's reaction to Lawan likely wasn't a matter of like or dislike. Paul had been his client for years, and here came Paul back to the States with a younger wife, changing his will, making Lawan his executor, and refusing to sign a prenup. Hampton had been right to react with caution, but he'd been more wrong than right, given what Robert now knew.

Lawan said, "While you were working, I arranged a meeting with Hampton's firm."

"Sounds like a great first step."

"I think so, too. The meeting is at two thirty. You have time for lunch before you go."

"Whoa. What about you?"

"I'll stay here with my guests. That way, you can talk freely to Mr. Bergen about me or anything else."

"Lawan, I'm not your lawyer, the estate's lawyer, or the foundation's lawyer."

"I want your opinion of him. Can you go as my friend?"

Looking at her, he found it impossible to refuse.

"Okay, but you'll need to reschedule. I can't show up in Century City looking like this."

Old jeans, a T-shirt, and his Reefs. The Reefs high end, but still.

"Sure you can. They call you the Beach Lawyer, right?"

CHAPTER 24

An hour after eating leftover party barbecue, Robert drove from Palisades Riviera to one of many Century City high-rises. Belkin and Daniels occupied the twelfth and fourteenth floors. In the firm's soaring two-story lobby, he cooled his heels, waiting for Hampton.

He called Philip Fanelli and left a message. Then he made a call to Jerry Baugh, and also texted him. Maybe he could persuade him to open up about his former employer and his fund's investments.

His eye was drawn to a freestanding partition covered with historical photographs chronicling the rise of Century City. He walked over for a closer look. Named after the *Century* in 20th Century Fox, his 150-plus acres had belonged to silent-movie cowboy star Tom Mix, who'd sold it to Fox back in the twenties.

According to the written captions, in the fifties, Fox studio head Spyros Skouras decided under financial duress to sell what had become the studio's back lot. The asking price: $50 million. In this case, the villain had been *Cleopatra*, the over-budget hoped-to-be blockbuster starring the world's hottest couple: Elizabeth Taylor and Richard Burton. That deal had been often dubbed the worst real estate deal of all time. Century City was now worth billions of dollars.

The worst of all time? Hyperbole, no doubt. Then again, it was Hollywood. "A business where," he'd once heard, "there is no penalty for lying."

Philip called him back. Robert heard salsa music playing in the background.

"Robert Worth, to what do I owe this extreme honor?"

"Hi, Philip. Real quick—"

"No, please, I insist, take your time. I'm at dance class with my beloved fiancée. As I told her, 'This call from Robert has all the earmarks of a true emergency.' A lengthy emergency call."

He pictured Fanelli getting dressed down by a dance instructor and liked what he saw.

"Then tell me, Mr. Astaire, have you heard any talk around town that the Three Thirty-Three Hedge Fund might be a Ponzi scheme?"

"Too bad being a jackass doesn't qualify his fund as a Ponzi. Their CPAs are . . . ?"

"Michaels and Fingelson." A large accounting firm, two buildings away from this one.

"Do you know if Reid ever guaranteed his investors a high rate of return?"

"Not that I've seen or heard about. But he gave one client a hard time getting his money out."

"That can happen for a variety of reasons. Is Reid in a never-ending process of raising new money?"

"Just the opposite. I believe the fund's been closed to new money for a while."

"Bernie Madoff told new money his fund was closed, too. That was part of Madoff's reverse-psychology pitch."

"Right, then Madoff would break down, let you in because you're *such a close friend.*"

"Exactly. On balance, I'd say Three Thirty-Three's on the up-and-up."

"Because . . . ?"

"Madoff promised new money and did deliver a consistent high rate of return. Year in, year out, no one can pull that off. To hide it all, he hired a no-count accounting firm for his so-called audited financials. Michaels and Fingelson? Reid's fund would be *relatively* small potatoes to them. Certainly not make-or-break. With their client base, they'd have no need for such low-level shenanigans. Plus, I know Fingelson—not that that matters, but it does—and he's a straight shooter."

Robert heard: "Robert Worth?" and turned around.

Speak of the devil: Hampton Bergen with his fifty-year-old hand outstretched.

To Philip: "My best to Ginger Rogers. Gotta go, thanks."

He stood, shook Hampton's hand, and they headed down a long, curving hall. Occasionally, it widened for assistants' pods—he'd seen a hospital organized the same way.

Hampton said, "Lawan told me to expect you. I'm surprised she's not with you."

"I hear you."

That was all he offered. Let him wonder. So far, he knew quite a bit about Hampton and about Lawan's legal situation; Hampton knew nothing important about him.

Hampton said, "I envy you."

"How so?"

"Beach Lawyer? Who wouldn't envy that?"

Robert nodded, making him work for it. They stopped at an open door with the name *Jasper Wolff* beside it. Jasper was behind his desk, squeezing a grip ball, eyes glued to his screen.

Hampton said, "Jazz, this guy's the Beach Lawyer."

"Oh, man, that's you?"

"Looks that way," Robert said.

Before Jasper could get going, he caught an incoming call and closed his door. A few doors down the hall, they entered Hampton's office. A brilliant view west caught the still fogged-in coast.

"That little girl, you saved her life, got her all that money back. Four million, right?"

Robert nodded.

"In some circles, that's real money," Hampton said.

Here we go. This guy worked two thousand-plus billable-hour years and earned at least $1 million. Half that after taxes, so let the dick-swinging commence.

Robert said, "Here's how I look at it, Hampton. I took down a half-million-dollar fee for ten days' work. My overhead? A new pair of jeans, which I save for big meetings. And my law partners' share of it? Exactly zero. So in *my circle*, and *in most circles*, I'm getting by."

"Okay, I get it."

"What's there to get?"

"You're a cool maverick, and I'm a grind. That about right?"

"I don't know you, and you don't know me, but you took the meeting, so I don't need any shit from you for showing up."

"Then what do you want, Worth?"

"Lawan asked me to come as a friend, so here I am. Right now, I'm glad I came so I could see if her negative opinion of you was fair."

Hampton's eyes narrowed. "I'm interviewing you to keep her as a client?"

"Hadn't thought of it until you mentioned it. But big picture, Hampton, check this out. Paul might've been worth a billion dollars, but that doesn't make him a big client. Big clients get into trouble, have ongoing compliance issues that burn tons of time. Paul's in limited partnerships, LLCs. Those documents he can read and understand, and the terms are almost always nonnegotiable. For that, he doesn't need much of your help. His estate? That poured over into the foundation, so there won't be any probate to guide Lawan through, meaning that fees for that piece of business are minimal, too. My best guess? In a typical year, you were lucky to bill Paul thirty thousand dollars."

He'd seen the firm's bills in Paul's files and saw no need for Hampton to know that.

Hampton said, "I liked Paul a great deal, respected him. We got along very, very well."

A nonanswer answer, but not quite as hostile.

Robert asked, "If Paul had been doing something important, legally, think you'd have known about it?"

"Like what?"

"Making a big financial move."

"Anything worth knowing, I'd have known about it."

Flat-out wrong. Hampton had no inkling that Paul had tried to self-solve his withdrawal from 333.

"Here's what I'm seeing, Hampton. I think you figure you can cut Lawan loose or keep her and the foundation as clients. For thirty thousand a year, you're good to go, either way, long as she doesn't generate any bad press for the firm."

Hampton's color rose. Good. Hearing that, any decent guy should be pissed off.

"Feel free to get out of my office."

"I made a lot of mistakes practicing law. You're making one right now."

Hampton stood up. "Get going, Worth, I have real work to do."

Robert kept his seat. "You're not making a mistake talking down to *me*, okay? Know what I think about your business relationship with Paul?"

Hampton shrugged. "No idea, and no desire to know."

"But Lawan cares, and I think Paul believed you were a damn good lawyer. Otherwise, he'd have fired you. It's not up to me to second-guess him on that, so I won't. But when it comes to having his wife as a client . . ." He stopped, switched gears. "What would your wife do if she

151

came through your front door and found you brutally beaten, bled out, and dead in your house?"

"Call the police, pick up the kids . . ."

"Lawan sat with Paul's body until the police came. Blood and all, she didn't want him to be alone. After that, being Buddhist, she chanted with monks at Wat Thai to send his spirit on its way. In fact, she still has one more night of chanting. And you know that prenup you wanted for Paul so badly?"

"The one he has in place?"

Hampton looked proud that he'd insisted on the prenup; Robert would've felt the same way.

"*That* prenup, yeah. She talked him into doing it. Not you."

"Think what you want, I—"

"Some clients are worth getting to know. I had a client like that once, and knowing her helped me more than it helped her. Paul and Lawan's party, you were a no-show."

He looked down. "I had other commitments."

"Should've come anyway, brought your wife. It was a blast. And your firm's *Godfather* flower arrangement with an unsigned card, and you calling her at all hours? What's Lawan supposed to think about you?"

A knock on Hampton's doorjamb. Robert turned. It was Jasper from down the hall.

"'Scuse me, Hampton."

"Yeah, Jazz, what brings you into my world?"

"I read about that situation you got into with your client, the young girl," Jasper told Robert. "How'd you get wind of who was behind it all?"

"You were damn lucky from what I read," Hampton interjected.

As the three of them went back and forth on Delfina's case, Robert's eye was drawn to Hampton's credenza photographs. Every lawyer has them: the photographs that say, "This is who I really am." The shot that brought Robert to his feet—Hampton at the Wild Card Gym in Hollywood, posing with Julio Cesar Chavez Sr., Robert's favorite boxer.

Robert asked, "You and *El León de Culiacán?*" One of Chavez's many nicknames.

"Yep. Chavez Senior looked like he was ready to step inside the ropes, go fifteen with whoever wanted some."

"Good to go, bet he was."

He cautioned himself—don't start liking this guy.

And as he sat here talking shop with them, he wondered why Paul hadn't used Hampton to deal with Trevor.

Robert interrupted. "This firm must handle a ton of wealthy individuals like Paul."

Jasper said, "Quite a few. If you have any throwaway clients down on the sand . . . ?"

"If they're not strung out too bad, I'll throw 'em your way." He asked Hampton, "You guys don't handle the Three Thirty-Three Hedge Fund, do you?"

Hampton shrugged, didn't offer more.

Robert said, "Let me put it another way. I know directly from Lawan that Paul invested in the Three Thirty-Three Hedge Fund. You know it, too. Now. Do you also represent the Three Thirty-Three Hedge Fund?"

Satisfied, Hampton said, "No, we don't."

Jasper added, "But if you're looking for commodities exposure, Reid's definitely wired."

Robert tried to get them talking. "Didn't Reid make his first big killing in uranium?"

Hampton said, "According to Reid, he bought it going up, shorted it coming down. Quite a few of our wealthy clients have placed funds with Reid over the years."

And there sat an answer to one of Robert's questions: Lawyers love to talk shop with each other. Even more, they love being heroes to their clients. If Paul had come to this firm to handle his situation, somehow, some way, word of Paul's intention to withdraw from the fund would leak out to the firm's other wealthy clients.

Words like this, spoken over lunch: *Can't tell you who it is, but I hear one of the big boys in 333's pulling out. All the way out. But you didn't hear it from me.*

Off that leakage, other investors would start pulling out of Trevor's fund. The more withdrawal demands, the more difficulty Paul would have getting his own money out.

A few more minutes of bullshitting law, and Hampton walked Robert back down the hall. He surprised Robert by asking, "This Thai temple you mentioned. It's over the hill?"

"North Hollywood. Wat Thai."

"And the chanting for Paul starts when?"

"Around seven. And I know what you're thinking."

"Do you?"

"You want to wear a tank top and go barefoot."

Hampton smiled. "How'd you know?"

"Just a hunch. Don't do it, Hampton. Sign out front of the temple says tank tops are disrespectful to Buddha."

CHAPTER 25

As the elevator let Robert out in the main lobby of the office building, two men in slacks and blazers had their backs to the door. Both craned their necks to check out something in the lobby.

"I'm leaving my wife tonight," one of them said.

"Don't bother, she's mine," said the other one. "What was she in?" "*Mission: Impossible? Die Hard?*"

Now Robert saw their dilemma: Lawan sat in the building lobby in jeans, a leather jacket, and dark shades. Mysterious. She definitely had the look of a movie star. As he walked toward her, he noticed how still she was. No cell phone, her hands in her lap, and he wondered about the last time he'd seen someone in LA just sitting.

She stood and made *wei* as he approached; he did his clumsy best in return.

Lawan said, "I know how much I've already imposed on you—can we sit for a minute?"

They sat down.

"By the way, I'm glad I met Hampton Bergen," he said.

"Why is that?"

"He's a top-notch lawyer, and Paul knew that. I'm gonna go out on a limb and say he's a solid man."

"Solid? Not sure what that means in this context."

"Highly competent. Decent."

He left out his hunch that Hampton would appear at her temple tonight—time would tell.

Lawan said, "It must seem odd how I reached out to you."

"A little, but every time you *reach out*, I learn more that helps Reyes."

"Good. The reason . . ."

Tears streamed from beneath her sunglasses; she left them on.

"Whether or not you came to Wat Thai, I would've found you anyway. Paul really liked you, and I remembered that."

"I barely talked to him . . ."

"Paul watches . . . Paul watched people. He watched you after the movie screening and said you were an unusual person."

He nodded his thanks. "Coming from him . . ."

"The fact you knew Reyes in the first place, had him as a client, was unusual, but coming over to watch what he shot?"

"Hate to say this, I was there trying to get out of doing something for Reyes."

"But you showed up, and that meant something to Paul. Oh, he liked your car, too. That it was old and wouldn't start, and how you reacted when that happened."

"Asking another car to hook up to my jumper cables?"

"The way you behaved about it, I think. I wasn't there, so I don't know, but it brings me joy that he was right about you."

A thud against the plate-glass window. He looked outside at the large open-lawn area. Hans—or was it EJ?—had bounced a wet tennis ball against the window. Now EJ—or was it Hans?—caught it. Both of them took off when Erik showed up. With cupped hands, Erik put his face against the glass, peered inside. The third child. Seeing Robert, Erik gave him a thumbs-up.

Lawan said, "Priya and I tried to take the boys home, but they wanted to ride with Uncle Robert. So did Erik. He's a . . . a *solid man*, too, isn't he?"

"Very solid, yes."

She looked outside at Erik. Seated on a concrete planter, a boy on each knee. All of them squinting at the window. She almost smiled. Hard not to, but he could see sorrow still tearing at her behind those dark lenses.

She said, "Priya and I are going back to the house. Then she's driving me to Wat Thai tonight. I'm afraid you're stuck with those three boys outside."

They headed for the door.

"Whenever I think sadness might take over, I remember the source of my grief is love."

"Does that help?"

"It makes the pain worthwhile."

Priya waved to them from behind the wheel of the Yukon. As Lawan got into the Beast with her, he understood why she chose to be around this happy family. Surely, she was closer to other people in LA. But just as surely, being around the Jacobsons helped Lawan keep her grief at bay.

CHAPTER 26

After a detour for takeout from In-N-Out Burger—*fries only, don't tell Mommy!*—all four males reached a momentous decision: *Let's go to the beach!*

Low tide had created a knee-deep lad wonderland, allowing Robert and Erik to sit on the sand while the boys scoured the flat-sand bottom for sand dollars. They tried to convince the boys that sand dollars could be spent; the lads, sadly, refused to buy in.

Robert brought Erik up to speed on Paul's files and his Century City meeting.

Erik said, "So, Three Thirty-Three isn't a Ponzi scheme. But what you're saying is because Paul wanted his money out, he and Trevor fought in public. Three days later, Paul was dead. Looks like Trevor's alibied up by Jerry's retirement party at Sprocket."

"We'll need to check out Sprocket to make sure."

Erik nodded. "If his alibi holds up, Trevor must've hired someone to kill Paul."

"Same way I see it. What'd you learn about the house alarm?"

"According to the maid, the system's nothing fancy. Paul didn't arm it at night unless Lawan was home."

"And Paul had been expecting Reyes."

"Did you know the maid wrote down the code by the keypad in the pantry?"

"No, I didn't." Robert considered the implications. "If someone had used the code to get in, that might point to an inside job, but they didn't need to use it. I keep wondering what the killer knew when he showed up at the door. Maybe he knew Lawan was gone, maybe not. Maybe he was prepared to kill them both if she got in the way."

"Or he planned to kill her, too, all along."

Robert said, "Let's say the killer shows up at the kitchen door and doesn't know the code. What's he plan to do? Break a window, break in, kill Paul and Lawan and anyone else who gets in his way?"

"Possible. But the alarm goes off with the broken window. This killer left no prints in the house or on the baton—that from a cop friend—and was smart enough to frame Reyes. You really think he'd ever consider busting in like that?"

"No way, that's hood-rat style, smash-and-grab."

They gave the alarm question sixty seconds of silent thought.

"Anything?" Robert asked.

"In-and-Out fries are awesome."

"Damn tasty," Robert said. "I see the alarm situation like this: it's two a.m. The killer had the code when he showed up. But seeing the unlocked kitchen door, the killer didn't need to use it."

"Best version yet, far and away."

They walked down the waterline.

Robert asked, "That drone today. Think it had a camera?"

"Definitely. Perv boy hovered his bird in front my wife. She'd been swimming, wind was blowing—don't make me spell it out."

The Asian Sensation in a wet one-piece. Hard to blame young Bryan, especially when Erik was having so much fun treating the kid like *America's Most Wanted*.

"I didn't notice anything," Robert lied. "Why don't we rough up Bryan, get him to fork over any party-night footage?"

"He pulled a backyard flyover that night?"

"Yep."

Erik shucked his shirt, looked at the ocean, and yelled, "That punk Bryan's goin' down!"

He took off running and dove into the water. Surfacing, he howled. The Pacific must've been colder than he thought. About to take the plunge himself, Robert's iPhone barked on the sand. He sprinted back to it, but he was late.

Jerry Baugh had returned his call; Robert dialed Jerry's number.

"Jerry, Robert Worth."

"Helluva quick callback. Sure you're a lawyer?"

"That's what they tell me. Any way we could get together tomorrow?"

"Want to play golf at Riviera?"

Riviera Country Club. Upscale, exclusive. On occasion, Howard Hughes had landed his Sikorsky airplane on its eighth fairway to impress Katharine Hepburn.

"It's been a while since I played. I—"

"Problem is, I'm not a member of Riviera. How does Balboa sound?"

A public course in the San Fernando Valley.

"What time?"

CHAPTER 27

The next morning, on his way to Balboa Golf Course, Robert passed the site of the 2017 Skirball Fire. One of seven major LA fires that year. Flames had jumped the 405 from the east, shutting it down, then climbed the western hillside, threatening the Getty Museum. It had scorched, but not destroyed, the vineyard at Rupert Murdoch's Bel-Air estate, once the home of Victor Fleming, the director of *The Wizard of Oz* and *Gone With the Wind*—and the stable of Clark Gable's favorite horse.

He crossed Mulholland Drive, and the San Fernando Valley spread out ahead, trying to shrug off a stubborn yellow cloud of smog.

His phone rang with a callback from Reyes' PD, Anita Yates. After minimal formalities, she got right down to it.

"When we talked earlier, you asked me to confirm that LAPD never questioned Trevor Reid. That is correct. They did have his name from several party guests who voluntarily called in about his altercation with Paul Dickerson. But once they focused on Mr. Reyes, LAPD dropped Reid altogether."

"With the evidence LAPD had, hard to blame 'em."

"Let's do anyway. That altercation will add to reasonable doubt."

She'd selected her investigator yesterday. A senior guy who'd worked several other murder cases. None on the Westside, she told him. Reyes had been right. Her investigator would be getting his Westside feet wet on Reyes' case.

Anita said, "I plan to subpoena Ms. Dickerson for the prelim and use her to attack the burglary predicate for special-circumstances felony murder. She's agreed to a second interview beforehand."

"One suggestion, Anita. Make sure you explain to her exactly what's going on. Some guy shows up at her door with a subpoena, I'm not sure what she'd think."

Much as he admired Lawan, she was always just a plane ticket away from Thailand anytime she chose to leave.

Anita said, "I'll hand her the subpoena at our interview and explain everything. Offer her a ride downtown the day of."

She went on. "I just saw Mr. Reyes. When I mentioned you were headed to Sprocket later today, he wanted me to remind you that their Cobb salad is—his words, not mine—*off the chain*."

Sounded to him like Anita was getting the hang of Raymundo Reyes.

❦

Twenty minutes later, Robert spotted Jerry seated on the patio outside the Balboa Golf Course grill. Robert grabbed a chair, and they ordered coffees.

Jerry said, "We'll grab a quick bite here, head over to the practice range before—"

"I can't play. Been years, and I'd only slow you down."

"C'mon, we all hit our share of worm-burners."

"I'm not here for golf, Jerry. I wanted to talk to you about Paul's death."

Jerry looked down. Shook his head before looking back at Robert. "Can you believe it?"

"No, I can't. Don't know how much you read about the case, but the man they arrested is a friend of mine."

"A friend of Paul's, too. I met him at Paul's house that week. Raymond something?"

"Raymundo Reyes. I believe they arrested the wrong man."

"Who in God's name would do something like that to Paul?"

He decided on the fly—if Jerry passed along their conversation to Trevor, so be it.

"All I know is, my friend didn't do it."

"Didn't the police find the murder weapon?"

"Yes, they did. But several people witnessed Trevor's behavior toward Paul. You were at the party—you know what I mean."

"Sure, I saw it, too. But Trevor, a killer? Not in this lifetime."

"If you know anyone else who was sideways with Paul, I'd love to hear about it."

"Look, Trevor's a known jackass. A notorious jackass, but that night, he was throwing me a retirement party downtown."

"Oh, really?" Robert lied.

"I mean, Trevor has dustups with people all the time."

"But Paul Dickerson didn't have any dustup that I'm aware of. Not ever."

Jerry stood. One of those college athletes who'd kept in shape with thick veins in his ripped forearms.

"All this shit going on, and none of it will bring back Paul. You're trying to help Mr. Reyes, I understand, but I'm under a tight nondisclosure agreement with the Three Thirty-Three Hedge Fund. I'm not about to violate it. You want to know about me and Trevor, that's a different story, okay, and it started in LA."

Jerry tossed a few bills on the table, and they headed toward the range.

"College, right?"

"Before college. Way before."

CHAPTER 28

"What's it that our boy Reid does inside that building all day?" Sonny asked Chet.

"Makes money, right?"

Parked in a tow-away zone on Canon Drive in Beverly Hills, Chet and Sonny eyed RJ and Trevor Reid. Both stood on the sidewalk across the street after exiting a glass office building.

"Instead of watching this pair," Sonny said, "we could be laid up down in Long Beach with those two thick gals live over on Sycamore."

"What's the point laying up after gettin' ourselves free and clear on Paul D? We're freelancers now, entrepreneurs, building for the future."

"You say so."

Chet had warned Sonny before about having enough money to quit full-time crime. Sonny, though, was lazy inside his mind, so Chet had at him again.

"It's not like you and me can start turnin' tricks if things get bad, a'ight? You rather pin down some new money while we can or go broke down the road, start sacking groceries on your sixty-fifth birthday?"

"We got some already set aside."

"Life tables give us thirty, thirty-five more years aboveground, and what's plenty now's not plenty then. Gotta think about inflation, a rainy-day fund for lawyers, bribes, shit like that."

Sonny nodded the way he always did after Chet had worn him down. "What I asked before about Reid—he walks off the elevator first thing and grabs an expresso. What's he do afterward?"

"Checks the stock market, looks at what's what over in China, and like that."

"Then what?"

Chet said, "Goes for one of his runs, manicure, trims his eyebrows, then a massage, or he orders in a blow job."

Chet realized his mistake too late. Ordered-in sex always reminded Sonny of his ex-wife, Gwen. The one Sonny despised. An after-lunch special—that's how Gwen had met the guy she'd dumped Sonny for. A millionaire who'd made a bundle in the jerky biz, Gwen had told Sonny. That accounted for Sonny always asking jerky questions at checkouts like he'd done the other day at 7-Eleven.

Normally, Chet's B.J. comment would've taken Sonny on a spew-filled detour to Gwen and the Jerky King. For now, though, Sonny stayed focused on Trevor Reid, across the street.

Sonny said, "All day long, not much on Reid's plate."

"Nighttime, too. If he feels like it, maybe he'll take a midnight cruise like he did the other night."

"What kinda boat name's *Marguerite*? If I had a yacht like him, I'd name it *Mister Fornicator* or *The Ramrod*, something cool like that."

How about *The Gwendolyn*? Chet was thinking.

Much as Sonny still acted torn up over Gwen, he had never once tracked her down. Seemed to Chet like Sonny'd rather stew in Gwen-hate than see her. That was fine with Chet. When he'd finally found Gwen, they'd got it on like he'd hoped starting out, and he could see why Sonny missed her. Girl was wild with daddy issues and a ginger on top of that.

Gwen had told him in bed afterward, "The only mistake I made worse than marrying Sonny was marrying Brophy."

Brophy. The Jerky King's real name.

"Wasn't really a jerky king," Gwen had told Chet. "He made jerky for all the ones already sellin' jerky at the checkout counter, so he's always worried about beef or turkey prices goin' up, and his customers being pissed off at him about his prices."

Beside him, Sonny said, "Here we go. Here comes Oldsmobile Jack."

What Sonny sometimes called Dav Concha, a guy who floated in and out of the big picture.

Across Canon Drive, Dav pulled up in his Delta 88, his drop-top down. RJ got into the Olds, riding shotgun. He put on a white captain's hat; Dav saluted him.

Chet said, "That pair in the Olds, couple of winners, aren't they?"

"I'll say."

And there went Trevor up to RJ's door. He slapped that captain's hat off RJ's head and screamed at him. Then Trevor leaned into the back seat and picked up a black-and-white puppy. Trevor whispered in the puppy's ear, set it back in the Olds.

Sonny cranked the engine and asked, "What's it with Reid and that pup?"

"Beats me."

And it did.

CHAPTER 29

Jerry striped a range ball drive more than three hundred yards from the practice tee and teed up his next range-ball victim. Robert sat on a bench, talking to him.

Jerry said, "I've known Trevor forever, but I met his father first. Trevor's dad was British, his mom, Welsh or Scottish, and they were some kind of half-assed royalty over in England. What's below earl?"

"Baron, maybe?"

"Anyway, Trevor's dad had a seat in the House of Lords and never went. Had a business, too, but he was selling family heirlooms to keep it afloat. He got a divorce, wife remarried, and Big Trevor moved to the States—Hollywood Hills—with Trevor in tow."

"How old was Trevor?"

"Five, six. Big Trevor started working as a front man at one of the studios. Called himself a producer, got his name on a couple of B pictures, but he had a righteous golf game, was a great raconteur, dated starlets, and a big drinker. With that British accent, royalty on top of that, Hollywood ate it up. So did I."

"How'd you meet him?"

"Riviera Country Club. My family was not quite middle class. My dad worked his way up from caddy to head greenskeeper. Big Trevor was a member, and because of my dad, I got to hang out there summers, hit balls, and play for free. Big Trevor saw I could hit it a mile, so he'd make long-drive bets, use me as a shill. 'You tosser,' he'd tell the mark, 'I bet you can't outdrive that thirteen-year-old over there.' After a while, we got to be close. Hell, he even gave me a piece of the betting action."

"Where was his son in all this?"

"I'd see him around the club, but he was just a . . . He rubbed most people the wrong way."

"Big Trevor's cool, so what happened?"

Jerry slammed another drive. Robert almost felt sorry for the ball. Jerry shook his head.

"Don't know. You want to think Trevor's the way he is because he was a short kid. But back then, he was my size. Big, but a jerk."

A big jerk. That worked.

"When Senior had money, Junior was a jerk, and when Senior lost it, Junior didn't miss a beat. Still a jerk."

"How'd his father lose his money?"

"Booze, picked up too many dinner checks. Then some dirty people used him to pick up a package in Mexico, bring it back over the border, no questions asked. But he's the one who got popped. Even in prison, the other inmates loved him."

"You went to see him?"

"If I didn't say it already, I loved that man. Larger than life. He never said so, but I'm pretty sure he paid for my private-school tuition in LA."

"That doesn't happen every day."

"Sure as hell doesn't, and he asked me to keep an eye on Trevor." In a decent British accent: "'Bit of a wanker, my son, but you'll see to it, won't you, Jer?' I didn't know what *wanker* meant back then, but I promised I would."

Looked like Jerry, at Big Trevor's request, had spent years toiling as Trevor's link to humanity.

A woman in her forties set down a bucket of balls at the next station. Wearing a short golf skirt, a visor, and shades, she had tanned legs that went on for quite a while. He pictured a beauty pageant in her past.

"And in college?" he asked Jerry. "You had to be a big deal playing Division One ball. How'd Trevor handle that?"

"Didn't care. Somehow, he found enough money to come to school—I think his dad hid some from bankruptcy court—and came to rest on my couch."

"Early nineties?"

Jerry nodded. "Ever read our *Barron's* interview?"

"I did. In college, Trevor got interested in stocks, and through you, he met those Qualcomm guys. Then he networked his contacts into his first hedge fund."

"Right, that was the Marguerite Fund. He named it after his wife."

"If you two ladies plan to keep yakking, take it somewhere else."

That from the pageant contestant. Jerry glared at her.

"Listen up, miss, we'll take it wherever we want to take it, and you'll either like it or lump it."

"*Lump it?* What the hell does that mean?"

Robert wondered if good-guy Jerry had disappeared and evil Jerry had just shown up.

Jerry said to her, "I don't know what *lump it* means, miss. I'm not all that bright."

"If I'd known that, I never would've married you."

They were smiling at each other. Jerry introduced his ex-wife, Kay Baugh, then pulled his phone from his pocket.

Robert heard him answer and say, "I'm not about to drive over there. I'll talk you guys through it." Then to Robert and Kay: "Gotta take this one, sorry."

Kay said, "Thought you'd retired, Jerry?"

Jerry didn't answer and moved away for privacy.

Kay shook her head. "Retired and the office still calls. 'Jerry, the security cards don't work; Jerry, can you come to the vault to help us with *blah blah blah*.'"

What Robert had just seen—Jerry taking a call from the 333 Hedge Fund—told him that Jerry had a postretirement deal with them. Most likely, they'd put him on as a consultant for a few years, and he'd work with them to ensure a smooth transition.

Kay asked, "You play?"

"In high school. Not in years."

"You thought I meant golf?" She winked, handed him her driver. "Let's see what you got."

He gripped her club, surprised how the feel came back to his hands, and addressed Jerry's teed-up ball. Trying to forget everything he'd ever learned except *Keep your head down*, he took an easy swing. Good contact, good result.

"Nice swing, but I'm a little disappointed in your weak follow-through."

Weak follow-through? He looked at her. *Really?*

She gave him a genuine smile. "I need some new come-on material. You playing with us today, or what?"

"Not today, a little too much already on my plate."

Using Jerry's driver, he laced a few good ones, and a few not-so-good, and remembered how much fun golfing had been. Years ago, he'd played with his father and Uncle Robert at Silver Creek Valley Country Club. Uncle Robert—an overbearing, belittling dickhead—cheated at golf and gave himself four-foot putts.

When her ex-husband came back, Kay said, "Jerry, he was flirting with me. Do something!"

"You have my full blessing, Robert. I'll instruct the bank to stop all alimony payments ASAP."

Still a fun couple. Bet they'd been great to vacation with and probably still were.

Jerry said to Robert, "We were talking about Trevor Reid."

Kay said, "Jerry always leaves out the part where he gave Trevor his start. The part where Trevor's nothing if he hadn't known Jerry Baugh. Trevor leaves out that part, too."

"Not always," Jerry said.

"That *Barron's* article was written years ago, Jerry. That was the last time Trevor gave you credit for anything."

"C'mon, Kay, let's not go into all that."

As if Jerry hadn't spoken, Kay said, "Before the Marguerite Fund, Trevor had been in and out of straight brokerage jobs after college. Bad at taking orders and even worse at giving them."

"Hard to imagine," Robert said.

"Back in the early 2000s, Jerry was invited on a salmon fishing trip to Russia, and they let him bring a friend. Jerry ran out of normal people to ask, so he invited Trevor. Once they reached Russia, Trevor showed his ass to the other guys soon enough, so Jerry had to babysit him."

She set another ball on her tee. Her hand was shaking, and her color rose. Angry, he believed.

"One night, Jerry and Trevor went into the only bar in the only town. Jerry'd had a few pops and started meeting people. One of them—what was his name?"

"General Sergei Popov. An engineer by trade. It was after the fall of the Soviet Union, and he had a whole corps of engineers sitting around with nothing to do."

Kay said, "Popov started shooting his mouth off to Jerry—*not to Trevor, to Jerry*—about Moscow's state arm that invested in all sorts of stuff."

Jerry said, "Gokhran. It controls the country's sales of precious metals, including the platinum-group metals. PGMs, they're called."

"Never heard of Gokhran," Robert said.

Kay said, "Same here, but Trevor knew what it was. *Because of Jerry*, by the time the guys who owned the fish camp left the country, they'd paid Popov a ton of money for his men to clear out the river channel, and Jerry made a friend for life. Popov started telling Jerry—*not Trevor, Jerry*—about *Gock-whatever's* plans."

Jerry said, "Whether the agency planned to keep supply off the market or release supply into the market. Their decisions made a big impact on the price of these metals, up and down. And Trevor played it. Off our success with those trades, Trevor raised a ton of money from investors, and we started the Marguerite Fund. That's when Trevor made his first killing going long rhodium."

Kay asked Jerry, "And how was it again, dear, that Trevor knew about rhodium?"

"Because of me, dearest."

Kay said to Robert, "Popov liked Jerry and wanted nothing to do with Trevor. Sound familiar?"

Jerry said, "Popov's calls went on for three, four years. One day he stopped calling, disappeared from the face of the earth."

"Got caught?" Robert asked.

"Must've. He vanished."

Robert wondered if that metal, rhodium, was in the 333 Hedge Fund's portfolio today. After all, Paul's hostility toward Trevor had started in large part because of Trevor's secret investments.

Robert gave it a shot. "How much rhodium is Three Thirty-Three invested in today?"

Jerry said, "Here are the precious metals. You got gold, symbol *Au*. Silver, *Ag*. Platinum, *Pl*. Palladium, *Pd*. Rhodium, *Rh*. Iridium, *Ir*. Osmium, *Os*, and ruthenium, *Ru*. Bet you anything that *if* Three Thirty-Three is invested in *any* PGMs, it's one of those."

"That was all of 'em, right?"

Jerry gave him a wink.

Kay said, "Using General Popov always sounded kind of sleazy to me."

Jerry said, "Might've been sleazy, but Trevor's lawyers cleared it. If it had been illegal, do you think I'd be telling your brand-new fiancé, Robert, about it?"

Kay wasn't ready to move on from Trevor.

"Trevor has an argument? Trevor's always right. Trevor marries Marguerite? Right again. Trevor sells his run-down Malibu Colony beach house for top dollar? Yeah, right."

Kay fielded a call from her vibrating cell phone, which had been lying on top of her golf bag. She said to Jerry, "It's Daze on the line, the second love of your life."

"Daisy, my daughter," Jerry told Robert. His face lit up saying her name. "That label on my sauce? Daisy designed it." Into Kay's phone: "Daisy, how are you—and before you ask, the answer's *no*."

Robert asked Kay, "You don't believe Trevor got top dollar for his Malibu house?"

"Great location on Latigo Shore Drive, that's about it. Last time I was there, years ago, it needed a million dollars of work, easy. And that's just the cosmetics he'd let slide. The ocean's been pounding his pilings to death for at least twenty years."

"What happened with Marguerite?"

"What do you mean?"

"The hedge fund that went under. What happened?"

"Oh, the fund, not the woman. When the whole country nearly melted down, all the investors pulled their money out. Jerry and I were still married—we lost all of our profits in Marguerite since day one and more, and we never did invest in Three Thirty-Three. But to Trevor's credit—and I hate to say it—his Marguerite Fund investors did better than most."

Jerry stepped back into the conversation.

"Kay, what say let's not relive ancient history?"

"Why not? I didn't sign an NDA on the Marguerite Fund; neither did you."

"Bad memory lane, Kay." Jerry's voice took on a slight edge, asking Robert, "How will your questions help get your friend out of jail?"

"I'm not sure. But the more I know about Trevor, I think, the better for Mr. Reyes."

Jerry said, "Try this on, Robert. Trevor's an asshole. Trevor's not a murderer. Kay? Sound right to you?"

"If you put *tremendous* in front of *asshole*, yes."

Kay's light touch had slipped away, along with Jerry's. Undercurrents Robert couldn't identify swirled between these two. Then again, a divorced couple with a child was lucky to have undercurrents instead of a flood of hostility.

"Sorry for busting in, Jerry, Kay. Thanks for everything."

"Before you get going," Jerry said, "got something for you in my trunk . . ."

CHAPTER 30

A case of Cannonball BBQ Sauce jiggled on the front seat beside Robert. Each bottle's label featured a cannonball trailing flames, flying past a saguaro cactus. For the two spicier versions, Jerry had told him, either *Spicy* or *Spiciest* appeared inside the cannonball.

Label's cool, Robert was thinking. Designed by their daughter—*Daisy* to her dad, *Daze* to her mom. Proud parents who couldn't hold their marriage together.

Robert made it from the 405 onto 10 East, on time to meet Erik at Sprocket downtown. Their plan: locate a Sprocket valet, a Latino whom Reyes and his mother knew from East LA, and learn what they could about Trevor's alibi.

He cobbled together a new picture of Trevor based on what he'd learned. According to Jerry and Kay, Trevor's investors had abruptly pulled out of the Marguerite Fund both during and after the Great Recession of '08 and '09. Sounded like nobody had gotten burned too badly. Lost their profits, not their shirts, when it closed down in 2010. No doubt Trevor believed if all his investors had stayed in his fund, they'd have all prospered. No doubt, too, Trevor didn't want to get burned like that again by his own investors, or have CNBC anchors feed him a load of crap about it on national TV.

Trevor's business needs explained his fund's strict rules—narrow gates—for investors to exit the 333 Hedge Fund. Not to mention his broad discretion as fund manager to override a request like Paul's—*for the good of the fund.*

From a business point of view, his motives were understandable. Trevor was a self-described *conviction investor.* If his fund had precious-metals positions he didn't want to sell, Paul's request for a massive exit could have caused him real problems. Even so, none of that justified his behavior toward Paul, a friend who'd invested in the 333 Hedge Fund and believed in Trevor at its outset.

As traffic ground to a stop on the I-10 East at Crenshaw Boulevard, Robert thought about Reyes going to trial. Had he gathered enough for a jury to believe that, just maybe, Trevor had either killed Paul or had him killed? Enough reasonable doubt for a jury to set Reyes free?

He'd made progress, but that was still all he really knew. What a jury needed to hear for reasonable doubt remained a mystery, even to lifelong criminal lawyers.

Recalling Kay's diatribe about Trevor's Malibu Colony home pulling in top dollar, Robert asked Siri to Google *LA County Registrar, Recorder of Deeds.*

Then he said, "Trevor Reid, Latigo Shore Drive, Malibu."

As he waited, a text from Erik popped up on his phone: Sprocket. Dining room. Join me for lunch.

Lunch at Sprocket with Erik? They weren't members. Who said anything about lunch?

CHAPTER 31

Once Robert made it downtown, he exited on Sixth Street, took a left on Olive Street, and parked underground. By the time he'd grabbed a coat and tie from his back seat and escalatored up from this exhaust-rich underground world, downtown LA's notorious air smelled downright pastoral.

Three city blocks later, he stepped through Sprocket's Art Deco entrance into its cool black-marble foyer.

"Sir, how may I help you?"

A man emerged from dim light. *Andre,* his gold name tag read, his lowered voice calibrated to preserve the aura.

Robert lowered his voice, too. "I'm meeting someone in the dining room."

"Mr. Worth for Mr. Jacobson?"

"That's me."

"Right this way, sir."

A long, quiet hall led them to the dining room. Chandeliers dangled, waiters bustled, and a handful of members dined. None so large or as content as Erik Jacobson, who was finishing his meal. He shot Andre an oversize thumbs-up. Andre's eyebrows arched, but he gamely returned the gesture.

By the time Robert had taken a seat, he was, if not ready to join, glad to be here.

"Lunch?" he asked Erik, as a waiter started clearing Erik's plates.

"Which sounds more impressive? Join me for lunch at Sprocket, or join me for lunch at the Poke Shack?"

"A toss-up."

"Know that guy who sucker punched Reyes in the joint?"

"The East LA cousin, yeah."

"Well, Gabriela squashed that beef. She went over to that family's crib, got after the cousin with her cane. Nobody lifted a hand to stop her."

"And word gets back to Tower One—lay off Raymundo Reyes?"

"Like greased lightning."

"Why are we eating—?"

The waiter interrupted for his order; Robert went with the Cobb salad in Reyes' honor.

"Hear it's off the chain," he told Erik, who ordered two pieces of chocolate cake. "All we planned to do here was talk to Peanut Lopez." Reyes' valet contact.

"Peanut's shift doesn't start till two, so I had time to kill."

"We're not members. How are we getting lunch?"

"I went up to the office, talked to membership, and told 'em I was born Sprocket."

"A mover *and* a shaker. What about member recommendations?"

"Needed two. The mayor's a member, so I gave up the mayor's name, and I gave up Trevor Reid."

"You told 'em your occupation was what? Loose cannon?"

"Told 'em I was an inventor in the digitally compressed aerodynamics field. True, right?"

A handheld fart machine. Erik had invented it; Robert had helped him license it. Guess that qualified.

"And I was currently employed as lead investigator for the public defender's office."

Technically true? No, an outright lie.

"Erik, I don't want you to—"

"What's gonna happen? They gonna contact the mayor?"

"No, they'll call Trevor Reid, and he'll wonder who's down here asking questions using his name."

"Erik Jacobson's who's asking. Hope he finds out I'm LAPD retired, snooping around his life, and shake up that shithead."

Erik's style grated against Robert's sense of order and logic. Even so, he ceded the point. He didn't like being wrong, but it had happened before.

"How was your salmon?"

"Portion could've used man-sizing, but tasty."

Robert's Cobb salad took center stage in front of him.

Erik said, "Menu said smoked bacon from Tennessee sets their Cobb apart."

After a few bites, Robert agreed. "Erik, do not come near my bacon."

"Never crossed my mind. Asking around about Jerry's retirement gig, a banquet waiter said Jerry's ex-wife and daughter cut out early." Kay and Daisy. "Jerry and Trevor hung on till around two a.m."

"Two a.m.? Shit. Trevor's Sprocket alibi's gonna hold up." He checked the time. Fifteen minutes till Peanut Lopez checked in. "Enough time for dessert?"

"What's your smoked Tennessee bacon taste like?"

Erik was already reaching for a piece.

❧

By the time Robert made it around to the valet station, back of the building, Erik had headed back upstairs to membership to evaluate his Sprocket dining experience.

Peanut Lopez had just clocked in when Robert approached him.

"Ticket, sir?" Peanut asked.

About fifty, Peanut wore a yellow-and-black Sprocket jacket and cap.

"I didn't park here. Raymundo Reyes says you pretty much run the place."

Hearing Reyes' name, Peanut's easygoing expression deserted his face.

"Known that kid forever, and he's no killer. Gabriela wanted me to talk to either Erik or Robert."

"I'm Robert." They shook hands. "I don't believe Reyes killed anybody, either. Had a few questions about the night of Jerry Baugh's banquet. Remember it?"

"Yeah, I was on till the bitter end. Now, *Señor* Jerry's a top-notch dude. Talks *to* you, not down to you. And when he came down late-late, he's all messed up. Handed out some hefty tips, said it would be a while."

"Until what?"

"Till he saw us again. He'd just given up his membership."

Made sense. Jerry, retiring, had cut down on nonessentials.

"How messed up was he?"

"Kinda teary-eyed. More messed up like that than drunk. Anyway, we got him an Uber, and off he went home. Wish all of 'em were like *Señor* Jerry."

"Hold on—what about Trevor Reid?"

Peanut didn't bother hiding his distaste. "Boy didn't get beat up enough when he was coming up."

"But he and Jerry left together, right?"

"No, they were hours apart."

"Wait—you're sure about that?"

"I'm sure-sure. An old member picked him up."

"How old?"

"Not *old* old. I mean a onetime Sprocket member. Didn't pay his dues, and they booted him a few years back. Hold on." He called out to another valet, "Hey, dude, what's drop-top Olds' name?"

Robert asked, "Dav Concha?"

"Right, *Dav the Shell*. The Shell's gone downhill since I saw him last. Looked pretty rough."

Concha. Spanish for *shell.* The last time he had seen Dav, he'd been with RJ, puking in the gutter after Paul's party. Dav Concha on a downhill slide.

"How'd you know about Concha's membership status?"

"*Mi tía* works in accounting, knows everything goes on here. Anything else you need to know, *Roberto?*"

"What time did *Señor* Reid leave with Dav the Shell?"

⁕

Robert and Erik ramped onto the 405 freeway in the Bronco, headed west from downtown.

"Night of the party," Robert said. "Your waiters were wrong about when Trevor left Sprocket."

"Waiters? Wrong? Impossible."

"Night of Paul's murder, about midnight or a little after, Dav Concha picked up Trevor, and they left together."

Robert explained what little he knew about Dav, RJ's drinking buddy.

Erik asked, "Any way they were headed over to Paul's?"

"Why not? From Sprocket to the Palisades Riviera, late night? How long's the drive?"

"Half hour, tops. You can prove what you're saying, that could be good for Reyes."

"Unless they have an alibi for where they went next. Good chance they do, but any kind of reasonable doubt Anita can throw against the wall helps Reyes."

Erik nodded. "But Peanut knows Gabriela and Reyes. Longtime family friend, biased as hell. They'd tear him a new one on cross."

"What's cross?" Robert joked about his total lack of trial experience. "Try this out for me. I want you to bundle up Paul, Trevor, Jerry, RJ, and Dav."

"Okay, they're bundled."

"Now, start off with San Diego State, back in the nineties. Then add the Three Thirty-Three Hedge Fund and Three Thirty-Three Film. To those, add Paul's party, front yard and back, then finish up with Sprocket. What do you have?"

Erik gave the question quite a bit of thought before saying, "One way or another, those five men are interconnected."

"Not each of them at every spot—I mean, RJ didn't go to San Diego State with them. Still, they're all connected."

"This Dav Concha's still pretty murky to me."

"Same here. Maybe we can fix that."

He called Lane Lang from 333 Film and left his callback number.

Robert said, "Got another puzzle piece for you. You're Trevor Reid, and you're getting a monster cash call to exit from Paul. So you tell Paul, 'Not happening, Paul.' But you're smart and down the road, who knows what will actually happen, so you sell your Malibu Colony beach house to increase cash on hand. According to Golden Fritts, Trevor sold it in record time for a record price."

"And?"

"What if Reid told Golden to lie about the sales price?"

"We could check the records."

"Already did. Trevor got four million less than Golden said in real estate news."

Erik nodded. "Trevor's feeling pressure from Paul wanting out of the fund?"

"Let's put it this way. After living there a decade or so, Trevor took a four-million-dollar hit off what the public was told."

"Another reason for Trevor to hate Paul. Is the timing right?"

"Perfect timing. The Malibu house was listed a week after Paul's second exit try."

"Like it, another nail in the Trevor coffin."

A few minutes later, Lane called back. After exchanging hellos with Robert, he put her on speaker and told her Erik was listening in.

She didn't mind. "Getting me into Paul's party, you're my hero. Met a guy there—not a showbiz guy."

"A guy-guy?"

"An if-this-works-out-we-move-to-Scottsdale guy."

She told him 333 Film would shut its doors next week. Robert got down to why he'd called her.

"Mind telling me what you know about Dav Concha?"

"Anything specific?"

"Paul Dickerson, Trevor Reid, Jerry Baugh, Roland Jakes, and Dav Concha. Seems like Dav's an odd duck in that mix."

Lane said, "Not really. Dav went to San Diego State the same time as Trevor and Paul. Way back when, Dav's family owned tons of Hollywood soundstages where they shot bunches of TV shows. *The Rockford Files*, remember that one?"

Robert said, "In reruns, sure."

Lane said, "Rockford had that guy Huggy Bear, right?"

Erik said, "No, that was *Starsky and Hutch*. Angel was Rockford's guy."

"Oh, right," Lane said. "But anyhow, the way I heard it from RJ—and from Dav's bragging, too—Dav used to be a hotshot stockbroker with Beverly Hills offices. Because of his family money—they hadn't blown all of it yet—Dav had tons of contacts and clients in LA after grad school. Confident as all get-out without much backing it up, but then he screwed things up for himself. Remember those pictures in our office stairwell— some fishing trip Dav bragged to me he'd set up for them in Russia?"

"Sure, back when Dav was riding high," Robert said, his mind working.

"Trevor wanted me to take down the shots with Dav in 'em. Hard to blame him. I mean, by then, Dav had moved from Beverly Hills to Culver City, way before it was up-and-coming."

"Where's Dav's office now?"

"Unless he's gotten the boot, somewhere off Santa Monica Boulevard and Purdue. He joked about his view of the West LA Police Department."

Erik said, "When LAPD pulls Dav over for DUI, that'll be convenient."

They heard Lane laughing. Robert saw the logic of Trevor eighty-sixing those shots of Dav. Dav had become a known screwup. Trevor didn't want to be associated with him publicly.

Robert asked, "Did Dav have any trouble with his brokerage license?"

"According to RJ, hell yes. Dav screwed up a time or two, got fined by those broker honchos."

"Right," he said. She meant FINRA, the agency that oversaw broker licensing. He wished her luck with Mr. Scottsdale; she asked him to give Reyes her best and signed off.

Erik said, "So Dav knows all of 'em. Goes way back with Paul, Trevor, and Jerry."

"More than that. Trevor started his first fund with Jerry's help, even partnered with Jerry on it. Even before that—sounds like *Dav helped Trevor, too*. Dav introduced his wealthy Hollywood clients to Trevor and invited Jerry on the Russia fishing trip."

He explained to Erik about General Popov, the Russian agency, Gokhran, and how Trevor got his start from the general's inside scoop.

"Turns out that over time, Trevor was the only one of these guys with real talent, so he moved onward and upward."

He turned off the freeway onto Overland Avenue. "How're you fixed for time tomorrow?"

"Good to go. Want me to bring a duckling with street smarts?"

"No, but keep him warming up in the bullpen. Know what I'm thinking?"

"Pretty sure. You're wondering why, if Trevor took down Dav's pictures—why'd he leave Sprocket with Dav the night of Paul's murder?"

"That's the question."

He began laying out a rough idea of what he had in mind for tomorrow. Erik kicked in his own two cents along the way.

Erik said, "If we're gonna go that route, I need to make a run down to Redondo."

Redondo Beach. The third beach community south of Venice.

"Why Redondo?"

"That's where I can buy the best off-the-rack spy gear."

CHAPTER 32

That night in his living room, Robert was on the Department of Corrections website, mulling over an appointment with Reyes. He heard Gia coming up the wooden stairs. A tiny part of him wished he didn't look forward to hearing that sound as much as he did.

Tonight's gym class. Whore Dance Class, she called it.

"Filled with grown women who must've missed out on being sluts. They're so nasty in class, grinding, hair tossing, humping like strippers. So outrageous, I can't quit class."

Gia took a seat beside him. He kissed her without looking. She squeezed his earlobe, moved in close to look at his screen.

"Going down to see him again?"

"Want to, but the drive down and back burns up most of the day."

"If I were in his shoes, I'd want you on the outside, trying to help me."

He showed her the jail's list of strictly prohibited items.

Reading the list, she said, "No weapons or ammunition? Really?"

"And no marijuana, cocaine, heroin, or speed. No carabiners, ropes, or climbing-assisted implements? Is that some kind of joke?"

"You can't go anyway." She read another rule: "Shorts shall cover customarily covered areas of the anatomy, including the buttocks and crotch area."

"Hey, if I can't wear short-shorts to jail, what's the point?"

She noticed a small jewelry box with a ribbon on the table. The magic size.

"Go ahead, for you." She reached for it. "Can you get out of work tomorrow?" he added.

"Probably. Boss man likes me okay."

"Likes you? He wants to have your baby." A gentle nudge. "Open it."

She opened the box. Inside, a cheesy-looking gold-bar necklace on a bed of cotton. Crude lettering etched into each square side: *24 K GOLD.* A piece of jewelry she would never buy. He'd picked it up after he and Erik hatched their spying plan.

"It spoke to me," he said.

"What'd it say?"

"It said, 'My sweetest love, you're my one and only sidepiece!'"

She gave him a long, grateful hug. "You lunatic! What's wrong with you?"

"Tomorrow, you'll need to wear it. Your undercover assignment involves that necklace, a push-up bra, and the seduction of a male subject."

"You?"

"Nope." Off her hint of disappointment, he added, "Only a partial seduction."

Robert FaceTimed Erik for a status report on the eavesdropping equipment they planned to use tomorrow. On his office desktop, Ducky Joe swam circles in a small plastic tub.

"Does your new receiver work?"

"Priya's downstairs. Let's see." Erik called out through the open door, "Boys, tell Mommy to start talking!"

Erik put on headphones and showed Robert a receiver the size of a large paper clip. At the same time, he pointed a plastic parabolic mike at his open office door.

Priya's actual voice called out from downstairs: "Can you hear me, Erik? Is this good? Is it working? Hello? Hello? Boys, can Daddy hear me?"

Erik took off his headphones and said, "Receiver and mike work."

Priya and the boys came to his office door: "Daddy? Did you eat all the boys' doughnuts?"

"Mighta had one," Erik said as his picture disappeared.

CHAPTER 33

An hour ago, Chet had followed the Delta 88 into an underground parking garage. Right away, Chet knew he'd messed up. One of those CO_2 warnings was posted right in front of their parked car.

Sonny said, "Coulda parked on the street, not have to breathe death air."

"It's meant to warn the weak and the pregnant. You either one?"

"I'm not weak. I have allergies and conditions."

Sonny read the sign out loud: "Breathing the air in this parking garage can expose you to chemicals including carbon monoxide and gasoline or diesel engine exhaust, which are known to the State of California to cause cancer and birth defects or other reproductive harm. Do not stay in this area longer than necessary."

Sonny said, "We don't need to be down here at all. So anytime at all down here is *longer than necessary*, and look at the small print. They updated the warning last year because this air's bad for you."

Chet said, "I looked it up, all right?" And he had. This wasn't his first parking-garage-sign rodeo. "All they did was add *Warning* in bold, plus a black exclamation point."

Even so, they sweated their asses off in the garage, their windows rolled up, with the air conditioner off.

Chet's thoughts keep turning to Mexico, to Hobie's Ensenada beach house. He'd finally found it on Airbnb, where Hobie rented it out—it had a four-star rating and got raves about the local guy, Pablo, who came running whenever you raised an eyebrow.

Beside him, Sonny said, "Car like that, at his age, Dav's trying too hard. 'Lookit me, I'm still young.'"

"Him and that RJ punk hanging out? That much I get. But Dav *and Reid* up in Beverly Hills? Normal circumstances, they're not palling around."

"Can't see it, either."

"How come, then, we keep seeing Dav with Trevor on that yacht?"

They'd followed Dav around plenty enough to get the gist of his life: Sausage McMuffin breakfast, at work by quarter to ten. Lunch at a cheap sushi buffet. Boogies bar at two thirty. Dinner in a booth, then passed out at his low-end apartment about ten, ten thirty. Rinse and repeat.

Every so often, though, Dav got squared away and met Reid on that yacht. Whenever he did, other people came along. Nice-looking couples, usually, driving clean cars, wearing deck shoes. Most times, too, RJ would be waiting on board, wearing that captain's hat.

It all made Chet wonder two things: What're they up to? And which one—Dav or RJ—gave them the quickest route to another easy score?

Chet asked, "Remember that day Dav had his passport picture shot?"

"Yep. This CO_2's killing me."

"Maybe you're pregnant," Chet told him. "A new passport picture means passport renewal."

"Probably."

"We can keep trying to figure out what's what, or just grab one of them, squeeze him, and get going."

"Which one?"

"Not sure yet."

But squeezing Dav was Chet's odds-on favorite.

CHAPTER 34

Sitting in Dav's office lobby, Erik wasn't surprised when Dav rushed out for their meeting. Earlier that morning, with Robert listening in, Erik had set the meeting for twelve thirty. Erik's story to Dav—he'd sold his business and had a few million bucks he needed to invest, pronto.

Then Erik had called Dav's office twice to say he was tied up in traffic. When Dav had tried to postpone, Erik dug in—meet today, or forget about it. Dav had relented.

In Dav's lobby, it was pushing 3 p.m. by the time Dav rounded the corner.

"Erik Jacobson," Dav said. "Dav Concha."

When they shook hands, Erik felt Dav's palm sweat. "Sorry I'm late."

"LA traffic. Worse every day," Dav said.

"Not really." Contradicting himself on purpose. "Men's room?"

Dav pointed the way they'd just come. "Other end of the hall."

By the time Erik took a seat in Dav's office, Dav's internal cocktail alarm must've been jangling hard inside his skull, his usual two thirty with RJ a receding oasis.

Dav's office was pretty much what he and Robert had guessed: A no-view view, a low-end Staples desk, and a credenza with pictures from Dav's glory days on it. A limp-dick broker with two FINRA violations, hanging on by his gnawed-down nails.

"Again," Dav asked, "where'd you say we met?"

"Oh, c'mon," Erik said. He'd never offered that information.

"I don't recall you telling me."

"Front yard of the Dickerson estate? You handed me your card, said to drop by anytime."

That exchange had never happened.

"Oh, yeah, yeah. What the hell's wrong with me?"

You're a drunk, for starters.

Dav asked, "Said you had right around four million to put to work?"

"Hell yeah. Money never sleeps!"

The title of the *Wall Street* sequel nobody liked that much.

"Not if I can help it," Dav said, eyeing his watch.

The afternoon sun started heating up the office. Dav's forehead prickled with sweat. He talked about Erik filling out an investor questionnaire, Erik's investing experience, risk tolerance, and the value of a diversified portfolio.

"Diversity, Erik, is the cornerstone of good investing. Diversity of sectors, diversity between large and small cap stocks, and geographic diversity."

Erik gave Dav a lost-in-thought look.

"What's on your mind?" Dav asked. "These are important decisions. Nothing's off-limits."

"Okay, then. I thought diversity was all about me getting along with people different from me."

Erik watched his ignorant answer land hard on Dav's plate.

"Excuse me, Dav." He texted Robert: Five more minutes. "Sorry about that."

Dav said, "Now. Again. About diversity."

While Dav repeated his spiel, Erik stood and crossed to Dav's credenza, looked at his photographs.

The earliest: Dav in tennis gear with Andre Agassi and Steffi Graf. Dav in black tie with James Garner—Jim Rockford in the flesh. Another one on the set of *The Andy Griffith Show*—Don Knotts held up Deputy Barney Fife's single bullet.

Then a faded shot: Dav with Jerry Baugh and Trevor Reid in fishing vests, a rapids-filled river behind them.

Erik bet this was the Russia fishing trip Lane Lang had mentioned. A copy of one of the photos Trevor had wanted removed from the film office's wall.

Another shot: Dav and Trevor on the flying bridge of a pleasure yacht; then Dav with a graying Asian couple on that same bridge. Recent photographs, judging by Dav's bloat, his puffy eyes, and receding hairline. The name *Marguerite* appeared behind them on a ring buoy.

"Now that shot you're looking at?" Dav said.

Erik picked up the shot of Dav and Trevor. "This one . . . ?"

"That's me on my good friend's luxury yacht."

"Looks like a ton of fun."

"It is, Erik, but investing's not all fun and games."

As Erik took his seat, Dav eased over to the credenza, parked his ass on one corner of it. He focused Erik on the photo of himself and the Asian couple.

"See these two, the ones with the big smiles?"

"They just win the lottery, or what?"

"You want to joke around, okay by me. He's a dentist in Hacienda Heights, she's a full-time mom—they don't have a worry in the world. Not anymore."

"Bet she was his hygienist before they married."

"How do you figure?"

"Her hands." At this point, he could've said, "Her nostrils," and Dav would've agreed.

"Know the best thing about my job?"

"The hours?"

Another derailing comment. By now, cocktail hour must seem to Dav like an impossible dream. To Dav's credit, he didn't flinch. He knelt down and locked eyes with Erik.

"What kind of appetite you have for risk, Erik?"

That was as far as Dav got; his desk phone buzzed.

"I told my secretary no interruptions. Excuse me." Dav picked up his phone, winked at Erik. He listened, then: "What? Say what? *He said what?*"

Dav hung up, looking alarmed. "Bear with me, this'll only take a minute or two."

Erik checked his phone—five minutes had passed since he'd texted Robert. Right on time.

🙙🙛

Twelve minutes later, Robert watched from behind the Bronco's wheel as Dav's Delta 88 flew out of the underground garage, almost getting air off the inclined ramp.

Another minute and Erik banged out of the front door of the office building, rolled past the dead landscaping, and slid inside the Bronco.

Robert told him, "Dude. You lit Dav up!"

"Man on fire. Gia ready over at Boogies?"

"On her barstool, prim and proper. Has a good view of Dav and RJ's booth."

Erik asked, "Could you hear her okay from outside?"

"Good enough. I don't know what happens when Boogies fills up."

"We park close enough, our parabolic mike'll pick up her voice, no problem."

After looking into the law, Robert had decided that Erik shouldn't wear a mike at Dav's office. California's criminal code required two-party consent to listen in on or record conversations if the communication was *confidential.* Getting Dav's consent? That notion was DOA.

Gia's situation differed legally. Even with no one's consent, Gia would be at a bar, a public place where privacy expectations of the recorded party—hopefully, RJ and Dav—dropped to almost nil. So Gia ran an almost nonexistent legal risk by wearing a transmitter.

Driving over to Boogies, Erik filled in Robert about meeting Dav.

"Now, over to my left, Dav has his old shots with Don Knotts from *The Andy Griffith Show* and James Garner from *The Rockford Files* era."

"Yeah, back when his family had soundstage money, but showing you he's still a big deal."

"And little people like me better listen up. So I'm sitting there, playing up being a moron—*don't say it*—and he comes out from behind his desk, closing in on Mr. Gullible."

"Not his first time doing it?"

"Well rehearsed, and he said it like he meant it. Oh. Saw Dav's picture in Russia, fishing for salmon with Trevor and Jerry."

"Getting to know our guys better, aren't we?"

"Gettin' there. Now, Dav, he showed off a Hacienda Heights couple with him on a yacht. Thanks to Dav, they're now living the good life, and then he goes down on his knees, locks eyes with me. Socks didn't match, he's so close I coulda slapped him, and just when he's asking me about my appetite for risk, you dropped your bomb out in the lobby."

"I was too early. What was he trying to sell you?"

"I never found out. How'd it go at the front desk?"

"Said I knew *Detective* Jacobson was with Mr. Concha, but I needed *Detective* Jacobson ASAP. Before Dav came out to see what was going on, I told her I'd better feed my meter and split."

He didn't want to run the risk that Dav, even vomiting, recognized him from his tussle with RJ outside Paul's party. "What happened when Dav came back in his office?"

"Started grabbing his stuff, said something business related just came up. So I jumped in, loose cannon blazing. Told him I *was* a detective and asked what he knew about Paul Dickerson's murder."

"How'd he take it?"

"Looked like he might stroke out, but I didn't let up. 'What's your connection with Trevor Reid? Where were you the night of Paul Dickerson's murder? Why were you and Trevor Reid joyriding after Sprocket that very night?' He *ran* out of there."

"Shittin' bricks, good. Wonder what'll happen at Boogies?"

CHAPTER 35

Gia sat at the bar and checked the bar menu again. Behind her, RJ
sat in a booth, his legs stretched out across the bench seat. All around
the bar, a boogie-boarding theme. Slick boards, one with a shark bite
munched out of it, hung on the walls. Monitor footage showed boogie
boarders catching waves on their bellies, on their knees, at the Wedge
down in Newport Beach. Rover even caught one on his own canine
board.

With a mike in her jacket's lapel, a transmitter in her purse, and a
glass of white wine on the bar, she watched Dav come through the door
and walk past RJ, headed to the men's room.

From her transmitter, she heard Robert say, "Gia, come in, Gia."

"Gia, here. What's your twenty, lover boy?"

"You know my twenty." His location.

"How'd it go with you-know-who?"

"Better than I thought. *Señor Oso's* with me."

She looked through the big front window and waved at them across
the street.

"Quit screwing around, the bartender'll hear you."

"You mean my main man, Steve? We're already tight."

"How'd Dav look when he came in?"

"Freaked out. Went straight to the men's room, I'm guessing for a little you-know-whatski." A bump of coke. "Dav's coming back. I'm gonna tee it up. Gia, out."

She clicked off. Bartender Steve was right there, so she started up with him.

"Hey, Steve. Was there a guy in here earlier, asking for Gia Marquez?"

"If he was here, he didn't ask me."

"No guy was sitting around, looking like he'd been stood up?"

"Mostly regulars this time of day, and I know 'em all—like it or not."

"Meaning the loser lied to me, right?"

Steve shrugged. "Romance, what're you gonna do?"

She gave him a scowl, part of her act. Then she heard RJ calling, "Steve, oh, Steve, where's my drink at, bro?"

Steve said, "Not a mind reader, RJ. Helps to say it out loud."

She kept her eye on Steve, who reached for a bottle of call-brand tequila.

"Same ol'?" Steve asked RJ.

"Same ol' same."

As Dav joined RJ in the booth, Steve asked, "What's up with your wife, RJ? He's never late getting here."

"Got hung up at work."

"Work? Dav works?"

"Heyooo."

Ed McMahon's trademark shout-out to Johnny Carson. Lane Lang had been dead-on about this bar, where everyone knew Dav and RJ's names. Corner of her eye, RJ waved at a couple of girls at a two-top. Their matching *Heche En Venice* boardwalk-stall T-shirts told Gia they were tourists, working on a slow buzz to carry them past sunset on into the night.

Getting her act in gear, she slipped off her conservative linen jacket and Hermès scarf. Her tank top tried and intentionally failed to conceal her Victoria's Secret push-up bra. She stood, hiked her skirt midthigh, and reddened her lips—Tom Ford's Open Kimono.

Once she'd slipped on a pair of cat's-eye shades, she eased back onto her barstool, then slowly swiveled to face in RJ's direction.

The tourists had just made it to RJ's booth, but he leaned around them and caught her act. She bet she could read his mind; it was telling him: *Damn!*

The two women took a seat, but RJ stood up. Dav took RJ's arm and had a few heated words with him until RJ shook him off and headed her way.

Her phone rang, an old-school tone. Had to be Robert, watching from outside. Her phone was still ringing when RJ made his first pass.

"Hey, babe. How does Patrón sound to get started?"

She didn't answer. Just stared at her phone screen like it was alive.

"Asshole," she said to it.

"Whoa."

She glanced up at RJ, wondering if he recognized her from outside Paul's party. So far, not a glimmer. Capri Drive had been dark outside Paul's house; that plus RJ's intoxication.

"How about a do-over?" RJ said. "Hello, babe, how does Patrón sound to get us started in the right direction?"

His off-center grin must've worked in his twenties. Looked like he counted on his tan now to cover his booze bloat and puffy eyes.

"Why are *you* here?" she asked.

"I come here a lot, but I never saw you here before. Believe me, I'd remember."

She knew his line before he'd said it. But why say so and come across so hard so soon?

"Then you have no idea why my boyfriend had me wait for him here—where *you say* you come a lot—and then pulled a no-show?"

"None. I don't. Your boyfriend, do I know him?"

She decided to go right at him.

199

"He kicked your ass, night of Paul Dickerson's party, and now he tells me to wait for him here. What's up between you two wankers?"

"Oh? That guy I scrapped with."

Scrapped with?

"Don't play me and pretend like nothing's going on."

"C'mon. I see that guy again, and it's on!"

Steve set down her white wine then, or she'd have laughed out loud. She made a big deal out of quizzing Steve about RJ really being a regular here. Once Steve signed off on RJ's bona fides, she said, "Sorry. Small world, I guess."

"Westside LA is Smallville. White wine? Sure that's it? Say the word, Patrón's on me."

She took a sip of wine, acted like she was thinking it over. Her phone lit up, Robert again.

"Listen to this," she told RJ, hitting "Speaker."

"Hey, babe," Robert said. "Listen, you at Boogies?"

"I'm listening."

"You're not gonna believe it, got a call from my old firm—remember Philip?"

She made a disgusted look at her phone. Then she pointed at RJ's tequila—*one for me, too.*

While he ordered, Gia told Robert, "Tell Philip to blow me. And you? Leaving me here without calling? But you know what? You did me a favor, and made it easy."

"Babe! Don't!"

Babe again, a word he never used. He and Erik had to be getting off on his *babe* routine.

"Don't *babe* me, you dickless loser. You were a real man, you'd give me what I needed, whenever I needed it, and even when I didn't!"

Gia didn't know who she was channeling. Whoever she was scared her a little.

She left Robert hanging as their Patróns came. She slammed hers back, signaled RJ to order another.

"Hear that?" she asked Robert.

"Hear what?"

"The sound of me—screwing another man!"

"Heyooo," RJ said.

❧

"Heyooo," Erik said to Robert in the Bronco after Gia hung up.

Through separate headphones, they listened to Gia's transmission from inside.

"You're what, Italian?" RJ asked.

"How'd you know?" Gia was half-Chinese, half-Latino.

"Got my sixth sense working overtime."

"Aren't you something."

"Remember the movie? Had Bruce Willis in it—not cool Bruce, dorky Bruce—he's already dead but doesn't know it."

"*Sixth Sense*, think I do. Oh yeah, and the Haley Joel kid, right?"

"That's the one. I guessed early that Bruce was already dead."

"Like I said, aren't you something."

In the car, Robert asked Erik, "Do all men sound as lame as RJ?"

"We sound great if they like us. If they don't, doesn't matter what we say."

"At least I got this necklace off him," Gia was telling RJ. "Probably fake like him."

"Here we go," Robert said to Erik.

Through Boogies' front window, they could see RJ leaning in for a closer look at Gia's gold-bar necklace.

Erik said, "He's going for the gold, dude, don't look."

Robert kept looking anyway. RJ leaned in, reaching for the gold bar. "Jesus," Robert muttered.

"Who bought her the bling?" Erik reminded him. "Suggested she wear that push-up?"

"Want me to remind you about perv boy Bryan's *Baywatch* flyover?"

"The one-piece wasn't *my* idea. You want to get between Priya and *Baywatch*, be my guest. Any word on young Bryan?"

"Lawan told him to bring her a flash drive of his footage from party week. Does Priya go for David Hasselhoff?"

"She ever met him, she'd dump me and the lads in a second. KITT's on display at a museum somewhere, okay, we'll go. That talking car's as close as I want her to the Hoff."

"The Hoff bigger to her than Bieber?"

"In her village? A Thai woman her age? The Hoff's bigger than Buddha."

❧

Inside Boogies, Gia and RJ kept eating the house specialty, crab tacos, while she kept the ball rolling about her necklace. She'd taken it off, and RJ was squinting at it, looking for a hallmark.

"Twenty-four karats, that's the best, right?" Gia asked.

"Not for gold, and this isn't twenty-four karat anyhow. It's white gold, meaning they added silver, a lot of it, so it wouldn't be so easy to bend or scratch."

"So this is white gold and silver posing as twenty-four karat?"

"'Fraid so, babe."

She wrote Robert a text and showed it to RJ: You cheap a-hole! Necklace not 24 karat. Fake like you! And soft like your Jimmy! She let the text go.

She told RJ she was in law school and asked what he did in LA. He told her about being in *the industry*, what movie people like calling their business. He planned to start working for his uncle at his hot-shit hedge fund up in Beverly Hills.

It didn't take her long to get Trevor Reid's name on the table. Front and center—where Robert had wanted Trevor to be.

She said, "I met Trevor at Paul's party. How can you stand working for a jerk like that?"

"Gotta know how to handle him. He pushes you as far as you let him push, and when he sees you won't back down, he's cool."

"No way he's cool. He's a jackass."

"Cool for a jackass, though, right?"

In the Bronco, Robert and Erik listened to RJ telling Gia a Trevor Reid story. How Jerry Baugh and Trevor had driven down to Huntington Beach so Jerry could show Trevor a secure vault that the fund used to store precious metals.

RJ said, "Trevor doesn't want to go, but his guy Jerry'd already told him, 'Hell yeah, you're going because you need to see how it works, and your fingerprints need to be on the access card.'"

Then RJ said, "They get all the way down there, and Trevor forgot to bring his driver's license, and get this, babe. It's four p.m., and he left it out in Malibu. So who's gotta go to Malibu, then haul ass down to Huntington Beach before the vault closes?"

"Bettin' it was you," Gia said.

"Bingo!" R.J. said.

"He actually said *bingo*?" Erik asked Robert.

"Reyes said bad dialogue was RJ's specialty. Sounds like Trevor's fund would fall apart without RJ running the show."

RJ said, "And guess what? I get down there and Trevor'd already split. Didn't even bother to call me."

"Jackass," Erik said.

"But cool," Robert added.

❧

Inside the bar, Gia asked RJ, "How big's your uncle's fund?"

"He keeps it under a billion." Winking at her about that big number.

Gia said, "That small? I thought hedge funds dealt with real money."

Her critique sideswiped RJ's ego; he flushed, hearing *real money.*

"Funds like his don't want to be big. They want to be nimble. They get too big, they can't invest in smaller situations because any gains can't move the profit needle enough cuz the pie's too big."

Needles and *pies.* A mixed metaphor, but she got it.

She caught a text from Robert, showed it to RJ: Babe. Please don't leave me hanging!

RJ helped with her answer. He suggested, Met a cool guy. A lot cooler than you!

She let that text fly, and they high-fived.

"If there was something I could make money on," Gia asked RJ, "something Three Thirty-Three was doing, you'd tell me, wouldn't you?"

"Couldn't, babe, no matter what. That gets me into trouble, but I'll say this—the fund's balls-deep into PGMs."

"That band from Athens, Georgia?" She sang a couple of bars from that song "Everybody Hurts."

"No, no, that's R.E.M. PGMs are short for *platinum-group metals.* There's only ten of 'em in the group, so I'm not telling you anything, but I'm telling you everything, wink wink."

"Starting to think you and Uncle Jackass aren't tight like you said. But that's just me."

"Me and Unc? We're tighter'n a well digger's ass."

Tighter instead of *colder*, RJ making a joke. Gia laughed for real— the joke was funny, and she was knee-deep into a Patrón buzz.

She said, "Who's gonna know if you tell me about those metals, if it's just pillow talk between you and me?"

Her pillow-talk promise pierced RJ's haze, even hammered.

"I want to tell you . . . ," he started.

She stood up for a trip to the ladies' room.

"There's wanting and there's doing. You a wanter or a doer?"

"A doer, babe, all night long."

❧

"You a wanter or a doer, babe?" Erik said, jerking Robert's chain.

"Don't start up with me, or we'll scrap for sure." Using RJ's lingo.

Robert took off his headset, caught Gia's phone call from Boogies' ladies' room.

"Babe," she said, "I think he's coming around."

Babe, still? She was loaded.

"Gia, I don't think he knows jack about Three Thirty-Three's investments. I'm gonna pull you out of the operation. You blow your cover, I can't use you in Budapest next spring."

"You sure? Whatever he knows, I think he'll tell me."

"I know, but—"

Erik said, "Hold up. He's talking to Dav."

Robert looked through Boogies' window—Dav and RJ sat at the bar. Gia's coat hung on her stool back, still transmitting.

Erik relayed their conversation to Robert and Gia:

"Dav's saying he's not gonna get stuck with the tab for the two broads—his words—from Altadena . . . RJ's telling him to chill out, he's taking her—Gia, he means—back to the *Marguerite* . . . Dav's saying, 'All the stuff's sitting out, let me go to the boat first, clean it up.' Then some more I can't quite make it out . . . and now RJ's telling Dav he's not letting Dav have the gate code to get on board . . . Dav's saying Trevor trusts him totally, so give him the goddamn gate code, and RJ says forget it because Trevor told him specifically don't give Dav the gate code." Erik added, "Ouch—that was me talking."

Through the window, Robert saw Dav headed back to the booth solo. He thought it over. The *Marguerite*. Named after Trevor's deceased wife. The yacht pictured in Dav's office photographs; the yacht where Dav and RJ just said *all the stuff's sitting out*; the yacht requiring a gate code for access. Could be their only chance to see what was on board.

He knew that men, drunk men in particular, can be charming until a switch goes off. Then bad things happen fast. One of many reasons why Gia carried pepper spray in her purse tonight.

Gia picked up on what he was thinking. "You'll be listening in, Roberto, and I won't go below deck. Once I'm on board, I'll grab something to bust him with, or Mace him if he tries to get jiggy."

She hung up.

Erik asked, "Get jiggy?"

Robert finished the Will Smith song title. "Wit' it. She's loaded."

CHAPTER 36

As darkness fell two blocks down the street from Boogies, Sonny and Chet sat on antique metal chairs. An antiques and curios shop owner had them set out on the sidewalk. Both painted white, the chair's metal bands created spring tension so they could lean back in them.

Sonny said, "Every liquor store, every gas-up and shop, every grocery store. Every one of 'em's selling jerky. All different flavors—spicy, extra spicy, and vegetarian—and most all the clerks are gnawing on a piece they keep under the counter."

Most all the clerks? Sonny'd seen two clerks eating jerky, ever, and wouldn't let go of it. Obsessing on things and on people, that was Sonny's nature. Chet had to put up with it as long as he needed to use it.

Chet asked. "Given any more thought to Mexico, us two getting down there like in the movies?"

"Mexico's a cesspool of unknown bacteria and disease, Chet. The water, the chow, the ocean."

"Not if you're careful what you eat, where you go."

"Even if. You ever think about how in the movies, they never make it to Mexico?"

"Did in *Shawshank Redemption*, right? Morgan Freeman, one who played God that time, he got down there and met his buddy from the joint. Last scene, they meet on the beach, fade out."

"Morgan's in Mexico, a'ight, on the beach, a'ight, but he's sanding a boat. Goin' all the way to Mexico to do manual labor in that god-awful heat? You shitting me—and add the heat to my I-ain't-going-to-Mexico list."

Chet thought about gotta-get-to-Mexico movies. Most of 'em were old. Made sense—it's hard to get lost anywhere in the world anymore.

Maybe Sonny was right about *Shawshank*, but what about *The Wild Bunch*, Sam Peckinpah's movie? The *Wild Bunch* gang made it across the border and had a kick-ass time in a Mexican whorehouse. But in the end—damn, Sonny was right—the whole bunch got gunned down by Mexican soldiers.

Thelma & Louise? Nah, those two broads never made it across the border. At least they'd picked up young Brad Pitt, and one of 'em—was it Thelma or Louise?—laid one on Brad all night long.

What about Quentin Tarantino's movie, had George Clooney and that other guy in it? Harvey somebody. They made it across the border in a RV, parked at the best truck stop of all time. Why the best? Cuz Salma Hayek's strutting her stuff up and down the bar, damn near naked, until they find out the hard way—whoa, all these Mexicans are vampires! Even Salma!

He bet he could prove Sonny wrong if he thought about movies some more, but forget it. Those were just movies. In real life, comman-deering Hobie's Ensenada crib for free and having that local guy, Pablo, hop to was the best idea he'd had in a while.

"How do you like them?" a salesgirl asked about their metal chairs. "Aren't they awesome?"

Sonny said, "More comfy than they look."

Chet said, "Nice retro look. Had 'em on our front porch grow-ing up. They started rusting out, time I left home. Bet anything Mom tossed 'em out."

"Bet she did," Sonny said. "What's holding up my meat loaf, Mom?"

Sonny messing up that *Wedding Crashers* line, Will Ferrell yelling to his mom back in the kitchen.

Sonny grabbed his crotch, winked up at the girl. "Meat loaf, sweets?"

She scowled, went back inside the store.

Chet asked, "See that Bronc up there, across the street?"

Sonny looked at the car.

Chet said, "Pretty sure I saw it parked outside Dav's office. A guy sitting behind the wheel."

"Two guys sitting in it now. Sure it's the same one?"

"Vintage paint job like that? Don't see that many around. Put it with that Bronco we saw over in East LA, and you start asking yourself."

"Asking what?"

"What's that Bronc doing wherever we go? And what's the Bronc got to do with those two jagoffs in the bar?"

Sonny didn't answer. Looked like he was brooding about something.

He got his answer when Sonny said, "Who does that bitch think she is?" Meaning meat-loaf girl inside the shop.

Chet didn't answer—like walking on eggshells, handling Sonny. A real pain in the ass till you needed somebody to start breaking eggs.

CHAPTER 37

"Not gonna lie to you," RJ told Gia. "I'm only part owner of the yacht."

"Which part?"

Well after dark, he punched in the code for the gate that barred entrance to the gangplank leading out to the *Marguerite*. Gia guessed the yacht was right at sixty feet. Sleek, red and white, with a flying bridge up top. A nice ride, no doubt about it.

"Can we take 'er out?" she asked, already knowing the answer.

"Not tonight, I gave the captain shore leave."

Sure you did. So full of shit. Then she thought over RJ's routine: *I'm in the industry; office on Abbot Kinney; access to a sixty-foot yacht.*

Must work wonders in LA, where outsiders climbed inside by hooking up with whomever they believed were the right people. She wondered if any of the women ever pulled back the curtain on RJ's industry rap: *What movies have you made—specifically? No, not in development—made. None? Then how'd you pay for this yacht? You didn't? Aren't you just a spoiled errand boy for a rich uncle?*

When the gate swung closed, she checked—no code box hanging on this side. One handle twist and she'd be outta here. Top of the yacht's gangplank, RJ snagged his white captain's hat off a wall peg and slapped it on.

"Welcome aboard, mate."

She eyed the generic emblem woven into the fabric: two rearing lions, squared off for a fight. So much to make fun of, she didn't even try.

A puppy started yapping somewhere on board.

RJ said, "Damn you, Petey, shut up!"

He took off to find the puppy; she checked out the main deck.

At the stern, an open-air seating arrangement. Leather sofas formed a U around three coffee tables. With Robert, sexy as could be; with RJ, a waste of time.

Inside lay the galley. Modern appliances. The rest of it, slick and sleek. On a laid-out towel rested a bowl of puppy chow. Beside the bowl, puppy crap on the teak deck.

"Uh-oh."

She spilled some puppy chow across the floor, giving RJ something to do besides her. A black-and-white border collie pup dashed in, sat down, and looked up at her.

"You must be Petey. You're in deep you-know-what, Petey."

She set her purse on the countertop. As she scooped him up, RJ wasn't far behind.

"Trevor's dog. Petey. P. Diddy. Pee-on-the-deck Diddy. Only living thing in the world Trevor doesn't yell at. Sometimes I have to drive that beast up to Beverly Hills just so Trevor can tell it hello."

Must've forgotten his king-of-the-world persona.

"Somebody's been a bad dog," she told Petey. "Did you make a big mess for *el capitán* to clean up?"

"No effin' way!" RJ said, grabbing a towel and dropping to his knees.

She strolled the rear deck, cradling Petey. It didn't take long to see *the stuff* RJ and Dav said they'd left out. The *stuff* Dav had wanted to *clean up* before RJ brought her on board.

Several document stacks rested on the dining room table. Given her ten-year stint as office manager at Fanelli & Pierce, she knew closing documents when she saw them. She moved closer to sneak a look at the parties' names, always at the top of page one.

R.J. said, "Hey, babe, ditch the Petester, and let me show you the view from up top."

She backed away from the documents, strolled back to the galley, and grabbed her purse.

"Okay, but the Petester wants to come along, too."

❧

Parked a hundred yards from the yacht, Robert and Erik kept an eye on Gia from the Bronco. Following Gia here in the Uber, and now, on board, they'd lost contact with her transmitter.

"Interference from all the electronics gear on these boats," Erik had guessed.

Now, Robert watched her on the yacht's main deck. Then he lost sight of her.

After thirty seconds more, he opened his door. "This was a bad idea."

"Got her, on the stairs," Erik said, pointing at the yacht.

Robert closed his door and watched Gia with RJ as they made it all the way up to the bridge.

"What's she carrying?" Erik asked.

"Looks like a cat."

Once Gia and RJ reached the bridge, its tinted windshield and dock-light glare blocked their view of her.

Erik caught a call from home.

Why are you with Uncle Robert? Where are you? When are coming home? Do you think Ducky Joe can hear us talking? Can Uncle Robert come tuck us in later?

Erik answered patiently. A great dad, a loving husband. Something for Robert to shoot for if and when the time came.

"Uncle Robert can't tuck you in tonight, guys, but he will another time. He promises."

Robert was about to promise them out loud when his eye caught a large object—*a body?*—tumbling off the bridge. The object bounced off the yacht and splashed into the water.

In an instant, he was sprinting toward the gangplank, shucking his shirt as he ran.

***

About a minute before Robert started running, Gia made it onto the bridge with RJ. Once he latched the gate, she set down the squirming pup. She had to admit, the view was dramatic. All around the yacht basin, boat lights dappled the water, and even though the water was nastied-up with diesel fuel, that was easy to ignore from up here.

She could even see the Bronco, facing her way. She almost waved, caught herself in time.

"Dig it?" RJ asked.

"Not bad."

She was about to excuse herself for the downstairs ladies' room. The only hard part would be convincing him to wait here. That would give her time enough to lift whatever she wanted from the documents and hit that gate.

RJ said, "Take the wheel, babe. One night, we'll definitely take 'er over to Catalina, drop anchor in Avalon cove."

Avalon cove hadn't worked out for Natalie Wood in the early eighties; she'd drowned there. A cloud of suspicion followed her husband to this day.

Behind Gia, a metallic object thunked onto the deck.

She looked down. Saw RJ's belt buckle at his feet, along with his pants.

RJ asked, "What do you think of this, babe?"

213

She made a half turn, saw him holding up her Mace, grinning. He must've swiped the canister from her purse while it was on the counter.

Stomping down on his foot, she raised an elbow and twisted fast and hard. Hoping to break his nose with it, she caught his windpipe instead.

Her blow sent him stumbling back, his shoes trapped inside his trousers. Before she could even think about grabbing him, he flipped over the rail and disappeared.

She ran to the rail. Looking down, she saw nothing in the dark water.

"Oh, no, please."

A second splash. Looking toward that gate, she saw—*was it Robert?*—swimming toward RJ.

She gathered Petey and hurried down the stairs. She didn't want to think about her legal situation—she'd been in the right, sure, but killing RJ for dropping his pants?

By the time she reached the yacht's boarding stairs, Robert was holding on to the gangplank, panting. She jumped down, locked hands with him, and pulled him up.

The sound of a vomiting man reached them.

"You okay?" he asked.

"Yes, where is he?"

He jerked his thumb toward the heaving sounds ten yards away.

"Swimming in, I think, crabmeat vomit."

"Never saw that before."

"You don't want to see it. Think it was those crab tacos you two were wolfing down."

"Not the ten shots?"

"Couldn't be that. C'mon, let's go."

"Let me grab a couple of things."

Gia ran back on board. The puppy was whimpering, and she petted him on her way to the document stacks. She thumbed through a set marked *copy*, checked the signature page, and stuffed it in her purse.

Holding up Petey close to her face, she said, "Hang in there, Petester."

She noticed the bone-shaped dog tag. Saw that his name was not Petey or any of RJ's variations.

By the time she left the yacht, RJ hung off the gangplank several feet below her, crabmeat strands laced in his hair. She knelt down.

"What were you thinking?"

"Swear to God, I wasn't gonna do anything. I thought you'd laugh about the Mace."

About stealing her Mace? As close as he'd been, he'd never touched her. She actually believed him.

"Think I'm an alcoholic," he said, blubbering.

"With any luck, babe, you're just an asshole."

CHAPTER 38

In the Bronco, Erik drove; Robert and Gia rode in the back seat. Gia was lying down, her head in Robert's lap. He looked over the documents Gia had pinched from the *Marguerite*.

They were familiar. He'd seen an identical set of documents on Paul's computer documenting Paul's investment in the 333 Hedge Fund. The documents in hand were for new money coming into the fund.

Erik said, "But Trevor said he stopped taking new money?"

"He bragged about it during a CNBC interview, but that's not what's going on here. This new investor only dropped a quarter-million bucks into the fund."

Gia asked, "It's not illegal for him to raise money, is it?"

"No, not at all."

He tried to match up what'd he'd just learned with what he already knew. A few minutes later, as Erik turned onto Lincoln Boulevard, he wrapped his mind around a new scenario that would give Trevor another reason to kill Paul.

"See how this sounds, guys. Not long ago, Trevor tells the world that he's not raising money anymore for the fund. Fair enough, he wants to keep the fund small enough to be, as RJ put it, nimble. But here comes Paul, wanting to withdraw a ton of money—maybe ten percent or more of the fund. Trevor tells Paul no—maybe the fund had losing positions he thought would turn around, who knows. Then *no*, again, and finally, *hell no, because I say so.* But nobody ever said Trevor wasn't smart."

Up front, Erik asked, "Not ever?"

"Not once in his life, and because of Paul's ask, Trevor sells his house in Malibu and sells it fast. Gets Golden to lie about the top-dollar sales price in a press release."

Gia asked, "And you think Trevor put that money from the house into his own fund?"

"If and when he needed to put it in, yes, and, yes, he's raising money every way he can. From his own assets and from new money, like in those documents. I thought Trevor shut down Three Thirty-Three Films because RJ was an idiot and didn't get the job done. What about getting out from under all that rent, all the salaries?"

Gia said, "Rent on that Abbot Kinney building has to be a hundred thousand a month."

Robert added, "Or more. Same time, he raises money from small investors on the side. And he uses Dav to do it. For all I know, he uses other brokers, too."

Erik asked, "Why not go to his other investors and raise money from them?"

"I wondered about that. Say you're Trevor, and you go to one of your big boys to kick in another twenty million. That investor's sophisticated, not a dentist from Hacienda Heights, and he knows the game every bit as well as Trevor does. So he's gonna ask Trevor, 'Why do you need new money, dude? You told the press the hedge fund was closed to new money.' What can Trevor *not* tell them? 'I'm raising new money because smart investor Paul Dickerson's pulling out of the fund.' Because? Anyone? You, the big guy in the front seat?"

Erik said, "Like you said, the big boys would want to know why. And then the big boys start talking to the other big boys, and pretty soon all the big boys are saying, 'Better safe than sorry. I'm getting out of the fund, too.'"

Robert said, "And Trevor's fund would be cooked. On board the *Marguerite*—what better place to close small-ball investors than on board a yacht?"

Gia said, "Other than RJ, it was impressive."

Erik said, "You take a big boy out to the *Marguerite*, they'd be saying, 'A sixty-footer? That's a dinghy where I come from.' But you bring a Hacienda Heights on board? They're thinking, 'Welcome to the big leagues.'" Then he asked, "How does Trevor leaving Sprocket with Dav, the night of Paul's murder, fit in with that theory?"

Gia answered. "Maybe somebody offered to put in a million and wanted special treatment, so Dav drove Trevor to the marina to put on a late-night show."

Robert said, "Maybe a lot of things, but explaining his own alibi is Trevor's problem, not Reyes'. Because Trevor left Sprocket early, a jury might believe that he killed Paul, or that Trevor and Dav killed Paul, or had him killed. That and whatever else Anita can come up with that might've driven Trevor to murder."

He dove deep into what he'd learned from the internet; from Paul's files; from Lawan, Gia, and Erik; and from Trevor himself.

"Here's what I'm thinking. Paul wants to pull eighty million out of Trevor's fund. A major hit, and Trevor won't let him out. Paul persists, so Trevor raises money from his own assets and from new investors, sells his Malibu pad for under market, and closes down Three Thirty-Three Film. Uses Dav, too, and possibly other brokers, to raise money from small investors. All that and he raises twenty, thirty million."

Gia said, "Makes sense. Tell me about Trevor coming to Paul's party."

Robert nodded. "Hat in hand, Trevor reaches out to Paul by email, asks if he can come for ten grand. Even buys a couple of thousand-dollar cheap seats for RJ and Dav. Paul says sure, Trevor shows up, and what happens? Trevor offers Paul a partial withdrawal, and Paul turns him down because—on principle at this point—Paul wants nothing to do with Trevor anymore. After all the trouble Trevor's had coming up with the twenty million, Trevor loses his mind with Paul and gets gut-kicked for his trouble. Angered and humiliated by everything Paul has put him through, Trevor Reid killed Paul Dickerson, or hired someone to do it for him."

Gia asked. "Why's he raising money that night if he knows Paul's gonna be killed? He doesn't need to raise money, does he, with Paul dead?"

A great question. One that he couldn't quite nail down.

"How's this? Trevor's withdrawal problem might not disappear, even with Paul's death, so he keeps raising money. And no matter what, Lawan's withdrawal from his fund would be easier to deal with than dealing with Paul had been. Or maybe all the back-and-forth with Paul made Trevor realize he needed a rainy-day fund, no matter what."

So far, Lawan's lack of interest in Paul's finances gave Robert's first scenario quite a bit of credibility. They kicked it back and forth without a clear resolution. As he continued to grind through new facts, he knew that eventually all the pieces would fit.

When Erik got out of the Bronco at home, he left Gia with this parting shot: "Good to know I'm still top investigator on this case."

CHAPTER 39

"You smell worse than RJ," Gia told Robert in the dark, hosing him off from her perch on the wooden stairs up to their apartment. His stench came by way of the funky marina water he'd just swum in. She twisted the hose nozzle and generated a pencil-thin spray against his soapy body.

"Careful where you point that thing."

"Who's your top investigator?"

"Retired LAPD officer Erik Jacobson."

"Who?"

Damn, her aim was good.

"You! You are, babe!"

"*Babe?* That word gets flushed tonight."

Another strategic hose blast. He turned his back to her, not quite in the nick of time.

"Gia Marquez is my top investigator!"

She gave the nozzle a twist off and stood up. "Was that so hard?"

A bad choice of words after she'd assaulted his privates.

"Where's my towel?" he asked, shivering.

She reached for it on the step behind her.

Another female voice said: "Oh, I'm sorry!"

On the walkway beside the main house at the front of the lot, Lawan turned away from Robert's nude body. His thrown towel hit him in the face, and he quickly slipped it around his waist.

Gia walked toward Lawan. "Don't worry about it, Lawan. What's up?" Lawan held up a letter-size envelope.

"I have the footage from Bryan's drone, but I didn't mean to—" Robert said, "It's okay, there's no bell at the front gate."

He dried his hands and took the envelope. Inside it: a flash drive.

Lawan said, "That's all of Bryan's drone footage from the day and night of the party. I came down earlier, didn't want to leave it in your mailbox."

"Good move," Gia said. "Why don't you come in?"

"You sure?"

"If you have an extra five seconds, we'll give you a tour."

A few minutes later, Robert had dressed; a kettle of water heated up on the stove. Gia and Lawan sat on the couch in the living-slash-dining room. He took a chair across from them.

Lawan was in the middle of telling Gia: "When I saw no one was home, I went down to the beach and walked to one pier, then to the other pier, and back here."

"That's how far, Robert?"

"Seven, eight miles."

"I stopped, had a lovely dinner at a café down on Washington."

He asked, "Did you meet with Anita Yates again?"

Lawan nodded. "She made sure I knew what was going on. Just tell the truth about what I know in the preliminary hearing, and if the district attorney—the DA—starts acting ugly, she'll step in."

Gia said, "Don't ever lie to the DA. If you don't know, say that you don't know. If you can't remember, just say so, and don't guess at an answer just to be helpful."

Looked like Lawan tracked Gia's advice, but he couldn't be sure. More small talk followed: what Joshua Tree National Park looked like, *glamping*—luxury camping—in the desert.

Lawan's desolate look had just registered with him when she burst into tears.

Gia took her hand. Tears began streaming down her face, too.

"It's okay," Gia kept saying.

Of course it wasn't okay. Lawan had been putting on a brave face for the last few days. He waited, helpless, until Lawan had cried herself out.

"Oh, my God," she said. "I'm so sorry."

Gia took her hand. "I can't imagine what you're going through."

Robert said, "Let me check on the tea," then noticed Gia reaching for her own stomach. A moan escaped her.

"What's wrong?"

Gia leaped over the coffee table, dashing for the bathroom. "Boogies! Crabmeat!" she yelled before the bathroom door slammed. Seconds later, the sound of Gia retching reached the living room.

"Something she ate," he said, lame as could be.

"Want me to check on her?"

Given Gia's concerns about him and Lawan, and Gia hugging the toilet bowl, he knew what Gia would want him to say.

"Better not, but thanks."

After a moment's quiet from the bathroom, Lawan asked, "Do you still think Trevor Reid killed Paul?"

"I think he's responsible for Paul's death. I'm not as sure as I'm going to be, but I'm getting there."

"Because of money?"

He nodded. "That's the simplest answer. That and ego."

"Then Paul died for no good reason."

"No good reason to a normal person, but Trevor's not normal."

Anger flashed across her face. *"Kaw pen kwai."*

"Sorry?"

"He is a water buffalo. Stupid, stubborn. I have the most unkind thoughts about him."

"You're not alone. From what Jerry Baugh told me, Trevor's own father thought he was a wanker, too."

"I know that word from Paul. *Wanker* and *kwai* mean much the same thing. If our friend Reyes is set free, will Trevor Reid go to jail?"

"Not necessarily, but I'll work with Anita and try to make sure it happens."

She seemed comforted hearing those words and stood. "I'd better get home."

"Thanks for the flash drive. I'll get to it soon as I can."

They went the door; she turned down his offer to walk her to her car.

She said, "Hampton Bergen came to the temple. I found him much different from how I remembered. Calmer and quite kind. He said you were a good guy. For a lawyer."

"That's a lawyer joke."

She smiled. "In Thailand, our lawyer jokes usually involve snakes and crocodiles."

Once she left, he parked himself on the floor outside their bathroom and rapped gently on the door.

A moan. A flush. A halfhearted heave.

"Do not come in here. Maybe ever."

"I won't. I swear."

"She's gone?"

"She's been gone."

"Could you two hear me?"

"Barely."

He heard her blowing her nose. Another flush.

"Liar! Uh-oh." Another retch. "She's so nice, I hate her."

"No, you don't."

"Bet she offered to see if I was okay."

"No, she didn't. She couldn't've cared less."

"Oh, God, when did you turn into such a liar?"

He smiled, put his head against the door.

"Look, you're my top investigator. You're my only girl. We're trying to make babies together, so don't be hatin'."

"I'm not hatin' on her. I like her a lot and feel so bad for her. Poor thing, God. Please go to the store and get ginger ale and a revolver."

"Will do."

"I'm getting in the tub." Their cast-iron, claw-foot tub. "When you get back, you'll want to look in my purse."

"Why?"

All she said was, "Petey. P. Diddy. Pee-on-the-floor Diddy."

CHAPTER 40

A half hour later, Robert slipped Gia a ginger ale with cracked ice through a sliver in the bathroom door.

Her weak voice said, "Did you look in my purse?"

"Not yet."

He went into the living room and dug through it until he found a dog collar. Back at the bathroom door, he asked, "You want a dog?"

"RJ called the puppy *Petey* and *P. Diddy*. Look at the name on the dog bone."

Etched into the silvery, dog-bone-shaped tag were the letters *Pd*.

"Damn, that's the symbol for palladium."

"Knew it was one of those platinum-type metals."

He scratched the tag with his key; it was very soft.

"Bet the damn bone's made out of palladium. Just when I thought Trevor might care something about a fellow mammal."

The puppy was nothing but Trevor's superstition prop. Naming the dog after his primary conviction investment fit a career-long superstition pattern: the *Marguerite Fund* and his yacht for a deceased wife Trevor claimed was lucky; *333* because they were lucky numbers; *Rain Dunes* for uranium; *Hey Gee*, a racehorse he'd owned when silver had been his top investment; and now *Pd*, or Petey, for *palladium*.

"Remember RJ's story about Trevor and the Huntington Beach access card?" he asked.

"Uh-huh. Access to a vault, right?"

"Yes. Did RJ mention the access card in the Uber or on the yacht?"

"Not that I remember, but I was pretty deep undercover by then."

Deep drunk.

He recalled Jerry fielding a call from the fund at the driving range. After he'd moved away for privacy, Kay had told him that her ex kept fielding calls about the fund's *access cards to the vault*. Like Gia said, RJ had mentioned a Huntington Beach vault.

His best guess: Kay and RJ had been talking about the same vault— the one in Huntington Beach where the fund stored its precious metals.

Where the fund stored its *palladium*.

"You alive in there?"

"Hanging on."

He brought his laptop to his bathroom door perch and Googled *precious metals+vault+Huntington Beach*. Several sites about secure vaults came up.

Made sense—there was a ton of money down there, not to mention world-class surfing. Among the sites listed, only Prestige Vault looked sophisticated enough to hold millions in palladium—maybe tens of millions of dollars' worth.

Prestige had been a private safe-deposit box company for over thirty years and wasn't subject to any reporting regulations about what went into its boxes. Owners could either make shipments to the facility by registered USPS mail, or make deliveries themselves. Prestige offered numbered vault accounts, entry by access card, plus a fingerprint pad on the door.

An article in the *Orange County Register* reported an attempt eighteen months ago at unlawful entry in the early-morning hours.

"A half-baked attempt, if that," Prestige management had pointed out.

Robert looked up *palladium* and found a chart of its price. Over the past year, palladium, *Pd*, was down well over 30 percent.

"Prestige Vault down in Huntington Beach. That's where Trevor keeps his fund's palladium."

A quiet voice: "Does that matter?"

"Palladium's price was down huge when Paul made his withdrawal request."

"Does that matter, too?"

"I know this. Trevor says he's a conviction investor. That means he doesn't want to sell it until *he* decides the time's right."

"Lemme know when you know, okay?"

Later that night, she slid into bed beside him, pale and weak. He made sure to tell her he was all in for baby-making so he could hear her say—*just once*—that she wasn't up for it.

For a while, as she snuggled against him, they watched Bryan's drone footage on his laptop. Over five hours of footage on that flash drive, it turned out.

Bryan had flown over Lawan's neighborhood, always circling back to the Dickerson estate. Every so often, a Flower's Flowers van pulled into the driveway; Lawan or the maid walked in and out of the house to meet catering trucks; workers arranged orchids onto tree trunks and tables; Paul drove out the driveway; Paul pulled back in; Paul stood in the backyard with Jerry by the rib-smoking pit.

Hours later, a sharp noise from Robert's laptop woke him. He turned down the volume and saw that he'd reached drone footage of Paul from the night of the party. Standing on the bandstand, addressing his guests with the microphone.

He recalled the moment. Backed up the footage until he caught a snippet of Trevor pushing Paul in the back, Paul kicking him. Fast-forward to Paul on stage. Robert saw Gia and himself as Paul told his guests to grab squirt guns.

Here came the sprinklers, and soon enough, at the edge of the frame, Robert caught a flash of Gia barreling him into the infinity pool. Soon after, Paul and Lawan and a swarm of others had jumped in, too.

It was the last time he could recall laying eyes on Paul Dickerson. Midjump into the pool, holding hands with Lawan. Smiling and howling and so much in love that the memory pained him.

Robert kissed his own sweetheart's cheek, her mouth open, snoring softly. Reaching to stop Bryan's footage—he'd watch it all with Gia—his eye caught movement below the infinity pool.

He slowed down the footage, brightened his screen to the max. Backed up twenty seconds and watched again in slow motion.

When forty-odd guests had piled into the pool, a slo-mo wave sloshed over the lip of the infinity pool, cascading into the canyon.

He made out two figures in the canyon, twenty or thirty feet below the pool, soaked by that wave of water. Two shadowy males who'd been paralleling Paul's overgrown rear property line on foot.

These two had no business being on the canyon side of Paul's rear fence at night—or during the day, for that matter. No doubt in his mind—the pair had been watching the party in progress. Getting to know the layout, and the man they would kill for Trevor Reid two short days later.

Son of a bitch, Trevor—gotcha.

He no longer wanted to stop at creating reasonable doubt for Reyes' preliminary hearing or his trial. Now he planned to prove that Trevor Reid had paid two men to kill Paul Dickerson.

CHAPTER 41

The next morning, Robert showed Gia the drone footage of the two men. She was still weak from food poisoning but stoked at seeing it. They agreed that the pair were interlopers; then she headed out to her job.

He drove over to Erik's house and picked him up. Before driving over to Lawan's, they detoured to Beverly Hills and parked in front of Trevor's office building.

Given that Trevor knew Robert's face, Erik delivered a large envelope to Trevor's receptionist. Inside it: Pd's collar—the *Pd* dog bone remained with Robert. So did the set of investment documents that Gia had pinched from the *Marguerite*.

Postdelivery, Erik slid back in the car.

"That oughta light a fire under Trevor's tight ass."

Robert said, "Bet you Dav's gettin' twitchy, too, after your meet-and-greet yesterday."

"Already called Dav's office. So far, he's a no-show."

Driving over to Lawan's house, Robert decided to call Jerry Baugh and light another fire under his ass, using buzzwords that might get him revved up enough to throw some of it Trevor's way.

When he didn't answer, Robert left a message: "Jerry, it's Robert Worth. When you can, give me a call. Lots of stuff going on, lots of new leads on the killer. Trevor's yacht, that dog living on board, the vault down in Huntington, the drone footage night of Paul's party. Also, I had a few more questions about Trevor to run by you."

Erik grinned, hearing Robert's vague but ominous message. "Love it!"

As they pulled into Lawan's driveway, Robert said, "Lawan's at Brentwood Security asking for whatever footage they might have of the neighborhood for the day of her party."

"Didn't Reyes' case file have all that footage in it?"

"No. The DA wasn't focused on the party. He was interested in the day before and the day after Paul's murder."

"So what're we doing here?"

"Snooping around her backyard, trying to find where those two guys were hiding out."

Five minutes later, they found an elevated spot behind the property's rear fence line. They photographed a tramped-down spot in the ground cover—a place where he believed the two men had been standing.

Careful not to disturb the area, they faced the house and had a near-unobstructed view.

Robert said, "The back doors of the house were wide-open that night. These two could see through the house, all the way into the front yard."

"Kitchen door's on their right, bedroom's upstairs, easy to see it all."

"Then the sprinklers went off, guests starting running around, and our guys had seen enough."

"So they headed out," Erik said.

A small animal trail led slightly downhill to the pool side of the lot; they followed it and stopped below the lip of the pool, twenty feet overhead.

Robert said, "Guests piled into the pool, and a big wave dropped down on 'em."

"Where were they headed? Over to Will Rogers?" Across the canyon.

"Dunno yet. Look at that."

One, maybe two sets of footprints. Looked like one of the killers had slipped in the pool's deluge. Something else for the LAPD to take a look at.

Skirting the footprints, they followed that animal trail along the side of the canyon. Stayed with it until it merged into a hiking trail they both knew: the Sullivan Canyon Trail.

Erik asked, "Couple guys watch the party, get wet, hike up Sullivan Canyon at nine p.m.?"

"Looks that way."

"Why not park in the neighborhood?"

"Night of the party, we walked up here because of all the traffic. Neighborhood parking's mostly permit-only. A great place for the killers to get jammed up, maybe stopped by Brentwood Security."

"So they hike six miles up the trail up to Mulholland?"

"These guys are planners. Maybe hiking *away* from the neighborhood makes sense."

"Then let's hit it, man."

They started up the long trail up to Mulholland. A half mile in, they slowed at a set of stairs leading down to the canyon floor.

Robert asked, "Think all that Nazi LA folklore is true?"

"Hell yes."

Before World War II, a group of intellectuals bought eighty acres of the canyon below them and built an enclave. Middle of nowhere, even today, at one time even featuring a water tower. The plan supposedly was that once the Nazis took over America after the war, the ranch would've served as a Nazi headquarters.

Erik asked, "How'd that work out for you, Adolf?"

"Four miles to go. Want to keep talking, or pick up the pace?"

"Go for it."

For the next two miles, they jogged uphill, then slowed to a walk halfway to the top.

Robert said, "You're not gonna like this—after what she pulled off on the yacht last night, I had to give Gia my top investigator slot."

"Oh yeah? In the back seat last night, her head was clearly in your lap."

"You saying my decision was biased?"

"Sayin' you're a man, she's a woman, and my history on the case makes *me* top dog."

CHAPTER 42

Before noon, Chet found Dav's key under his doormat and slipped into Dav's apartment with Sonny. With Dav down at his complex's pool, they took their time looking around. A few pictures of young Dav with TV stars here and there, but nothing of interest until they came across Dav's expedited passport envelope.

Chet opened it, took out Dav's passport, and showed Sonny the passport photo.

"Remind you of someone you can't stand?"

"Not really, gimme me a hint."

"No hints. Where's the fun in that, Son?"

Truth was, Dav didn't remind Chet of anyone. With any luck, Sonny would sort through his catalog of hatred and resentment and come up with his own answer. Sometimes self-help worked better on Sonny. Made it less obvious what Chet was up to.

Down at the pool, Dav swam laps, his blender resting on a nearby table, plugged into a socket. Chet and Sonny walked through the pool gate. Chet opened Dav's sealed plastic container resting on a plastic table. Healthy fixin's: mangoes, blueberries, and an oddball fruit he'd seen in the store but couldn't name.

Sonny had already fixated on the pool's signage:

PERSONS HAVING CURRENTLY ACTIVE DIARRHEA OR WHO HAVE HAD ACTIVE DIARRHEA WITHIN THE PREVIOUS 14 DAYS SHALL NOT BE ALLOWED TO ENTER THE POOL WATER.

Chet wondered at this sign's message, too. You had a pool, then what? Check everybody's drawers for diarrhea? Say, "Give me your whereabouts and bowel movements for the last two weeks"? How was that supposed to work?

Dav made it to the end of the pool, threw his arm up onto the pool's coping, sucking wind.

"Hey," Chet said, holding up the mystery fruit. "What's this one called?"

"A pomegranate. I just washed it so . . ."

"Seeds on the inside?"

"Yeah?"

If Dav had any sense, he'd have noticed that he and Sonny vibed prison in their Triple Five Soul knockoff jeans and jackets.

Chet said, "Seeds on the inside, what's the point in washin' it?"

Without answering, Dav took off for a lap that would put him by the exit gate.

Chet had tossed Sonny the pomegranate.

"Before he runs off, get him to show you the seeds."

Sonny walked down to the far end of the pool. Dav had stopped swimming, blowing hard from another short lap. Sonny squatted in front of him and set his pomegranate on the coping.

Dav looked over at Chet. "What's going on? What's all this?"

"Ask him that's standing in front of you."

Sonny told Dav, "Know what? You remind me of somebody."

"Who?"

"If I told you, bro, where's the fun in that?"

He motioned Dav to lean toward him. When he did, Sonny slammed down his fist on the top of Dav's head. His chin smashed open the fruit and banged off the concrete, and blood gushed onto the brilliant purplish-pink pomegranate seeds.

Dav was whimpering by the time Chet winked at Sonny and said, "We better get Michael Phelps inside before he bleeds out."

❧

Once they wrangled Dav up to his apartment, he was compliant in full. They even let him get after his freezer vodka to cut through the pain. Then they sat him down and made Dav let them in on what he'd been doing with Reid and RJ on board that yacht.

Dav told them, "It's legal for Trevor to raise money, but I can lose my license if anybody ever filed a complaint."

Chet asked, "What you're doing, how's it illegal?"

Dav tried explaining, but whatever law Dav might've broken sounded like a technicality. Like a lawmaker had decided it might make them look good back home with the voters.

Chet asked, "Why the passport, Dav? What's cookin', my man?"

"Had plans to leave the country for a while."

Sonny asked, "With what to spend? Me and Chet have our stakes, but you look dog-ass broke."

"I do all right for myself."

"No, you don't, Dav Man," Chet said. "See, your shitbox here, it'd be cool just out of college—*hey, come on over, we got a pool at my place*. But your passport has you pushing fifty, and once upon a time, you were a young stud, had your picture taken with TV stars."

Sonny said, "Here you are driving a rusted-out Olds."

"Not anymore. I got rid of it."

Dav tried to shut down about what he had planned, but Sonny heel-stomped Dav's bare right foot and made it clear that clamming up wasn't going to fly.

So Dav puked up what he had in mind for screwing Trevor Reid.

Chet and Sonny liked Dav's whole plan, except for one thing.

"He's not asking Trevor for enough stacks, is he, Sonny?"

"Not near enough."

CHAPTER 43

In another hour, gassed from their uphill jog, Robert and Erik reached Mulholland Drive. Named after the engineer credited with bringing water from the Sierras to LA, this wasn't the movie-familiar road, paved and curving, where countless scenes had been shot, most recently in *Nightcrawler* and *La La Land*. This dirt-and-gravel fire road ran along the Santa Monica Mountains' spine for miles and miles after paved Mulholland ended east of here.

Robert and Erik split up looking for . . . they didn't know what. Ten minutes later, Erik's echoing *hallo* reached him.

When Robert caught up with him, Erik led Robert along a faint trail. Urine and reefer-smoke odor grew stronger with every step until they reached a clearing. Ten or so rambling millennials squatted here. Brush had been cleared, tarps hung between trees. A firepit centered the site. Worse-for-wear trail bikes and several Bird scooters leaned against trees.

Erik said, "This is Amabel. Been here about a month."

"Anabel?" Robert asked.

"Amabel," the girl said.

The least-stoned among them, a young woman with a shaved head. As Amabel walked them back to the road, she relayed what she'd told Erik—the night of Paul's party, she'd seen a vehicle hidden on Mulholland.

She said, "They parked off the road, and it was *way* after dark when they came back."

Robert asked, "That long ago? How do you remember that?"

Stoned as you are, he was thinking.

"Their headlights flashed on our camp, and we all started freaking out. Thought we were getting busted, till we figured out what they were up to."

"They?" Robert asked.

"Two guys in the front seat. Didn't look to me like fire department dudes."

Erik asked, "You mean fire marshals?"

"Dunno know if they's marshals or what. What the side of their car said they were, that's what I'm sayin.'"

"Their car had a . . ." Robert almost said *insignia*, decided against it. "The car had fire department markings on it?"

She nodded. "Two circles, the size of cantaloupes. Car was white, too."

Erik asked, "By car, you mean . . . ?"

"I mean a car-car, not an SUV car."

Robert said, "A sedan."

She nodded. "A white Taurus with the two cantaloupe-size circles on the doors."

"You sure it was a Taurus?"

"On the trunk of it?" She placed pointed fingers to each side of her head and wiggled them, like horns. "There was, like, a zodiac sign, like Taurus the bull."

"Why didn't they look like fire department dudes?" Robert asked.

"Guys wearing camo and ball caps?"

She shrugged. Robert gave her twenty dollars, and Amabel took them back to the clearing. They asked around about the two camo-wearing dudes and came up empty.

Huddled with Erik, Robert said, "Our two guys, wearing camo, drove a dummied-up fire marshal's car."

Erik nodded. "A white Taurus sedan, standard fire department issue, I think. But these fire trails get locked down tight at sunset."

They'd both seen the thick, round, yellow bars at the foot of their Topanga Fire Trail hike.

"So how the hell'd they drive a car out of here?"

One quick way to find out—they each downloaded the Bird app and commandeered two scooters from the campsite. The scooter's charges looked decent, and the millennials were cool with their taking them once Robert's fifty-dollar bill landed in their dope kitty.

Ten minutes later, they rolled east, past the intersecting West Mandeville Fire Road; another fifteen minutes put them at the trail head where Mulholland proper started.

That round, yellow swinging bar was open. Locking that hollow metal bar to the post was simple. Unlocking it, not as simple. Inside the hollow bar, two padlocks had locked the bar into place, and bolt cutters wouldn't fit inside the padlock aperture.

From the blackened, scorched metal, they could see that the killers had blowtorched both padlocks.

Robert said, "So they had a torch already in their car."

"Like you said, they're planners."

When they reached the big church on Mulholland proper, Robert caught a text from Lawan: Brentwood Security won't show me any surveillance info. Sorry.

Erik texted Uber while Robert called Anita Yates. Once she picked up, he told her he was on speaker with Erik; Reyes had told Anita that Erik was working his case.

Robert said, "We know a lot more that connects Trevor Reid to Paul's murder."

He told her about the two men watching the party, blowtorching the Mulholland barrier in a Taurus with a bogus fire marshal's insignia.

Anita said, "Need to see that drone tape, ASAP. I'll get some people moving to preserve the footprints, the squatter's testimony, and torched lock."

"Are we there yet?" Robert asked her.

"Enough to kick Mr. Reyes during his prelim? I doubt it. The DA basically just has to put a warm body in the defendant's chair. But we're closer than I ever thought possible to outright acquittal at trial."

"Erik here, Anita. Give your investigators a heads-up—the girl at the campsite is Amabel Gelman . . . that's right, *Amabel.* She may have warrants, so I'd get somebody up there before she bolts."

As their Uber pulled up, Robert said to Erik, "I want to find out why Lawan struck out with Brentwood Security. You still want to bird-dog Dav?"

"Think I'll show up at Boogies later today. Let's see how much Dav digs *that* coincidence."

CHAPTER 44

Inside the Museum of Ice Cream downtown, Sonny scowled at the art displays alongside their group tour. Chet liked the fake ice-cream cones, Popsicles stuck into walls, and ice-cream-sandwich swing set.

Good, clean fun, bright colors, happy people. And Sonny.

"What's the problem?" Chet asked, even though he already knew the answer.

"I thought they'd show us ice-cream-making machines, the history of ice cream, shit like that. Not plastic bananas hanging from the ceiling, giant gummies, and Good & Plenty tubs for lying down in."

"I see. You were expecting something like ice cream through the ages."

"Sure. Who wouldn't?"

Chet had deliberately misled Sonny about the museum's program to keep Sonny sour with fresh slices of anger and resentment.

"My bad, man. That website I read was flat-out wrong."

"We better get going before I say something to somebody."

Nobody needs to see that.

Outside, they headed toward their rooms.

"Dav Man," Sonny said. "Think he'll score tonight?"

"Believe so."

"Not gonna rabbit on us, is he?"

"Don't see how he can go anywhere serious with no passport or credit cards."

Those they'd taken, leaving Dav his driver's license in case he got pulled over. That and $100 should keep Dav in town until tonight.

Chet went over in his mind whom Dav might remind Sonny of, somebody already living on Sonny's shit list. A long list, but Chet still came up empty. Maybe it didn't matter. There were other things that could cause Sonny to turn on a dime.

Take Paul D. He'd surprised them—already dressed, coming down the stairs. Their masks not even pulled down yet. But there he'd stood in the hall, looking right at them in their jumpsuits and booties.

And boy, Sonny had lit him up fast with that baton. Paul D. went down fast and never moved a twitch after that. But Sonny had kept after him, and Chet had decided to let Sonny go on, making the overkill look more personal than what it was.

Not what the one who'd hired them had asked for, but Chet had cared more about misleading the cops than anything else. Besides, motive for killing Paul D. didn't matter anyway once that Latino pulled in the driveway, and he'd figured out how best to play out that lucky stroke.

On the sidewalk, Chet stopped, looked back at Sonny. Still stopped on the corner, looking down at the sidewalk.

Walking back to him, Chet wondered: Maybe he stepped in chewing gum and wanted to scrape it off without getting hemorrhagic fever.

"Remember Findley?" Sonny asked.

A guy Sonny'd met in prison. He'd insulted Sonny about those moles on his face, called him *Chocolate Chip*. Sonny had caught up with Findlay down the road and drowned him while he was filling up a kiddie pool in his backyard.

"Findley, sure do. How come?"

That's all Sonny had to say. But he saw what Sonny was driving at. Their boy, Dav, reminded Chet a little of Findley, too.

Sonny said, "We already made a deal with Dav about the money split. We gonna live up to it, or what?"

"Live up to it? C'mon, Son, stop kiddin' around."

CHAPTER 45

Lawan brought two espressos out to the Bronco from Brentwood Country Mart. Once they were headed over to Brentwood Security on Sunset, Lawan told Robert why the head of the company had stonewalled her.

"I told Ms. Lester who I was, what we wanted to see, but she'd already turned over everything the DA asked for. In her mind, that was the end of it."

Best he could recall from Reyes' file, Brentwood Security had furnished the DA with dashcam footage of the day before and the night of Paul's murder. That, plus the written logs covering the week leading up to the murder.

Nothing, though, for the day and night of the party.

"They tell you why you couldn't have a look?"

"Company policy in cases like this."

Cases like this? His pulse quickened with irritation.

He guessed that the security company wanted a subpoena from either the DA or Reyes' attorney. That way, the company was complying with a lawful court order, not simply disclosing unrelated, otherwise private, information from this neighborhood.

He understood its point of view—and would've advised his own client to do the same thing. But putting himself in Lawan's shoes, he thought the company's position was asinine.

They pulled up to a nondescript mall office off San Vicente Boulevard. Lawan pointed out a woman in her forties coming out of Dunkin' Donuts. Head high, erect posture, a no-nonsense haircut—he guessed either ex-military or ex-LAPD.

"That's her—Carla Lester."

"Let me see if I can shake something loose."

He caught Carla as she was about to open her Town Car's door.

"Ms. Lester, Robert Worth. I'm an attorney, a friend of the Dickerson family. Ms. Dickerson is in my car."

She shook Robert's hand; he led with an exaggeration.

"Ms. Dickerson is quite upset by what you told her earlier."

"Upset? Why?"

"For starters, she just lost her husband in, arguably, the safest neighborhood in LA. A quick word about what she needs, and I'll be on my way."

One look at his hiking attire, and she dismissed him with an eye roll.

"Told her my position already."

"Just take a minute, hear me out. I know you already cooperated with the DA, but what Ms. Dickerson wants to see involves neighborhood activity around their party."

"She asked already, and I already told her—"

"If you don't listen up, your company policy's about to get a ton of unwanted scrutiny."

"Doubtful," she said, crossing her arms.

He showed her his last incoming call: *Anita Yates*.

"She's the attorney for the man accused of killing Paul Dickerson, and right now she still has a choice. Either go wide with her subpoena of your security footage or go narrow. *Wide* might cover a month or two. *Narrow* might be you dealing with me. All I want is to take a look at your stops sandwiching the Dickerson party."

"Anybody can call the public defender's phone number. Nice try."

"Wake up, Ms. Lester. That call was incoming. Widow Dickerson, you'll be glad to know, hasn't said word one—*yet*—about how well your company did securing her neighborhood the night Paul was beaten to death."

He could see Carla giving in; she kept protesting out of habit.

"We followed every procedure correctly, and we stand by all of our actions."

Robert seriously doubted her company had any liability for Paul's death, but any prospect of a civil lawsuit was never welcome.

"Suit yourself," he said. "Brentwood Security's about to test-drive a saying I never believed."

"Being what?"

"That there's no such thing as bad publicity."

She chirp-locked her Town Car.

"Let's see what I can do."

⁊

The security company offices looked oddly elegant for a strip mall, probably decorated this way for Carla's upscale clientele. Robert and Lawan took seats in front of her desk; each of them grabbed a view of Carla's monitor.

Carla said, "We have dashcams, body cams, and mikes. These days we have to be so careful."

Robert said, "I know, lawyers. Who needs 'em?"

Carla glanced at him—not sure yet what to make of him.

"According to my summaries, the day of the party and the day after, we had a total of eight stops in Palisades Riviera." She showed them the log on her monitor; write-ups appeared for stops, numbered one through eight. "Three stops, I won't share with you without a subpoena. I will, however, reveal this much. Each stop involved the same neighborhood resident. On each stop, his vehicle was parked, its back door open, with two individuals in the back seat. Let your imagination run wild, and believe me, it would if I identified the men involved."

Someone famous, screwing in a back seat. But no fire marshal sedan yet like the one that had parked on Mulholland.

"Fair enough, let's see the other five stops."

The next two stops on the company dashcams hadn't involved Palisades Riviera–permitted vehicles. One a Nissan SUV, the other a Camaro. Smoke pouring from the Nissan's driver's window. Carla's officer approached the Nissan.

Carla said, "Given the volume of smoke, my officer assumed the driver was vaping pot. Turned out, he was vaping CBDs, which are legal."

CBDs—a nonintoxicating anti-inflammatory found in marijuana.

Carla said, "Same was true for the Camaro, but the passenger was smoking, not the driver. Moving on, unless you see something earth-shattering."

"Nothing yet," he said.

Next, a Flower's Flowers van had parked on the side of the road. The passenger's door was open. A man knelt on the sidewalk, coughing. A security officer pulled up behind the van and approached the driver's side.

Lawan said, "For our party, they made deliveries most of the day."

"We were well aware of them, Ms. Dickerson."

He couldn't put his finger on what bothered him about the van—he was still hoping to see a fire marshal sedan.

Carla moved on to a Toyota pickup with lawn mowers, weed trimmers, and garden hoses overflowing the bed and overhead rack.

"The last daytime stop before the party, this truck. Had a flat tire, put on its flashers."

"Wait. Let's take another look at the flower van."

Carla took them there; his problem with the van dawned on him.

He pointed at the two back windows and asked Lawan, "Those two windows? Remember the van we saw in your driveway?"

She nodded. "After going to court, the day we ran into Gretchen."

"That van had flowers and vines hand-painted onto both rear windows. Like they were a continuation of the vinyl flower arrangement on the back doors. But this van's rear windows are both clear, see-through."

"I remember. You're right."

On his phone, he found Flower's Flowers' website. He showed Lawan its photographs of the Flowers family and their fleet—every rear window they could see had those hand-painted rear windows. A distinctive, decorative add-on for their upscale clientele. Carla pulled up the website and took a closer look, too.

"Could we look at your officer's body cam for that stop?"

Into it now, Carla worked her keyboard. As her officer approached the van's driver's-side window, the driver rested his elbow on the window frame, his hand gripping the doorframe above. The body cam moved closer with her officer.

The van driver wore a cap and dark glasses and gave the officer—from what little they could see—a smile. His arm, plus his cap and shades, blocked his face almost entirely.

Officer: "Everything okay here?"

Driver: "Except for his allergies, Officer. Is it ragweed season or what?"

Officer: "When the wind picks up, it'll blow pollen off these mountains, even off the desert."

The passenger climbed back in the van; his face not discernible in the shadows. The driver turned away from the camera and looked at the passenger.

Driver: "You done with all that?"

The passenger nodded.

Officer: "Headed up to the Dickersons'?"

Driver: "On our way."

Officer: "All right, then, have a good one."

Driver: "You too, Officer."

Carla said, "Dammit. No facial ID on either of them."
Lawan said, "I think I saw—"
He stopped her. "That's okay, Ms. Dickerson. I think we have what we need."
The remaining stops were nonevents. Once Anita called Carla from downtown, Carla agreed to furnish everything the company had on or near the party date and to look through her database for a shot of the van's occupants. A love-in by the time the call ended, and Anita seemed to be her sedate version of thrilled.
Outside in the Bronco, Lawan asked him, "What do you think?"
"The driver's arm blocking the camera? I don't think that was random. The driver knew what he was doing."
"You think he was a security guard?"
"Or a cop, or . . . I don't know. He wasn't carrying a baton, so . . . ?" He shrugged. "Sorry about stopping you inside. It's not a good idea to speak freely about a case."
"I understand. What I remembered, those two men in the van made the last delivery. I let them in the front door. It was a very busy time, caterers everywhere, gardeners misting orchids, Jerry's barbecue pit outside, a liquor-store delivery, house cleaners."
"And after you let them in?" he asked, his pulse quickening with the question.

"Yes, they each brought in a potted Royal Thai orchid, saying it was a gift from the owners for all the business we'd given them. And the one, he sneezed, same as on Brentwood's tape. We went back to the kitchen, put the orchids on the counter, and then . . . I don't know. Something came up, I can't remember . . . and I told them to . . . I don't really remember."

"Can you recall what they looked like?"

"Vaguely. Not large for *farang*." For Americans. "One was white, very white."

"Pale?"

"Pale, yes, and quite thin, the one who sneezed. The other was dark, maybe Latino, or Asian. Maybe both. Much darker than the sneezer. Oh, and the sneezer, his face had . . . not freckles . . ."

"Acne?"

"No, a funny word. In English, the same as a small burrowing animal."

"Moles? He had moles on his face?"

She nodded. "Not disfigured, but you'd notice if you met him. So many people came in and out of the house at that point, I thought the party would be a big mess. Then Paul showed up and smoothed everything out. At least, he made it seem that way."

When she mentioned Paul, he wanted to comfort her, but her loss called for more than bromides—and bromides were all he had to offer.

"So they could've been in your home another minute or another . . . ?"

She shrugged. "A half hour more, I wouldn't have noticed. Who are they?"

"They were part of a plan to kill Paul."

"Hired by Trevor Reid?"

"Had to be."

On his drive back to Ozone from downtown, Robert called Jerry Baugh and left *another* message about getting together. More to prey on Jerry's mind—hoping that he might rile up Trevor off the text—than to actually meet again.

As he pulled onto Neilson Way, Erik touched base about their favorite broker, Dav Concha.

"Today, the guy doesn't show at work—*or at Boogies*," Erik said.

"Missed Boogies? That's big."

"Something's up with the Dav Man. Bartender Steve—no fan of Dav's—tells me he's run up a six-hundred-dollar tab. I got his address from Steve, might snoop around his place."

He told Erik about the Brentwood Security tapes, the Flower's Flowers van, and Lawan's recollections of the two men.

"Day of the party, our two guys delivered orchids to the house in what had to be a bogus van. By eight o'clock that night, they'd switched to the fire marshal Taurus, parked it on Mulholland, and hiked down to surveil the party."

Erik added, "After getting soaked underneath the pool, they hiked up and drove out Mulholland in the Taurus. Jesus, these guys don't mind doing prep work."

"Big *huevos*, too, going inside with flowers. That's when they could've picked up the alarm code."

They noodled through that idea. The code had been written down on the pantry wall. Even though the killers hadn't needed the alarm, this piece of the puzzle fleshed out his theory of the murder—that the killers showed up at the kitchen door with an alarm code that they hadn't needed.

They wondered about how the killers went about altering the Taurus and the van.

Erik said, "Easiest way these days is having 'em vinyl-wrapped."

He agreed. "Easy on, easy off. Except for the van's hand-painted back windows. Had to be that the killers were thinking: 'What kind of person would ever notice something minor like that?'"

CHAPTER 46

The next day, Robert headed to the Valley on a whim, an impromptu visit to Jerry's home. His approach: keep the conversation casual at first. Pretend like he hadn't already left Jerry a message with all his wild questions. Ask good-guy Jerry about buying some Cannonball BBQ Sauce, tell him how much he liked Daisy's logo.

After that, he'd try to get Jerry to stir the Trevor pot again. Tell Jerry that every single piece of evidence he'd discovered pointed toward an innocent man being in prison—and toward Trevor being behind Paul's murder.

Driving past the Getty Museum again—it hadn't gone anywhere—he realized he'd driven to the San Fernando Valley twice in one week. A personal best or worst, depending on how you viewed the Valley.

Jerry lived on Edgewood Avenue in Reseda, a bedroom community ten miles shy of Calabasas, home of Justin Bieber, a slew of Kardashians, J. Lo., Drake, and other celebs who craved total privacy one day, worldwide publicity the next.

Once he exited the 101 onto Van Owen Avenue, Jerry's house wasn't far. On Edgewood Avenue, tall trees loomed over stucco and board-and-batten ranch houses; owners parked on the street or in attached garages. An oasis of peace and quiet, ideal for garage sales, lemonade stands, and high school car washes.

Two long blocks ahead, a low-slung red sports car roared toward him.

On this street? What an a-hole.

The car hogged the middle of Edgewood, so Robert pulled to the curb.

To his surprise, the car braked to an abrupt stop one block ahead. The driver got out. Checking addresses as he started driving again, Robert saw that Jerry's house would still be two blocks ahead of him. He passed the sports car—a Maserati—and glanced over.

Trevor Reid stood in a front yard, screaming at Jerry's ex-wife, Kay. A girl in her early teens dropped her golf bag and ran inside the house.

Robert was confused—did he have the wrong address for Jerry? Did Jerry and Kay still live together? He pulled over to see if the situation would escalate. Once Kay spoke to Trevor, it did. He could hear Trevor yelling through his closed windows and jumped out.

As he drew nearer, Trevor screamed at Kay, "Next time you see Jerry, tell him he better keep his mouth shut about the fund's investments!"

"Hey!" Robert yelled, closing fast.

Kay kept backing away. Trevor still berated her, his fists balled. That brand of anger—Robert had seen it on the boardwalk. Insane rage, and you never knew how far it could go.

"Trevor!" he shouted. "Back off, goddamn it!"

Kay pointed at Robert. "Trevor! Look behind you! Get out of my yard!"

Trevor whirled, saw Robert. He leaned down and grabbed a driver from that golf bag.

"You dick, Worth! I'm gonna kill you!"

Really? Robert had seventy-five pounds and six inches on the guy, but rational Trevor wasn't at home, and here he came. Trevor liked long-distance running, didn't he? Robert doubted that he was a close-combat expert.

His hands up, palms out, Robert stood his ground.

"Trevor, just stop, man. Calm down!"

Trevor kept coming. One of two things had to happen next—Trevor swinging the driver like a baseball bat, or raising it overhead and swinging down. Trevor picked door number two. Once Robert saw the club's head going for the sky, he stepped close and stuck a hard left jab into Trevor's pointed nose, ready to double up if the insanity stayed at this pitch.

It didn't. Trevor's nose started bleeding. With most people, the sight of their own blood brought them back to reality. The club fell from Trevor's hands.

Robert didn't care—he popped Trevor's nose again on general principles, and it gushed more blood.

He scolded himself for how much he loved that sight. Trevor bent over, trying and failing to keep blood from staining his suit. Grabbing Trevor's lapels, Robert slung him back toward his car. Trevor stumbled and hit the lawn on his ass.

Kay yelled, "Out of my yard, Trevor! Or I'm calling the police!"

Robert said, "Better do it, big man, or she'll whip your ass next."

Trevor stood up. "Why're you in my business, Worth? You have no business with me or with my company. Leave me the fuck alone!"

"You're talking nonsense, Trevor. Get lost."

"Go away!"

Those words from Daisy Baugh, inside her mother's front door. Kay went to her daughter and held her until Robert made sure Trevor had driven away.

An Uber stopped in front of the house.

Kay told Daisy, "Everything's okay now, Daze. Please thank Mr. Worth, and make sure to apologize for being late for your golf lesson."

Daisy picked up all the clubs and thanked Robert for helping out. A well-mannered girl, good-looking like her parents, and still a little shaken.

Once Daisy rode away, Kay said, "What the hell? I don't know how to thank you."

"Not a problem. Do I have the wrong address for Jerry?"

253

"No, he's two more blocks down Edgewood, same way you're headed. If he's home, he might be in his shop. If not, the office might've badgered him into going to Hollywood about those access cards."

Postdivorce, the couple lived on the same street. He realized that his divorced parents had done much the same thing—minus the goodwill that existed between Jerry and Kay.

Kay thought of something. "Know what, Robert? I *do* know how to thank you. I'll tell you about Marguerite."

"The fund?"

"No, the woman. Or as those who knew her liked to call her, *that bitch Marguerite.*"

❧

On Kay's rear deck, Robert worked on a tall glass of iced tea; inside, Kay looked for her wedding album. Behind him, he heard the soft gurgle of the Aliso Canyon Wash.

He already tried to persuade Kay to file an incident report, but she'd declined. Even so, he knew that, when and if needed, Kay could be subpoenaed to describe Trevor's rage today.

She set the album in front of him alongside a well-worn manila envelope. Even though Jerry had been Trevor's best man at Trevor's wedding, she didn't take him on a gauzy trip down memory lane.

"See this one? Trevor and Marguerite's wedding day."

Similar if not identical to the wedding shot on the film office's stairs. This one: an eight-by-ten: Trevor, Marguerite, Jerry, and Kay, left to right. All posed in formal wear, the placid Pacific Ocean behind them.

"Was the wedding at Rain Dunes?" he asked. The Malibu house Trevor had recently sold.

She nodded. "Uranium, right? Great view, stupid name. Beside Trevor, that's Miss Thing."

Everything about Marguerite caught his eye—dark, wavy hair, tall with a slender body, full lips, part Spanish, part French, he guessed.

"To her face, I liked calling her *Madge* or *Maggie*."

"How'd she like that?"

"About as much as she liked me. All four of us went to college together. Jerry was a stud, even back then. Trevor didn't have a pot to piss in yet, but it was clearer every day he was gonna do well. I was considered . . ." She shrugged.

"Great-looking? Stunning?"

"Aww, let's leave it at hot, but Marguerite had that European accent, exotic looks, descended from nobility—*she said*—and was the ultimate prize. Can I still say that?"

"I know what you mean."

"Know when Jerry met her?"

He shook his head.

"March third. Let me back up—Jerry met her before Trevor did, and dated her for a while. Then she realized that Trevor was all about money, and really, who was Jerry? A former football star, popular as could be, the one everybody liked."

"I can still see that."

"I always saw it and fell in love with him instantly. But Marguerite . . . ?"

"That bitch?"

"She wouldn't let Jerry go. Not that she wanted him—or that they were even lovers. She wanted him in her quiver. Like a butler or a valet so Jerry would always hop to when she wanted something. Ever hear of Prison Max?"

A publicly traded company. It ran private prisons in several states, including California.

"I think Trevor mentioned that company at Paul's party."

"Giving Jerry a hard time about the fund's investment in it?"

"A very hard time."

"Jerry always felt slighted, belittled by Trevor, and wanted to make his own investment pick. To prove himself to Madame, I always thought. So he spent close to six months, back and forth to Kern County, researching that private prison. On Jerry's recommendation, Trevor's fund invested millions of dollars up there, and you know the rest."

"That was the last time Trevor let Jerry pick an investment?"

"Yes, and Trevor likes to tell anybody who'll listen."

"Preferably in front of Jerry."

"Exactly. Know when Jerry first met Marguerite?"

"March third, you said."

"March third at three p.m. Are you seeing it yet?"

A moment later, he did.

"Third day of the third month at three o'clock? Three thirty-three, like Trevor's hedge fund."

"The two lovebirds came up with the numbers."

Lovebirds? Jerry and Marguerite.

"Marguerite sold Trevor on the name—some mystic bullshit, a good-luck number from Asia. And after all, Marguerite had her heart set on it."

"How'd you find out where the numbers originated?"

"At a class reunion. *She told me.*"

"She what?"

"Oh yeah, she got off on telling me. 'It was the date and time I first met sweet, sweet Jerry.' She knew I wouldn't tell Trevor because Jerry worked for him. She'd deny it anyway, so what was the point?"

"Wow." That wasn't enough. So he added, "Damn."

"Next time I saw Marguerite, I was with Daze, and she had the balls to bribe our daughter."

"With what?"

"Anything Jerry and I couldn't afford. Daze told me, 'I don't like Marguerite.' I said, 'You don't have to like everybody.' Marguerite even

256

tried calling Daze at home, before kids had cell phones. That end run wasn't going to work. Ha!"

"Helluva a lot to deal with."

"Think so? Know what *marguerite* means in French?" Before he could say *no*: "It means *daisy*. I didn't find out till years after Jerry and I—only Jerry, now that I look back on it—named our girl."

Daze to her mother, *Daisy* to her father.

"That's why you call her *Daze*?"

She nodded. "Trying to put the origin out of my mind. I mean, she's my daughter, and I couldn't love her any more than I do."

She nodded again. "Want to know why Jerry and I are divorced?"

She showed him another photograph from the manila envelope; its subject matter embarrassed him to look at.

"Jerry hid this shot from me. When I found it four years ago, he told me it was a gag, that he'd forgotten about it. It wasn't a gag."

Another eight-by-ten: Rains Dunes' lawn the day of the wedding: Jerry in a tux, Marguerite in her wedding gown, the pair standing arm in arm.

Just the two of them. Heads touching. As if the wedding had been theirs.

"*That's* why I divorced Jerry. The final straw, it's called."

Her face flushed; she stood. So did Robert. He didn't know what to say next. She did.

"Want to come inside and start some trouble?"

She'd had a world-class terrible day; he tried reaching for humor.

"Better not. My girl planted some kind of fidelity chip on me."

"Got it."

She stared down at the damning photograph.

"Why couldn't they just act like normal people and screw each other behind my back?"

CHAPTER 47

Jerry's ranch house layout was the mirror image of Kay's. From the driveway, Robert saw the fierce glow of an arc-welding torch through Jerry's garage-door window.

The front screen door was open; Robert walked through it. He took his time making his way to the kitchen, where another door surely opened into a laundry room or directly into the garage.

Nothing of interest caught his eye in the living room or the kitchen; he stepped through the interior garage door.

Ahead of him in the dark, Jerry worked in a welder's mask, arc-welding metal to metal, the flame a brilliant golden blue.

Jerry didn't notice him; Robert waved his arms.

"Jerry? Yo, Jerry!"

Jerry saw him, cut the torch's power, and flipped up his mask. The room went totally dark; Robert's pupils dilated, his vision spotted from exposure to the torch's blaze.

"What are you doing in my garage?"

"Door was open, you didn't return my calls, and—"

"What's eating you, digging into things that don't matter—why!"

Jerry's dim form started coming at him. Not a raging runt like Trevor—this was six four, 220, of in-shape, ex–college jock. Great hand-to-eye, knew his shop's layout, rightly pissed off enough to do damage if he managed to lay those big hands on Robert.

Robert kept backing up, blinking his eyes to regain his vision. His heel caught a power cord taped to the floor. He stumbled, recovered. Jerry was still drawing closer when Robert's hand gripped a table behind him.

Grasping for a weapon, he found something heavy. Felt like a wrench.

A weapon? What are you doing? You're trespassing in this man's house! Get outta here!

"Jerry! I'm leaving! Okay? I'm gone!"

He dropped the wrench, raised his hands, and groped his way back toward the kitchen door. Thanks to a minute slice of kitchen light, he made out a button near the doorjamb. Lunged for it and hit it. The garage door creaked open, a burst of daylight spilling onto both men.

The violent charge left the room. Jerry's hands came down.

"Trevor's just been out here, chewing my ass about a goddamn dog collar. His yacht? What's wrong with you?"

"I told you—"

"Your friend's in jail? Not my problem. I don't know him, and I don't care. Sending your girlfriend onto Trevor's boat with RJ? Leave me out of it! All of it!"

Robert started tossing out ideas to see what might get traction.

"My problem—Trevor is still raising money for Three Thirty-Three and lying about it."

"The fund's closed to new money."

"Guess Trevor kept you out of the loop once you were leaving. What else didn't he tell you?"

Jerry motioned him outside, into the light of day.

"C'mon, move it. Outta my garage."

Robert went along but kept spitballing.

"Is the fund's biggest position still palladium?"

Jerry didn't answer; he stopped walking, looked at Robert.

"Still keeping it all down at Prestige?" Robert asked. "They had a break-in; you might want to tell Trevor to look into it. Oh, wait, that's beneath him. He's a visionary."

Jerry looked exhausted, almost gray.

"All I care about is my family's Cadillac medical, my payout, and the NDA I signed with the fund. Whatever you're fishing for, you won't catch it here. Get in your car, and get gone."

Robert headed for his car. "Might want to check on Kay. Your pal Trevor just went off on her."

As Robert got behind his wheel, Jerry's garage door started closing. Pulling away, he saw Jerry in his rearview, jogging up Edgewood toward Kay's house.

He liked both of them. Could be all the compressed violence he'd just experienced, but he felt a little sick. Somehow, interfering with these lives on Edgewood Avenue saddened him.

❧

When traffic on the 405 snarled into a sea of pulsing red-and-white brake lights, Robert had plenty of time to think.

Exotic Euro-bitch Marguerite first came to mind. From what Kay had said, that other woman lacked the traits he'd witnessed in sociopaths he'd encountered in the past. Not that Marguerite was normal. She qualified as a resource the world would never deplete: jerks, jackasses, bitches, and douchebags.

So Trevor had won the prized Marguerite and married her, but Jerry still loved her, and Kay had always felt like a consolation prize. She still loved Jerry, who loved a dead woman, who, like Trevor, had never loved anyone.

A real circle of trust.

Just then, Gia called him.

She said, "This is Deputy Marquez. I've had complaints about *Robert Logan Worth*. Hear he's been a very bad boy."

"Hey, Marquez, did you know the Valley's where all the LA weirdness really goes down?"

"Not the boardwalk?"

"No, you *expect* weirdness on the boardwalk."

He told her what had happened with Trevor, Kay, and Jerry. Kay hitting on him didn't make the cut.

"Could we have some *normal* tonight?" he asked.

"Normal with my number-one guy? Sounds about right."

CHAPTER 48

The next day, Robert met Anita downtown at the criminal court building—CCB, to insiders like him. They headed over to Tower One, across the fringes of Chinatown, and met Reyes in a visiting room.

Reyes nodded through the update on what they'd learned, and particularly liked that the drone had discovered the two men watching Paul's house that night.

"What'd I tell you about the Beach Lawyer, Anita?"

"He's got a future with my office—as an investigator."

Reyes said, "That dummied-up fire marshal ride, tell me how you see that workin'."

"Normally," Anita said, "no one pays attention to a city vehicle—they're too common in LA."

Reyes said, "Makin' 'em smart for goin' that way."

"Yes, but we're looking into something else. We've had reports from your neighborhood that a fire marshal's sedan was cruising your street in East LA not long before the baton was planted on the porch."

"Kinda grabs you with both hands, don't it?" Reyes asked.

"You could say that," Anita said. "We were already in touch with the fire department to rule out their people having overnight business up on Mulholland. Just as important, we'll ask whether any fire marshals had business on your street. If not, even more pluses will go into your column."

"*Pluses* like springing my ass at the prelim, or like I'm buying tickets for Super Bowl Seventy-Five?"

Robert helped her out. "That's a couple decades from now."

Anita said, "My best guess? Pluses that put you somewhere between the two. Like I told you, the prelim is the DA's playpen. He need only show that it's more likely than not Mr. Dickerson was murdered and that you killed him. The DA can still put you at the residence near the time of his murder, middle of the night. He'll come up with a reason you two argued, and we'll defend against that. Now, at trial, reasonable doubt will come into play."

She looked at Robert. "You know most of what I know. What are his chances at trial?"

On the spot. He looked at Reyes. Knowing for a fact that he was innocent made the question even harder to answer.

Reyes said, "C'mon, *Roberto*, grip it and rip it."

He gave it some thought. "Okay. Take the drone footage of the two guys watching Paul's, their bogus fire marshal sedan, and the flower van. Now, put both guys inside the house with Lawan making a fake flower delivery. I think that at trial, those items alone will definitely create reasonable doubt for a jury."

Reyes asked, "Reasonable doubt out that ass. Right, Ms. Yates?"

"*Out that ass*, in my opinion, too," she said, with that soft accent of hers. She asked Robert, "And at my client's prelim?"

Robert said, "For Reyes to get kicked at prelim, I think Anita would need to connect the two guys to Trevor Reid in a concrete way. I mean, we have our theory about *why* Trevor Reid wanted Paul out of the way, and it holds water, for the most part. But actually showing a link between the two men and Trevor Reid—proving the link—that would put you on the street again after your prelim. In my opinion."

Anita said, "That's as good a take as mine."

Reyes said, "Then, shit, *amigo*. If I'm gonna get sprung at the prelim', you best get crackin'."

CHAPTER 49

Rather than get crackin', Robert called Gia on his way home from Tower One. Tonight, they decided, they'd follow their normal-night menu. Go for a swim, eat a casual dinner near home, and try their hand at baby-making.

"The fog's rolling in," she said. "When you get home, let's open the windows."

They did that sometimes, letting the fog float inside their candlelit Ozone pad. Their normal menu started to fray when he hit a traffic snarl and grabbed a new call from Erik.

After he told Erik that he was roadkill on the I-10, Erik said, "The jammed 405 yesterday, the jammed 10 today. Aren't you something?"

"Yeah, living the dream."

"Dav, Dav, Dav. Where do I start with the Dav report?"

"I'm not going anywhere."

"Well, what I'm thinking is, Dav's getting ready to split town."

"Did he happen to tell you when?"

"In a way, yeah. First off, he sold his Olds and bought a 2013 Camry."

"Check."

"A couple hours ago, he dropped off a mountain of dry cleaning. Looked like a year's worth."

"Half check."

"I hear you, so how's this for a full check? Nosing around the complex, I find out Dav's apartment's coming up for renewal next month. And he's not renewing."

"After how long?"

"Twelve years."

"Double check."

"I ran across some of Dav's mail from the Department of State—US passport office. Unless Dav's working deep, deep undercover, they just mailed him a new passport."

"By *ran across*, you mean?"

"Old school, Beach. I went through his trash bags."

"Then leaving town makes Dav's big bar tab a nonissue to him."

"Way I see it, too. Then there's Dav's trip to Triple A. I saw him grab a few road maps, all for Baja Peninsula; then he talked to one of their reps."

"Dav didn't see you?"

"Couldn't see me unless he spotted me first, and he didn't."

"Think he's driving his Camry down to Cabo San Lucas or what?" The southern tip of Baja Peninsula.

"I see him more headed to Loreto or San Jose del Cabo on the Sea of Cortez."

"Cheaper than Cabo San Lucas, that's for sure," Robert said. "He doesn't need a passport for a short visit. But for an extended stay, he'd be an idiot to go without one."

"Sooner than later, Dav's gonna be gone for good, but he's gotta be hurting for money. Even in Mexico, a guy his age needs quite a stash to call it quits and kick back for the duration."

"Then there's those two FINRA beefs. Lawyer's fees and fines would've dinged him pretty good."

Erik asked, "How much you figure Dav's made on the side, raising money for Trevor?"

"Hard to say. If Trevor raised ten million and Dav caught five percent of it—that's half a million. If he caught ten percent, that's a million. Did he pay taxes on it? Let's say yes."

"So, you don't know."

"No idea, I'm just trying to sound smart. But I buy your theory big-time—Dav's not long for LA."

"I'll keep an eye on him tonight; tomorrow he's yours. Before long, though, I bet he makes a run for the Mexican border."

"Like they do in the movies."

CHAPTER 50

A little after nine that night, Robert and Gia finished their meal at James' Beach on North Venice Boulevard. They'd just asked for the dessert menu when Erik texted him: Call me, ASAP!

Robert called him back, put him on speaker for Gia; Erik started talking right away.

"Gotta go home, family crisis."

Gia asked, "Priya and the boys okay?"

"Hell no. Ducky Joe's gone MIA. Somebody left the top off his pen and, you know, predators."

"Okay, so tomorrow, I'll take over with Dav and—"

"No, not tomorrow. Right now."

Robert signaled for the check.

Erik told them, "Last hour or so, Dav's been yakking like a crack-head on a small, cheap cell phone—not his iPhone. Incoming, outgoing, pacing on his two-foot-wide balcony, biting his nails, hoovering Camels—and still not drinking, far as I can tell."

"So, we'll drive over there and—"

"Hold up, he's in the parking lot, walking toward the gate, still blabbin' on that burner."

Robert slapped down two hundreds and headed out the front door of James' Beach with Gia. "On our way."

Erik said, "Okay, good. Wait! There's Dav's Uber. First time in a decade, he's sober. *Now* he calls Uber?"

Outside James' Beach, a heavy fog had rolled in and kept rolling. Robert and Gia jumped in the Bronco and took off on Venice South, headed inland. A few miles more on Venice, they'd be close to Dav's complex.

Robert told Erik, still on the line: "We're headed your way."

"I'm on him, and he's . . . Let's see . . . his Uber's turning onto Venice. Now he's headed *your* way."

A few blocks after the Bronco cleared Lincoln Boulevard—a mile and a quarter from the Pacific—the fog lay behind them.

Erik on the phone: "He's still rolling toward you on Venice. You'd better turn around and wait for him."

Robert wheeled the Bronco to Venice North, facing the way he'd come. Gia climbed in the back seat and rolled down the window behind him. On her knees, she scoped out traffic coming their way.

Robert asked Erik, "What's the make of the Uber?"

"Hard to believe—a silver Prius." Like every third Uber in LA.

"Don't worry about bugging out on me, *Oso*, Gia's taking over the case now."

Baiting the bear. Robert held up the phone, so Gia and Erik could do their thing.

Erik said, "Gia? If she's in the mix, let me be clear on this. Dav's *my* find, not hers. And after you two follow him and bust open this case, Dav goes in my column, not Gia's."

Gia said, "Got two words for you, *Oso. Stakeout sex.*"

Erik groaned.

Looking in his rearview, Robert said, "Is that Dav's Uber coming?"

Gia said, "Yep, I can see the Beast behind it."

Erik said, "See you then. I'm peeling off."

Once Dav's Uber passed, they followed the Prius' taillights toward the beach, back into the wet, quieting quilt of fog.

Ten minutes later, at the far end of Marina Peninsula, Robert was idling beside a deserted, fogged-over construction site. He watched Dav's ride stop on Speedway, fifty yards ahead. Dav got out, and the Prius drove away.

Dav stood alone, his fog-bleared image lit by a single streetlight.

Gia asked, "So stakeout sex is . . . ?"

"On hold."

Dav raised that burner phone Erik mentioned, spoke to someone, and moved toward the beach. At that point, a condominium building blocked him.

Gia asked, "He's meeting somebody, right?"

"Has to be."

Dav had just taken one of the pedestrian-only streets that ended at a sidewalk paralleling the beach. After the beach sidewalk, only the hyperdark sand and ocean. He'd come here to meet someone either on the beach or in a condo off the beach sidewalk.

"Gonna see what's up," he said, opening the door.

Gia got behind the wheel. "Anyone who shows up, I'll get their license plate, take a picture."

He ran toward the street Dav had just taken. Before rounding the corner, he peered around the building. Dav had moved on. Robert ran to the beach sidewalk and caught Dav walking toward the wide North Channel between Playa Del Rey and Marina Del Rey.

Other than the occasional dog walker, this area was deserted this time of night. With the fog, even more so. Many of these condos were unused second homes, so he eased onto the sand, away from what little light those condos threw off.

With the fog working in his favor, he began tracking Dav.

Two blocks later, the beach sidewalk ended at the North Channel. Dav took a ninety-degree turn toward the ocean. The jetty sidewalk put him on course for the North Jetty. A 400-yard straight shot—channel to your left, sand to your right—until the jetty sidewalk ended.

An isolated meeting place if you didn't mind the gull guano littering the dark-gray granite foundation.

He knelt until Dav was fifty yards out on the jetty sidewalk, then dashed toward the channel and wound up behind him. Not too far behind, he guessed—Dav had disappeared in the thickening fog.

Walking the jetty sidewalk, he stopped. Looked behind him. Far as he could see, no one was tracking him.

Another hundred yards out on that sidewalk, he realized he risked running up on Dav.

Just then his peripheral vision caught movement: Dav on a narrow sidewalk perpendicular to this one. Robert recalled an under-the-sand public restroom at the narrow walkway's end. Dav disappeared down it.

Rather than follow Dav, he decided to circle around. To make a beach run for the spot behind those sunken restrooms. From that vantage point, he'd be looking down into the underground stairwell.

As he was about to make his dash, a solitary male figure wearing a hoodie jogged from the ocean toward the restrooms. Robert knelt, froze, and watched the figure, who wore a backpack.

A short adult male. A delivery or an exchange about to happen, he guessed. And he guessed, too, given the man's stature, he was looking at Trevor Reid.

Trevor disappeared from Robert's view as Trevor closed on the bathrooms. That gave Robert an opening, and he took off running for that vantage point overlooking the stairs. Digging through the sand, he'd made it halfway when Trevor emerged up the men's-room stairs, his backpack gone.

Robert dove belly-down on the sand; Trevor started jogging back toward the ocean.

Not sure about service out here, he texted Gia: Trevor leaving. Jogged from ocean. Parked where? Pier?

He took off again, made it another forty yards, then saw two men and went belly-down again. They'd taken up the same position he'd wanted for himself. At a railing, with a view into the stairwells.

They leaned over the railing, talking to someone below. Ten seconds later, Dav joined them with Trevor's backpack, and the trio high-fived each other.

Two men had killed Paul. Why were these two here? With Dav?

Dav tossed the taller man a cell phone—probably that burner he'd been using earlier. The man crushed it underfoot against concrete, fished through the remnants.

For the phone's chip, he guessed.

Dav slipped off the backpack, knelt, and unzipped it on the sand. All three checked out the contents, shared a good laugh about it.

Dav stood. The taller of the other two—the one with facial moles?—slipped an arm around Dav's shoulder. Said something that made Dav laugh.

Then it happened—the taller man's arm snaked around Dav's neck. He mounted Dav's back, wrapping his legs tight around Dav's torso. Pulling Dav's head back, his legs locked in place, the man took Dav to the ground. With Dav locked in, he was choking Dav to death.

The other man zipped up the backpack, slung it over a shoulder, and watched his partner. Looked like the two killers talked to each other all the while.

When Robert couldn't stand the sight anymore, he stood up, and shouted, "Hey! Hey! Hey!"

The one standing looked over. Robert knew he'd be a dim figure, same as they were to him.

He yelled again, "Let go of him!"

271

The one standing reached inside his jacket—Robert knew a pistol came next. He took off running as fast as he ever had. Keeping to the darkest spots, he decided to make tracks back to the Bronco.

Reaching the beach sidewalk, he sprinted back the way he'd come. At the pedestrian street Dav had first taken, he rounded the corner on the fly, slipped on a patch of sand, and went down hard. Back on his feet fast, he made out the gunman in the mist, headed his way. A good runner, long strides. And fast. The other man must've stayed behind, finishing off Dav.

At Speedway, Robert looked for Gia. The Bronco, gone. She must've gone after Trevor. Out of harm's way. Good.

He started down Speedway, back toward the channel where Pacific bent around the end of Grand Canal. Forget that. He headed in the opposite direction. Toward Washington Boulevard. Toward cars and people and lights.

Halfway to Washington, a stroke of luck: a lit-up townhouse to his left. On the second floor, through a floor-to-ceiling window, he saw people milling around, heard music pulsing, a party in progress.

Bounding up twenty-two exterior stairs, he made it to a second-story door. Banging on it, he shouted, "Let me in, please!"

An eyeball at the peephole. A female voice. "What's up?"

"Let me in. I'm in trouble and—"

"Hold on, I'll find Alfred."

He peered around a corner of this stairwell, back the way he'd just come. Out on Speedway, the gunman had already stopped. Must've seen these same lights—he looked right at Robert, headed his way. Another ten seconds or so, and the guy would reach the bottom of these stairs.

Robert: lit-up and defenseless.

A male voice behind the door asked, "What's the problem?"

No time to negotiate entry with Alfred. "Call the cops!" he yelled.

Instead of taking the stairs down, he leaped from the landing into darkness. When he hit the ground, his right ankle gave way. He'd felt worse sprains, but a bolt of pain shot to his brain. Outrunning his pursuer might've just been scraped off the table.

He scrambled alongside the townhouse—into darkness and fog, thank God—and made it to a back alley.

Across Pacific Avenue lay Grand Canal with its steep-sloped, overgrown, thirty-foot banks.

He made it across Pacific to the dirt trail paralleling the canal. No one yet visible behind him. A quick hop over the split-rail fence, and he'd be history to anyone but a bloodhound.

Grabbing the top rail, he stopped.

"Shit!"

The canal bank had been clear cut. Making that jump would put him out in the open or in tide-shallow canal water. Take your pick—both could be death traps.

He hobbled farther up the dirt trail, wondering where the gunman had gone. Fifty yards ahead, the pedestrians-only Lighthouse Bridge, deserted, like the peninsula's walking streets.

The bridge's middle arch spanned the 150-foot canal; a quarter arch at either end anchored the bridge to the ground.

Underneath that closest quarter arch lay a shroud of total darkness, and with any luck, the usual homeless camp. Witnesses. People to raise hell and, for a few bucks, to make tons of noise.

Behind him, a single car headed his way. Three hundred yards back down Pacific, creeping along behind fog lights. Hobbling again, faster, in more pain, he pictured two men inside. Each one scoping out his own side of Pacific Avenue.

Robert made it to the bridge, sat on the bank. He zipped three quick texts to Gia. Skidded on his ass down the steep bank to the bridge's base and crept underneath the first arch. No humans in sight, but they'd left behind an eclectic assortment of trash, waste, and a busted-up shopping cart.

He sat down, his back to the arch, tried calling 911, then realized—sitting under God only knew how many feet of concrete slab—*No Service*.

❧

Ten minutes earlier, Gia read Robert's first text: Trevor leaving. Jogged in from ocean. Parked where? Pier?

She'd driven up Speedway, paralleling the beach, toward Venice Pier at Washington. Every block she passed, a pedestrian-only street gave way to the beach. Given the fog and the darkness, she couldn't see anything at all beyond the beach sidewalk.

Rather than risk driving all the way up to the pier, she stopped halfway. Turning on her emergency flashers, she left the Bronco and plunged onto the beach to locate Trevor.

If Trevor had shown up jogging, she agreed that he must've parked at the pier. Her plan: to wait halfway out to the shoreline. Once there, she crouched in the darkness and fog and could still make out the shoreline and the beach sidewalk.

Checking for more texts from Robert, she came up empty: *No Service*.

"Great," she muttered.

Made sense. The Pacific made up half her current location and had exactly zero cell towers.

She looked up. Saw nothing at first, then her eye caught a moving form. The top half of a bobbing torso at the waterline.

Had to be Trevor, running on the low-tide hard pack, though she couldn't say with any certainty who was beneath the hooded sweatshirt. She got an angle on him and took off in the deep, soft sand. Even so, he gained on her in the hard pack until she made it out of the soft sand.

274

She kept up with him, losing sight of him now and then in the fog as they headed toward the pier. Away from the jetty, the fog became spotty, thick one moment, thin the next.

Her confidence grew—Trevor was headed for the pier parking lot at the terminus of Washington. Trevor's beach business tonight had to be illegal. He could have used a car and driver or Uber, but each had its own paper trail and witnesses.

Just ahead, Venice Pier jutted into the Pacific. She looked around; Trevor had disappeared.

Dashing into the parking lot, she ran to its only exit. With her iPhone in hand, camera ready, she stood on a truck's bumper and scanned the lot.

Here and there, people strolled down rows of cars. A chirp, an interior car light. A couple getting inside. No Trevor.

Had he kept running up the beach? As she thought about hitting the sand again, an engine roar reached her. Not a Harley rumble—a high-performance car shriek.

She turned landward just in time to see a low-slung sports car tooling inland on Washington. Could've been Trevor's Maserati—the one Robert had seen in the Valley. Hard to say.

As she jogged back to the Bronco, her phone vibrated in her pocket. Three texts from Robert, coming in all at once now that cell service was back.

Call 911; Under lighthouse brij; 2 guys coming.

Shit. How far back to the Bronco? A quarter mile at least.

❧

Once Dav had stopped twitching, Sonny ran back to their car, parked at the boat channel. Chet had just made it back from chasing that witness and told Sonny how he'd lost the runner after a near miss at a townhouse party.

Now, as Sonny drove the Taurus slowly up Pacific, Chet scanned his side of the road for the witness. By the witness's shouts at them on the beach, Chet knew he'd seen Dav's murder going down. Could the witness ID them in all that fog? Why'd he been there anyway?

"Any way Dav had somebody along for backup?" Chet asked.

"Never see him with anybody except RJ and Trevor."

"Wasn't RJ—I'da run that doughboy down easy. Thing about Dav is, he feared us. Thought he'd meet up with us tonight, split Trevor's money, and get going."

"That witness. By now, he's long gone."

"Let's give it one more shot. Hit your flashers."

Their emergency flashers blinking, they stopped at a bridge spanning a wide canal. Both got out. To the right of the bridge's entrance, a path led down a steep bank to the muddy canal. Even from up here, bum-camp smell invaded his senses. He knew better than to ask Sonny to go down.

It could be the witness had holed up with a group of batshit crazies. Half of 'em ex-cons anyway with bike chains, ball bats, knives, and who knew what else.

Sonny said, "Unless he can swim through mud, he's not in the canal."

Chet motioned for quiet. Motioned Sonny onto the bridge with him. Pointed at their feet.

Sonny nodded. Then it dawned on Chet—why keep quiet? If the runner was under there, hearing them talk might flush him out.

❧

From under the ten-foot-wide bridge, Robert saw a car's fog lights diffused yellow in the fog above. The two men hadn't driven past; they'd parked up on Pacific Avenue.

He tried to jerk a cast-iron wheel off the shopping cart to use as an ersatz weapon. Nothing budged until one end of the cart's push handle came loose. Grabbing its free end, he worked it back and forth till it broke off in his hand. An up-close weapon, if need be.

Nothing could hide the gagging-inducing stench of human waste. Even so, quick and quiet, he slathered his face and hands with what he prayed was mud and dimmed his phone.

Under the quarter arch where he'd hidden, an acute angle formed where it dove into land. He lay down, wedging his body into that angle. If someone grabbed only a quick look, they'd miss him.

He noticed the fog starting to lift. What had helped earlier no longer did.

His best option? One of them came underneath here—the one without a pistol. Given half a chance, he could jump the guy with his own weapon. Knock him cold. Or whatever.

He heard footsteps on the bridge above him. Moments of held breath later, he heard the killers' voices.

⁂

Chet spoke to Sonny, louder than he normally would.

"Lost him after that party, but he was headed this way. That much I'm sure of."

Sonny got the idea. "We stick around long enough, betcha he'll show up here."

"Don't you know it."

Chet slid over the bridge's six-inch-thick concrete railing onto a three-inch ledge. Leaning out, gripping the railing with his right hand, he could make out half of the ground area under the first arch.

"See anybody under the bridge?" Sonny asked, even louder.

Chet didn't make out anyone. Then he wondered: Was that a body jammed in tight against the piling? Left-handed, he drew his pistol from his waist.

"Not yet, but I know he's down there."

Now that he'd located the witness, he started to have fun with it. "Check my pistol, would you? See how many rounds I got left."

As he spoke, he was already aiming at what should be the witness' prone body. Too bad about any gunfire noise and the left-handed shot—he couldn't pass it up. His finger found the trigger, and he squeezed it.

❧

Weapon gripped tight, Robert wedged even closer against the piling base. Kept telling himself—*be still.* Nearby, a fog-dimmed human shadow appeared on the glistening canal mud. Next came part of a man's face looming above, fifty feet away, as Robert's pursuer leaned out from the bridge's railing.

Robert heard the pair talk about him. About knowing where he'd hidden, about having a gun, and checking the number of rounds.

Eyeing the channel, he wondered: any way he could burrow into its mud, somehow keep breathing, until they—

A gunshot sparked off the concrete, ricocheting above his prone body. No accident—he'd been spotted. He had to leave his hide, was about to jump and run, when he heard the familiar roar of a straight-line six engine.

❧

Sonny saw it first and said, "Hey!"

Chet was still leaning out from the railing when the car barreled over the sidewalk onto the bridge. Its brights flashed on, lit them up, that damn vehicle doing thirty or more, headed right at Sonny.

For an instant, Sonny wondered what lethal bacteria lay inside that filthy canal muck. Then it was too late—the vehicle bore down on him, and he hopped over the railing, knocking Chet's hand loose, taking him along, too.

The blanket of filth came up fast. Even though he tried turning away, Sonny hit face-first, felt that nasty ooze cram up his nostrils and spill down the back of his throat.

Through his clogged ears, he heard Chet asking, "You alive?"

Sonny had no idea what health problems lay ahead. In a way, he wished he could've answered *no*.

CHAPTER 51

Off the sound of his Bronco's engine, Robert was already on his feet when the two men tumbled into the channel. No splash, no thud. A sound somewhere in between.

He heard Gia laying on the horn, and he scrambled up the canal bank. His swelled ankle hurt, sure, but the thought of Gia waiting powered him through it. Ten seconds after he felt concrete underfoot, he was inside the Bronco.

Gia floored it across the pedestrian bridge into the Marina Strand Colony. They held hands, squeezing hard, still silent. She took Dell Avenue into the other canal district, hung a right, braked at the end of Linnie Court.

Robert hugged her for a long time, then looked into her eyes.

"You saved my ass, baby."

"Your texts, they all came at once, I didn't know—"

"Gia, you saved my ass."

She kissed him on the mouth, even with his lips covered in God knows what. Who cared? They were alive, and together, and they held each other until she started crying.

Normally, they would've already called the LAPD, met them at the beach bathrooms, and walked them through what they'd seen. But Robert said, "If I met with the cops, they'd have legit questions. *Why were you there? Who was with you? Do you know the parties involved?* And whatever else they might think of."

"If we—especially you—held anything back, I'm worried about misleading the LAPD in a murder investigation."

He agreed. "Or hurting Reyes' case. Did you see their car on Pacific?"

"Sure, its fog lights were on, flashers, too. Think it was white."

"Any markings on the side of it?"

"Like a fire marshal? Not that I could see."

Before going into Walgreens for ice and ibuprofen, Robert found a pay phone on Lincoln Boulevard and called the Crime Stoppers hotline. He kept it simple and anonymous: less than an hour ago, there had been an assault, maybe a murder, next to the sunken peninsula restrooms; the assault had involved two men, average height and weight; they could be white, Latino, or Asian, not black; the men appeared to know the victim; they drove a midsize white sedan, could've been a Taurus; and at least one of them had been armed with a pistol.

"Another man had entered the bathroom with a backpack and left without it. The victim wound up with the backpack before they assaulted him."

That was the essence of what he knew. He left out his own Lighthouse Bridge chase. Disclosing it now would lead to irrelevant questions: *Why were they chasing you? Why'd you run? Where was your girlfriend? Why'd you stop at the party?* Making it more about him than the two men. So when the Crime Stoppers operator tried to dig for more, Robert signed off; they had a crime scene and plenty to go on for now.

Reyes remained his top priority for now. If later he thought differently, he'd be happy to tell it all to the LAPD.

Once Robert and Gia made it back to Ozone, they parked in a public lot, not in the alley beside their apartment in case they'd been followed, their identity unearthed, or they'd already been on the killers' radar.

First, Gia hosed him down in their yard—she liked hitting him with that stinging spray—and he soaped himself even harder than he had from the harbor water. Afterward, they decided to stay the night in the main house's master bedroom overlooking the Ozone walk street.

As it stood, he and Gia were still trying to reach a decision.

In the upstairs master bedroom, with two ice bags emptied into a cooler and four Advil in his belly, Robert jammed his foot into the ice until he couldn't take it anymore. A few minutes later, after a pull of brandy, he repeated the process.

Finally, they felt free to speculate about what might have happened tonight.

He asked, "What did you actually *see* that you can be sure of?"

"A short man in a hoodie on the beach. Anywhere from, I dunno, five seven to five ten. Then he got into a high-end sports car and took off."

"Maserati, maybe?"

"Could be, probably, I don't know."

"Red?"

"Halogen streetlamps, a long block away?" She shrugged.

In his mind, he had no doubt—he'd witnessed a blackmail exchange on the beach. Dav knew that Trevor had kept raising money after telling the world his fund was closed. Knowledge that Dav had gained from his own participation in the raise. Knowledge that could do terrible damage to Trevor's fund if the financial world became aware of it.

Broke or close to it, Dav must've planned to collect a big payday for keeping his mouth shut and, like Erik said, drive down to Baja. With his new passport in hand, maybe drive down to Mexico and stay for good.

In bed, they speculated about what he'd seen after Dav and Trevor's backpack swap.

"When Dav walked up to the two guys, they started joking around. Looked like, 'Great job, Dav, way to go,' that kind of rap. Then Dav handed over his phone, and the other guy took its chip and nuked the phone."

"Dav's burner that Erik mentioned?"

He nodded. "Dav thought they were getting ready to split the money and opened Trevor's backpack. Took out a stack of bills and started laughing. Wasn't long after that, ten seconds, maybe, that one of the guys started choking out Dav, took him to the ground."

She said, "Wait. What if *Trevor* hired the two guys to kill Dav *because* Dav was blackmailing him?"

He thought about it. "A triple cross? Trevor lets them keep his blackmail money as payment for killing Dav?"

"Something like that."

"Guess Trevor could've done that; he already knows them. But why not just pay them to kill Dav at his apartment? Or behind Boogies? Going to all this trouble to make the money drop, I think Dav teamed up with our two guys."

"I think you're right."

Finally, it dawned on him exactly why he'd been so tight-lipped about going to the authorities. If he'd told them he believed the jogger was Trevor Reid, the LAPD would show up at Trevor's office tomorrow—or at his home tonight—and question him. Trevor would have no choice—he'd lawyer up and shut his mouth.

That's not what Robert wanted. He wanted first crack at Trevor Reid.

❧

Around two that morning, Robert rolled off their mattress. He went to the rear bedroom and scoped out the Love Shack below for unusual activity. All quiet, so he went into the master bathroom to urinate.

He washed down two more ibuprofen—the swelling had subsided, along with much of the pain—and noticed the iris-themed wallpaper, its seams darkened by decades-old paste. Different irises, all purplish, scripted names below each one: Japanese, Siberian, Crested.

As he eased his foot into the ice again, he wondered if irises would do well at the beach. Surely, no other flower could be as high-maintenance as the orchids at Paul's party.

He liked the feel of this house. A few creaks and groans, but so what? Gia liked it, too. Maybe buying it would be the best way to go. Great problem to have, he decided, as he lay back down beside her.

His mind turned to Reyes' project, *Walk Street Hits*, and Trevor's hedge fund screwing that up with its reservation-of-rights letter. He recalled trying to negotiate with Trevor, who'd replied: *Take a deep breath, lawyer man. No need to get pissed off—it's your client's problem, not yours.*

His last thought of the night before sleep enfolded him, brought a smile to his face.

Not anymore, Trevor. I'm gonna make it your problem.

CHAPTER 52

The next morning, Gia left the big house for a motions call at her firm in Westwood. These days, court motions were often handled over the phone, not face-to-face in a courtroom.

"Mandatory attendance," she told him. "Like sex tonight."

"Any way I can get out of it?"

"Yes, but I'll have to hold you in contempt."

Two hours later, he finished drafting two releases on his laptop. One of them, for his own signature, dealt with disclosing what he now knew about Trevor's investments. Another release dealt with Reyes' initial legal problem.

He planned to present both releases to Trevor, then learn what he could from Trevor's reaction and pushback.

Erik called in. "An hour ago, like you wanted, Petey's palladium dog bone and your message for Trevor to call you, along with your phone number, were delivered by messenger to Trevor Reid's office."

"Great, and I still need you rest of the day."

"Lads are available. A hundred bucks per?"

Robert's phone rang—a 310 area code. Looked like Trevor, already calling.

"Sorry, I have a strict height requirement. Get ready to roll."

"Hello?" Robert said, answering the new call.

"Robert Worth?"

He recognized the voice. "Yes, Trevor, thanks for calling."

"I'm calling because you knew my good friend, Paul Dickerson. No other reason than that."

Being careful in case Robert was illegally recording the call, but laying it on a little too thick.

Robert said, "Wonder if we could meet today? Sooner the better, as far as I'm concerned."

"Well, let's see. What suits you today?"

"I'm all the way down in Venice, but I'll leave it up to you."

Trevor decided on Brighton Coffee Shop, a block or two from his office.

"Can you make it there in an hour?" Trevor asked.

"Give me an hour and a half. I don't want to keep you waiting."

Robert hung up and immediately called Erik.

"You still up in Beverly Hills?"

"Close enough, why?"

"See if anybody makes a fast break from Trevor's office building toward Brighton Coffee Shop."

"On it," Erik said.

Then Robert filled in Erik on what he wanted to happen.

❧

A few minutes before the agreed-upon time, Robert walked into the Brighton diner, a corner joint with burgundy awnings. Like the Pantry on Pico, this place had survived the ongoing purge of LA spots that failed to be the latest thing.

At a two-top facing the door, Trevor sat on a long, shared bench that served four separate tables. At the table next to Trevor, a male customer, early forties, took his time on a Denver omelet.

Robert sat down across from Trevor, each dispensing with a handshake.

Trevor went first. "You want something? Let's hear it."

"Couple of things."

On the way here, Robert and Erik had discussed a general game plan: more bomb throwing, get Trevor to make a mistake; then watch him making it.

Robert touched his iPhone screen, slid his phone across the table. Trevor read what appeared: Unidentified Man Found Dead on Marina Del Rey Beach.

Trevor looked up. "And?"

"Wonder who it is?"

"If I was a mind reader, I wouldn't be here."

"I could talk more freely if you told Denver omelet to split." The man at the next table.

Trevor refused to act surprised. Without looking at Denver omelet, he said, "Brabson, leave a twenty and go."

Brabson did as he was told. Robert heard a familiar voice behind him tell the waitress he didn't mind sitting at an un-bused table.

Erik took Brabson's place beside Trevor on the bench, facing Robert.

Robert told Trevor about what Gia had seen. "Last night, a friend of mine was near the Venice Pier. Couldn't be positive, but my friend was half-sure you were in the neighborhood."

Trevor didn't rise to the bait. "Good for your friend."

"With all the riffraff down there, doesn't seem like a place you'd hang out. Then again, lots of people have secret lives."

"Get to it, Worth."

So far, Trevor appeared unfazed.

Robert pulled a document from his jacket pocket, slid that across the table.

"That release is for your signature."

A two-pager. Trevor read it over. The document made it clear that Trevor and his companies released any rights they had or might have had in *Walk Street Hits*—and specifically repudiated Trevor's reservation-of-rights letter.

That letter had derailed Reyes' negotiations with T-Mack, the problem that had brought Reyes to Robert in the first place.

"Back to this nonsense?" Trevor asked.

"He's in prison, charged with murder. His project is worthless."

"His project was always worthless without my backing. What's in it for me to sign?"

"Cheering up a guy who's getting ready to do life."

"Again, I get what?"

Robert showed him the second document, this one four pages long.

"Sign that first release for my client. If you do, you and I will both sign this second release, in which I promise not to disclose what I know about your fund's investment in the metal your dog likes so much. Neither will anybody else who might've learned about your investments from me." He stood. "Read it, take your time."

He went into the men's room, waited a full thirty seconds, and called Erik.

Erik answered with: "Time's money, dude. Talk to me."

"Is he reading?"

"Yep."

"Like skimming or reading?"

"Door number two, my friend. We always aim to please at EJ Inc. Say, why don't you drop by my house this weekend? We'll fire up the grillski."

Laying it on, talking too loud, having fun.

"Did he sign anything?"

"What am I, a mind reader? Bring whatever beer you want when you come."

Erik hung up.

Robert felt on edge, borderline nauseated, and wondered if the ibuprofen flooding his bloodstream had caused it. Or if his edge came from doubting himself.

Erik texted him: TR reading. Checked in w office. Casual conversation.

So far, this meeting felt off. Way off. A dead man on Marina Beach? Looked like Trevor didn't know the headline was about Dav. That made sense. Far as Robert's *friend* spotting Trevor in Venice? Even if the friend could ID Trevor, so what? Washington Boulevard was a mile away from the murder.

Still, that edge ate at him, his pulse kicking up a notch. He bent over the toilet, salivating, breathing deep. Had to be the ibuprofen, didn't it?

The feeling passed; then a single thought grabbed him by the throat.

Am I wrong? Can I be wrong about Trevor Reid having Paul killed? What about Lawan and Reyes? Erik, too, and Gia and Anita. Have we all been wrong all this time?

Erik texted him: He just signed both docs.

Robert splashed water on his face, toweled off, and pushed through the door. Took his seat without speaking.

Trevor said, "Simple. Done."

He checked Trevor's signatures on Reyes' release.

"I'll get his signature and send you a copy."

"You'd better. That's on you."

"Did you read over the second release carefully?"

The release that prohibited Robert from revealing the fund's investments.

"I've read hundreds of releases. You'd like to think it's complicated, but it's not. Not if you can actually read and know what to look for."

"Sure you read Section Twelve?" The subpoenas section.

Without looking at the document, Trevor said, "*Subpoenas?* If you get subpoenaed by a court of competent jurisdiction, you can be forced to tell the court whatever you might know, or think you know, about my fund's investments. But that's the only situation when you can discuss my investments."

"Does that bother you?"

"Why would you ever get subpoenaed? You in some kind of trouble?"

"I'm not, but my friend, Raymundo Reyes, is. And I saw Paul kick your ass three days before he was murdered. Could be that Reyes' lawyer would be interested in what I think about that. Maybe issue me a subpoena so I'll talk about that fight and why I think it happened."

"Try this. Are you currently subject to a subpoena?"

"No, I'm not."

"Then what's your problem? I already signed what you wanted."

Robert's doubt drilled him between the eyes. Trevor Reid seemed completely unconcerned about any link between his fund's investments and Paul Dickerson's murder.

Trevor simply did not care.

Trevor said, "You don't look so hot, sport," his version of a smile bubbling up.

Robert found himself picturing the purple-iris wallpaper he'd stared at last night. *Flowers.* Was he thinking about the Flower's Flowers van? No—a critical question about real flowers came to him.

The purple-and-white orchids at Paul's party.

He wondered how much Trevor knew about them.

"Have any use for flowers, Trevor, or could you not care less?"

"When you can tell me how to make money off flowers, I'll care. But it's a volatile business, subject to changing taste, disease, EPA constantly up your ass. If I wanted to speculate on farmland, there's ways to do that, but flowers? Did I mention irrigation, delivery, theft? Think it's good business for you, Worth. You can lose your ass bringing beauty to others and feel good about yourself."

So much for asking a simple question.

"You just mentioned flower delivery."

"Among several other things."

"What about the flowers delivered to Paul's house? I know a lot about them—do you?"

"As much as the next person. Certainly more than you."

"Remember what kind of flowers they were?"

"Do you know what makes orchids unique among flowers? They have both male and female reproductive organs. That way they can go fuck themselves, same as you."

So far, Trevor ran true to form. The smartest person in the room, enjoying himself. That much Robert had hoped for. But Trevor's attitude about the murder hadn't changed, and rested where it always did—between arrogant and sour. Not angry or nervous about where the orchid's question might lead. Flop sweat trickled down Robert's back as he watched his whole theory about the case—his entire reasonable-doubt scenario for Reyes—dissolving before his eyes.

He tried once more: "Remember what color those orchids were? Or were you too busy with Paul kicking your ass to notice?"

Trevor checked his watch, looking bored. "Who's still around? Me or him? And since you asked, Alex Trebek, some of the orchids were purple, some were white."

"Everybody knows that. Here's one you don't know. What kind of orchids were they?"

A cloud crossed Trevor's face. "Did you look it up beforehand? You need to one-up me that bad?"

"Either you know or you don't. Hey, there's gotta be worse things than you blanking on something irrelevant like this."

Trevor flushed with anger. That's when Robert knew: Trevor had no idea the flowers had been Royal Thai orchids.

To be sure, he asked, "So even if I told you the orchids were Marquez Royals, you'd still think I looked it up?"

He'd just named them after Gia.

Trevor said, "Of course you did, but look. My compliments; consider it your very own summit of Everest."

Trevor stood up, tossed a twenty on the table.

"All this trouble to get a release on a piece-of-crap movie project? Don't know whether to admire or pity you. Oh, wait. I *do* know."

Robert kept his seat as Trevor walked out.

Erik read to him off his iPhone screen. "You should've asked him how many species of orchids in the world. The answer, Trebek, is twenty-eight thousand. And he was right—they can screw themselves. Damn, who knew?"

In spite of Erik's droll patter, Robert sat mute, lost in a sea of unpleasant thoughts.

Erik noticed. "What's up with that pop quiz you gave him?"

"*Royal Thai orchids.* You heard—he had no idea what they were."

"No, you stumped him. We had 'em in Paul's front yard, too, and I didn't know the answer. How'd you find out?"

"It doesn't matter how *I* knew. *I* didn't have Paul Dickerson murdered. And killers I hired didn't show up at Paul's the afternoon of the party with a Royal Thai orchid delivery. All those species of orchids— *how'd those two fake delivery guys know to bring Royal Thai orchids?*"

"Oh, shit."

"No way around it—the two guys knew Flower's Flowers was delivering all the orchids to the party. And they knew what species of orchid to deliver in that fake Flower's Flowers van."

"That fake van," Erik said. "They needed time to wrap it with the company logo, too. That's impossible unless you learn who's delivering orchids the day of the party."

Robert hated the direction his reasoning led him. "Whoever was working with the two killers knew that Flower's Flowers was delivering Royal Thai orchids to Paul's house on the day of the party. And they knew about it at least a few days, maybe a week, beforehand."

"Lawan? C'mon, I can't believe that."

292

"I can't, either. And I don't."

He couldn't fight his conclusion.

"Jerry Baugh."

"What? I thought he wore a white hat," Erik said.

"Great guy, a terrific guy. Good father, good ex-husband, good friend."

"Then how do you figure Jerry?"

"The party. That night, Jerry told me straight up that the orchids were Royal Thai. I didn't know that until Jerry told me."

"I can't believe—Jerry had Paul murdered?"

"Hear me out, okay. Let's say you're Flower's Flowers, and Paul Dickerson ordered *a ton* of Royal Thai orchids."

"A ton of 'em, definitely."

"A big order like that comes in, and Flower's Flowers doesn't just say, 'Sure, Mr. Dickerson, we have them in stock. We'll run 'em up there right now.'"

"Hell no. They'd definitely need lead time to put together an order that size."

"And Trevor didn't have anything like that much time. I saw the email thread where Trevor asked Paul if he could come to the party. Paul received Trevor's email just three days in advance."

"Spur of the moment?"

"Like that, yeah. You saw Trevor just now. To this day, he has no clue what kind of orchids were at Paul's. But the fake flower-delivery guys had time to wrap the van like Flower's Flowers *and* to bring the right kind of potted orchids up to the Dickerson estate."

"You're saying Jerry's the one who had plenty of time to figure all that out. The alarm code, too?"

"Even the alarm code. Let's start with what I know for sure. Jerry was up at Paul's well before any guests arrived. Even dug a pit in the backyard. Bet anything he was in and out of the house all that week before the party. Even if Paul didn't give his old college friend the code just to make his job easier, Jerry could have seen it on the pantry wall."

Erik nodded, mimicked Jerry. "Sorry to bother you, Lawan, I need some pepper, aluminum foil, need to use the men's room."

Robert nodded. "I mean, Jerry didn't just call Paul one day and say, 'Heads up, I'm digging a hole in your backyard.' Guarantee you, Jerry knew the alarm code, saw it on the pantry wall, maybe. It wouldn't surprise me if Paul gave Jerry the code just to make his job easier."

"Old college buddies. So Jerry hands off the code for the killers to use the night they came for Paul."

"Got it. But Paul didn't set the alarm, so the killers didn't need the alarm, after all. Then tell me: If the killers already had the code, why go to all the trouble of making an orchid delivery and dummying-up their van?"

"Because they're planners, pros. Why take Jerry's word for the layout at Paul's—*for anything*? Their asses were gonna be on the line for first-degree murder, and they wanted to look around, see for themselves. With all the party confusion, Lawan said they could've been inside her house for a half hour or more."

"Are you hurting Reyes' case right now? His whole defense was gonna be making Trevor the bad guy."

"That's for Anita to decide once I tell her. But you saw Trevor just now . . ."

"He didn't seem worried about the right things. About *anything*. Almost hate to ask, but why'd Jerry do it?"

"Dunno yet. Do me a favor, and find our valet again down at Sprocket. His aunt works in bookkeeping. Ask her when Jerry's retirement party was set up and who paid for it."

"Then what?"

Robert's mind was moving too fast, about to explode. He needed to slow down. An idea was trying to reveal itself, but he had no clue what the idea might be.

CHAPTER 53

In a Koreatown spa off Olympic Boulevard, Robert sank into an herbal-tea Jacuzzi, letting its light-green liquid swirl around his body. The sauna's website had promised its treatment regulated hormones, detoxed the body, and promoted beautiful skin.

All he wanted from the sauna was a quiet place to sort out his thoughts.

Reaching back, he realized how he'd overlooked Jerry. Good-guy Jerry, cooking barbecue at the party; Jerry with his own bottled barbecue sauce, the labels designed by his loving daughter; Jerry managing to take Trevor's gratuitous abuse in stride.

He pieced together his conversation with Jerry at the driving range. That day, Jerry had appeared concerned about Reyes' plight. Had even opened up about his modest upbringing, how he was the son of a greenskeeper, and how much he'd loved Trevor's father. All of it true, no doubt.

In the misted room, he wondered why Jerry had spoken to him at all at the range. All Jerry needed to say was, *Sorry, Robert, I signed an NDA. Wish I could help you with Reyes, but I can't.*

An obvious conclusion presented itself: Jerry had no idea Reyes was going to show up at Paul's that night, get framed, arrested, and charged with his murder.

He had never *planned* to frame Reyes. At the driving range, Jerry must've actually felt guilty about Reyes' plight. But only up to a point—the point where Jerry's own life might be impacted.

Later on in Jerry's garage, Jerry had no longer cared about Reyes' incarceration. After getting reamed out by Trevor, Jerry's new posture became: *I don't know Reyes, and I don't care.*

What about Trevor's alibi versus Jerry's?

Trevor's partially blown Sprocket alibi had bugged Robert all along. Why would Trevor tarnish a tight alibi by getting in a car with Dav Concha for a money raise on board the *Marguerite*? Even to raise, say, $10 million. If Trevor had planned Paul's murder, Trevor would want his own ass covered. That way, were he ever questioned by the LAPD, he could tell them—and the financial press—that he'd been at Sprocket with tons of witnesses.

But Jerry's alibi—not leaving Sprocket until 2:00 a.m.—was rock solid.

What was it the Sprocket's valet, Peanut, had told him about Jerry? He'd been *teary-eyed* leaving the club. Now Robert looked at Jerry another way—he'd been emotional at Sprocket, sure, but not because he'd retired or given up his membership.

Jerry had teared up because Paul Dickerson's murder was taking place, right then.

Paul's murder. On Jerry's say-so.

The same type of tears Jerry had shed privately at Paul's party. Not tears from barbecuing or from Trevor's humiliating insults. Jerry had stood as a welcome guest inside Paul's home. Yet Jerry already knew at the party that soon his friend would be dead.

Robert rose from the Jacuzzi, grabbed a towel, and sat on the tub's edge, sweat pouring out of him. His visitation with Reyes was in less than an hour; he still had plenty of time.

He recalled reviewing Paul's business file. He'd come across Paul's withdrawal email thread with Trevor. Before things got nasty, Trevor

296

had turned over Paul's request to Jerry. Jerry's emails to Paul had been helpful and courteous, the tone you'd expect from two college buddies.

Jerry's tone versus Trevor's nasty put-downs—that had diverted Robert from the obvious: months ago, *Jerry knew*, just like Trevor knew, that Paul wanted to withdraw from the fund.

Why, then, had Jerry defended Trevor at the driving range? Hadn't Trevor abused him for years? Why not get even with Trevor, throw him under the bus?

Had Jerry been defending Trevor, or defending the fund? Or was defending one the same as defending the other? Or had Jerry been somehow defending only himself?

He couldn't say. But he still believed that Paul's withdrawal from the fund lay at the heart of Jerry having Paul killed.

Paul was your friend, Jerry—why'd you need him to die?

CHAPTER 54

In a Tower One visiting room, Reyes' face lit up reading Trevor's signed release of *Walk Street Hits*. Seeing Reyes' expression made Robert's day. He planned to hand over the release to Anita ASAP to secure Reyes' signature.

Reyes asked, "How'd you go about squeezing the hedgehog to sign off?"

"I followed Erik's advice, started throwing bombs and lighting fires. T. Reid Three couldn't take the heat."

He watched his mention of Erik sink in with Reyes.

Reyes said, "Erik and Priya had *Mamacita* over for dinner—she loves being around those two boys and *Patocito José*." Ducky Joe. "Thank Erik for doing that for her, would you?"

Erik? Not E-Rik? That might be a first.

"Will do, and don't take this the wrong way: even though your legal problem is cleared up, your project is still worthless."

If not, Reyes might run afoul of qualifying as an indigent and lose his public defender.

"I feel you, but you still on the books for ten worthless points."

Reyes told him that while he'd been in his cell, the rest of his movie story had become clear as a bell. Once he could sit down with it, he could blow through the rest of his screenplay.

Robert kept nodding—whatever Reyes needed to talk about to relieve stress was okay with him—but his mind was elsewhere.

On his way over to Tower One, he'd called Anita and told her what he believed about Jerry. They decided to let her make the call on when to tell Reyes. She had no trouble continuing to raise reasonable doubt using Trevor. Whether that reasonable doubt had a basis in fact? A different question altogether.

"Two theories of reasonable doubt isn't Reyes' problem," she'd told him, "as long as I present truthful facts to the court."

When Reyes wrapped up his screenplay talk, Robert had a few questions.

"Before Paul's party, did you see a lot of good-guy Jerry around the estate?"

"All the time. Always pitching in, always lending a hand. That's how Jerry rolls."

"Any idea how long the party had been set up before the night of?"

"Gonna say six weeks, easy."

Robert told him about Dav's death and about Paul's killers' involvement.

"I'm still trying to connect why the two men killed Paul and then killed Dav. So far, I don't see any link. Maybe there's not one."

"Bet anything the two killings ain't random, *Roberto*."

"How so?"

"Guys like you, *Roberto*, you accustomed to being around rich folks, but most criminals ain't ever seen serious money up close. You told me before, them two killers hid behind Paul's, scoped out the gig. Before that, even, that pair had to be spookin' around, looking at the cast of characters, and what you think they thinkin'?"

"You tell me."

"They thinkin', 'What's those people done so special they get to have all that extra stuff? Where's my slice of it at?'"

Made sense so far.

"See, in movies and books, hit men are smart, hafta look sharp, live in a bitchin' domicile, drive a nice ride, and all the rest. But in real life, they just want to take shit that don't belong to 'em and get themselves paid."

Robert could feel that same thought from the sauna trying to grab him, then recede.

Reyes said, "Think about them two. Already got paid for killing Paul, but once I pulled up at Paul's and they planted that baton, I give 'em an out. They free birds, baby, and they sayin', 'Coast is clear, let's stick around, scoop us up some real money, easy money, off all these rich dudes.'"

"*Real money.* Like whatever they took off Dav Concha and Trevor."

"Like that, yeah. Money's gettin' more real by the minute, and your everyday, bona fide criminals? They gonna run circles around citizens like Dav and Trevor, and whoever else they maybe got their eye on next.

"The two of 'em woulda been right thinkin' they got away with killing Paul. Hadn't been for you and Gia and . . . you know . . . being on Dav's ass."

"Won't hurt to say his name again."

"You and Gia *and Erik*, a'ight. Now. How'd I know all what I just said?" A trace of sadness creased Reyes' downcast eyes. "First time I went up to Paul and Lawan's, saw all their comforts, I had that where's-mine-at feeling, too. Then Paul took up with me, talked to me man-to-man, and it shames me way down deep, as far down as you can go, when I look back on my thoughts."

Robert was touched by Reyes' words, and Reyes was verging on tears when the door opened. A prison guard stuck his head inside.

"Time's up, Raymundo."

Robert stood, same as Reyes.

"I believe in you, Reyes. We all do. And we'll do everything we can to get you outta here."

Reyes told the jail guard, "Hear that, Smiles? Might as well let Mr. Innocent go now."

Looked like Smiles got a kick out of Reyes' patter. "Little thing called a trial, Raymundo."

"Smiles here's one of the good ones. I get outta here, I'm gonna Yelp 'Tower One Smiles' five stars."

It wasn't until Robert walked down the hall that he focused on the ASP baton hanging from Smiles' belt, one like he'd seen several times before.

Seeing it, the thought that had receded earlier grabbed him by the throat.

Prisons. And prison guards. Not security guards or street cops. No. Prison guards.

The killers hadn't been police. Not Erik's Eagle Scouts who'd found the baton on the porch.

Why not prison guards? Good-guy Jerry had a connection to prison guards, didn't he?

As he stepped from Tower One onto Bauchet Street, he tucked away his answer: *Prison Max.* That failed investment Jerry had recommended to Trevor. The total investment wipeout in Trevor's first hedge fund.

How had Trevor described the investment to Robert at Paul's party? *Prison Max—Jerry's greatest hit.*

CHAPTER 55

That afternoon, Chet and Sonny were clearing out of their short-term rooms downtown. Looking back on killing Dav the night before, Chet thought about the best thing about falling into that canal mud: Sonny had dropped all his jerky talk.

After falling into the ooze, they'd driven to a CVS in Westchester. Chet went in alone. He'd bought Betadine—Sonny had wanted Betadine for gargling, too—rubbing alcohol, eye drops, and mouthwash.

A half hour later, at an isolated do-it-yourself carwash off La Cienega, they'd hosed each other off with the water wand. Sonny had rubbed alcohol all over his naked body—his face twice—then poured Betadine up his nose, pinching shut his nostrils till he gagged.

Chet had put his underwear and T-shirt back on while Sonny dumped all his filthy clothes in the trash can and started to get in the passenger seat.

"Uh-uh. I can't have a nudist riding shotgun. Lie down on the back seat, and stay down."

For the most part, that hose-down and antibacterial orgy had taken care of Sonny's smell, but it didn't do much for his state of mind. All the way downtown, he'd been stuck on the same channel.

"Need to take my antibiotics, Chet. Need to take 'em right away."

"Soon as we get to our place, have at it."

"Think I'll take the rest of the bottle."

"How many more's in it?"

"Twelve or so."

"You want to get sick for real, take twelve or so of those two-a-days."

"Just watch me."

"What ought to bother you—if there's a BOLO on this Taurus, two males driving it around."

"That Bronco driver didn't grab our tags. Didn't even hit its lights till he crossed Pacific and jumped the curb onto the bridge."

"You sure?"

"I's watching it. Let's unload the Taurus tomorrow at that Kia lot out in Alhambra. They'll treat us right."

Chet saw that for the bad idea it was. They'd take the Taurus to another lot, in the Valley, say, not in Alhambra where they'd bought it. No, they'd take whatever beatdown in price a Valley salesman dished out and stick with the cargo van. Now that Hobie had cleaned off the flower-company vinyl, it was just another vehicle cruising the SoCal dream on the streets of LA.

Today, Chet finished packing up the beach money. The $400,000 they took off Mr. Hedge Fund and Dav. He crossed the hall to Sonny's room and stepped through the open door.

"Why don't we swing by Hobie's on our way to *Mehico*?"

"However you say *Mexico*, Chet, I'm not going."

"Free place on the beach, you still not in?"

"Free? Hobie tell you that?"

"Not yet, but we talk to him right, why wouldn't he?"

"He's done giving us freebies to save his brother's ass. Push him too hard, and he goes to the cops. I'm for getting outta LA, either goin' home or goin' someplace not so nasty."

"Like North Dakota?"

"Whatever's opposite of Mexico—where I ain't going, no matter what you say or how you say it."

As they started down the hall with their bags, Chet's burner rang. He picked it up and listened. Then he cupped the phone.

"Guess what, Son? *It's her.*"

CHAPTER 56

That night, back in the Love Shack again, Robert packed an overnight bag for his drive north to Bakersfield tomorrow morning. That city, up in Kern County, had been home to Jerry's recommended investment—a private-prison location owned by Prison Max. That particular location had gone belly-up, losing all the fund's investment.

From their bed, Gia had listened to his new narrative: that Jerry had hired two former prison guards to kill Paul.

Now, she said, "Hard to believe it's Jerry, but you have better answers about his guilt than about Trevor's."

"Wish it wasn't true."

"Me, too." She asked, "Prisons can go bankrupt?"

"Privately owned prisons like the one in Bakersfield can go under. Check my laptop."

She opened it on the bed and started reading an old article. The byline belonged to Trish Vise of the *Kern County Gazette*. She'd covered the local prison story from day one.

While Gia read, he told her, "I called Trish, told her I was interested in learning about Prison Max. First thing she asked me: 'What's it worth to you?'"

"Our First Amendment at work."

He smiled. "Trish's retired, gave off a weird vibe on the phone, so I told her I was a lawyer working on my first screenplay. That it was going to center around a prison situation."

"Her vibe was that weird?"

"A retired reporter looking to swap money for information? Something about her, I couldn't see myself telling her I'm looking into Reyes' case."

Gia looked up from the article. "Prison Max? Never heard of them."

"A publicly traded player in the private-prisons sector. What do you think about that article?"

"Interesting. Prison Max planned to shut down one of their locations in Bakersfield. Before they did, local authorities asked them to hold off. The closure would've had a big ripple effect on the local economy— losing jobs, all the businesses that feed into a prison. And what do you know—Prison Max gave the locals six months to figure out how to raise sixty million dollars to buy the prison. Who knew prisons were so damn fascinating?"

He whipped a rolled-up pair of socks at her; she batted them away.

He said, "The locals hired an investment banker, put together a prospectus, and raised the sixty million from private equity. If you can handle the excitement, read that bookmarked article."

She started reading again. "Uh-oh. Smuggled cell phones, smuggled weapons and drugs, violent guards on the take, a cover-up by prison officials."

"After raising all that money, it took just eighteen months before the feds shut it down. I bookmarked the prison's bankruptcy file, too. Interested?"

"Not quite. This Prison Max facility was the only investment Jerry ever recommended to the fund?"

He nodded. "Trevor gave him a shot, and Jerry blew it. According to Jerry's wife, he spent the better part of six months going back and forth, digging into how the prison worked. Even so, the fund lost every nickel of its nine-million-dollar piece of the deal."

She said, "Bakersfield. So you think that's where Jerry Baugh first rubbed elbows with corruption."

"Yep, and with violent men who carry batons."

"It makes total sense, but it's unbelievable. Anita's already doubled down on your Trevor-did-it theory. What'd you tell her about Jerry?"

"Everything. All the facts that looked bad for Trevor are still okay for Jerry—the dispute over Paul withdrawing, the fight at the party, two men watching Paul's party, the fire marshal truck, and the flower van. It's up to the DA, not Anita, to poke holes in her reasonable doubt."

"*Pero, Roberto*, why did Jerry kill Paul?"

He zipped his bag closed.

"I don't know yet, but he did."

"So now I'm with a screenwriter. Is that a step up or step down from Beach Lawyer?"

"Just a solitary man with a keyboard and a story in his heart. You tell me?"

CHAPTER 57

The Bronco overheated only once, climbing the long grade of Interstate 5 known as the Grapevine. As Robert had explained to Gia more than once, the Bronco was temperamental, not undependable. Hard as she rode him about his car, he believed if he ever got rid of it, she might leave him.

Once he made it to the Tejon Pass, it was downhill sailing to the flat floor of the San Joaquin Valley. Just as he picked up Highway 99, the Golden State Freeway, Erik checked in.

"*Sawaat dii khrap, amigo.*" Erik's blend of Thai and Spanish.

"You don't hear that every day," Robert said.

Erik had contacted Peanut, the Sprocket valet, about Jerry. Peanut, in turn, had quizzed his aunt in accounting about Jerry's retirement party.

"Think you're gonna like this. Jerry's party was ordered five weeks before Paul's murder. According to Peanut's aunt, Jerry paid for the gig himself."

"Jerry paid for his own party. Not Trevor. After twenty-plus years, Trevor didn't pony up when Jerry left."

"A consensus prick. No longer a consensus murderer."

Robert said, "At least five weeks before Paul was murdered. That's how long Jerry had been planning his alibi and the murder."

"Looks that way to me."

Robert took the Golden State Freeway for another hour. As he neared the airport exit, he recalled Trish's corroded voice telling him: "You'll exit at the airport in Bakersfield. If you hit Merle Haggard Drive, you've gone too far."

Country-music legend Merle Haggard hailed from nearby Oildale, he'd learned, and often sang about his own prison experience. Haggard had been a favorite of Luis', the Worth family farm manager. Robert could still picture Luis strumming "Sing Me Back Home," Haggard's mournful tune that captured the regrets of a prisoner facing up to what he'd done.

One day, he hoped, that Merle Haggard song would describe Jerry's own feelings, locked in a prison cell.

※

"You have arrived at your destination," Robert's Waze told him.

In front of him, the LaZee Suzan Mobile Home Community. Looked to him like Suzan herself had been in charge of upkeep.

A cargo van pulled in behind the Bronco, then swung around him. For some reason, his eyes followed the van into LaZee Suzan. Why? Was he expecting a Flower's Flowers van to tail him? Did he secretly dream of replacing the Bronco with a van? He smiled at the thought of pitching Gia a cargo van with shag-carpeted walls as his Bronco replacement.

A few turns after entering the gate, he pulled up in front of a shaded mobile home, last painted, it looked like, when AOL ruled the internet.

He got out. Trish Vise pushed open her rusting screen door. Wearing a stained sundress and leopard-print slides under swollen ankles, she looked nothing like her pert byline photo.

"Any trouble finding the place?" she asked, letting loose a robust cloud of cigarette smoke.

"Not a bit."

She stubbed out the smoke on her metal doorjamb, dropped it into a Yuban coffee can full of butts on the ground.

"Come on in, I won't bite."

Inside her nicotine-infused home, he took a metal kitchen chair across from her worn-out recliner. Beside her, a TV table arrayed with prescription pill bottles.

Trish said, "A screenwriter, huh? Read my series of articles about the prison and just had to know more?"

"What happened up here? The prison closing, then getting bought with private money—that's unusual. Anything you can tell me about it would be helpful."

"Oh, the whole thing was a full-on shit show."

As the window-mounted AC unit chugged on, she fired up a Brand X smoke and went over things he already knew: the threatened prison shutdown, the money raised by outsiders to take over the prison, the corruption, and the federal shutdown a year later.

If possible, he wanted to lead her to Jerry without being too obvious. He already knew that only a handful of outside investors had been involved.

"Did you get to meet any of the players who invested?"

"Every one of 'em, but most of 'em flew in private, left quick as they could."

"From what I've heard, those guys can be pretty eccentric."

"Eccentric? That's one way of putting it."

"Any standouts?"

"Yes and no. I mean, there was a pair of 'em. Jerry and Trevor. A real odd couple."

"Odd couples work great in movies. Why were they odd together?"

"First off, see, Jerry was up here quite a while and was popular in town. But dickless Trevor, he was in and out the same day, like most all of 'em. Even so, he managed to rub people the wrong way."

"You're saying Trevor wouldn't thrive doing time?"

"Oh, he'd'a been popular in the joint, that's for sure. Now, Jerry Baugh?" She smiled, saying his name. "All the time Jerry spent here, taking people out to drink at night, he knew the place inside and out."

"A people person, huh?"

"Blow a few hundred in a bar up here, you're everyone's newest and best. Always figured Jerry either had a shitty home life or something to prove. No other reason to stick around here long as he did. But yeah, everybody dug Jerry, including me."

Something to prove? To Trevor . . . to Kay . . . to Marguerite?

"What interests me is all that money coming into town, then the corruption. In the script, there would be some hyped-up violence around all that."

"Your hook, sure. White hats and black hats trapped in one place. Maybe they take a money guy hostage?"

"Not a bad idea." And it wasn't, if he were writing a script.

She directed him to the bottom drawer of a filing cabinet against the living room wall. He slid open the drawer; its dry tracks screamed for WD-40.

"Take out those two fat accordions, and don't look at 'em."

Accordion files. He pulled them out, walked them to her kitchen table, and sat down.

"Those files're all my background work on my prison series. Not gonna find it online anymore because the paper went belly-up, and all that data fades away after a while. Want to keep 'em overnight, copy 'em, whatever, that's gonna run you five hundred."

"Well," he said.

He had that much on him. Another $1,000 in the car.

"Pay to play," she said, rattling one of her pill bottles.

"Think I can come up with that much."

As he stood, a white sedan pulled up outside. A muscle-car engine throbbed, rattling the louvered windows till its engine shut off. Two men in front was all he could see. Tensing, he watched the driver getting out, coming to the door. A skinny redneck in jeans, 7-Eleven shades, and a faded Def Leppard tank top. No surprise to farm-boy Robert, a mullet topped off the look.

"That's Tony," she said. "I'm expecting him. Open the door, would you, and don't say a word."

He stood, felt the makings of a setup. Trish's metal baseball bat leaned against the wall behind the door. Tony—the one knocking, down on the second step—wouldn't be a problem. Robert would kick Tony hard enough to do real damage. The one in the car—he'd go after him and their car with Trish's bat and see what happened after that.

He opened the door and stepped back. Tony came inside, looked at Trish.

"The hell's going down, Trish?" Meaning Robert.

"Old friend of mine from LA. He drove all the way up here, same reason you dropped by. Wink wink."

Tony asked, "So we still on or what?"

"On as hell, Tone, but you're in a bidding war. And I need to see another bill from you before you go back in my bedroom and pick up what I left out for you."

"A hundred more? *Shiiit.*"

"Hundred's pocket money down in LA, ain't it, hotshot?"

She jerked her head Robert's way. Tony glared at him; Robert shrugged. Tony reached for his wallet.

"A'ight, *shiiit.*"

"Look on my bed, same old same."

Tony headed into the bedroom. Where no doubt a stash of prescription OxyContin lay on her bed. Tony came out, trying to look sour about her price gouging but already wiping drug-eager palms on his jeans.

Outside, Robert watched Tony hop off the stairs, jump behind the wheel, and peel off with the other dope fiend.

Trish said, "You're the cool head, aren't you?"

"I was raised out in the boonies, knew a lot of guys like him."

"You see Tone tailing you, call me, and I'll take care of it."

He left $500 on her TV table and grabbed the two files.

"What time you need these back?"

"Tomorrow, anytime, and bring another five hundred when you come. A carton of Hump filters, too, if you can find 'em."

"Another five hundred for . . . ?"

"I'm holding back something from you—if I can reach 'im, I have a contact down your way who just might blow your mind."

She began coughing, held up a finger to hold him, digging deep for whatever lurked in her lungs. When she was done, eyes watering, she said, "Don't call here after eight tonight. Gonna eat dinner, watch my shows, and maybe dance with Charley right after that. Wink wink."

At a motor court off the Golden State, Robert shampooed and showered again. Spending two hours inside Trish's mobile home ranked even with rolling around in canal mud.

"Dance with Charley?" he wondered out loud.

In this lifetime, he didn't want to know what she'd meant. Toweling off, he remembered driving out of LaZee Suzan. Tony had parked his van a hundred yards down the road.

Slowing down, Robert had rolled past them. Looked like Tony and the shotgun passenger had already nodded out on hillbilly heroin. Another farm boy he hadn't seen in the back seat had been getting ready to fix and didn't bother looking his way.

Even so, off Trish's warning, he'd parked in the next-door lot rather than in front of the motor court and pulled the shades to his room.

That night, digging into the first accordion file, he thought Trish might've snookered him. Most of the contents were her articles and story notes dealing with the prison closure's impact on the community;

313

how the shutdown might affect local political races; photographs of city council members, half-baked protests, and the like.

But the second folder's materials started during the money-raising phase, when Jerry had been in town. Robert came across a folder from her paper's photographer filled with group photographs.

Together, they covered the entire staff at Prison Max. Each shot gathered various staff sectors in front of the prison gate, all of them smiling. One big happy family.

When he came to a group shot of the prison guards, he studied it carefully and noticed a man with several large moles on his face.

The caption ID'd the guard: *Sonny Mars.*

Lawan's white guy with moles on his face. The bogus deliveryman who'd sneezed inside her house. One of two men who'd beaten Paul to death. The man he'd watched choking out Dav Concha.

"Hello, Sonny Mars," he said out loud.

He studied the group shot. Nothing else jumped out at him until he came across an article that covered Sonny's arrest for domestic violence. According to the police report, the violence had been "on the person of his wife, Gwendolyn."

A third party had been involved, a man Sonny had gone after with his baton. According to Gwendolyn, the man escaped unharmed through the master bedroom's sliding door. The bedroom where, again according to Gwendolyn, she'd been showing off her new bathroom tiles.

Sonny Mars. A violent man who liked using his baton.

Further into the photo folder, he found a series of eight-by-elevens that hadn't made it into the paper.

Taken at a local bar, over time. Jerry appeared in half the shots, buying all the drinks, no doubt. In one picture, Sonny and Jerry shot pool. In several other pool-shooting shots with Jerry, he and Sonny were with a third man.

That third party looked either part-Asian or Latino. That mixed-ethnic look jibed with Lawan's description of the second deliveryman inside her house.

Flipping back to the first group shot of prison guards, he came up with the third man's name: *Chet Archer.*

Chet Archer, Sonny Mars, and Jerry Baugh shooting pool. Together in one shot. Tight. Three bros.

He set aside the file. Connecting these three men, actually putting them together in one shot, surged adrenaline into his system, and he burst onto the second-floor landing.

He ran down the stairs, sprinted across the parking lot. Little to no nighttime traffic here, so he ran a couple of miles up the frontage-road shoulder and jogged back the way he came, then dove into his motel's mobile-home-size swimming pool.

A half hour later, he was back in his room, dried off, putting together a quick narrative and timeline. Without that, he'd have a hard time explaining to Anita—and to himself—his reasonable-doubt theory about Jerry and the two guards.

The way he saw it now, Jerry's history with the killers had started long before Paul's party.

2013:

Jerry came to Kern County/Bakersfield:

Met Archer/Mars.

333 Hedge Fund invested $9M in Prison Max.

2014/2015:

333 Hedge Fund lost entire $9M.

Six months ago:

Paul tried/failed to withdraw money from 333 Hedge Fund.

Jerry decided to retire.

Trevor and Jerry—both in the email loop about Paul withdrawing money.

Five/six weeks before Paul's murder:

Paul's party set in motion.

Jerry's Sprocket party set.

Jerry hired Archer/Mars, former prison guards.

A week/ten days before Paul's murder:

Jerry/Jerry's BBQ became part of Paul's party.

Jerry gained access to Paul's house/property.

Jerry learned about Royal Thai orchids; Flower's Flowers delivering to party.

Jerry/Archer/Mars prep for murder at Paul's home.

Three days before Paul's party:

Trevor asked to attend/Paul accepted.

Day of party:

Bogus Flower's Flowers van stopped by Brentwood Security.

Archer/Mars bring Royal Thai Orchids inside house, witnessed by Lawan.

Night of Paul's party:

Trevor/Paul fight.

Note: Random event. Jerry had no control over it.

Archer/Mars watch from backyard/canyon.

Archer/Mars hike out to fire marshal Taurus on Mulholland. Amabel/squatter youth witness.

Night before and day of Paul's 2:00 a.m. murder:

Jerry and Trevor at Sprocket party.

Trevor leaves early w/ Dav Concha. Whoops! Trevor didn't know about murder.

Later, Jerry leaves Sprocket.

Same time—Archer/Mars murder Paul.

Reyes shows up at Paul's. Random event.

Archer/Mars see Reyes.

Later that day:

Reyes framed by Archer/Mars.

Day after that:

Reyes arrested on boardwalk.

That was that for his timeline. He believed that over time, Anita could prove all of it.

What still eluded him: *Jerry's motive.*

He still believed Paul's attempted withdrawal had triggered his murder. But Jerry had nothing invested in the fund. Kay had even backed up Jerry about that fact at the driving range.

Still, Jerry had protected the fund by giving Trevor an alibi. No way on earth that Jerry would murder Paul and protect Trevor just to keep his medical plan and a consulting contract.

And so . . . ? And so . . . ?

Still crapping out, he got into bed, tried to fall asleep, and failed. Still in bed, agitated, he pulled up the prison bankruptcy file he'd bookmarked on his computer down in Venice.

Early on, he came across several motions that had been filed by prison creditors objecting to a decision the bankruptcy trustee had made about a particular debt. Nothing stood out to him. Within six months, the trustee had prepared his *Trustee's Final Report to the Court and Application for Fees.*

Every creditor had been notified, a list of all prison creditors attached to the report. After a thumbnail calculation, he figured that senior creditors got twenty cents on the dollar and general creditors—the

Marguerite Fund appeared on that list—came away empty-handed. A total loss.

At Paul's party, that wipeout had prompted Trevor's suggestion that Jerry repair lawn mowers in his garage. That Jerry put up a neighborhood sign: WILL SHARPEN BLADES.

As he scrolled through the list of stiffed general creditors, he came across:

Edgewood Consultants, Inc. Consulting services: $100,000.

The name jumped out at him off of his garage musings. Edgewood Avenue was Jerry's address in Reseda. The street where he and Kay each still resided.

A trip to California Secretary of State's website yielded a company mailing address: Edgewood Consultants on Edgewood Avenue in Reseda. The listed officers: Gerald and Katherine Baugh.

To him, that meant one thing: Jerry Baugh was corrupt, way back then, and not very clever about it.

Somehow, Jerry had worked out a $100,000 payoff from the prison, surely for directing the fund's money into the prison investment. He had taken a bribe but must've submitted a legit-looking consulting invoice to the prison. They'd never paid it, though, and his unpaid invoice had gathered dust until the bankruptcy trustee had come across it.

He wondered how Jerry had reacted when he received a formal notice from the bankruptcy court that his bribe had become a matter of public record.

Bet you freaked out when you saw that letter, didn't you, Jerry?

Jerry must've been financially strapped back then. Robert could imagine Daisy in an expensive school, the Great Recession, other bad investments—who knew at this point? Add to the list Trevor's abusive treatment, losing Marguerite to him, and whatever else found its way onto a lifetime of grievances from Trevor.

All those things and surely more had led to the corruption of Jerry Baugh.

And Kay? He doubted she knew anything—he hoped not—but for Reyes' case, he didn't care.

Now Anita could also allege that Jerry was corrupt from the outset. That he'd taken a bribe. That he knew the two prison guards. She could use Brentwood Security footage and Lawan's testimony to put Archer and Mars in a Flower's Flowers van, then inside her home the day of the party. Bryan's drone footage would reveal the killers watching her house that night. The millennial camper could put their fire marshal Taurus on Mulholland. Once the two former prison guards were located and questioned, Reyes' situation would only get better.

As Robert finally dozed off at daybreak, he believed that Reyes had an excellent chance of release after his preliminary hearing.

Sorry, Anita, after his *prelim.*

❧

After a few hours' sleep, he grabbed a late breakfast at Zingo's Cafe on Buck Owens Boulevard, the latter named after Owens' nearby Crystal Palace concert hall. Listening to Owens' "Act Naturally" duet with Ringo Starr on his headphones, he worked his way through sides of biscuits and gravy, hash browns, and avocados.

In his booth, trying not to sing along with Ringo, he glanced though the plate-glass window. A Brinks cargo van pulled to the curb.

Again, he thought about calling Gia, messing with her about his van-for-Bronco swap:

"What's wrong with shag-carpet walls? Don't come a-knockin' if this van's a-rockin', baby."

Two men got out of the van in matching uniforms. Robert's eyes bored into them.

His gaze stayed with the two guys coming through the door, then shifted back to their van.

His mind began to speed up, touching down on things he'd learned since Reyes had first brought him his option problem on the boardwalk.

"Excuse me, sir. Everything okay?"

"Prestige Vault," he said to himself.

"More coffee?"

He emerged from his thoughts and saw the waitress.

"No, thanks, just the check."

Outside, in the quiet of his Bronco, he went online and looked into the price of palladium. Today, that metal traded for about $900 an ounce. For ease of calculation, he rounded up the price to $1,000.

The largest palladium bar offered for sale online weighed ten ounces and cost $10,000. To invest in $1 million worth of the metal, Trevor's fund would need to buy a hundred ten-ounce bars. For $10 million worth of palladium, a thousand ten-ounce bars. And so on.

After he'd converted from millimeters to inches, each bar's rough dimensions equaled three inches by two and one-quarter inches. About half the size of an iPhone.

Stacked on top of each other, that million-dollar stack of ten-ounce bars would be twenty-five inches tall. Quartered, the stack would still be eight inches high and would weigh about sixty pounds.

He believed that those dimensions accounted for only a small percentage of the fund's palladium holdings. With palladium as Trevor's $750 million hedge fund's biggest position, his investment could easily equal $10 million. Probably much, much more.

And $10 million worth of palladium? That alone would weigh about six hundred pounds. What would Jerry need if he'd planned to move it from one location to another?

At that point, he knew enough to make his next call: Prestige Vault in Huntington Beach. Trying to stay calm, he closed his eyes until he found himself speaking to Oswald Dodds. Robert introduced himself as a wealthy individual investor. Naturally, he was concerned with privacy and wanted information about storing a large quantity of palladium bars.

Oswald first assured him that Prestige differed from banks in that the depositor was anonymous, both to Prestige and to third parties.

"We're tailor-made for your situation, sir. Our vault door automatically locks down each night. To enter during business hours, you always need a preissued card keyed to your handprint. Once inside our vault, or in a viewing room with your belongings, your privacy is once again assured."

"I liked what I saw on the website, but I had a few nuts-and-bolts questions."

"Glad to help out."

"If I wanted to remove my metal bars—there'd be quite a bit—how does that work?"

"Well, for that kind of thing, we have a secure loading dock in back, and a Bobcat forklift."

"Would you require me to hire a security firm to move my metals?"

"Like Brinks, Garda, Loomis?"

"Like that, yes."

"No, that's not a requirement."

He sagged momentarily, then asked, "What would happen if I showed up to move—I'll use a big number—six hundred pounds of gold bars?"

"Oh, well. I mean, that would be . . . for that kind of bulk—what're you thinking about doing? Loading all that in the back of your SUV?"

"Of course not. A cargo van, something like that."

Oswald said, "For that much precious metal, Mr. Worth, if you failed to hire a legitimate secured van like Brinks, you'd be asking for trouble. Those vans come with an armed driver and a second armed guard riding shotgun."

Two uniformed van guards in a Brinks van.

He said, "Not using, let's say, Brinks again, for that much metal. That would be noteworthy to you?"

"Noteworthy and extremely foolish. I can't think of once where a transaction like that has happened. I mean, we're covered on our end—we notify each cardholder on our books about every withdrawal. But once you leave our premises, you'd be on your own, and there are all sorts of people out there, believe me. And for the extra cost, it's damn well worth it. Listen, if you want to drop by—"

"I know I've taken a lot of your time—one last concern."

"What I'm here for, sir. Shoot."

"I saw an online report that you'd had a serious robbery at your facility."

He'd overstated the report to get a reaction out of Oswald and wasn't disappointed.

"Robbery? How about an attempted—I don't know what you'd call it. More like two drunks on the roof with crowbars, but somebody called the cops, and it wound up in the local paper. Business defamation, if you ask me—but you try making that work in court."

He thanked Oswald, clicked off, and stared straight ahead. Two pieces of information that Jerry and Kay had revealed at the golf range came back to him.

On the practice tee, Jerry had fielded a call from the fund. According to Kay, the call probably involved a problem with access cards. And that someone wanted him to come over to the vault.

Later, on Edgewood Avenue, Kay had told him that Jerry lived down the street from her house. That he would either be in his garage or over in Hollywood—dealing with the cards.

A vault in Hollywood. Not in Huntington Beach.

Didn't take long for Robert to nail down the only vault in Hollywood comparable to Prestige Vault in Huntington Beach: Hollywood Famous Metals.

With that piece in place, he'd finally corralled the reason why Jerry Baugh had hired two former prison guards to kill Paul Dickerson.

※

On his laptop in Zingo's parking lot, Robert typed in another piece of Jerry's murder timeline.

Eighteen months before Paul's murder:

Jerry hired Archer/Mars to stage a half-assed break-in @ Prestige Vault.

Jerry/Archer/Mars called local cops about the break-in/gave Jerry excuse to move palladium.

Jerry/Archer/Mars drove a wrapped van that looked like legit Brinks van.

Archer/Mars posed as legit security at Prestige.

Jerry/Archer/Mars moved metal via Brinks van to Hollywood Famous Metals.

He stopped typing, noodling through what came next. He recalled how pliable and easy-to-scratch Petey's palladium dog tag had been. Online again, he watched demo videos of guys in workshops melting down palladium, pouring it into precast molds.

Jerry had moved a small fortune in palladium from the vault in Huntington Beach to a new vault in Hollywood. Robert decided that he'd made one stop along the way: his machine-shop garage on Edgewood Avenue.

Quite a garage stop that had been. That's where Jerry had substituted palladium for . . . Robert didn't know for *what*, but he had a pretty good idea.

He Googled the weight of lead, *Pb*, versus that of palladium, *Pd*.

Lead: 707.96 pounds per cubic foot.

Palladium: 712 pounds per cubic foot.

Easy enough for Jerry to substitute ten-ounce lead bars for ten-ounce palladium bars. The lead bars could be preformed in a mold, weighed out in advance, and substituted with minimal effort. After the switch, Jerry, using Archer and Mars, would've checked the tainted batch, including the lead bars, into the Hollywood vault. Their checked-in weight would match up closely enough with the bars he'd checked out of Prestige.

Any weight discrepancy between what had left Prestige and what he'd checked into Hollywood Famous Metals would've been minuscule.

Jerry's substitution left him in possession of as many palladium bars as he'd decided to steal.

Nice payday, Jer.

He went back inside Zingo's and ordered a coffee to go. While waiting, he compared why Trevor—and now Jerry—each seemed like such a good candidate for killing Paul.

Both men had shared a common goal: neither had wanted Paul to withdraw from the fund.

Trevor's motive, he'd already pieced together: If Paul's withdrawal had become public, withdrawal requests by other investors would surely follow. Trevor's fund, his own investments, and his reputation would be damaged by forced sales of fund investments, including palladium—*the price of which had been way down all year.* Selling this conviction position was anathema to Trevor, given that palladium was surely his largest position in the fund.

Right, Petey?

Jerry had his own reasons for wanting Paul's money to stay in the fund. But Jerry's *actual motive* for killing Paul differed wildly from Trevor's theoretical one.

Jerry feared that massive sales of physical palladium, caused by Paul's withdrawal, would reveal his own switch of lead bars for palladium.

Would Paul's murder ultimately have kept Paul's money in the fund? What about Paul's widow, Lawan? What about Paul's estate and his lawyer, Hampton Bergen?

Jerry had known Lawan as Paul's wife, recently married to Paul and from Thailand. With Paul's massive estate to deal with postmurder, the sale of Paul's interest in the fund, and so the metal, would fade away for quite a while. On top of that, Jerry surely knew that Trevor would do everything in his power to delay any estate action for as long as humanly possible.

Jerry hadn't pulled off the mythical perfect crime. Far from it. Only a crime that had been almost impossible to link to Paul's murder.

Day one, Jerry had started scrambling to protect himself after Paul's bombshell request. All Jerry needed: the passage of time between his own retirement and the detection of his switch of lead bars for palladium. Time, plus as many people as possible who would have access to the Hollywood vault and the palladium.

With any luck, Jerry's crime wouldn't be unearthed until all, or most of, the palladium had been delivered to a new buyer. Detection of the lead bars—and of his crime—could be years away.

By that time, Jerry Baugh, former COO of the 333 Hedge Fund, would be a distant memory. One of many people who'd had access to the fund's Hollywood vault. One of many people who might've pulled it off.

In that event, insurance claims would surely be filed. Just as surely, claims investigators would contact Trevor. Would Trevor point the finger at his retired COO? No way. He'd cover for Jerry, too, because Jerry's theft reflected both Trevor's poor supervision of the fund and his own poor judgment.

In a future hypothetical confrontation, Trevor would no doubt tear Jerry a new one, but that tongue-lashing would happen in private. If Jerry had a mind to, he might deliver a few choice words of his own: "You're right, Trevor, I ripped you off. What're you gonna do about it, you pathetic little man?"

Jerry and Trevor; Marguerite and Kay; greed and need. All of it mixed together into a toxic brew that had fueled Jerry's free fall into corruption, desperation, and finally murder.

The shame of it all, that a wonderful human being, Paul Dickerson, had paid the ultimate price.

CHAPTER 58

It was almost 2:00 p.m. by the time Robert made copies of Trish's files and pulled up to her mobile home. He was trying to think up an excuse to leave the file on her doorstep when she appeared at the door.

"There you are, studly."

He got out and came to the screen door with her files.

"Any help?" she asked.

"Every little bit helps," he said, downplaying its importance.

"I called around. Think I found that mother lode I promised you yesterday."

"Your other contact?"

With all that he'd learned from her files, he'd forgotten about her other source.

"If you did your homework last night, you've seen her before."

He drew a blank, shrugged.

"Patty Stokes. In one of the prison-employee group shots."

"I might've copied that photograph. I'll take a look at it."

"Patty worked in the warden's office as executive secretary, knew everything going on inside. You'd be missing out if you didn't ring her up. Oh, wait, did I mention her number's unlisted?"

She stuck a Post-it to her doorframe.

"You find me that other five hundred, her number's right here."

Why not? He fished five bills from beneath the passenger-side floor mat and handed them over.

Once she counted it, he snagged the number off her doorframe.

Trish said, "Now, look, she's expecting your call, but she used to work for the warden and gets squirrelly talking to strangers."

"Makes sense. Inmates get out, come looking to settle a score."

"You got that right, hotshot. Patty lives down around Long Beach somewhere. Give her a call—I vouched for you. She'll want a few bucks to talk, but talking to that tough little broad'll be a trip."

He'd just about slid behind the wheel again when Trish called out.

"Hey, Worth. Where's my Humps?"

Her Camels. Was that a little bump and grind behind the screen door?

"Next time, Trish," he said, and got the hell out of there.

CHAPTER 59

Robert was halfway home when he noticed how low he'd let his phone charge sink. He called Anita to update her on Jerry's link to Chet Archer and Sonny Mars. Her office told him Anita wasn't available. One of her clients under house arrest had gone off his meds and barricaded himself inside a tire store over in Carson.

The prisoner's only request—the report was on Channel Five, her office said—was that he turn himself in to Anita. Bringing her his latest news in person would have to wait.

He connected with Gia—a short call. She was about to step into an interns' meeting and wouldn't make it home until late. Philip and his fiancée, Dorothy, had invited them to an early dinner at Bistro Fresca, and Gia had decided to take them up on the offer.

Too bad. His shag-carpeted van routine would have to wait.

Over time, Gia and Dorothy had become quite close. Even Philip had turned the final corner on Gia's bad acts from when she'd worked at Philip's firm with Robert.

Darkness was falling as he crested the Grapevine and reached out to Erik. He related to Erik how Sonny Mars and Chet Archer fit into Paul's murder. How and why Jerry had substituted lead bars for palladium in his garage, leaving Jerry with palladium to sell whenever he saw fit.

"You identified our two fire marshals, our two orchid delivery guys. Way to go, lawyer man."

"Once I get hold of Anita, she can work out the last mile between Jerry and his hired guns."

Alibis, phone and bank records, finding out who had vinyl-wrapped the two vehicles.

Erik said, "I'm still having trouble with Jerry's retirement-party alibi. Why did Jerry give Trevor a Sprocket alibi, too? If Reyes hadn't been framed, Trevor might have been a likely suspect after that fight with Paul at his party. Tough luck for Trevor, right?"

Robert liked going over settled facts with Erik. Too often, the ex-cop poked gaping holes in them.

"Why did Jerry give Trevor an alibi? Take One, roll camera." Robert cleared his throat. "Even though Jerry was free and clear of the fund, if Trevor became a person of interest in Paul's murder, the fund would suffer massive, maybe total, liquidation."

A long silence. Had he missed something? He had no Take Two in his quiver.

Finally, Erik said, "Got it. And once the fund liquidated, regardless of why, and started shipping palladium to new buyers, Jerry's theft wouldn't stay secret for long."

"Nailed it, *Oso*."

He told Erik about Trish's Long Beach contact named Patty Stokes.

"Think you need more evidence?"

"Taking to Patty can't hurt."

"Then wait till tomorrow. I'll ride down with you."

"Might be fun. Maybe drop by Manhattan Beach on the way, grab a stool at El Tarasco."

A locally famous Mexican food joint. They put a pin in El Tarasco for tomorrow, and Robert signed off.

Ten minutes later, he checked his Waze. For some reason—a topless hitchhiker? A spilled crate of bootleg DVDs?—all routes to Venice showed up as ominous red lines. It would take him hours to get home, even more sitting around in traffic jams.

He eyed Trish's Post-it on the dash: Patty Stokes, along with her Long Beach area code. So he called her, and Patty picked up on the second ring.

He ID'd himself the same way he had to Trish: Robert Worth, a lawyer working on a prison-based screenplay. Like Trish had told him, she'd already teed Robert up with Patty.

Patty said, "An innocent man in prison, denied justice and fights for his freedom? It's been done to death."

"Maybe a few more twists and turns along the way."

"Inside, they're all innocent, just ask 'em. Trish told me you're paying, or we wouldn't be chatting away like this."

"I can pay you what I paid her."

"Look, I'm already paying Trish a two-fifty finder's fee, so it'll be an even thousand coming my way."

"That's a lot of money."

"Hey, this isn't Trish talking. I held the keys to the kingdom at the prison. Every money guy who flew into town met me. And the guards? I know the skinny on all those degenerates, same as I do half the prisoners. It's your dime, mister."

"Trish brought up a guard named Sonny Mars. She'd written him up in the paper."

Not exactly true, since he hadn't mentioned Sonny's name to Trish.

"A degenerate and an abuser. Call him *Chocolate Chip* to his face, and see what happens to yours."

The moles Lawan had seen on Sonny's face.

"Chocolate chip?" he asked anyway. "What's that all about?"

"Try to picture a scene, Mr. Screenwriter. It's me with my hand out. Same scene. Picture you slapping some bills into it."

"I hear you. Interested in meeting tonight?"

She told him that every day she walked twenty thousand Fitbit steps; today she'd fallen way behind.

"Tell you what, I'll be into my hill walk by then. Can you make it to San Pedro by eight?"

"Looks like if I went downtown, took the Harbor Freeway, I might make it."

"Eight sharp, yes or no? I'll tell you stories'll curl your hair if you have any."

"Eight sharp, then. Where in San Pedro?"

She wasn't ready to tell him.

"Nobody ever called me a pushover, okay? You'd better be who you say you are. If not, I will defend myself."

"Look me up online."

"Already have, Beach Lawyer."

"Then where do you want to meet?"

"*The Usual Suspects,*" she said.

"The movie?"

"You're the screenwriter. Figure it out," she said, and hung up.

CHAPTER 60

When Robert stopped at a money machine in San Pedro, he Googled *San Pedro+The Usual Suspects*. His search took him to iterations of the Korean Bell of Friendship in Angel's Gate Park. That massive metal bell hung inside an elegant open-air pagoda on a hillside overlooking the Pacific.

From the online photographs, he recalled *The Usual Suspects* scene where a bunch of bad guys, ones he'd liked, met a bunch of other bad guys, ones he didn't, and they all talked tough.

Several hundred yards down the hill from that bell, South Gaffey Street ended. That's where he pulled into Point Fermin Park, a few minutes early, got out of his car, and looked around.

Even in the dark, he made out the form of an enormous, spreading tree.

A female voice called out: "Ficus macrophylla. For the unwashed, that's a Moreton Bay fig."

Patty stood thirty yards away on Gaffey. Her hair in a brush cut, wearing spandex walking shorts and an Under Armour windbreaker over a modest sports bra.

He walked over, his hand extended. She pulled her hand from her windbreaker and showed him a Mace canister.

"Don't disappoint me," she said. "Seven fifty for me now—two fifty for Trish. Throw another five hundred my way if you like what I tell you."

Their deal just changed; already here, he didn't care.

She took his up-front money and, without a word, started speed-walking up Gaffey. He came along.

"Remember the bell scene from the movie?" she asked.

"Word for word," he lied, smiling so she'd know it.

"A cool location—they shot it like the bell was in LA—but a great movie."

"Been a while, but I thought so, too."

"What's your main character's name?"

Right, his screenplay.

"Erik with a *k*."

"Erik? Shit name for a hero unless it's a Norwegian prison."

"Some people call him *Jake*."

Only Reyes, and then *Yake*, but still.

"*Jake*, there you go. So what can I tell you?"

"On the phone, we talked about Sonny Mars. You called him a degenerate. Why not start there?"

"A wife beater for starters. Back then, up in Kern County, that was the end of it, but I always thought Mars was capable of sowing true darkness. Him and that other one, looked to me like they egged each other on."

"You mean Chet Archer?"

"Yeah, Archer, but what I said's not right. More like Archer egged Mars on, getting under Mars' skin, winding him up. Now, in your movie, a guard could be corrupt, a borderline psycho like Mars. Then you could get into his life after he clocked out for home. You know, the local bowling team, Little League, Thanksgiving dinner, that kind of normal stuff."

"And the guard is anything but. Good idea, I like it."

If he'd been writing a movie, her ideas weren't half-bad. They reached the top of the hill and turned around.

"Anything left in your tank, Worth?"

"Just enough. Being a lawyer, I have a pretty decent feel for how those money guys think. Don't think it's been done in a movie. Maybe one of 'em gets taken hostage."

"Not a bad angle. Met 'em all—all those who bothered showing up."

"Some didn't?"

She nodded. "This was a big deal to the community; small potatoes to them. They'd look at the numbers and decide what to do from back in New York or wherever."

He hoped she didn't need prodding to come around to Jerry; she didn't. A few minutes later, she brought him up.

"Hard not to like Jerry Baugh. Played Division One ball for a minute, wife and kid at home, well liked. But something . . . something about him didn't quite add up."

"Hey, that's another good angle—a corrupt money guy gets taken hostage. Ever get to the bottom of Jerry?"

Looked like she was thinking it over. They reached the bottom of Gaffey, headed back up.

"Not really. He was a big deal in a small town, liked it a little too much. After seeing that belittling turd he worked for, can't say I blame him. After a while, I'd see Jerry with Mars and Archer huddled up around town. Like maybe they'd got their hooks sunk into Jerry."

Or vice versa, Robert was thinking as they reached the bottom of the hill.

She said, "Let's see, up and down Gaffey, that's another nine hundred steps."

"Where's your Fitbit?"

"At home. I know all my walks so well, I don't need it anymore. Ever been to Sunken City?"

"Never heard of it."

"Getting over there, taking a lap once around the big field, that's another eight, nine hundred steps. C'mon, that's my last leg."

She led him to a fenced-off area onto a dirt path. Across an empty field to their right came the muffled roar of heavy surf banging against whatever lay below.

Patty said, "Back in the twenties, some genius developers built a subdivision out past where this field ends now. With erosion and the waves beating on these cliffs, the houses they didn't move fast enough fell into the ocean, concrete foundations and all."

The metal fence around the three- or four-acre field was serious: ten feet tall with sharp metal spikes topping off each vertical bar.

"Never heard any of that."

"Living up in LA, you wouldn't. Down here's a world apart."

They reached a gap between the square bars. Someone had managed to bend out the one-inch-thick square bars.

She went through first and didn't wait. He sucked it up, squeezed through, and caught up with her. They walked clockwise around the field's perimeter.

He said, "You mentioned Baugh, Mars, and Archer huddled up. Any idea what they were up to?"

"Could've been anything, long as it was illegal. Why the state never figured out a way to take away those two's pensions is beyond me."

They reached the far end of the field. Patty kept up her strong pace as they first circled near the cliff.

"Don't get too close. Dimwits die out here all the time when land gives way underfoot."

She beckoned him to follow her. Another fifty yards' walk put them at the edge of a rock-filled ravine leading down to the beach. A combination of shifting land and erosion must've caused it to form. Waves broke on the beach below, and seawater, compressed into the ravine's chute, ran halfway up to where they stood, over graffiti-covered rocks.

Patty said, "You feel stupid enough, that's the way down."

She started their walk again, several yards back from the cliff.

Again, he asked, "Any idea what those three guys might've been trying to pull off?"

"Top of my list? A bribe from the prison. There was some talk about some hot money making its way into Jerry's pocket. Dunno if Jerry ever pulled it off or not."

Even though he'd figured that one out, he didn't let her know.

"This Jerry guy—what do you know . . . ?"

She stopped. Looked over his shoulder, back at that fence gap they'd slipped through.

Her tone sharpened. "You liar. You said you came alone!"

His eyes followed hers. "I did."

Two men. The second had just made it onto the field. Before Robert could speak, a sharp jolt surged through his body, starting at his neck. His knees buckled, and he dropped onto the ground.

Patty lowered a stun gun; Robert's blurred vision revealed the two men coming their way.

"Hurry up!" Patty yelled.

They broke into a run.

The stun gun's first shock wave began to pass; he rolled away from her, made it to one knee. Tried reaching for her face, her hair, but his fingers slipped through her gelled brush cut.

This time, she jabbed his shoulder, followed him to the ground, and kept up the pressure. His body writhed and twitched as if demon-possessed.

She knelt beside him. He caught her savage look as she jammed him a third time. This surge went on longer, maybe five seconds, but his spasming muscles, uncontrollable, made her torture seem eternal.

"He knows you both!" she called out.

"Not for long," said the closest voice.

Robert made out a telescoping baton in Sonny Mars' hand.

Tall and thin, he'd killed Paul and Dav. Robert's life was next in line.

The cliff's edge, six or seven feet away, was his only way out. He had no idea if the drop-off was sheer. If so, he guessed the drop at forty feet.

Patty held him down, her right hand on his throat, her head at his beltline. With every ounce of strength he could muster, he snapped up his left knee and caught her flush on the jaw. She folded across his torso.

Sonny Mars wound up, raised his baton, aiming for Robert's head. Patty's deadweight held him down. Grabbing her windbreaker, he jerked her body toward his head.

A wet sound came from her skull as Sonny's baton struck her foursquare.

"Shit!" Sonny screamed. "Aunt Patty!"

Hugging himself, Robert rolled toward the cliff. On his last rotation, he saw the stars first, then the dark horizon, and last, the drop-off.

Then he was headed down. The drop wasn't sheer.

Twisting, he put his feet out in the lead and slid on his ass down a steep, loose-shale slope.

What came next—a rock shelf, harder than the surrounding shale. Once he hit that shelf, he flew into the air, falling now, tumbling out of control.

The ocean came at his face, and a split second later, he hit the water. He sank. How far, he didn't know. His feet found the bottom, his knees bent, and he sprang for the sky.

Surfacing, he blasted salt water from his mouth and wondered: *How lucky can I get?*

Two grateful gulps of air. He looked around, tried to get his bearings. His feet touched bottom, and the water got shallower—fast.

The reason why—an incoming wave. An eight-foot face. White water feathered its crest. He'd been in the ocean enough to gauge that it wouldn't break on shore but against the cliffs not far behind him.

Standing in just three feet of water now, then two feet. The next wave's strong seaward pull left him with only one choice—dive under the wave and come out the far side.

He started his move too late. His mind flashed to Erik's story—that surfer who'd died at Boneyard up in LA. Then the strong undertow sucked his feet from beneath him and shot him feetfirst toward the oncoming wall of water.

 ॐ

Chet took Patty's wallet out of her jacket and put it into his own. After he and Sonny rolled Patty over the cliff, they watched her limp body tumble down the steep slope like an unstrung puppet. She disappeared over the lip that Worth had crested a minute earlier.

The whole time, Sonny kept blubbering. "I killed her. I killed Aunt Patty."

"No, you didn't. It was an accident. Worth's the one who killed her."

Chet knew the truth differed: nobody had killed Patty in the field; she'd still had a decent pulse when he'd rolled her over the cliff.

Chet had decided it was time for their mom's sister to move along. After all, she'd told them that he and half brother Sonny stood to inherit her house in Long Beach. That, plus Aunt Patty had a belittling way about her that he didn't much care for.

He puzzled through how her plan to help them kill Worth tonight meshed with what had just happened instead.

Yesterday, Trish Vise from up in Bakersfield had called Aunt Patty, who'd been one of Trish's newspaper sources from Patty's days in the warden's office. Trish filled Patty in: a lawyer named Robert Worth was driving up to talk to her about a screenplay he had in mind.

When Aunt Patty had called him and Sonny yesterday, it didn't take long to see that Worth—traveling to Bakersfield behind his bullshit screenwriter pose—had figured out the prison angle between Jerry, Sonny, and him and was digging up ground better left undug.

How Worth had pieced things together, Chet had no idea. But he had. Then Trish had laid the solution to Worth in Aunt Patty's lap. Trish thought she and Patty could carve a few more dollars out of Worth for helping him out with his prison screenplay.

He and Sonny had been in Aunt Patty's kitchen when she took Trish's second call.

Playing along, Aunt Patty had told Trish, "Sure, Miss Trish, never hurts for a gal to pick up a little spare change, so keep me on that Worth money train.'"

They'd been watching, too, when Aunt Patty took Worth's call. Making him work for their get-together, giving him cute clues about *The Usual Suspects*.

Aunt Patty had been fired up about the whole scam. Maybe she felt like she was reliving her glory days in the warden's office, back when she could zap any prisoner who'd looked at her the wrong way—and a few who hadn't.

To be fair, though, Aunt Patty had a soft spot for him and Sonny, being that she'd raised them once their mom had taken up whoring and shooting dope full-time.

Before meeting up with Worth tonight, Aunt Patty had left behind her Fitbit and phone at her house in Long Beach. That way nothing would put Aunt Patty at Sunken City, the spot they'd decided on as the best place for Worth to die and disappear into the ocean.

In the field now, Chet took Sonny's elbow and slow-walked him over to the ravine. On the way, he drilled one thought into Sonny's brain—*Worth killed Patty, not you.*

At the ravine's edge, Sonny wiped his eyes. "I'm gonna go down there."

"Don't. Surf like that, he's probably dead, same as Aunt Patty. Wait here. If he comes up, nail him. I'll go get the car, and we'll be across the border in a couple hours."

"The border?" Sonny asked.

Chet didn't answer. What still bothered him—who else knew what Worth knew? Patty's name, for instance. Their connection with Jerry Baugh and Paul D.'s. murder. On that, only time would tell. Anyhow, the situation with Worth and Aunt Patty had worked out okay so far. Both bodies would be fish chow soon enough. So he'd go get Hobie's key for his Ensenada rental, they'd chill out in Mexico and wait for the dust to settle here. Come back to the States in a while and take charge of Aunt Patty's place.

"What'd you mean by *the border*?" Sonny asked.

Seemed like Sonny's voice was louder than before.

"Yeah," Chet said. "We take off for a month or two in Mexico, come back, and sell Aunt Patty's house. Or move in, whatever we want."

"What'd I tell you already?"

Before Chet could kid around with his *Mehico*-for-Mexico bit, Sonny cracked him across the face with that baton. As Sonny raised the baton to rain down death on his half brother's head, Chet wondered why he'd never seen it coming.

CHAPTER 61

Boneyard . . . Boneyard . . . Boneyard . . .

That surf spot's name kept rolling around inside his head.

Robert opened his eyes and found himself in a couple of feet of seawater. His arms felt like someone had taken to them with a baseball bat, his right side scraped raw and burning from salt water.

Where he'd wound up after banging into that cliff: all around him lay algae-slicked, canted foundations of the houses Patty had told him fell from that subdivision.

Seaward, he could see the next set of waves building. He had maybe thirty seconds to get out of this break zone, or he could die here.

His own personal Boneyard? Not if he could help it.

Standing, he made out the mouth of that ravine again. His only way up and out. But this time, from the ravine's mouth, Sonny Mars stepped out onto the beach, his baton dangling from his right hand.

Going through Sonny—getting to that ravine—that was his only way out.

On his first step toward Sonny, Robert saw him turn tail—the next set of waves now incoming—and take off running into the ravine, back the way he'd come.

Robert saw his chance and began slip-sliding on the rocks and foundations toward the ravine. Looked like he could make it there in time, no problem—until he stepped on a tilted concrete slab, lost his footing on the green slime covering it, and slid eight feet to its base.

The first incoming wave was closing, twenty yards away. He decided: not another cliff bang! He pulled himself to the top of the tilted concrete slab. A cavelike opening had formed underneath its landward lip.

If he could slip inside the lip, the wave's force should pass over him.

By the time he scrambled into his ersatz cave, the next wave was almost on him. Slipping his arms around a half circle of exposed rebar, he grabbed his elbows with opposing hands and hung on tight.

Even so, he glimpsed the wave's hollowed-out shape as it rose on the angled concrete and started to pass over.

A moment of total quiet—one deep lungful of air.

Then he was submerged inside the pull and suck of the passing wave, his eardrums pressured as the wave's force tried to pull him from his shelter and into the cliff again.

First, the water sucked out his feet and legs, pulling them landward and up. His body followed, fluttering like a flag as the wave yanked his jeans around his knees.

The wave's power slowly subsided. His feet and body dropped to the beach. He released the rebar and gulped in grateful lungfuls of oxygen.

Seconds later, he pulled up his jeans and took off for the ravine without looking—Sonny or no Sonny, he had to outrace the next wave. To draw even with that ravine's mouth and escape the deadly cliffs.

He drew even with the ravine—that was as far as he made it. For some reason—a sandbar, the ravine itself, a smaller wave—the next wave broke farther out than the others.

As he dashed for the ravine's mouth, he heard the wave's weight pound the beach, booming behind him.

Its churning, boiling white water caught him up in it. Fighting to keep his head above water, he was carried, out of control, toward the ravine.

Toward Sonny Mars, he believed.

Closer and closer, human flotsam along for the ride to this wave's final destination from God knows where.

No way could he explain what happened next—sea-foam and salt water pelted his face, blinding him as he rose into the ravine with the surging ocean.

His knee slammed into a rock, but his body kept going, hands out in front now, fending off whenever he could. Giving up to the force of it, he protected his head with both arms and hung on tight to himself.

Seconds later, his body weight settled on the ragged rocks beneath him. The water receded, and a sudden quiet enfolded him.

Dry. Land.

He closed his eyes and thanked the powers that be—

A man's cough broke the night.

Twenty feet below him, Sonny barked up seawater from deep inside his lungs. Robert slid and slipped down until he was just above him, one eye on the ocean below.

"Foot's jammed," Sonny moaned.

Robert saw the baton still clutched in his hand. From this higher ground, he looked out at the next wave, on its way. This one looked larger than the last. He stepped on Sonny's wrist. Was that a wristbone breaking? Pinned it to a rock and pried the baton from his grip.

"Gimme a hand, would you?" Sonny asked.

"Sure, Sonny."

He paralleled Sonny's body down the rocks, well out of the killer's reach. Made it down to Sonny's foot, wedged tight into the rocks. The thought of freeing him had never entered his mind.

"You're right. Jammed in tight."

Even so, he couldn't count on Sonny not fighting free. Before he could ask himself why, he raised the baton and cracked Sonny's free ankle, turning it soft where metal struck bone.

Sonny howled in pain. Robert liked the sound, knowing that he'd struck that blow for Paul and for Lawan. For Raymundo Reyes and Gabriela, too.

Murder for hire? A prison guard, in jail for life with no parole? Ouch, he was thinking.

He raised the baton again. Imagined the number of head blows it had taken for Paul's murder to look like a crime of passion. He eyed this degenerate's kneecap—as good a place as any to start.

He lowered the baton. It was easy to see himself forgetting to stop at the knee.

"Get me out!" Sonny said. "This water's filthy!"

"Hope so. Don't run off, Chocolate Chip, I'm going for help."

As the next wave began its frothy ascent, he scrambled up the rocks, barely ahead of it. Sonny's cry for help below was drowned out by, he hoped, a burning lungful of contaminated salt water.

He crested the ravine, up and out.

In the flat field, the first thing he noticed: Chet Archer's dead body on the ground, his savaged face and skull a pulped mess.

The Bronco keys had somehow remained in Robert's pocket through the ocean's recent beatdown. Old-school keys, not electric, undamaged by the water. He didn't bother checking his iPhone; that had fried in the salt water. He patted Chet's pocket, felt a cell phone, and decided to leave it there for official data retrieval.

Patty Stokes' wallet lay on the ground—he almost missed it in the dark. Inside, he found her driver's license, along with her street address in San Pedro. After dropping the wallet where he'd found it, he limped across the empty field, squeezed back through those bent-out vertical bars, and made his way slowly to his vehicle.

Nearing the base of Gaffey Avenue, he saw a large male figure at his driver's-side window, cupping his hands against external light and peering inside. The pain in his ribs stabbed him as he stopped. Was there another person in the puzzle that he'd missed?

The large male turned from the window—Erik Jacobson caught Robert's eye. Then the Yukon, double-parked uphill on Gaffey.

"Erik," he said.

Erik approached him. "Dude, you okay?"

"Barely."

Erik took one look at his disheveled state and gave him a hug.

"How'd you know?" Robert asked.

"I called in Mars' and Archer's names, then pulled up their address in San Pedro, where you were headed. Once I saw that, I asked for the same dope on Patty Stokes. Live on the same street, all three of 'em, so at that point, I started burning up your phone with texts."

He recalled that before his Gaffey walk with Patty, she'd told him to turn off his phone.

"Missed 'em, and my phone's history. Good to see you, man."

"Same here. C'mon, I want to show you something over at Patty's."

On the way, Erik first called the Long Beach PD and told them about the two bodies down by the ocean and the man trapped in the ravine. Robert then ran down for Erik what had just happened, and as they pulled up to Patty's two-story stucco home, Erik pointed out a white cargo van parked in front.

"That it?"

"Matches the make I saw on those security tapes. I'm betting that's the Flower's Flowers van, all cleaned up."

On their way back to LA, Robert called Anita, caught her at home, and debriefed her, too.

Anita said, "I can't come to grips with what you're saying—we can actually prove that Mr. Reyes is innocent. This kind of miracle never happens. You know that, don't you?"

"Glad I didn't know that going in."

The way they left it, Anita would call a judge at home. After a trip to the ER, Robert would help her fill in the blanks of her writ of habeas corpus. Known in legal circles as *the great writ*, it demanded that a prisoner be brought before the court to determine whether he should be released immediately.

Then he made another call. Closed his eyes so he could see Gia's face again.

"Hey, baby, I might be a little late getting home tonight . . ."

"Why?" she asked.

Then he told her what had happened.

CHAPTER 62

Two mornings later, Raymundo Reyes walked out of Tower One a free man. That afternoon, Jerry was arrested, cuffed, and read his rights in a sand trap beside the eleventh green at Balboa Golf Club. At the same time, the LAPD executed a warrant on Jerry's home. Behind his house, in a sunken homemade concrete vault, police dogs found five triple-sealed turkey-basting bags filled with palladium bars.

All told, Jerry had stolen three-quarters of a million dollars' worth of that metal.

Even the arresting officers agreed that Jerry was a good guy—he'd joked to them that his arrest would save him from finishing up a terrible round of golf. Robert doubted Jerry's good humor had held once he'd been charged with murder-for-hire, a special-circumstances murder that qualified for the death penalty. At a minimum, he'd be in jail till death, right alongside Sonny Mars, who'd nearly drowned in the ravine.

According to news accounts and Anita, Trevor Reid had been brought in for questioning about both Paul's murder and Jerry's arrest. On the heels of Trevor's public nightmare, Lawan had reached out to Robert with news of her own: Hampton Bergen had passed along rumors and whispers he'd "heard around town": major investors were lining up to withdraw from Trevor's fund.

Lawan had already instructed Hampton to move full speed ahead with the same course of action.

No doubt lingered in Robert's mind—those *rumors and whispers* had come from inside Hampton's firm. True to form, they'd whispered the withdrawal news to set themselves up as heroes—the very problem with his own withdrawal that had concerned Paul Dickerson from the outset.

In spite of all his efforts, Trevor's second hedge fund would surely follow in the footsteps of the Marguerite Fund, adding another failure to Trevor's hedge-fund-guru column.

Robert wondered again about Jerry's motives for killing Paul. Was it really about money? Not really, or more accurately, not *only* because of money. Robert laid the initial blame for Jerry's downfall on Trevor's acid personality and the churning resentment Trevor had engendered in his only friend over the years. Robert couldn't fathom an otherwise-normal person murdering an innocent man like Paul. At least Jerry's personal slippery slope, from corruption all the way to murder, fell within the realm of Robert's understanding of flawed humanity.

Five days after Reyes first saw daylight over his head, Robert meandered up the boardwalk for their late-afternoon meeting at his office. Lately, he'd been thinking about Trevor's scowling approach to life and his fund's largely undeserved misfortune. Sure, Trevor had positive traits—intelligence, even loyalty, after a fashion, to old friends Jerry and Dav and to his nephew by marriage, RJ. Then it dawned on him that focusing on Trevor's positives was a bit like opining about a man-eating tiger—*they say he was a good provider for his family.* It simply didn't matter.

A storefront T-shirt cliché caught his eye and verged on summing up Trevor's overall situation. Stenciled across its front: *Karma's a Bitch.*

Minutes later, he sat down with Reyes at his boardwalk conference table. Their first order of business: the trial lawyers pursuing Reyes like rabid dogs with promises of big civil judgments against the LAPD and the city.

Robert asked, "You decided what you want to do?"

"Way I see it, if I'm LAPD, on the evidence they had, I'd toss Raymundo Reyes in jail, too, not give it a second thought."

Robert had heard that sentiment from him in Tower One; seemed he still felt the same.

"Sure, I can hire one'a them cop-chasers, tell him to make my case, and I bet anything we'd squeeze a payday from out the city. But sitting here with you, smelling Hawaiian Tropic body butter in the air, I only know one thing f'sure: I am the luckiest *güey* on Planet Earth."

"Not gonna argue with you."

"Besides that, LAPD worked hard as hell to get me out, and LAPD helped out Gabriela while I was inside."

LAPD meant Erik.

"You thank LAPD personally?"

"Went over to his house last night, had us a tête-à-tête in the backyard."

"How'd it go?"

"I brought one'a my *Walk Street Hits* posters for his boys, signed it for 'em and everything."

Robert winced—Reyes might've pushed things too far, too fast with his new best pal. "Oh."

"Don't freak out on me, *jefe*. Erik's the one asked me to bring over the poster."

"Makes sense. He loved your movie big-time."

"Now I get it why you two *güeros* so tight. He's a . . ."

Across from him, Reyes looked down, choking up.

"I hear you. He is."

Reyes had discovered for himself: Erik Jacobson was a large man in many ways.

"But you, *Roberto*? You're the one who put your ass on the line, you're the one who—"

"Reyes, don't thank me again. Seriously, when you start crying, dude, I do, too. Word's gonna get around I'm soft, gonna lose my boardwalk cred, and who needs that?"

Reyes grinned. "Let me tell you how Mister Ten Percent's doing."

Reyes' new nickname for him because of his ownership in *Walk Street Hits*. Reyes showed him a series of texts from studio executives. Serious guys. So serious, even Robert had heard of them.

Reyes said, "Already turned down an offer for all rights for five hundred thousand, sight unseen."

Robert wasn't surprised hearing that. Reyes' release from prison— Reyes, Gabriela, and Anita outside the criminal court building—had even caught national buzz for a day or two.

"Taking your time with it, good."

"I'm all about wait and see. Figure out who wants to make a movie, and who just wants to piggyback on my arrest, look Hollywood righteous by making a deal with me."

"Like what you're doing, but don't take too long."

"I won't. Oh yeah, and all the execs're asking about who's that blonde Uma I cast in my movie, who represents her."

"And you said?"

"Told 'em Gigi Marquez is the new Greta Garbo, baby. All she wants them to do is leave her be."

Robert grinned. To the film community, Reyes' answer would only add fuel to whatever Gigi Marquez–fire might exist. Nothing generated more interest in Hollywood than hearing: *Get lost. She doesn't care about being in movies.*

Reyes said, "So far, I like this letter best of all of 'em."

He showed Robert an email from T-Mack, the Irish producer who'd been genuinely interested in Reyes' project before Trevor had interfered. Even then, T-Mack had treated Reyes with courtesy and respect.

Finally, Reyes' decision to be up front with T-Mack about Trevor's offensive reservation-of-rights letter bore fruit.

Dear Raymundo,

Way over here in Ireland, I was unaware of your legal entanglement until you were actually released. How out of touch can one human being be? Surely with *Walk Street Hits* under your belt, you will now have the filmmaking world at your feet—which is, I think, the very best place for it.

I plan to follow your career with the utmost enthusi-asm. If there is any way I can help out, let me know. I am so very happy for you!

Reyes said, "*Legal entanglement?* Sounds like T-Mack's been talkin' to you."

"That's a cool letter. T-Mack's keeping his hat in the ring without putting any pressure on you."

"We gettin' together next week. Pip-pip, mate." His accent needed a lot of work, but his thought process was rock-solid.

They headed up the boardwalk together toward Ozone.

"Gia says you can't make it to beach karaoke tonight," Robert said.

"Got a dinner in town. It winds up early, I'll break for the beach."

"We're bringing in a deli platter from Bay Cities, serious desserts from Urth. Sorry you're gonna miss out."

Reyes nodded, wrestling with the decision. "You order that triple-layer cheesecake?"

"Let me think—hell yes. Did you know Erik does a serious Mick Jagger?"

Reyes stopped. Looked at Robert, surely picturing a 260-pound Mick strutting his stuff at sundown.

"Does he do Mick's chicken dance?"

"Hot lips, pouting, the whole package. Priya's singing 'Sugar,' and Gigi usually goes with something by James Brown. Delfina's coming too, I think."

"Aww, man, Delfina? You killing me. What're you singing, *mi abogado?*"

"Think I might get an important phone call when my turn rolls around."

Reyes held up his phone.

"You sing karaoke tonight, and I slip outta my dinner in town."

A no-brainer—he'd already planned to sing "My Girl" to Delfina, same as Jesus did for her in the desert.

"Done."

※

A new northern swell was on its way that night from who knew where. On the beach before sunset, Gia pulled him from the others for a quick walk down the beach to the Venice Jetty. Both of them liked standing on the hard pack, holding hands, sheltered from chaos behind the piled granite boulders, the waves pounding the barrier and sending sheets of white spray, tinted pink and gold with sunlight, high above the jetty's jagged-rocked rim.

Good a time as any to run his Bronco-to-van routine on her.

"There's something I wanted to talk to you about."

"Same here," Gia said. "I saw Priya this afternoon. She wanted me to try out something she bought."

"She buy you a mullet wig?"

"No, smaller than a mullet, it came in a box. More like a game, really."

"How'd you do?"

"Well, it wasn't that hard. There were only two answers, positive and negative, and I lucked out."

Her words seemed playful, lighthearted, until the real game dawned on him: a pregnancy test.

"*Exactly* how did you do?"

"Instead of James Brown tonight, I might go with 'Old MacDonald Had a Farm' or 'Hush, Little Baby.'"

He pulled her close in and held on. She buried her face in his chest. When he finally found her eyes, she asked, "You happy?"

"Yes, sweetheart, very happy."

"You scared?"

"Not until you asked."

Salted mist blew across their faces, and the world trembled beneath their bare feet. He dug his toes into the sand and held on tight.

"Sometimes those tests are wrong," she said.

"When we get home tonight, let's take out some insurance."

She nodded. "What was it you wanted to talk about?"

"It can wait," he said.

At the moment, he felt like he didn't have a care in the world. But he knew, too, that everything in the world mattered more now than it had a moment before.

Walking back to join the others, they held hands like lovers do, and he wondered again that they'd ever found each other.

ACKNOWLEDGMENTS

For their early reads, essential research, and moral support:

Ana Shorr, Doctor Bobby, and T.J. Hall. Without all three, I might have thrown in the towel.

Ryan Gustafson, Jacqueline, and the Lads of Steel.

Sanya, Wijitra Pimros, Lila Pinnapa, and the monks at Wat Thai.

Hardwick Caldwell; L.H. "Hacker" Caldwell, III; Chris Fehr; and Mindy Freeman.

Rambling Steve Davis, Ben B. Philips, Jeff "Hikikomori" Gallo, Andrea Mattoon, Libby Duff, Elizabeth Woods, Happy Baker, Kay Kendall, Surfer Dave, and always, Sensei Rooney.

All the guys at Nick's up Speedway and at Urth Caffé, Santa Monica.

Attorneys Alan Wertheimer and Bret Carter.

My manager, Chris George.

My ever-intrepid and even-now-enthusiastic agent, Beth Davey.

Copyeditor Valerie Kalfrin and proofreader Jill Kramer.

Caitlin Alexander, my preternaturally patient, tolerant, and wildly talented developmental editor.

And then there's Liz Pearsons and her team at Amazon. For three Beach Lawyer books now, she has given all those people and groups above a reason to help out an unknown writer in the first place.

ABOUT THE AUTHOR

Avery Duff was born in Chattanooga, Tennessee, where he attended Baylor School and graduated summa cum laude. After graduating Phi Beta Kappa from the University of North Carolina at Chapel Hill, he earned a JD from Georgetown University Law Center. He then joined a prestigious Tennessee law firm, where he became a partner in five years, before moving to Los Angeles. Duff's screenwriting credits include the 2010 heist drama *Takers*, starring Matt Dillon, Paul Walker, Idris Elba, and Zoe Saldana. He is the author of two previous books in the Beach Lawyer series: *Beach Lawyer*, an Amazon Charts Most Read and Most Sold Book, and *The Boardwalk Trust*, a bestselling legal thriller.